BLACK CLOUD: HOW MANY LIVES CAN ONE INCIDENT SHATTER?

GEORGIE HARVEY AND JOHN FRANKLIN
BOOK 4

SANDI WALLACE

PRAISE FOR SANDI WALLACE'S BOOKS

'A beautifully written police procedural, where the characters are every bit as important as the plot. *Black Cloud* brilliantly captures the impact of small-town tragedy, as investigators struggle to cope even as they work towards solving an horrendous crime.'

CHRIS HAMMER, WINNER OF THE UK CWA NEW BLOOD DAGGER AWARD FOR *SCRUBLANDS*

'Aussie Noir at its best. Once again Wallace has tapped into the rural crime genre with an iconic sense of place beneath a black cloud of menace and intrigue. Her Georgie Harvey and John Franklin series just gets better and better.'

B. MICHAEL RADBURN, AUTHOR OF THE *TAYLOR BRIDGES* **SERIES**

'*Black Cloud* is absorbing and suspenseful, a perfect weekend read for the rural crime fiction lover. Wallace has struck that elusive balance between relatable characters, disturbing crimes and an urgent plot that drives the reader forward.'

L.J.M. OWEN, AUTHOR OF THE *DR PIMMS* SERIES AND *THE GREAT DIVIDE*

'Sandi Wallace's best yet! Engaging, fast-paced, and full of suspense.'

KAREN M. DAVIS, FORMER NSW POLICE DETECTIVE AND AUTHOR OF THE *LEXIE ROGERS* SERIES

'A gripping twist on the bushfire threat all Australians live with.'

JAYE FORD, AWARD-WINNING AUTHOR OF *DARKEST PLACE*

'Suspenseful, exciting, atmospheric rural crime; a riveting debut.'

MICHAELA LOBB, SISTERS IN CRIME AUSTRALIA

'The police aspect of this novel has depth and believability...this debut is a cracker.'

J.M. PEACE, SERVING QLD POLICE

ALSO BY SANDI WALLACE

Georgie Harvey and John Franklin series

Tell Me Why

Dead Again

Into the Fog

Black Cloud

Short story collections

On the Job

Murder in the Midst

Award-winning short stories

'Sweet Baby Dies' (*Scarlet Stiletto: The Eleventh Cut* – 2019)

'Fire on the Hill' (*Scarlet Stiletto: The Tenth Cut* – 2018)

'Busted' (*Scarlet Stiletto: The Eighth Cut* – 2016)

'Ball and Chain' (*Scarlet Stiletto: The Sixth Cut* – 2014)

'Silk Versus Sierra' (*Scarlet Stiletto: The Fifth Cut* – 2013)

Non-fiction

Writing the Dream (contributing author)

For Simon, much missed. And Ellen.

DAY ONE

WEDNESDAY 13 JUNE

CHAPTER ONE

'NOBODY COULD'VE SEEN IT COMING. AN ACCIDENT.' BOB Getty scrunched up his face.

Fifteen minutes into their interview, he'd done a full circle to the exact words he'd used at the start. Georgie Harvey laid a mental bet on what he'd say next.

'A good man's life snuffed out. Kaput. Dead.'

Word-for-word, same facial expression, identical pauses. He hadn't just used it earlier, but also on the *breaking news* report on Channel 7 last Friday evening. It'd been echoed in the print, radio and television media until the story was bumped from the spotlight by the murder of a baby boy during a burglary in Bendigo.

If Georgie worked for a daily, she'd be chasing today's headline, not talking to Getty on his farm in Gordon. The main perk of writing for *Champagne Musings* was leeway to follow her instincts on stories that'd lost traction in the mainstream. From her warm, comfy study in Richmond, Getty's quirks had signalled there was more to this situation than the initial news story. Standing in the iced-over paddock with her feet turning numb inside her boots, a niggle seeded in her mind.

She shuffled on the spot, and her feet prickled with the movement. She assessed Getty, re-running her editor's response, *You reckon there's a story, so find it.* Typical of any conversation with Sheridan Judd, she'd added, *Don't miss your deadlines though.*

In Georgie's silence, the middle-aged man repeated the words and gestures.

He's talking about his best mate's sudden death – sure it's not a reaction to shock?

She pretended to make notes, covertly watching Getty's eyes shift to the shed, float over a bunch of gas cylinders, then across the misty yard to the dam from where they'd pulled Allan Hansen's body.

Almost certain.

Her gut feeling was that he kept restating it so that he wouldn't forget or deviate. She'd seen it before. Her partner John Franklin told her crooks did it all the time, and he should know as a seasoned cop.

Hansen's drowning was no accident.

———

Constable Sam Tesorino's mobile went off. She scooped it up, noted the caller and grinned.

'Hi!' She restrained herself from adding, *boss.* 'Franklin! How's it going? You busy?'

'Just killing a few minutes while I'm waiting for Marty. Got to thinking, you've only six months left. You worked out where you want to go next?'

Since John Franklin's move from the Daylesford station, they often went days without catching up. Yet she knew that he

4

meant her next posting, when her two-year probationary period was up, and not holiday plans.

'Definitely the country but not a town this small. Regional, with a CIU – maybe Bendigo or Ballarat. That's if I have much say.'

Sam's chest tightened with an odd mix of gloom and excitement. She struggled to imagine moving on from Daylesford, even though it wasn't the same anymore. She had to transfer out in a step towards joining one of the squads. She wasn't sure which. The mounted branch used to be her dream. But after what had happened at Mount Dandenong last spring, she'd done a mind-shift from never wanting to deal with sex offences or homicides to thinking she could make a real difference in a unit like that, after a requisite stint in a crime investigation crew.

She saw the time. 'Shit.' With her mobile still pressed to her ear, she snatched her jacket from the back of her chair and gave the toilet door a sharp rap as she rushed by.

'Hurry up, Irvy.'

'Catch you at a bad moment? You got a callout?'

Franklin sounded strange. Could he be wistful?

'Haha!' She laughed. 'You miss the uniform, don't you? You miss us!'

He denied it.

'Yeah, right. Whatever you say. But yes, we should've left already – we're due to meet a nurse in Korweingi at 10.00am.'

It'd ordinarily only take fifteen minutes to reach the address in Korweinguboora, or Korweingi as locals dubbed it, but she'd wanted to allow longer in view of the weather.

Not going to happen now. Thanks, Irvy.

'Hang on,' she told Franklin, then hollered to her partner, 'Irvy, hurry up. I'll meet you in the truck.'

'What's the job?'

After grabbing the keys for the marked four-wheel drive, she juggled the phone to shrug on her jacket. 'A welfare check at a farm on Riley's Lane.'

'*Whose?*'

Sam scurried down the wet staircase and climbed into the driver's side of the truck. 'The Murray place. Alec and–'

'*Bel. Our local kindergarten teacher.*'

Her 'Yes' was drowned out by Senior Constable Grant Irvine slamming the passenger door, letting out three loud sneezes.

She shook her head. 'You look like crap, Irvy.'

He sniffed hard, complained in a nasal twang, 'That's nothing on how I feel. Bloody thanks I get for swapping shifts with Harty.'

Sam turned over the ignition. 'Gotta go, Franklin.'

'*Take it easy.*'

She laughed. 'The only trouble I'm going to get is from the grumpy bum sitting next to me.' Irvy wagged a finger at her. 'Hopefully, we'll be offered a nice hot cuppa though.'

———

Marty Howell glanced sideways, as he and John Franklin drove out in the unmarked station wagon. 'Bet you used to dream about popping on your suit for the theft of a bunch of pigs, didn't you?' He let out a little snort.

'Oh, yeah.' Franklin chuckled. 'It's right up there with our hundred-odd woolly friends that were nicked from Greendale last week.'

The older detective sobered. 'These cases mightn't be glamourous, but I get a kick outta cracking them.'

Franklin nodded, thinking of his farmer mates hurting enough without losing their stock.

'I like it when crooks make mistakes. I like it a lot,' Howell said, entering the Grant Street roundabout after a light van. He then took the first exit onto Bacchus Marsh Road, the car's tyres swishing on the wet bitumen.

Franklin watched his partner's face wondering what he was getting at. 'Yeah?'

'Think about it, mate. We've had a run of similar jobs, and most couldn't be pinned down to a specific day, let alone time. True?'

Howell zipped through the second roundabout. Only a month into Franklin's posting at Bacchus Marsh, he'd taken this route from the cop shop to Western Freeway plenty. It hadn't grown on him much.

He pulled his attention back to the conversation. 'Yep. The Greendale sheep could've been gone for up to five days before the owner noticed. Big difference to the pigs missing from Colbrook – we can narrow this one down to the past twelve hours. So assuming they're the work of the same mob–'

'They're getting sloppy or cocky,' finished Howell. He smacked his lips. 'I never doubted we were eventually gonna nab 'em. But now I warrant it'll be sooner than later.'

———

In her side vision, Sam saw Irvy thudding away on his mobile. He stopped, dumped his phone into his lap and plucked at the woven leather band on his wrist. It'd gone on non-stop since they'd left the station.

'Anything wrong, Irvy?'

He pulled out a wad of tissues and blew his nose, but didn't answer. Sam sensed him stiffen as they neared his house on the left. He twisted in the seat as they passed it, huffing loudly.

She forgot him and focused ahead, steering the truck by the

Sailors Falls car park. Steady rain ratcheted to a volley pelting the windscreen, and a patch of fog swallowed the truck. Sam checked the headlights and fog lamps – both were on and the wipers set at top speed. Shitty day – any worse and she'd have to pull over, but it'd definitely make them late.

She anticipated the dip, rapidly assessed the water over the road. Navigable in the four-wheel drive.

'God, it's cold, isn't it?'

The truck heater was on full blast but barely took off the edge.

Irvy didn't answer, too busy typing on his phone. Sam wrinkled her nose. She couldn't force him to talk. He really should've called in sick and stayed in bed. She hoped man flu was all it was because she wanted the real Irvy back, not this cranky version.

———

Georgie parked in Gordon's main street, running over her interview with Getty in her mind. She left the car heater on to defrost her feet. They were so cold she couldn't decide if her socks were wet.

Allan Hansen's home was next on her list, and she needed an opening that'd get her over the threshold. Her background research revealed the man had left behind a de facto wife, Jeanette Roselle, and two grown sons from a previous marriage. Every chance she'd find one or more of them there.

Could she go with the same approach she'd used for Getty? As the face of the news story, a follow-up with the guy had been an easy sell. She needed to come at it differently with the family. But how?

Georgie eyed the structures around her, ignoring a couple of men on the footpath chattering as they darted glances at her

1984 black Alfa Spider. Her course to Getty's place had given her a good overview of the town. It boasted a large church and two primary schools in addition to a small number of businesses, including the cluster she could see from here: a pub, a general store, a hat shop and a strange mixed business combining old wares, clothes, books and café. The nearby homes were predominantly lived-in as opposed to weekenders: cars in driveways, wheelie bins out of sight, chimneys smoking, gardens tended, and kids' play equipment, building materials, caravans or trailers in the yards. She guessed the residents rarely saw impractical classic convertibles in town mid-week. She'd given them something gossip-worthy.

What she needed was a good strong coffee from the café to kickstart her frozen brain and get this story moving. She'd hate this trip to have been a timewaster.

Sam concentrated on driving. Irvy was crap company, playing with his phone, and blowing endless amounts of snot from his nose.

'That was Sucklings Lane,' she thought out loud. 'So next turn.'

She spotted Riley's Lane and hooked onto it. The truck bumped along the narrow gravel road, the tyres slushing and spraying mud.

They swept past a round-topped shed and approached a wide gate hung with a sign etched with 'Goodlife Farm – A & B Murray'. They were at the right place. Wispy fog threaded around twin bare trees on either side of the driveway giving the place a haunting beauty. Sam grimaced at the black cloud bearing down from the south-west. Nothing sweet about that. Just dark and threatening.

'Can you get the gate, Irvy?'

He muttered, then released the passenger door. The cabin temperature plummeted. Sam shivered, shaking her head at him, clearly still grumbling while he moved to the gate. He quit it when two kelpies bolted down the gravel driveway, barking.

Irvy gave a *settle* gesture and spoke to them. The lead dog came close, quiet now, its white-blazed nose held high and red-coated chest and neck stretched up as it listened. Its mate stood alongside – two red-dog bookends, the second one slightly finer-boned and pure-coloured. They stalked Irvy as he opened the gate and swung it shut after the truck pulled through.

Sam drummed the steering wheel while he used his mobile, this time speaking, not texting. Not happy either. The dogs tracked his wild arm movements. He didn't say a word when he reentered the cabin, pocketing his phone. She didn't dare ask what was going on and inched the truck forward.

Old, spindly trees and an informal cottage garden around the timber house meant Sam had to stop near the adjacent shed. She left the motor running for heat and wipers, and took in the empty space.

'We seem to have beaten the nurse.'

'Yeah.' Irvy went to get out. The wind gusted, rocking his door on its hinges. He shoved a booted foot against it.

'Hang on. It's only ten now.'

'We can do this without her.'

Sam glanced at the rear-view mirror. No sign of the nurse who'd requested the welfare check. 'She'll be here any moment.'

The dogs watched on, dropping to their haunches when Irvy yanked his door closed. Sam hid her relief, then let central communications know they were at the address.

While they waited, Irvy plucked at his wristband. 'This is going to be a dud.'

'Possibly, but we have to complete the job.'

'They're probably not home.'

The place did have an empty feel. They couldn't make assumptions though. She said, 'Maybe the Murrays are asleep or down the back and haven't seen us.'

Silence inside the cabin, except for Irvy's snotty breathing. Sam's eyes followed a dappled grey as it trotted along the fence line to their left. The horse whinnied.

She floundered for something to say that might get Irvy to loosen up. The rain suddenly stopped, and the truck's wipers scraped over the windscreen. She clicked them off. No doubt it'd bucket down again any minute.

At a loss, talk about the weather.

'Think it might fine up?'

He twitched his shoulders.

'The last two nights were *so cold*, weren't they? I had to sleep in my tracksuit and socks.'

He didn't react.

'And how was that wild wind that blew up at 3.00am? I thought the roof was going to come off on Monday night, but it was even worse last night. Still gusty now, isn't it?'

He gave her nothing.

Sam tried again. 'We've probably had the equivalent of June's usual rainfall in the past fifty hours, don't you think?'

All he said was, 'Yeah,' and she surrendered.

Irvy glared at his mobile and mumbled to himself. He pulled out his mushed-up tissues and blew his nose. It went on forever.

'Gross!'

He pushed open his door and lumbered out. 'Not waiting.'

'Irvy!'

Sam switched off the ignition. He was already tramping across the yard. The two kelpies sniffed at his heels.

Sam exited, zipping up her police jacket. She tuned into an approaching vehicle and tracked a silver, compact SUV on Riley's Lane. It was unmarked. It could be Denise Zachary's own vehicle or from the hospital fleet. If it wasn't the nurse, it appeared that they'd be going ahead without her.

Sam met the SUV at the gate. She waved it through, indicating to park near the police truck, and hurried back.

The woman's black gumboots landed in a puddle when she emerged from the SUV. She laughed. 'Lucky I didn't wear my stilettos today.' Her boots squelched as she took a step towards Sam, tugging down her pink blouse with blue logo to cover a ring of bare flesh above her trousers.

'Sam? I'm Denise.' Strands of brown hair whipped in the wind, escapees of a messy, high bun hugging her round face, as she stooped to shake hands. When she straightened, Denise had a good eight centimetres on Sam. She glanced at Irvy pacing on the verandah deck. 'Your partner's keen.'

Embarrassed, Sam didn't respond. She led the way up an overgrown pathway. The dogs yapped and ran by.

'Freezing, isn't it? Hold on while I grab my coat?'

Sam shuffled for warmth while the nurse returned to her SUV and battled the wind to pull on a woollen coat. She heard knocking.

'Mr and Mrs Murray?' Irvy rapped again.

Denise made her way back up the path, and Sam continued towards the cottage.

Irvy sneezed, once, twice, then a third time, each progressively louder. He swiped his nose with the back of a hand while he opened the flywire door, then the main door. As Sam's foot struck the bottom verandah step, she smelt rotten eggs.

Can't believe Irvy farted.

She caught another whiff, and her stomach pitched.

'IRVY! STOP!'

She charged forward. He had too much of a lead and stepped inside. Denise yelled from right behind, 'Sam?' The dogs took up barking.

'NO!'

Irvy disappeared calling, 'Mr and Mrs Murray? It's–'

Sam shouted, 'GAS!' as she reached the top step.

A loud bang coupled with a whoosh and bright flash, chased by the flare of orange flames, a burst of heat. A scream. It could've been Irvy. Windows blew outwards, and the panes in the front door and its fanlight exploded. A dog's yelp pierced through the noise. Sam flew backwards, holding up her arm, shelled by shards of glass and splintered timber.

She hit the ground. Her skull struck a brick edging the pathway.

CHAPTER TWO

Marty Howell hummed a tune, and Franklin's mind drifted back to Daylesford. To Sam and her next move.

She'd be wasted driving the van for too long. She needed a few more years of general duties and experience in larger stations, then he could see her smashing through the extra training and exams to move up the ranks. Her empathy was the only thing to watch: a good and bad trait. Sam would fit well in a SOCIT team, be a smart investigator and great advocate for victims and their families, but he worried how dealing with child abuse and sexual offences would affect her long-term. Luckily, the brass had assumed as the rookie she'd been roped into their rogue investigation last year, and there was no black mark on her record—well, maybe just a smudge—unlike the rest of them. But he had no regrets considering what might have happened otherwise, and his mates said the same.

He took in the landscape as Howell steered the car along the Ballan–Colbrook route. Very different to the urban sprawl of Bacchus Marsh's centre and the distinctive steep, undulating hills and mixed farms around it. Bacchus straddled commuter belt suburbia and traditional country town with a population of over 20,000, making it nearly ten of Daylesford. And the patch for their crime investigation unit ranged over the Golden Plains, Hepburn and Moorabool areas. It made things interesting.

If he got the chance for official attachment to the CI team, would he take it?

Franklin pulled a wry smile. He'd jump at it. But District Inspector Eddie Knight's push me–pull you since October seemed to have no use-by date. It was wearing thin. He'd struggled but passed his sarge's exam while biding his time, seeing if what effectively amounted to work-experience kid in the detective's unit would come to more.

Still waiting.

———

Sam stirred and coughed. She wheezed, conscious of things in stages. Heat. Smoke. Muted sound. Tingling in the back of her neck – no, not tingling, a shooting ache. Her fingers found a sticky spot. It stung, and she pulled away. There was a horrible stench coming from somewhere. Confused, she couldn't think what it was, what to do. Pain scorched through the fuzziness. She was hurt. Badly. All over. But especially her head.

Oh, God! I'm on fire. Can't remember what to do.

She tried to sit up and swayed giddily, and then fell back to the ground. Dullness in her ears cleared to hissing, buzzing. Nauseous, her stomach rolled.

That's it, roll. Drop and roll.

Already down, Sam didn't have to drop. She tried to roll, but couldn't. She felt around – one of her legs was twisted sideways at an angle that was all wrong. The tips of her fingers probed melted material, flesh, and bone protruding the skin.

She screamed. Couldn't hear it.

Sam writhed and slapped at her body. Trying to beat out the flames. To detach from the singeing and melding of her skin, hair and clothes. She cried, 'Help!' but it disappeared into a vacuum of confusion.

Oh, God, this pain is unbearable!

Thoughts spun in her brain. Irvy. Denise Zachary. The Murrays. Who else was hurt? How long would it take for help to arrive?

She strained to lift up. A fresh level of pain hammered her skull. She yelled, 'Irvy?' thinking she was facing the cottage. Unsure, she shook her head. The movement made an ear pop. It still rang, but the roar of flames taking over the building was unmistakable.

Toxic fumes, the reek of burning flesh and hair, horrific pain. Sam flopped back, staring up blindly. Sick with the thought that they might've been set up.

———

The police radio crackled. Franklin was chuckling at something Marty Howell had said. But their laughter died when they heard '...*reports of a series of explosions and fire in the vicinity of Spargo Creek. Fire and ambulance dispatched.*'

Franklin plucked up the radio mic and gave the callsign for their unmarked CIU station wagon. He requested the address.

'*Still pending corroboration. Initial caller said Spargo–Blakeville Road, Spargo Creek.*'

The operator paused. Then said, '*Second informant stated Back Settlement Road, Korweinguboora.*' She stumbled over the pronunciation, emphasising the *r* in the first syllable.

'We're not far–'

Franklin cut off Howell, saying into the mic, 'Casualties?' He clenched the handset.

'*Unknown.*'

'We'll be there in,' he glanced at Howell who mouthed *ten minutes,* 'approximately eight minutes.'

After he'd signed off and activated lights and siren, he answered his partner's unspoken question. 'My old crew are in the area. Riley's Lane, which runs straight off Back Settlement Road in Korweingi.'

'Fuck.'

'Yep.'

Howell planted his foot, and the Commodore shot forward. Franklin grabbed the dash to stabilise against body roll.

At this rate, we'll be there in five.

Sam heard a sound that tore through her body, hurting much worse than her own physical pain. It repeated, while a dog whined in the other direction. She could tell the difference. Both were agonised. One was human.

'Hold on.' Sam's words rasped and cracked.

Sweet Jesus. Help us.

'It'll be all right.'

It's not going to be all right.

She was still burning.

Sam's eyes rolled at the spearing pain in her fingers as she fumbled the zip on her jacket. The fine movement of grasping and drawing the pull tab was impossible, so she yanked the jacket lapel as hard as she could, letting out a whimper of relief when the gap widened around her neck. She attempted to slip off the jacket like a jumper. It ripped her skin, and she let go, panting.

She clenched her jaw, blocking out her injuries. Somebody needed her. Irvy? The nurse? One of the Murrays?

She tried to swallow to make saliva. Managed, 'I'm coming!'

She rocked on the wet turf and slapped at the flames. Her bra had fused with flesh, the underwire blazing. Heavy on her skin, her equipment belt chafed. She blinked rapidly to clear her vision, scared of permanent damage.

It didn't help.

It's probably normal after a blast.

Couldn't stop the sinking dread with, *Nothing's ever going to be normal again.*

She talked over her inner voice. 'Shut up, Sam.' She had to hold it together for the other survivor. 'Survivors,' she rebuked herself.

It was all on her. And she had to quit wasting time. If they were set up, the perp could still be lurking or more booby traps about to go off.

After another round of fast blinks, Sam made out the hazy outline of her hand in front of her face and gasped. Then the other person moaned. Her gut wrenched in response.

Her best guess was that the person was further back from the Murray house. Denise had been behind her before. It had to be her.

'Denise?' she croaked.

The shrieks heightened.

Sam dug deep to call louder, 'I'm coming!'

She turned in the opposite direction, into the heat. 'Irvy? Where are you?'

He didn't answer. Sam's stomach lurched again as reasons for Irvy's silence ricocheted in her mind. None of them good.

Biting her lip against the pain, she sat up. She tried to stand, stumbled and gave up on getting upright. She pulled herself over onto her elbows and half-crawled, half-slithered, dragging her useless leg as she followed Denise's screams.

She refused to think about what the friction was doing to her burnt skin as she scraped along, snagging on bushes and shrapnel, or what she'd see when she reached the nurse.

CHAPTER THREE

GEORGIE SIPPED FROM HER TAKEAWAY COFFEE BEAKER AND nearly spat out her mouthful when Sheridan Judd said, *'To be honest, you haven't done much to impress me lately.'*

It hit a sore spot. All she'd written for the magazine in the past month, at least, was fluff and dull stuff. But every journo had dry patches. She still cringed.

Her editor went on. *'Finish your column and what's outstanding. Then take this week to recharge.'*

Innocent enough, except for the barbed edge. Georgie anticipated what was coming.

'And get me that brilliant story you said you were onto.'

Judd paused.

'Or don't bother coming back.'

Reasonably sure her editor had run out of steam and wouldn't actually dump her, Georgie said, 'I told you, there's a story here.'

There was something about the pretty township of Gordon that intensified the vibes she'd sensed at Getty's farm. All she had so far were her instincts and imagination. Yet she promised, 'I'll get you a top story...'

She broke off, distracted by the serious tone of the radio announcer.

'In breaking news, there have been reports of a series of explosions and an uncontrolled fire in the vicinity of the small town of Korweinguboora in central Victoria.'

Georgie turned up the volume.

'The number of casualties involved, extent of damage to property, and cause of the incident are not known at this stage. Emergency services have been called to the scene. We'll bring you further information as it comes to hand.'

She straightened in her leather seat. 'Something big's going down not far from here, Sheridan. I'm going to check it out. Talk later.'

Her editor was still speaking when she hung up.

———

Sam tried to fix on a positive. Blurry, excruciating sight was better than none.

It sort of helped.

She made out the shape of a person in the haze. They were upright and in motion. She slither-crawled in that direction, soon exhausted by the effort of moving what was probably mere metres.

A few feet from the nurse, her body took on fierce shaking.

She hadn't been in the job long, but she'd already seen too many victims of accidents and violence, several with horrendous injuries. A few that were dead. Scenes like that were always dreadful. But she wished she'd never witnessed *this.*

It was difficult to imagine that the burning woman was lucky to be alive.

Sam's hearing dulled as a woozy wash came over her. She recognised it was shock. She knew she couldn't give way to it. Denise needed her – she'd die without her help.

She took a shuddering breath. Smoke scratched her throat and swelled her airways. Her lungs strained. When she coughed, her ears popped, and noise burst back. More chaotic and louder than ever.

It took immense effort, but her 'I'm here, Denise' sounded reasonably controlled.

The other woman continued to shriek.

Sam drew from deeper inside to use her cop voice. 'You need to stop, Denise. Drop and roll.'

No reaction, and the nurse's erratic movement was fanning the flames, feeding the fire.

'Denise, please listen.' Sam struggled into a standing position, biting back her yelp at the sharp pain that shot up her leg. Listing to one side, she held up a hand, meaning it to be calming and authoritative. 'You know what to do from your training. Stop, drop and roll.'

It was no good. She couldn't get the message across.

Sam groped for ideas.

Take Denise to the ground and roll out the flames.

Impossible with a broken leg.

What then?

I don't know!

Oh, God. Yes, I do.

She'd have to use what was left of her own jacket to douse the fire. It was going to hurt, beyond anything she'd ever experienced before.

No choice. Rip it off. Do it fast.

With shaking hands, Sam yanked the material away from

where it had fused to her waistline, tearing her flesh. Finally, it was off. Panting, she blinked off dizziness.

Denise still appeared oblivious to her.

Maybe it did more to calm herself than the nurse, but Sam talked through what she was doing. 'I'm going to wrap you in my jacket and pat out the flames. Okay?'

Denise didn't answer, but she stilled and looked directly at Sam. Her eyes were filled with naked fear, and underlying that, trust.

Sam murmured as she worked, aware that she was going to hurt Denise by helping her. Her thoughts scattered when she took in the strips of skin peeling off her own red-raw hands.

Oh, God! Oh, God!

———

At full throttle, they made it to the Mineral Springs Hotel in Spargo Creek in record time. Most locals knew it as the Korweingi Pub, despite the five-odd kilometres separating the two places and the years since the last beer was officially pulled. It traded as an antique store these days, open only for short, random hours during the week and on weekends. Could often drive by and see no vehicles out front.

On their approach, Franklin clocked two women and an elderly man clustered near a couple of cars, talking animatedly. One woman pointed up the road and another nodded. The group turned and watched as their unmarked passed by, apparently mesmerised by the wailing siren and flashing blues-and-reds on the wagon.

He and Howell had exchanged few words since the initial call. Seeing as they'd sped along Spargo–Blakeville Road and taken the turn onto the Ballan road without spotting anything amiss, the first informant's version was clearly dodgy. Franklin's gut shrivelled. Worried because that put the incident in Korweinguboora, close to Sam and Irvy's welfare check at the Murray farm.

The radio crackled to life. Franklin took in the two words 'Riley's Lane' and grabbed up the mic.

'Two officers from Daylesford...' He faltered and tried again, adding their names. 'They were due at Riley's Lane this morning, to see Belinda and Alec Murray. Have they reported in?'

Franklin sweated on the operator's response.

'Not since they notified their arrival.'

He clicked off the mic. Slammed a fist into the dashboard.

Howell slowed behind several cars travelling in the same direction, possibly locals on their way to the property to offer help. All suddenly slowing to the speed limit. As if they were going to issue tickets right now.

'Why don't they pull over? Morons!'

Howell peered through the windscreen. 'Can't.'

Franklin saw the truth in that but fumed. Howell was hamstrung by the vehicles bunched up on the curving road. Without a clear visual for oncoming traffic, he couldn't gamble on space to cross over the centre line to overtake without risking a head-on. Likewise, overtaking on the left shoulder was out.

So much for the good time they'd made reaching Spargo Creek.

Franklin dialled out on his mobile. Unanswered, the call went to message bank. He disconnected, then tried a second number. Ended it and blew out a breath.

'Fuck.'

'Still can't get onto Sam and Irvy?'

'No.'

The wagon bounced over a pothole.

Franklin stared at the phone in his lap, dwelling on Sam

and Irvy. His colleagues until he'd been attached to Bacchus Marsh. His mates.

'They were on a welfare check.'

Howell grimaced.

'What's happened to them?'

His offsider didn't answer. Instead, he glimpsed his mirrors, clicking on the indicator, and deftly accelerated past the cars.

Both uncontactable. Why? Because they're too busy helping? Or because they can't answer?

They were the closest car to the address. First responders to what?

Howell decelerated, signalling right.

They were nearly there.

———

'How bad?' The nurse's voice rasped.

Sam floundered for words. Honesty would not help. But an outright lie?

God give me strength.

A man broke into her desperate prayer. He bellowed in a language she couldn't understand, not English or Italian. Then said, 'Hold on, we're coming.'

Sam wheezed, 'Thanks,' hoping he was real, not imagined. Then scared he was the perp who had set up the explosion – *if* it was an ambush.

'Get water, Vlatka!'

A female answered, 'I have got it, Sven.'

Feet pounded in approach. Other sounds made Sam think items were being dragged or thrown out of the way. But she still couldn't see their rescuers.

She crawled forward. Tried to yell out. Croaked, 'Have you rung triple zero?' It was doubtful they could have heard it.

But the woman spoke. 'Don't panic. The fire truck and ambulance are called.'

Sam slithered a bit further. 'My partner–' The words were indecipherable, and she collapsed backwards. Spent. Nothing left to fight with.

She blinked to be sure the apparition leaning over her was real. An older woman with a concerned round face. A bucket propped on her hip.

'This will be cold, I'm sorry.' She splashed water onto her.

Sam heard a hiss. Maybe the sound was only imaginary, but the liquid soothed fractionally more than it deepened her pain.

Denise was screaming. Sam felt herself fading. In the distance, a man cried, 'What on earth!'

In the next heartbeat, somebody shouted, 'LOOK OUT!'

A loud crash, the popping and snarling of debris and flames. Then Sam blacked out.

CHAPTER FOUR

THE CAR'S TYRES HISSED ON THE SLICK BITUMEN. WIND buffeted the little convertible, whistling as it crept through every tiny gap between the canvas soft top, glass and body.

Georgie gunned the accelerator, slipping past a tractor trudging along, half on tarred road, half on gravel. Trying to calculate when she'd get to Korweinguboora. Then jumping to her good luck at being relatively close by.

Maybe the magic story wasn't Allan Hansen's mysterious death. Maybe she'd had a kind of premonition leading her to be on the spot for a massive breaking story, all the better because of her connections with Daylesford. But if so, there might be a conflict over whether it could wait for the forthcoming issue of *Champagne Musings* or Georgie needed to sell it to a daily.

Her pulse thumped through her palms on the steering wheel, while her stomach turned. Several explosions and rampant fire couldn't be victimless. Someone had to be hurt – by property damage, if not physically. The same event that excited a journo or editor for its newsworthiness would leave people devastated. But finding and writing the truth was her job, so she brushed off the niggle.

Georgie slowed for her turnoff, then powered the Spider along the Ballan–Daylesford road.

What am I going to find when I get there?

————

A red Country Fire Authority tanker had beaten them to the corner of Back Settlement Road by seconds. Franklin recognised the crew-cab immediately – the primary voluntary fire brigade's appliance for Daylesford. Out quick, it probably held only a skeleton crew. The cumbersome truck took the left turn awkwardly, then paced up. It filled the width of the rough tarmacked road and rumbled with its siren blaring and lights flashing.

When Howell pulled the wagon in behind, the tanker blocked the forward view, so Franklin stared through the side window, expecting a tell-tale mushroom of thick dark smoke but wincing when he spotted it. Large and noxious looking.

He pointed. 'Over there.'

His offsider glanced and nodded, grim.

Neither spoke for a few moments. Bitumen turned to gravel as they wound through backroads that narrowed as they went. Sirens from the tanker and their car wailed out of sync, filling their silence.

Franklin lowered his electric window and sniffed. Even here, a couple of minutes from the farm, smoke and fumes impregnated the air.

He tilted his head and listened. He made out at least one siren well in front, possibly stationary and already at Riley's Lane. An appliance from another nearby fire brigade was his best bet.

Speedy response – this could turn out all right. Then, *Reports of several injuries,* on the police band dashed his hopes.

———

It occurred to Georgie that it was odd to be on this road without Daylesford being her destination. Not that Franklin was there anyway: he was posted nearly sixty kilometres away.

Her thoughts took a tangent from what lay ahead to Franklin. He had admitted to missing the crew at Daylesford more than he'd expected. And he was cynical about whether he'd ever be officially promoted to detective with the black mark from the investigation into the Savage kids' disappearance still shadowing him. So she could see what he was doing – playing down how much he was enjoying the new challenge in case it didn't pan out. She also got that he felt disloyal to his mates and his home town.

She turned her mind to the story she was chasing, driving by rote. Her left hand and both feet handled the gears, clutch and accelerator, while she was oblivious to the changes in landscape, from open pasture to forests of gangly gums, then a cypress pine plantation to her left as the road continued to wind and gently climb.

All the while, her thrill over the potential story alternately waxed and waned.

———

Howell dodged around a motley mix of utes, cars and trucks that'd arrived before them. Franklin figured some belonged to volunteer firefighters who'd come direct instead of joining the trucks at the CFA shed. Others would be neighbours pitching in. Fortunately, they'd showed nous and parked along the lane where the sides weren't channelling water overflow, leaving room for emergency service vehicles around the burning structure.

The Murray place.

Howell steered up the driveway, then far left of the frantic scene, braking beyond the round-roofed garage. Franklin pushed his door open as the wagon was coming to a stop. He leapt out, sidestepped the swinging car door, then took stock, squinting through a haze of black smoke. Assessing dangers, the situation. Seeking signs of life.

This was worse than bad.

He coughed as fumes stung his throat, noting a silver Holden SUV parked behind a marked police truck. He recognised the ding and scrape on the truck's rear quarter panel. It belonged to the Daylesford station. They had a sedan and a truck and occasionally an unmarked loaner, but in these weather conditions, Sam and Irvy would've chosen the truck for a farm job.

'Sam? Irvy?' Franklin's shout was lost. Overwhelmed by the crackle and roar of flames, yells between people, and tooting horns.

Six firies dived out of the Daylesford tanker they'd followed up Back Settlement Road. Donned in yellow hard hats, fire suits and gloves, moving with well-practiced cohesion, unravelling the thick heavy hose, extracting other equipment. There was a sense of suppressed urgency. Rushing could put the lives of their crew in danger.

Franklin ducked around the Daylesford truck and an ultra-light appliance from Leonards Hill, as the fire captain from the smaller town waved to his Daylesford counterpart and loped over to strategise. The bloke always took the four-wheel drive quick-attack ute home, allowing him to travel directly in primary response to emergencies. His team would be here soon in the tanker.

After hasty words, the two firies split up, apparently working through their RECEO list. Franklin knew it backwards and carried out a similar pattern of hazard check and prioritisation as he searched for Sam and Irvy.

Rescue if possible was always the number-one priority.

Protect life and protect property came into *check exposure*. Risks like arcing electricity wires or combustibles, and potential for the fire to spread to other buildings and vehicles.

The focus would then move to containment and ultimately extinguishment. Down the line, they'd overhaul the scene, ensuring the fire couldn't rekindle and making it safe for investigators.

He mentally logged what he noted as he called out, 'Sam! Irvy!'

Long grass around the house – but it was green and wet from the recent rain. A small mercy, particularly in these squally conditions. Dry fuel and blustery wind would've turned their house fire into a fast-running grassfire, and possible bushfire too, with Wombat Forest edging Korweinguboora in spots.

He didn't like the proximity of a clump of large trees. The closest structure was the garage. The nearest vehicles aside from the fire trucks were the two four-wheel drives in front of the garage and a couple in the attached carport. They'd need to keep the fire clear of these combustibles, watch for embers.

Franklin hopped over a thick hose, eyes watering as he approached the burning house. His breathing laboured as the smog of hot vapours intensified.

Where the fuck are they?

It was what – fifteen or twenty minutes since the first explosion? And already fire engulfed the Murray home. Even as he watched for a few seconds, the flames swelled. They whooshed high and hungry, chewing everything in their path and erupting through the roof.

The destruction made Franklin wonder about the order: the blast, then fire, or other way around? His stomach dropped.

Where are Bel and Alec?

The Murrays hadn't crossed his mind until now. He froze, staring at the house.

They're not in there with the two boys?

―――

Georgie passed the old pub with the half-painted mural on its windowless wall. She trailed a couple of utes, all driving above the speed limit. Probably all headed to the same place, so she wouldn't have to worry about missing the turnoff.

'*...on the situation at Korweinguboora,*' grabbed her attention.

She straightened in her bucket seat and increased the radio volume.

'*Unconfirmed reports have indicated that several people have been injured in a number of explosions and fire called in at approximately 10.00am this morning.*'

The announcer sounded hyped.

'*It is believed that at least two police officers from Daylesford are among the injured.*'

Georgie inhaled sharply. Her immediate thought was, *Franklin*. Relief, then guilt, and horror.

―――

Franklin backtracked, found the Daylesford captain.

'What do you know, Rohan?'

'Very little, so far. You?'

'Sam and Irvy are here somewhere, plus a nurse. They were due to check on the Murrays.'

The firie cast an alarmed glance at the house, then back to Franklin. He squeezed Franklin's shoulder and hastened back to his crew. They sprang into action—one member directing the nozzle at the structure, his mate helping manoeuvre the awkward hose—and pumped water from the belly of the tanker.

Franklin was a cop, yet he'd been on the end of hoses and involved in many and varied ways around more fires than he'd wished. As the firies worked, the house continued to collapse, oxygen fed the flames, fanning them higher and hotter. His years of experience told him that containment was the best they could hope to achieve here. The building was a lost cause.

God help anyone inside.

Franklin homed in on a small cluster of people fifty metres away. 'Sam? Irvy?'

Frantic yelling stopped him dead. Fragments of an exchange between several firies reached him.

'Heat's getting up to the LPG cylinders!'

'...can't let them go up...'

'...roll them out the way...'

'...can't get close...'

'Too late!'

'RUN!'

CHAPTER FIVE

THE EARTH SHOOK UNDER FRANKLIN'S FEET. WITH IT came a boom and an orange flash that cut through the black smoke. Several people cried out. Impossible to tell if they were hurt or merely scared.

Franklin realised he was rooted to the spot with his mouth open. As he snapped out of the daze, a warning, 'Look out!' came back-to-back with two further explosions.

There was a clamour of action, then a distinct, 'Clear?'

From a different direction, 'Anybody hurt?'

'No, Captain!'

'All good here.'

More blasts might be coming. Franklin needed to find Sam and Irvy and get them to safety.

That's if they're not already...

He let out a ragged breath. No way he'd finish that thought.

He scanned back to the bunch of people he'd been approaching before the blasts. Dressed in overalls or jeans, they were probably neighbours or friends of the Murrays. Were they safe there?

Depends on what we're dealing with.

He glanced at the chaos around the house.

Booby traps?

An aftershock trembled through his nerves. He'd been through appalling things in the job – *but this?*

He caught himself. He had to prioritise the safety of the civilians and his workmates – not necessarily in that order. After that, they'd untangle what had happened. The cause. Who or what was to blame. Deal with charges and the consequences.

Franklin started towards the civvies. One moved off. Before the circle reclosed, he glimpsed a body on the ground and broke into a run. He swore when a firie blocked his path. A stranger, so not part of the Daylesford crew.

He tried to push through, but the bloke gripped his arm.

'Step back.' His voice rumbled through a mask. 'We've got some injured folk.'

Franklin said, 'I'm police.'

The firie took a pinch of his suit jacket. 'Where's your gear? The old place is riddled with asbestos. Get your protective gear on. And then–'

Franklin yanked his arm free. 'They're my mates, get it? I don't care about procedure. I need to know that they're okay.'

He had seen enough to know that wasn't the case. And also to know who was writhing over there.

———

It couldn't be Franklin, but that didn't mean Georgie wasn't freaking out. Her stomach hollowed as her mind's eye panned over Franklin's friends. Hers too now.

Lunny? Sam?

She couldn't bear the thought.

Harty? Slam? No, not them either!

Franklin would be shattered if any of these four was hurt. They were his best mates. But the whole team was tight, there wasn't one you'd wish had been hurt over the rest.

Maybe the reports were wrong. No police casualties or nothing serious. Or they were from another station. She curled inside, guilty for wishing that, then obsessed over the Daylesford cops. Who might've been rostered on this morning?

Irvy? Or what's-his-name – the new guy?

She had to get a grip.

Georgie's mobile rang. She glanced to the cradle, saw Judd's name on the screen and let her editor go to voicemail. If her friends were involved, this wasn't a story now. It was personal.

She heard a growing cacophony of sirens and spotted an ominous haze. She floored the Spider, honking as she overtook a van.

———

The CFA bloke clapped Franklin's back and thrust a bundle at him. 'Take these. Ambos are coming.'

Franklin grabbed the items, grinding his jaw as he nodded. He jogged, splashing through puddles to the huddle of people, disregarding the phone vibrating in his pocket as he nudged his way through.

He sank into a crouch. 'Sam, it's me. Franklin.'

It took a moment, then seemed to register.

He didn't know what to do. Instinctively, he wanted to hold her. His fingers reached, then he brought his hand down.

Sam whimpered as a woman dribbled water over her. Her blue uniform was almost unrecognisable. She must've been struck full-frontal.

'We try to cool her down, but might be wrong thing in this...' The woman signed to the sky.

Franklin got her meaning. She was rightly uncertain. While it might soothe Sam's burns to a degree, in these freezing conditions, the cold water could be a mistake.

Oh, shit. Who's screaming?

Blokes were knotted together five or so metres away. Seemed to come from there.

Irvy? Or too high-pitched for him?

Franklin's eyes ran over a firie leaning over something – from his shape and size it could've been the bloke who'd stopped him a minute ago. Another bloke filled a knapsack sprayer from a caged water cube on the back of a ute. He joined the firie, who shifted, allowing Franklin to see a person lying on the ground. The side of a face and hair. Female. A second burns victim.

Brunette. Not Bel Murray.

The vic's shrieks twanged Franklin's already strained nerves. He skimmed over bunches of people, desperate to locate Howell. Couldn't see him and grappled with what to do.

Look out for his mates first—help Sam, find Irvy—or go to the woman's aid? There was a firie with her who'd have at least basic medical training. But by the sound of it, she must be in poorer condition than Sam.

He glanced at his friend and doubted himself. He'd seen burns victims in his time. It's unavoidable when you live in the country, even more so as a copper. Horrible household accidents, especially burns to kids from boiling water or stovetop incidents, were the most common, along with bushfires. They were hard to forget.

Some of the vics looked a whole lot worse in the days after copping their injuries than at the scene. In any emergency, you had to watch the quiet ones, like Sam. They could be beyond the initial stage of shock, their bodies shutting off from anxiety and pain. Declining blood pressure could put critical stress on organs that might also have been impacted in the primary trauma. Breathing could stop – particularly in cases of airway burns. Inadequately managed, shock was deadly.

Franklin spurred into action. 'Could I have a little space?'

The onlookers stepped back.

Trying to ignore the smell and his fear of getting it wrong for Sam, he assessed her vitals and ran a head-to-toe check.

Her pupils were dilated and her pulse thready. Blood was congealing around a wound to the back of her head, but it looked bad. His feeling was that they were dealing with an impact injury before or after the burns – whether she fell or was struck, he had no idea. She had a compound fracture to her fibula, bleeding around the protruding bone, and imbedded debris. He was scared to remove her clothing, knowing infection was one of her biggest risks, and for fear of hurting her more.

He remembered the bundle the firie had handed him. He'd set it down and forgotten it. A few plastic-wrapped, large burn sheets and gauze pads had never looked better.

Sam flinched when he applied a pad to her leg, holding it to the wound for a minute. Inspecting the pad, the blood was dark-coloured and the amount moderate.

He made a judgement call. Prioritise her shock. Wincing, he pressed a clean pad to the leg fracture, then cloaked her in a sheet. He put another gauze pad under her head to cushion the wound there.

Sam gave a faint cry.

Franklin caught the attention of the woman who'd been helping her earlier. 'Can you keep pressure on that pad on her leg through the sheet?'

'Yes.' She went into action with the air of a farmer used to helping sick or injured livestock. Evenly, she said, 'I am Vlatka. You are Sam, yes?'

Sam murmured, then squirmed, maybe trying to sit up.

'Best to lie still.' Vlatka maintained her hold on the pad but gazed at Franklin. Expecting him to lead.

He focused on a spot where fire hadn't left its mark – Sam's right ear and a thatch of black hair over it. He stroked the hair. 'You'll be okay, Sam.'

Will she?

She gasped, mumbled. He leaned closer and made out, 'Is Denise alright?'

'Denise?'

He glanced towards the other injured woman, racking his brain. Who was she? A friend or relative of the Murray family? He couldn't recall a Denise working at the kindergarten. Nobody jumped out from around town. Was she the nurse Sam and Irvy were here to meet?

His mobile buzzed inside his pocket. Whoever it was would have to wait.

———

'Shit, voicemail.' Georgie pressed disconnect before the beep. No doubt Franklin would be fielding calls, maybe in transit to the scene himself. He didn't need his phone jammed with unnecessary messages.

The car ahead turned after a paddock full of rusty junk and wrecks. She shot a glance at the black and orange funnel of smoke in the sky, and judged they were going to the same place. She shadowed behind.

Her mobile rang. She flashed through two candidates— Franklin, unlikely; Judd, more probable—and checking the screen saw it was neither. Not in her address book. She let it go.

The call rang out as Georgie's knuckles knotted around the steering wheel. She'd left the radio on for news updates, but reception was crackly and intermittent and could ghost to nothing any moment.

The rock riff on her phone went again.

———

'What's the go?'

Franklin jolted at the voice beside his ear. He'd missed Marty Howell's approach. Some of his panic ebbed, knowing his partner had his back.

Sam must've heard Howell and tried to rise.

'Stay calm.' Franklin eased her horizontal. 'Be a tick.'

He hoisted himself up. In a low tone said, 'Get onto D24 and let them know we have at least one member down.'

Howell agreed. 'And we're going to need the arson and explosives squad.'

'Yep.' Franklin whispered, 'Sam's in a bad way.' He summarised, 'Conscious, but second or third-degree burns mostly to her front, an injury to the back of her head, and an open fracture to her left leg.' He tapped his mid-calf area. 'Bleeding's subsided and she's in a burn sheet, but she needs the ambos here asap. And there's another injured woman over there.'

Howell followed his finger-point as Franklin sped on. 'Name's Denise, apparently. Might be the nurse Sam and Irvy were meeting. Don't know the status of her injuries...but it sounds bad.'

He took a breath, but dread made it ineffective.

Howell needed to contact communications HQ – urgently. But Franklin had to know. 'Any news on Irvy? Alec and Bel Murray and their two little boys?'

His partner's lips pulled. 'Nope. But when we're able to speak to Sam or Denise, we should be able to piece things together. The Murrays could've been out when Sam and Irvy arrived. Might be off visiting and blissfully unaware.' He glanced at the devastated house.

He'd skirted the question, avoiding the first part. Franklin clamped Howell's bicep. 'What do you know about Irvy?'

Howell did a headshake. 'The firies wouldn't let me near the house. The blaze is out of control, and they can't get inside.'

He stepped away, extracting his mobile radio, and Franklin deciphered what his partner hadn't quite said.

Irvy's unaccounted for. But it's assumed he's in there.

Meanwhile, the best the firies could do was an external attack until they got the fire under control and it was deemed safe to enter. Too late for whoever was in there.

His gaze went to the burning wreck as more glass shattered. With a heavy groan, another section of roof collapsed. The thud vibrated through the earth. Embers scattered. A fireball landed too close for comfort. Several trees were alight, driving the firies back.

He checked his watch. Ten or so minutes since their arrival. Seemed like longer, but also that he'd wasted every second.

Howell traded the radio for his mobile phone, and Franklin heard him say, 'We'll need extra bodies from the crew – anyone you can dig up.' He guessed he meant their CIU team, then his thoughts ping-ponged back to Irvy.

Their truck's here, but Irvy could've gone for help.

But wouldn't he have taken the truck? Something must've stopped him. Maybe Sam had the keys. Maybe he was helping a third casualty and the news hadn't filtered down the line yet.

Or maybe he's injured, and they haven't found him. Clear of the fire. Unconscious. So he can't call out.

Franklin frowned. Unlikely that Irvy was lying around and

hadn't been spotted. Even if the shockwave from the initial blast had sent him airborne, he'd only be so far from the house, wouldn't he? They couldn't miss him.

Howell broke into his thoughts. 'You see to Sam.'

His eyes were watery. Franklin hoped it was smoke-induced, not tears. If his mate lost it, so would he.

'I'll check on Denise and send an update. I've got bods from our crew coming, and I'll let Lunny know direct on his mobile and get as many from Daylesford as possible.'

Franklin watched him go. Imagining his old friend and boss's horror when Lunny learned about Sam and Irvy. And losing it anyway.

CHAPTER SIX

THE CALLER WAS THE ONE WHO HAD TRIED HER PHONE only a few minutes ago. Apparently, they thought it was urgent. Georgie decided it wasn't and she'd best keep the line open in case Franklin or one of the others rang.

Her phone beeped a moment after the last ring. They'd left a message this time.

'You'll still have to wait,' she was muttering when the radio transmission went to static. She killed the switch. Sirens were suddenly loud inside the cabin and exacerbated her guilt. She couldn't ignore the message – what if it was Franklin using someone else's mobile? Or not him, yet it had to do with Korweinguboora.

She called her voicemail.

'Miss Harvey? It's Hilda Getty here.'

The delay was long enough for Georgie to think there was nothing further.

'You met my husband earlier? Well...'

Another hesitation then, *'It'd be better to speak directly. Please phone me.'* She rattled off a number. Broke again for a lengthy pause and in a whisper added, *'If my husband answers...um...hang up.'*

Georgie's mouth widened. Curiouser and curiouser.

'No message please.' Hilda's voice had an anxious note. *'I'll see your number and will get back to you when I can.'* She repeated her number, and the message ended.

Her imagination reeling, Georgie missed the car ahead slowing before it turned without indicating. She almost rear-ended it. Swore as she stamped the brake and geared down, understanding when she saw a string of haphazardly parked cars.

She sent up a prayer to any god listening to keep her friends safe.

————

Franklin snapped out of his inertia and knelt beside Sam. 'How's she doing?'

The shoulders of Vlatka's thick, red flannelette jacket lifted to her ears, stuck for three seconds and dropped. Enough said.

Belatedly, he introduced himself. Adding, 'We're colleagues.' He motioned to Sam. 'Friends.'

'My husband Sven is over there.'

Vlatka directed her nose to the huddle around the other casualty. A man wore a similar jacket to hers but in blue, and Franklin guessed he was Sven. Matched in short rotund shape, they probably shared a wardrobe.

'We live on the next farm.'

He stroked Sam's patch of unmarked hair. 'Do you know the other woman?'

Vlatka shrugged. Her stomach expanded, testing the buttons on her jacket. 'No.'

He went to continue, side-tracked when Sam tried to sit up.

She said hoarsely, 'Irvy? Denise?' Wild-eyed, she flapped an arm, cried out and fell back. Her head bounced on the ground. Her body quivered with rapid, shallow breaths.

Franklin murmured. More noise than coherent words, while his mind churned.

Sam was still panting, but her teeth chattered intermittently.

'Are you cold?'

She didn't respond, bar a roll of her eyes. It looked involuntary.

Where're the ambos?

Her eyes rolled again, showing too much blood-shot white.

I can't leave her.

'Vlatka, see my colleague over there?' Franklin pointed out Marty Howell, standing apart, using his mobile. He took over putting pressure on Sam's leg. 'Ask him for the ETA on the ambulances?'

'I will.' She moved off.

He breathed with that small relief and went back to talking to Sam.

———

Sam floated in a strange way. Numb, not scared. Dreaming. Franklin was in her dream.

She thumped back to reality. Shivering, coughing and wheezing, all at once.

'Sam? Easy there, mate.' Franklin came into view, his brow cut in deep furrows.

She wanted to tell him not to worry but couldn't. Her dream pulled at her. At odds with yelling and crashing sounds. Then an approaching siren. That was comforting.

Help for Denise. And Irvy.

With a long sigh in her mind, Sam drifted.

―――――

Over twenty years in the force. Most of them at Daylesford, a soft, country posting by comparison to many stations around Victoria, especially Melbourne's CBD and suburbs. But still, he'd dealt with his share of crap, on and off the clock. This though...it'd have to be the worst of the lot.

'Franklin!'

He looked down on Sam. She hadn't spoken. Couldn't have. She was out of it.

I really am losing it.

He confirmed she was breathing. He'd have to put her in the recovery position. Watch the leg as he moved her. He shivered, aware he was sweating heavily, the perspiration turning to ice with the windchill.

At a touch to his arm, he jumped.

―――――

Franklin whipped around to Georgie. Smudged with dirt and smoke, but underneath the grime he was too pale. She saw why as she hunkered beside him.

She whispered, 'Sam?' Mind screaming, *Oh, shit. No. Why did it have to be Sam?*

She wanted to comfort Sam but was afraid – and she appeared to be unconscious. Georgie swung her gaze to Franklin and realised that he was staring at her as if he didn't trust his eyes.

She gave his thigh a squeeze. 'It's really me.'

He shuddered and pulled her in tight, then pushed back. 'Help me put Sam on her side.'

'She's unconscious?'

'Yep, but breathing.'

Thankful for that, Georgie said, 'Who's her partner?'

'Irvy.' His expression was stricken. 'We don't know where he is.'

Fuck.

He nodded as if she'd said it aloud. Then he peeled a sheet off Sam, and the acids in Georgie's stomach surged to the back of her throat. Their friend's injuries were so awful, she didn't know where to look. The sheet whipped in the wind, and Franklin rammed it under his knee.

'Be mindful of her leg,' he said.

A bloodied pad mostly covered that wound, but she saw enough for her imagination to fill in the blanks.

Poor Sam.

Together, slowly and gently, they transferred Sam to the three-quarter prone position. Franklin pulled out the sheet, mud-stained and mucky with stuff Georgie did not want to think about. He stared at it, brow wrinkled, confused.

She said, 'Better use a fresh one.'

Sam didn't stir while they covered her with their last clean sheet. Georgie watched her for a moment. Sickened and scared. And simultaneously compelled to draw in the details.

'Coming through! Paramedics! MAKE WAY!'

Georgie rose and beckoned to a pair donned in dark uniform with reflective vests. 'Over here!'

She glanced back to see Franklin's hand under Sam's nostrils and his face turn ashen.

CHAPTER SEVEN

'SHE'S NOT BREATHING!'

Panic fizzed in Franklin's chest.

Not Sam!

A strange numbness came next. Not a good feeling. No use to Sam.

People were saying stuff, but it was like being underwater – he saw their lips move, heard burbling, but couldn't understand. He flicked over the faces looming around him: Georgie's, a male ambo, his female partner. All this probably only took seconds, but it seemed protracted.

It was Vlatka that he settled on; the calmest. Time did another warp and the gap between her hand reaching out and the actual touch to his shoulder stretched.

Then he was back. Every sense sharp. Automatically in tune with the female ambo, carefully transferring Sam to her back.

He watched the deft movements of her blue-gloved hands complete a respiratory assessment, as he described Sam's condition.

'She—Sam—has been intermittently conscious and responsive...breathing until a moment ago. Suffering a rear-head injury, shock, lower leg compound fracture with moderate bleeding, severe burns to most of the body. Because of...' He broke off. Rephrased. 'Full secondary survey was difficult in the circumstances. Initial cooling with water by bystanders–'

The ambo cut in. 'For how long?'

'I think, ten minutes,' Vlatka supplied.

'Clean running water?'

'Buckets...'

Franklin wished he hadn't seen the ambo's cringe, reading her worry about infection. She leaned back on her heels. 'Breathing again.'

He exhaled, relieved and finished his summary. 'At that point, I prioritised Sam's shock and covered her – infection and heat loss, you know?'

The male ambo told him he'd done good. Franklin doubted it.

Then it was all go, with the paramedics continuing their assessment. Franklin filled anxious moments clocking their nametags—Cal and Zeenia—and leading introductions.

He picked up his situation report. 'The second casualty is Denise, but that's as much as I know.' He caught Marty Howell's attention and waved him over, but his partner shook his head. 'Serious, I think.'

Both ambos nodded.

'And there are several other people currently unaccounted for.'

Zeenia said sharply, 'Say what?'

'The homeowners, Belinda and Alec Murray, along with their two sons, who are around eight and two years old.' He rocked a hand to show he wasn't certain of the boys' ages.

The angles of her cheekbones sharpened.

'And Sam's partner, Senior Constable Grant Irvine, known as Irvy.'

'Oh, mate, sorry to hear that.'

Cal hooked Sam up to oxygen. It looked painful.

Thank God she's out of it.

'We need to examine Denise too, as first responders.' Zeenia rose and ran through a list for Franklin to monitor. She added, 'Another ambo and a MICA unit are on their way, but we're it until then.' She pulled his gaze. 'It's tough when it's one of your own, a mate, but you're doing good. Keep it up. Let us know if Sam's condition deteriorates.'

A lump filled the back of his throat. He especially appreciated her calling Sam by name, instead of *the casualty*. He didn't want them to leave, but Denise's condition might be more life-threatening than Sam's.

Georgie broke into his thoughts. 'What do you want me to do?'

He blanked. 'Don't know. Howell's spoken with Lunny and rallied our troops. The CI and Daylesford troops,' he clarified, unused to the outsider status of his detective's suit. Then he thumped his forehead. 'I didn't think of Kat. I don't want her finding out about this from some bitchy teenager.' Dread balled in his gut. 'So speak to Maeve. Ask her to get Kat out of school and explain as much as we know.'

Georgie extracted her phone.

That should've made him calmer. Maeve was like a nan to Kat and would do the right thing by her. And his daughter was a mature seventeen – had to be with a cop-dad as sole parent for all practical purposes.

But it didn't.

Kat and Sam were tight. Their failure to keep three local kids under their watch safe last spring, and the desperate hunt after they went missing, had cemented already close mateships between all of them involved.

This will crush her.

CHAPTER EIGHT

GEORGIE DIALLED OUT ON HER MOBILE AND RUBBED HER eyes. The thick fumes were irritating them like crazy.

The phone picked up.

'Maeve. It's Georgie.'

'Oh, love. Have you heard?'

'Yes. Long story, but I'm at the scene.' She sketched what she could on Sam, then Denise, dreading the inevitable question.

'And Irvy?'

The quiver in Maeve's words nearly undid Georgie. She cleared the smoky phlegm coating her throat. 'No news on Irvy or the Murrays yet.'

'Oh, no.'

Georgie tuned into approaching sirens. The volume of voices rose around her, driving her to the point. 'Franklin needs your help.'

Franklin clocked a car ablaze with strobes coming up Riley's Lane. With its fluoro-yellow outlined blue-and-white chequers and high-vis lettering, the highway patrol car was designed for obvious police presence. This one stood out like dog's balls even in the orange-black haze.

Right behind was an ordinary marked blue-and-white. A knot in Franklin's neck pulsed. Help had arrived, but if the blue-and-white was from Daylesford, the level of tension would skyrocket.

He checked on Sam—still out cold—and turned back to the cop cars as they came up the driveway. They entered the front paddock. Someone had moved the horses out back with the cattle, freeing up this area for a makeshift car park. Half a dozen vehicles already filled the corner.

A lone cop exited the candy car; two uniforms from the second sedan. Franklin recognised them all, though they weren't from Daylesford. A reprieve. He exhaled.

As the three conferred, he read their puffed-out chests, stressed manner. They weren't as personally connected, but each knew the whole Daylesford crew, having worked together on various occasions over the years and via semi-regular social gatherings.

He fixed on the highway patrol driver who kept handling his holstered weapon and barely looked at the other two. The HWP was doing what Franklin had failed to. Focused on Sam, he hadn't treated this as a crime scene with the perpetrators possibly still in the vicinity and the potential for more booby traps.

Friends or not, vics were vics – they needed to be made safe then handed over. And processes had to be followed. Whatever needed doing done.

Emotions had to be turned off, the situation dealt with. It's what cops do.

———

She pushed the disconnect key on her phone and hearing 'Georgie?' swung around.

'Marty.' She hugged the detective. 'I can't believe it. Sam... and Irvy...'

Howell's face turned into a hound's, all sags and sad. But he said, 'We stay positive, yeah?'

She bobbed her chin.

'Walk with me.' He indicated to a bunch of uniformed cops beelining to Franklin. 'They'll check-in with him, and he's tied up with Sam. We need to make progress before the circus really starts.'

Georgie fell into step with Howell. Despite having no intention to write this story, she dropped into journo mode as they approached a barn with a rounded roof. She took in everything in high-definition detail. The substance that makes articles transcend mere words on the page, takes readers into the scene.

The shed was a patchwork of steel cladding. A few shiny pieces, many with remnants of different paint colours—faded green, yellow, red, blue—and bearing various degrees of rust. It had double doors set back from the front posts by around a car's length, creating a carport in front of a garage. An eight- or ten-year-old Nissan Patrol with a snorkel and 'dads car' drawn onto the red-mud-crusted duco in wonky lettering sat adjacent to an older, cleaner Nissan Navara dual cab utility – presumably the mum's car.

On the left of the dual cab, a rope draped the length of the carport: a rudimentary clothesline. Sheets and pillowcases, and jeans, windcheaters, T-shirts and underwear in four sizes—male and female adult, child and infant—flapped as icy wind tunnelled into the shed, pulling at the multicoloured pegs. The bleached white cloth nappies and tiny romper suits, one with I'M THE BOSS, made Georgie's chest contract.

She tore her eyes away from the baby's clothes to where Howell had looped – a police truck and a smaller, silver SUV near the shed. The Holden Captiva had a BALLARAT decal; the letters were filled with the design on the Australian flag.

Circling the vehicles, Howell peered inside. He tried the truck handle: locked. He did an extended survey of the Captiva, still without touching it.

'It'll help to know who this belongs to—Denise or someone else—before the heavyweights arrive. If it's not hers, we have another MIA. Could be a vic, witness or suspect.'

'You didn't get anything out of Denise?'

'She could barely breathe, let alone talk.' He flinched. 'I was happy to hand over to the ambos.'

Georgie's mind went to Denise and Sam, and how they would come out of this.

Howell gave her an odd look, maybe wrongly assuming she'd judged him.

'I felt useless there with Sam,' she admitted. 'We leave it to the experts to do their thing and concentrate on ours. That's the best way we can help.'

He agreed, pointing to the Captiva. 'And that's the only thing we've got at present.'

He extracted a pair of disposable gloves and snapped them on. 'Sam knew Denise by name, so it's a fair bet that she's the nurse they were meeting. But even if that's true–'

Georgie finished for him, 'It doesn't automatically clear her.'

'Yep. Everything here is part of a crime scene – we don't know what's important yet.'

She thought aloud. 'Even the SUV placement behind the

truck could be significant. Could've been deliberate, to block them in.'

'True.' The word was clipped. Howell instructed, 'Step right back and duck down until I've got this open. Cover your head.'

She retreated around ten metres, watching him use the tip of his index finger to release the driver's door. If he triggered a device, Howell would go up and she probably would too. He was a smart cop and he'd made the choice. Hell, there was no choice. They had to pitch in.

With the same finger, he eased the door open. Held tense, then his shoulders loosened.

Georgie scrambled up and went to Howell.

He was muttering, 'Trust nothing and nobody and note everything. Until we know differently.' Could've been talking to her or himself.

She glanced over to the Murray home and the yellow-clad firies fighting the blaze. It looked hopeless. By the time the fire was safe, nothing would be salvageable: item or person.

If this was deliberate...

Her gut burned. People did it all the time: financially strained, money tied up in an asset that would be slow to move or would barely cover their debts at a quick-sale price.

Who said this's about building insurance?

She pictured the baby clothes pegged to the line. Didn't know what to think.

Trust nothing and nobody, like Marty said.

CHAPTER NINE

Franklin watched Sam's eyelids quiver. Having a nightmare, or trying to come to?

He heard, 'Mate,' and rose, glancing around to Stuie, who regularly rode the HWP unit in the area. They shook hands, then Hallsy the sarge at Trentham and her constable Benno both slapped his back.

Hallsy asked, 'How is she? And Irvy?'

Franklin kept a watch on Sam, filling them in as quietly as he could over the mayhem. He had to switch off from the sorrow on their faces, instead zoomed in on Sam.

He tossed up leaving one of the uniforms with her while he took the lead. Despite his earlier thinking about the requirement to focus on the crime scene, it was a crap decision.

'Hallsy.'

She nodded.

'I'll stay with Sam until handover to the ambos. Get things started, okay?'

The sarge said, 'Yes,' but Franklin specified it anyway. 'Do what you can to preserve the scene. Limit access to those that need to be here. Get names of everyone, especially witnesses. Me and Marty Howell will take statements later.'

He looked around for his partner, and caught sight of him and Georgie near the shed.

Shit. What are they doing?

There had already been multiple explosions. In the chaos, and with him tied to Sam's side, communication was snatched words when people passed. He had no idea if they'd ID'd the source of the blasts, or if there was risk of more. Meanwhile, Georgie and Howell were poking around a stranger's vehicle adjoining the garage. Either could hold explosives, tripwires.

They weren't even wearing protective gear.

———

Sam coughed, tearing her throat. She went to lift a hand, but one arm was numb and the other pinned. She forced open her eyes. It took her moments to clear some fuzz, then to make sense of an arm extended away from her and the other tucked into her body under a cover.

With a hacking cough, she managed to bring a hand to her mouth, startled by a mask tented over her face. She tried to pull it off and sit up.

'Leave it on, Sam.'

Franklin removed her hand. It hurt. Then she felt a small sense of relief that he was still there. And then she wanted to cry. If only she could rewind back to the moment when she'd jumped into the truck with Irvy this morning.

No. Further back.

Rewind to where he'd decided to come to work sick – if only he'd said no to Harty originally. If the first person at the door had smelt the odorant added to gas, none of this would've happened.

But that's why accidents suck.

She tugged at the mask, anxious to get up. On the ground, she was a victim. On the move, she was a cop, with purpose – helping Denise and Irvy.

She froze, questioning, *But that's why accidents suck?*

Her heart rapped a weird beat. Was it just an accident? That Irvy missed the danger sign of gas was freaky bad luck. But the rest of it?

She reverted to her earlier fear. *Oh, God. What if we were set up?*

———

Howell must've seen Georgie's shiver because he asked, 'You all right?'

'Yeah.'

But her mind was racing, processing different scenarios. If she had to rank what she hoped had occurred here, accident would top the list, insurance fraud second. She'd covered and studied too many graphic crimes to not consider viler possibilities though.

The Murrays could've been targeted – with or without provocation or warning.

And they could be inside. Maybe alive.

Murder–suicide or domestic murder happened far too often, and she couldn't stand either phrase. They watered down what it was.

Maybe paranoia, drug abuse, or a power or martyr complex inspired one of the Murrays to stockpile enough explosives to cause the maximal bang, damage and body count.

Maybe they're watching – enjoying this.

Looking at the black smoke billowing from the house, anger

heated Georgie's veins. If this was aimed at her friends and the nurse, she wanted whoever was responsible to pay.

Too soon for judgements.

She redirected her attention to Howell. He gazed into the Captiva's cluttered cabin, and she held back her questions while he catalogued the contents.

'Woman driver.'

Georgie leaned closer, and he added, 'Travel mug.'

She checked the console drink holder, noting a smear of light lipstick on the rim of the mug and a couple of black elastic hairbands circling it – the so-called non-stick type that always snagged her wavy, red-brown strands.

'But the handbag in the passenger well clued me up first.'

Their exchange of grins was short. There, then gone.

'You spotted the compendium on the passenger seat, Marty?'

'Yes.'

He continued scanning the vehicle, while Georgie's imagination took off. Say Denise wasn't the nurse – who was she, then? And how did she fit in?

Lover, accomplice?

Mastermind?

And then?

Something backfired. Maybe literally.

Listening to Howell mumbling to himself and the clamour around them, Georgie's mind leapt to Denise as a cash-strapped relo who'd inherit if the family predeceased her.

A couple with two little kids who probably have a huge mortgage and bugger all cash in the bank? I can't see it.

She scoffed, making Howell glance her way. He reached for the handbag.

'Sam!'

Franklin's warning had an undertone. He was scared. Not what she needed from him. But she stopped fiddling with the mask.

She lay panting. In time, her breathing, Franklin's face, and the world around them receded, fuzzing around the edges, along with her thinking. Aware enough of being pulled under again though.

Might not come out of this one. Must fight it.

She tried to roll over.

'Sam, take it easy. Rest.'

Her eyes settled on the burning cottage and the swarm of CFA trucks and firies. The fuzziness came on stronger. She couldn't let it take her without knowing.

'Irvy?' Her voice rasped, but she was sure Franklin understood because he looked gutted. Worse still, he didn't answer.

Oh, God.

The last place she'd seen her partner was now a wall of fire. The front entrance, windows and walls blown out; fire burned in.

A volunteer firie lugging large bolt cutters stopped just forward of where she lay. Sam tried to see around the figure. Hard, because they had their headgear off and tucked under an arm, enlarging the obstruction.

'Is that *Sam?*'

Franklin sprang up, grabbed the firie and dragged them aside. He was gesturing, angry, and the firie's gaze split between him and Sam.

Sam couldn't hear them, but two things struck her. The pity. In the firie's face and body language. And recognition. Talitha worked at Sam's favourite café and occasionally had drinks with the gang at the pub – when she wasn't training or on a call with the CFA.

Talitha's mouth moved, telling Franklin, *I'm sorry.*

He flung his palms. Talitha put a hand on his shoulder.

Finally, they both glanced her way.

'IRVY?' Everything that Sam could muster went into that word.

Enough, because it brought them to her side. She let her head flop, spent, fog lapping her mind.

Hold on until you know.

'Where did you last see him?'

No words possible, but she made the smallest lift of her finger.

'The verandah?' Franklin guessed.

She shut her eyes, opened them, trying to communicate *No*. Pointed urgently. Waited for them to get it. Hoped they would. Fought the pull of nothingness.

'The front door?' Talitha sounded distant.

Sam shut her eyes, but quicker than before to signal *Not quite.*

'Did he go inside?'

Yes. She did two fast blinks.

Franklin repeated it back as her mind coasted.

———

Georgie itched to help. 'Got a spare pair of gloves, Marty?'

'Should have.' He rummaged through his pants pockets, both external pockets in his jacket and then the internal ones. He tossed a set across.

She pulled them on and picked up the compendium, thinking aloud. 'It's a diary, day-to-a-page.'

'Got your purse,' Howell muttered. 'So where's your licence?'

She flicked through the diary, heard 'Gotcha' but kept going. He'd share anything pertinent. Before she read any entries, she assessed the handwriting. In her untrained opinion, the neat, bold, upright cursive script looked feminine, though not love-hearts-for-dots-above-the-letter-i-girly.

'One current Victorian driver's licence for Denise Zachary.'

Georgie glanced up.

Howell added, 'Who apparently resides at Bakery Hill, Ballarat.'

'Good to know for sure,' she said.

He agreed.

'Denise has several entries in for today.' She tapped the page. 'A 9.00am, which just says "office". Her 10.00am is "Bel Murray, farm visit" – she'd allocated two hours for the return trip.'

She went to skim over the previous days, but was distracted when Howell angled the purse so she could see a protruding business card.

'Denise works for BRICC.'

At her head-tilt, he explained, 'A regional cancer centre at Ballarat.'

Georgie read the card. 'Breast care nurse.' Heavy-hearted, she suggested, 'Bel has breast cancer?'

'Maybe.' He puffed out his bottom lip. 'But how does that translate to a welfare check with police?'

CHAPTER TEN

FRANKLIN GLANCED AT GEORGIE AND HOWELL, STILL poking around the SUV. Seriously, he should know better than to panic. The most acute danger had passed the moment Howell had opened the door.

They should've waited. But would he in their shoes?

A wind gust buffeted him, peeling back the corner of the burn sheet around Sam. He knelt and tucked it in. His mind pinged back to the SUV. There could be other triggers. The boot or bonnet release, glovebox lock, ignition.

He wanted to go and help, but Talitha had left, saying she had to cut the chain around a bunch of spare gas cylinders to move them, before hoisting the bolt cutters over her shoulder and pulling on her headgear. She had merged into the crowd and the fog of fumes in the air trapped by the moist black cloud above, and he'd lost sight of her.

Sam was back in the recovery position. Unconscious. Breathing, but for how long until her body stopped again?

Franklin yanked at a tuft of his short, sandy hair. He needed news on Irvy. When he'd asked Talitha, her *No, sorry* reiterated there'd been no change to the little he knew – they hadn't located any further casualties near the burning structure, and they couldn't enter while the fire raged.

Gotta find Irvy.

Can't leave Sam.

Oh, shit. Kendra.

He heard a pained moan and checked Sam. She hadn't moved. Then he realised it'd come from him.

Kendra would go out of her mind once she realised local coppers were involved and she couldn't get hold of Irvy.

They had a feisty marriage, spent more time on the phone than any couple Franklin knew, and for at least half of those conversations they were arguing or patching things up. With a fleeting smile, he pictured Irvy often winking, admitting it meant plenty of make-up sex. And their five kids and one-on-the-way validated that.

The idea of Kendra turning up at the scene, wondering where her hubby was, set his pulse thundering.

———

Marty Howell opened the glovebox and flicked through the contents. It seemed to Georgie that they'd already taken too long to go over the Captiva. They'd verified the owner and joined a few dots. Surely, they should move on now?

Impatient for action, she shifted to the rear of the vehicle and raised the tailgate. Called to Howell, 'What are we looking for?'

'Anything suss.'

Small help. She shook her head.

He caught on and barked a short laugh. 'I'm hoping we don't find a thing – don't expect to. But look for anything that might implicate the nurse in what's gone down here this morning. Anything that points to needing the bomb squad, as well as arson.'

A frisson went up Georgie's spine. She met his eyes over the back of the seats. 'So, accelerants, that type of thing?'

'Yep.'

Excited yells came over the roar of flames and pump noise, and she turned to see more of the house collapse and embers burst into the smoke haze.

Something started that.

Georgie flipped the lid off a plastic tub and peered inside. Suspension files sectioned brochures and forms branded with BRICC and other logos. She pocketed a couple out of curiosity and turned to concentrate on the corner of the boot.

She lifted a tarp, dropped it and stepped back. 'Whoa!'

Howell's 'What?' was sharp.

'Jerrycan. And it reeks of petrol.'

———

Franklin tore his gaze away from the sweat beads on Sam's brow and upper lip at the sound of another approaching siren. He glimpsed a white wagon with flashing blues-and-reds, part of its fluoro 'MICA PARAMEDIC' lettering and a single responder on board, female. He stroked the patch of hair near Sam's ear, letting out a deep breath. A MICA ambo was among the best-trained in the service, their vehicle a mobile intensive care ambulance – both were a bloody welcome sight.

Splitting his gaze between his friend and the ambulance, Franklin saw the van pull up where it couldn't be boxed in, and a tall, lean woman exit and complete a once-over of the hectic belt of land. She extracted her kit and did another scan. He rose and waved towards Sam. The ambo acknowledged him. She strode out, long-legged, confident, not running but covering the metres rapidly, while constantly sifting the scene. Undoubtedly processing the incident, determining obvious casualties and potential hazards, prioritising treatment and assessing the need for additional resources.

'John.'

He jumped at the voice from behind. Turned to Tim Lunny, Sergeant at Daylesford and his old friend when not acting as a father-figure.

Franklin was struck by the worry in his eyes. He strove for something reassuring. In the end, he managed, 'Sam is stable, and MICA just arrived.'

He ignored Lunny's unspoken question. His priority was handover to the ambo.

'Hiya. I'm Shannon.' The MICA ambo offered her hand to them both, then got busy kitting up with gloves and protective glasses, shooting off a string of questions to clarify Franklin's rundown of Sam and Denise.

'We could have more casualties.' He outlined what he knew. Hated that it was so little.

'Got that.' Shannon gave a sympathetic grimace.

She focused back on Sam for a few minutes, full of reassurance and warmth that Franklin was grateful for. She helped her with a green whistle, and before the pain relief could've kicked in said, 'How's that, Sam? Already feeling a bit better, aren't you?'

Shannon said it with such confidence, while nodding enthusiastically, that Sam's negative shake of the head turned to bobbing for yes.

Then from out of nowhere, with the briefest glance at Lunny, she said, 'How're you feeling there, mate?'

In his side vision, Franklin spied Lunny pressing on his left shoulder.

'Yep, yep. All good.'

He didn't look it.

———

Georgie seized the jerrycan and gave it a shake. 'Nearly full.'

She noted the relief and letdown that flashed over Marty Howell, reflecting her own reactions.

Good and bad in that almost-full petrol container. Good, because everything so far indicated to Denise's innocence. Bad, because that left them no closer to understanding what they were dealing with: accident or sabotage, and who, if anyone, was culpable.

Howell went on with his search, but for a minute Georgie watched the people around her and the unabating flames, then fell to staring at stains on the yellow-and-red sticker on the fuel can.

The yellow-and-red jarred in her mind. A memory trying to emerge, with the sense that it was pivotal. Was it relevant to what had happened here on the farm? Or to one of her stories – perhaps Allan Hansen's death?

CHAPTER ELEVEN

NEARLY MIDDAY, THE MORNING WAS PRESSING ON.
Franklin's brain randomly replayed the sharp drilling of
increasing rotor noise and vibrating *wuppa wuppa* of the rising
MICA air ambulance that had double-loaded the critically
injured Denise and Sam for transport to the trauma centre at
the Alfred Hospital in Melbourne.

He couldn't shake Sam from his mind. He kept hearing *soot
in the airways...stridor... we'll have to intubate* and seeing
Shannon do the procedure. Over and over.

He used that to spur him on. Made a judgement that the
firies were gradually winning against the inferno, not that there
was much left of the Murray house, or Bel's garden out front.
He had done a brief canvass of the property, spoken to a cross-
section of witnesses, and ruled out more casualties – aside from
any poor bastard inside the house.

What next?

A sound made him freeze, before he checked it out. It had
happened numerous times already today. Dreading Kendra

turning up. And almost as much, the inevitable flock of suits and officials.

At least one police officer critical and another MIA. One civilian down and a family of four also unaccounted for. A house destroyed by a fire fuelled by accelerants. Several exploding gas cylinders. Not yet known if all this was by accident, or by design.

The place would soon be swarming with specialist detectives and crime scene crews. The Goodlife Farm couldn't be less aptly named.

A voice broke into his thoughts. 'John.'

He pivoted to the newcomer, inhaling deeply.

'District Inspector, sir.'

'Eddie.'

Franklin nodded passively. He had given up on understanding where he stood with Eddie Knight. The DI could swing from cold to hot, from critical and threatening to proud and congratulatory in a flash.

He blanked his expression and summarised the situation, gazing at the most neutral part of the DI's face. His manicured sideburns.

'We're going to have to give them something.'

Franklin followed the DI's line of sight. With a punch to the gut, he clocked a few media broadcast vans and civvy vehicles amassed beyond the blue-and-white chequered police tape the uniforms had used to cordon off the front gate in a bid to control the scene. Almost impossible while they were still dealing with an active fire.

'I want you alongside. Stand united, all that. Brush yourself down and meet me at the front gate in ten.'

Without waiting for a reply, the DI coursed for Rohan Crichton. The man's radar couldn't be faulted in picking the senior fire captain as the one in charge, Franklin gave him that much.

Marty Howell appeared by his side. 'What's up?'

'He's giving an interview and wants me as a spare wheel. I've got inquiries to run.'

Howell's brows danced, and Franklin was relieved when he let his gaffe pass. He was basically a work-experience detective, his partner had the years under his belt. But this case couldn't be more personal, and he wanted to be front-and-centre of the investigation not cameras.

Embarrassment flushed his cheeks. He looked down and spotted muck on his trousers, pissed that Eddie Knight had taken about a minute to mention it.

He bent and rubbed off what he could, though as soon as he trudged over to meet the DI he'd accumulate more – and somehow, it'd fall right off his boss.

That pretty much summed up the differences between them.

———

Sam floated in semi-consciousness, listening to murmurs but unable to make out what was being said. The main speaker was a woman. Her tone was reassuring. She knew what she was doing and wasn't panicky, unlike the others.

Maybe it's not as bad as I think.

Who was she kidding?

She sighed, not sure it was out loud. The woman's voice faded.

———

Flanking the DI, Franklin lifted his head only once to where they were headed: the small pack of media mongrels hungry for anything they'd be thrown.

A pang of guilt said that was unfair. They were doing their job, and just because they looked excited, it didn't mean they weren't as horrified as everyone else. They played a role in serious crime. Some were good, ethical, intelligent, even made a difference to the results, like Georgie and her crime-reporter mate Matt Gunnerson with the MISPER case last spring.

He and the DI strode on, his boss muttering to himself, possibly practicing his speech. The closer they drew to the huddle of people around their broadcast vans, the noisier the babble. Journos already calling out questions. Sound and camera crews shouting directions about position, volume, and to *get the burning house in the backdrop*.

He reminded himself, *Just their jobs*. But anger burned up his oesophagus, filled his throat. He tugged at his collar. He caught a glance from the DI and straightened his tie while trying to stop visualising the news banners. Unsuccessfully.

Then they stopped, and were immediately circled by reporters with their mobiles thrust out to record the conference. Furry fat mics on boom poles swung in. On edge, and fearing he'd tell them what he thought, Franklin noticed one face in the huddle that gave him somewhere safe to look.

When their gaze met, Georgie gave him a head bob meant to be reassuring. Then she did what he understood all too well – took a sphinx impersonation, her eyes deep-brown pools that were alert but unreadable.

He spotted a phone in her hand, recording things. She was acting like them, more worried about filing for her magazine than Sam and Irvy. He couldn't look at her. Disgusted.

———

Franklin frowned and his face turned to a mask, but Georgie knew the tick of the pulsing vein at his temple and the clamp of his jaw so well. His tells when he was stressed or angry. So small, yet so revealing. She tried to catch his gaze, but he fixed beyond her.

She completed her test of the video function, then did a slow 360-degree sweep with her phone. The difference between her and the jostling group around her was marked. She wasn't mentally writing her opening paragraph or a title that her editor would redo anyway.

No, the video was purely for her reference, and out of deeply ingrained habit, not to quote in an article or tease out on Twitter. She was prone to taking down plenty of useless information via video or voice recordings and handwritten notes because, in among all of that, she'd generally capture helpful, possibly even vital scraps.

District Inspector Knight cleared his throat, and the volume of the rabble lowered. A number kept talking. Georgie felt breaths on the back of her neck. The male to her right bumped his pregnant-sized gut into her side. She snapped a look at him, but he missed it.

While the DI awaited silence, Georgie scoped the small crowd. Fast to gather, particularly those who'd come from Melbourne – someone's worst day making for someone's best news story. The trucks were from the city and Ballarat. A journo nearest the front half-turned, revealing the Channel 9 logo on her blue raincoat. Mic flags belonged to various regional TV and radio stations.

Knight shuffled on the spot. He drew back his shoulders and his decorated epaulettes winked. One of his hands clasped the other wrist. His dress uniform appeared immaculate, amazing for a press conference on a soggy road.

'Are we right?' he asked.

The Channel 9 reporter checked with her crew.

'Yep,' her camera and sound guys replied.

'Go ahead.'

Knight's chin steadied. 'At a little after 10.00am this morning, police received reports of a series of explosions,' he raised his hands and amended, 'or loud bangs,' he reclasped his wrist, 'and a house fire at this property.'

Journalists cut in, and Georgie strained to listen to the DI.

'Our first officers arrived within approximately fifteen minutes of the initial call, along with members of the Country Fire Authority, who continue to work to control the blaze.'

'How many people have been injured?' the man who'd bumped Georgie bellowed, nudging into her again.

Another butted in with, 'Can you confirm police casualties?'

Knight licked his lips and ignored both.

'At this stage, we are still gathering information. While there are many details I cannot provide at this moment, I can confirm that two police members were in attendance when the incident occurred here this morning. I can also confirm that paramedics treated a number of serious injuries at the scene before two patients were airlifted to Melbourne.'

That set off a frenzy of interruptions, but Georgie concentrated on the grim set of Knight's mouth. She sensed he was about to wrap up, and did a repeat arc with her mobile, probably capturing more armpits than heads in the tight-packed media huddle. She aimed the phone back at the DI.

'I trust you will respect the casualties and their families and not speculate on their identities, or upon what has occurred here in Korweinguboora today.'

Knight glanced at Franklin. They leaned in and murmured briefly.

Facing back to the crowd, Knight said, 'Our specialist

resources will attend shortly to help piece together events, and we hope to have further information for you soon.'

The man beside Georgie yelled, 'Do you suspect arson?'

He was loud and next to her ear, which thrummed in pain.

A female from ABC Radio called, 'Is this a domestic violence matter, District Inspector?'

Knight took a steely look. 'I'm sorry, but no questions at this time.'

He and Franklin swivelled on their heels and strode off.

CHAPTER TWELVE

AFTER THE DISTRICT INSPECTOR CONCLUDED THE PRESS conference, many of the journos squirrelled themselves away inside their cars or broadcast trucks, with a few using the latter as windbreaks. They filed their stories, then returned to gossiping among themselves. The more industrious sneakily approached CFA volunteers or witnesses, but if they weren't brushed off, they were curtly herded back by uniformed cops – often Franklin's best mates, Scott Hart and Mick Sprague from Daylesford.

Georgie hunted for Franklin and found him talking to a civilian – one of the neighbours, she guessed. When he closed his notepad and the woman trudged off in her muddy gumboots, she joined him.

'You okay?'

He gave her an odd look and didn't answer.

'Anything I can do?'

'Don't you need to phone your editor?'

His tone jabbed at her more than the words. She gave a sad headshake and turned to leave. Even after everything they'd been through and being an item for eighteen months, he still didn't quite trust her professionalism and loyalty, the barriers she'd constructed around her occupation and her friendships.

She took a few steps, then realised she was in the wrong. He'd misread her interest in the presser. His fight-or-flight response made him lash out rather than allow her in.

He hadn't moved when she twisted around.

'Not a journo here,' she called to him, approaching. 'Unless I can use it to help.'

His Adam's apple shifted up and down as he swallowed.

Georgie listened to shouts between the firies and the pump of the tankers, giving him a chance to reply.

In the end, she broke their silence. 'I'd better let you get back to it.'

Franklin breathed, filling out his chest. 'Ask around, but be careful not to lead the answers. Some people clam up with us, where they might chat with you.' He gazed over the property and back at her. 'Try to pinpoint what came first – fire or blast. Suss out any strange people or occurrences here lately. Anything unusual about the Murrays.'

She nodded. 'There had to be a reason for Denise requesting the welfare check, and that could be central to everything. But what's significant enough to cause all this? Relationship problems, an affair? Money, debt? Drugs, mental health?'

Franklin lifted his palms. 'People do fucked-up things for reasons we don't understand all the time.'

It struck Georgie that neither of them believed the Murrays were going to turn up unharmed nor that they'd be able to help them work out what had happened today.

CHAPTER THIRTEEN

AFTER MIDDAY, FRANKLIN RETURNED A BUNCH OF CALLS, surprised he hadn't heard from Kendra. She had his mobile number, and she'd used it plenty over Irvy's years at Daylesford. Once, when he was in court with his phone off and their little girl broke her arm. Another, when Irvy was doing a PD course, and his mum died; Kendra didn't want to give him the bad news in a message, and Franklin volunteered to drive down to Melbourne to deliver it personally. And on a bunch of occasions fortunately less fraught.

But not today. And as far as he knew, none of them had. He scrolled through his contacts and hesitated over Kendra's number.

Call her...and tell her what?

Better to wait until we know something more?

He scratched his chin, remembering how Bill Noonan, his original Daylesford sarge, used to bang on about *cat's on the roof* – confusing the heck out of those who hadn't heard the story of a bloke minding his brother's cat. It went that when the bloke phoned to check in, his brother blurted out, *Your cat died.*

Distraught, the first bloke told him he should've broken it gently, starting with, *Your cat's on the roof and it won't come down*, then called him the next day to say, *We got the cat down but it's not doing too good*, and finally broken the news a day or two later. The joke went on to finish with, *Mum's on the roof and we can't get her down.*

His mouth quirked at the memory, though this situation was far from funny. Figuring he should put the cat on the roof, he went to dial Kendra.

Stopped just before he touched the screen.

What if they had it wrong? What if Irvy was never here today? Or he went off on another job or a private task, and Sam had covered for him?

It wasn't plausible. He ticked off the reasons in his mind. Sam played things straight. She'd been frantic about Irvy and indicated he'd entered the house. And even if Irvy had gone off, it would have been on foot because he didn't have a vehicle, and surely, he would've returned at the commotion.

Franklin dropped his mobile in his pocket and inhaled the stench filling the air. They didn't know anything concrete. There was nothing to be gained by jumping the gun.

———

A woman walked into Georgie and mumbled, 'Sorry.'

Instead of moving off, she stood awkwardly, possibly desperate to unload.

'Chaotic, isn't it?' Georgie said.

The woman dipped her head, but her gaze was unfocused, and she swayed on her feet. She muttered, 'I can't believe it. I'm fixing the dam pump and there's this boom, and then flames lit the sky.' She flung up her arms, emphasising her description. 'And there were more blasts. *Here!* We're a quiet lot. This sort of thing doesn't happen to us. And Bel and Alec have lost everything. I can't believe it.'

Georgie commiserated, and the woman did a slow turn as if to go now that she'd said her piece.

'Do you have someone—'

'My son. And there is always Vlatka and Sven.'

She gestured to a paddock with the Murrays' cattle and a pair of horses loosely ringed around two figures, presumably Vlatka and Sven. Then she lurched away.

When Georgie approached the couple, she took one look at the skittish, young black-and-white cow that held the woman's attention and skirted it.

She joined Sven as Vlatka said, 'So exciting, eh?' and stroked the cow's upper back. Apparently talking to it, not Georgie.

The animal shuffled, hoofs squelching on the waterlogged paddock and eyes wary.

With few words needed, Georgie adopted Sven's rhythm, spreading feed for the herd.

'Don't they have enough food?' She skimmed over the lush paddock.

'A bit of roughage—dry feed—protects them from the wind chill.' The farmer smiled and patted his rounded belly. 'And a little treat soothes us all, yes?'

She found it telling that they assumed the Murrays weren't going to return soon to fend for the cattle themselves, but held back her questions.

The woman murmured to the fretful cow, 'Not ever seen this many people and heard this much noise in your life.'

Sven winked at Georgie. 'You watch now.'

Vlatka's soft drone went on as she extended the strokes with her hand. The cow stretched out its neck and let its ears fall. Then it nudged her shoulder and gave it a lick.

Georgie and Sven laughed.

A moment later his face fell, and he hurried to a cow hanging back. Blood trailed from its rear flank to hoof. The farmer's body blocked Georgie's view as he inspected the injury.

He called, 'She's cut herself. It is not very deep.'

Vlatka handed a bundle to Georgie, which she assumed she was supposed to give to Sven. The woman herself went on to reassure another large beast that was clearly rattled.

Georgie squatted by Sven, out of kicking range of the cows. She helped him steady the injured animal and clean the wound.

He spoke. 'Alec would not like that you are hurt.'

Weird how the couple talked to livestock like humans. But Sven's mention of Alec presented an opening for her questions.

'Have you and the Murrays been neighbours for long?'

'My family has been here since we came from Holland when I was a little boy. Bel and Alec moved in before Ethan came along.' He did a head-wave motion. 'The boy's – how old is Ethan, Vlatka?'

She made an exasperated noise. 'We went to his eighth birthday party last month, remember?'

Sven said mildly to Georgie, 'So nine years.' He tipped his hand, implying the number was approximate. 'But I've known Alec since *he* was born, yes?'

Alec was a lifelong local, while Bel wasn't necessarily – Georgie filed it.

The wound dressed, Sven rose with a light pat to the cow's rump and walked towards the fence. He began searching.

He didn't seem fazed by Georgie shadowing him.

'Look for tufts of hair, blood – where she might have caught herself.' He jerked a thumb back towards the injured cow. 'Might need repair.'

'Okay.' She inspected the fencing wire, mulling ways to keep Sven on the subject of the Murrays without being obvious.

He did it for her while mending a section of wire. 'They are a good family. Things have not been easy for them, but they hold together.'

She tensed. Was he alluding to a motive?

'Poor things. How's it not been easy?'

For the first time, Sven gave her an odd glance and hesitated. 'With Bel on maternity leave, money is tight.'

Georgie picked it as a half-answer. And that was all he was going to give for now.

CHAPTER FOURTEEN

FRANKLIN SPOTTED TWO SUITS CROSSING THE PADDOCK and muttered, 'Here comes trouble.'

'What's that, mate?'

He explained to Howell out of the corner of his mouth. 'Check out Mr Important – the bald bloke with barrel chest, beard and sunnies.'

His partner followed his gaze and smirked. Franklin presumed he agreed that only dickheads wore sunglasses on a wintery crime scene eclipsed by rain clouds and toxic smoke.

'And his crony, Bean-Man.'

They flicked to the second suited man who looked as if he'd been stretched on a rack.

Franklin predicted, 'Ds and coming this way. Guessing arson. Could be homicide or professional standards, if not.'

They'd all come...and some, depending on the outcome.

'Yeah, mandatory for this type of–'

A shout interrupted Howell. 'Franklin! Marty!'

Rohan Crichton waved and loped up to join them, a step

ahead of the two strangers. But he didn't get another word in before the bald bloke spoke.

'DS Ram Bruner.' Sunnies still in place, he offered his hand to Franklin and squeezed. He shook the others' hands, introducing his gangly offsider. 'DSC Pandu Darmawan.'

'Darma.' Putting out his hand, Darmawan used his free one to push his prescription glasses higher up his nose. Mauve plastic, the same colour as the shirt under his suit, teamed with a coordinating tie. On his bulky partner, both would've looked stupid, but they suited the lanky bloke's brown skin, and his grip was dry, firm but not deliberately crushing like Bruner's.

After Franklin filled in who was who, Darma said, 'Sorry for the circumstances.'

His accent held both an Indonesian and American twang; maybe overseas-born and English-language schooled by American expats or he'd done exchanges in the US. He sounded genuine.

'We're with arson and explosives. The rest of our crew are following.' Bruner gestured towards Riley's Lane, and Franklin spotted his mate Mick Sprague logging three more suits at the scene: two females and a male, all fresher-faced than Bruner and Darmawan.

Crichton joggled his helmet, reminding Franklin that the captain didn't have time to loiter and he'd come over for a reason. He lifted his brows in question.

'It's contained.'

Welcome words, yet his gut hollowed. He ran his gaze over the mill of people, thinned now by most of the neighbours and onlookers. Scott Hart, his other close mate from Daylesford, was in confab with Lunny, both at an angle away from them and best left out of it.

Anticipating what Crichton was going to say, Franklin said, 'Walk and talk.'

He strode off. They scrambled to catch up.

Crichton's deputy met them as the captain said, 'We're going in for a quick swoop.'

Nobody spoke for a minute or so – what was appropriate? The deputy handed out P2 face masks warning, 'You'll still need to keep back. Pre-1990s – it's bound to have asbestos.'

From memory, Franklin guessed the cottage had actually been pre-World War II with later tack-ons. 'I think the lean-to at the back would've been riddled with it.'

The firies nodded and fitted their breathing apparatus and helmets. Then they approached as a group, dodging hoses still trained on glowing coals and bands of flames.

The captain's voice was muffled when he said, 'The front of the house took the full brunt.'

Franklin gazed at what used to be the entrance – walls and windows blown outwards by the blast.

Understatement.

His next thought was, *And that was where Sam last saw Irvy.*

Irvy must have gone right into the house, or he would've been blown outwards with the walls and windows like Sam and Denise.

Georgie's phone had been running hot, and it rang yet again.

No preliminaries. *'What have you got?'*

'Little more than what the press conference covered, Sheridan.'

Her editor let out an exaggerated sigh.

'And the Gordon story?'

As if she'd been twiddling her thumbs since this morning.

'I haven't had the chance to progress it.'

'*I need something.*'

So much for *Take this week to recharge.* But she understood. Sheridan Judd wanted the inside scoop on what was happening here, while she recognised Georgie wouldn't provide it. But Judd hadn't achieved the rank of editor without clawing up and over people's feelings, and she relished holding the whip hand. She was flexing it now. In her eyes, Georgie was playing hard, so she was playing harder.

Georgie drew a breath, sucking back what she really wanted to say. This was her boss and the magazine her main income. 'As soon as I can.'

She'd barely disconnected when another call came in. The screen displayed a number that she'd missed earlier today. It could be important, so she picked up.

'*Miss Harvey. It's Hilda Getty here.*' She raced on. '*Anyway, while my husband's out...because you haven't rung...*'

Georgie apologised, despite only a few hours passing since Hilda's message. She explained, 'You have probably heard about the incident at Korweinguboora?'

Hilda made a vague noise of agreement.

'Well, I'm at the scene at present. Perhaps I could ring you back?'

'*I know something that I wish I didn't. I want to tell someone—you—and I am scared I will change my mind.*'

Georgie's pulse accelerated. 'Could you tell me now?'

'*Not over the phone. I can't risk him coming in and overhearing.*'

Him – her husband? Georgie's curiosity hiked, and she looked into the distance, picturing Bob Getty and his wife who she had only shared a few words with.

Hilda awaited her reply, but a shout and flash of movement caught her attention. Franklin's hands soared. Howell clawed the air, grabbing for him, then watched at a standstill.

Her excitement over the Gettys shrank as Franklin sagged forward clutching his temples.

CHAPTER FIFTEEN

Howell said something. Crichton stood frozen, holding a rake that levered a charred, cracked rafter and warped tin off what remained of the floor and substrate. Franklin moaned. There was no mistaking what lay underneath.

'Franklin?'

He turned, numb, as Georgie jogged up.

She said, 'Is it Irvy?'

It was like a mammoth wave was breaking over the top of him, which had happened a few times when he and Kat had visited his parents on the surf coast. Sound muted, skin burning as he scraped the seafloor, lungs crying for air. Scared he'd never swim out.

Georgie spoke again, her words lost on him. She wound an arm around him, gave him a squeeze, then let go.

Pull yourself together, Franklin.

'Has to be.' He shuddered.

Nothing left of the plastic, fabric and velcro of his equipment belt. But his pistol had survived.

They all watched in silence as the fire captain leaned over to check the figure. But in Franklin's mind there was no question that they were dealing with a fatality.

Crichton shook his head, confirming that Irvy was gone.

Best that way, considering what he'd copped.

Franklin called to Crichton, 'Leave it as you found it.'

It because he couldn't bring himself to say *him* or *the body* or *the deceased*. Not yet. And now, with at least one fatality—all the more so, a cop on a job—they had to preserve what they could of the scene. What was left of it after fire, multiple blasts, and tonnes of water.

Almost reverently, Crichton re-covered the form.

The arson Ds stepped up then. Even the arrogant Bruner had known to wait.

Darmawan patted Franklin on the back. 'I'm very sorry, Franklin.' He added to Howell and Georgie, 'For you all. Tough to lose one of our own.'

'Yep.'

The captain and deputy edged a little further into what had been the front room, obviously minimising disturbance of evidence and being mindful of hazards to themselves, including smouldering debris. Crichton hoisted his rake as they went, then together they jemmied back a wrecked couch that'd been overturned in the blasts or under the collapsing structure.

'Holy shit!'

They let it go. The deputy stood rigidly still. Crichton stepped back, his boots crunching on something. After hesitating, he rejoined their huddle.

Dragging off his helmet and breathing apparatus with trembling hands, he looked at Franklin. His eyes were brimming.

'Looks like the whole Murray family, mate.'

CHAPTER SIXTEEN

'WHAT'S GOING ON?'

Georgie recognised Lunny's voice, though she'd rarely heard him sound so frantic, as the sergeant came up with Scott Hart at his heels. He went to push through to the ruined house, and Franklin blocked them both with an arm.

Forced to stay metres back, the newcomers jostled for view. They couldn't fail to spot the boots under the rubble.

'Is it Grant?'

It took Georgie a second to realise he meant Irvy. Nobody at the station used his real name in normal circumstances.

'Fuck.' Harty swore up at the sky.

Moments ago, everything Georgie had felt was for Franklin. Fierce protectiveness combined with doubt. Torn by wanting to physically comfort him and being strong to help him through.

But the rawness of the two Daylesford coppers' reactions sent jarring coldness through her insides. And as the news sunk in properly, grief clamped her chest and settled as a gnawing pain deep in her gut.

From the moment they'd learned Sam had last seen Irvy entering the cottage, added with the fact that he hadn't been sighted since, Georgie had understood the inevitable. He was dead. But to have it confirmed...to see his body...nobody could be prepared for that.

Her hands balled as she watched Franklin. Grim, he showed them what Crichton had brought over, now sheathed in a rag.

Lunny said, 'Oh, Christ.'

Everyone else stared at it. No words.

Franklin cleared his throat. 'The firies are finishing a room search...they found the Murrays.' He jerked his head to indicate where.

Lunny turned the colour of his hair: shocking white. 'Are they...'

Franklin muttered, 'All gone.'

Georgie's fingernails bit into her palms.

'They're nearly done in there. Haven't alerted us to anything further.'

Five deaths plus Sam and Denise in critical condition were more than enough.

CHAPTER SEVENTEEN

FRANKLIN COULDN'T READ BRUNER BEHIND HIS DARK sunglasses. He'd made the right noises, offering his sympathies to them all, then re-flicked the cold switch.

'We can't be tripping over you. We'll let you know what we need and when.'

'These are our friends.'

'Especially why you need to back off a bit, mate.'

He nearly lost it. Pointed out, 'This is our patch,' thumbing at him and Howell. 'We'd have caught this case even if we hadn't been first responders.'

Bruner's chest swelled, inflating his suit jacket. 'Yes. But we were always going to be the ones driving it.'

Franklin spoke without thinking and couldn't recall the specifics of what he'd said immediately after. Something to the effect that he wanted in on everything. To personally inform Kendra. To see Sam's family in Melbourne. To find out why the nurse requested the welfare check. To pick apart what had led up to today's horror.

Bruner laughed without humour. 'So you want to be here,

and in Melbourne, and in Ballarat. Think about it.' He rapped his temple.

'I'm going to break the news to Kendra Irvine.'

'Let the coroner complete the initial—'

'His wife deserves to know,' Franklin tilted his head towards Irvy, 'from one of us.'

It was a miracle she hadn't turned up here. Or at least phoned one of them. Could she really have no clue yet? Nothing via the grapevine?

His throat constricted. What if she'd heard and couldn't deal with it, hurt herself instead of facing it? No, the kids would keep her grounded.

Bruner butted in, but Franklin stalked off across the paddock. Hallsy met him as he neared the unmarked CIU wagon.

She didn't have to say that she knew. It was written all over her.

'Anything you need.'

He nodded, surprised by Howell's, 'We'll let you know.' He hadn't noticed his partner following.

Franklin took a step and frowned when Howell didn't move. He was anxious to go, to reach Kendra before a callous journalist or gossipmonger.

Then he called himself an arsehole for being oblivious when the older detective said, 'But for now, keep an eye on Tim Lunny, yeah?'

CHAPTER EIGHTEEN

'MOST DAYS, EVERYONE GETS HOME SAFELY.'

The district inspector stared directly at the Channel 10 camera. He swallowed hard. The reporters and camera crews ringing around him—a much larger group than this morning—were silent, transfixed. Georgie knew that wouldn't last.

'But today we have had an officer and a civilian with injuries necessitating them to be airlifted to the Alfred Hospital. And although our investigations and formal identification are still underway, I can also confirm that,' he paused, 'tragically,' squeezed lips emphasised the word, 'a number of bodies have been located at the scene.'

He raised his voice over journalists throwing out questions. 'Detectives from the arson and explosives squad are in attendance, and with an arson chemist and other investigators, they will examine the circumstances around the fire and its cause. We are working to confirm the identities of the deceased so that families can be informed.'

Georgie could see DI Knight taking great care with his

words. He consulted his notepad and did another heavy swallow.

'As is required of a critical incident of this nature, a number of agencies are working in cooperation with police to complete this investigation thoroughly and expediently.'

As Knight conferred quietly with his media advisor, Georgie mentally listed those she knew of. Arson squad as lead, teaming with the state coroner and her staff, chemists, photographers and general crime scene crew, the homicide squad, and professional fire investigators with the CFA. In a fatality associated with police contact, and serious injury and death of members on duty, the professional standards command would also probe every detail, including Sam and Irvy's actions, keen to apportion blame.

Knight trod carefully around a few questions. He reiterated it was essential to 'allow time for full and proper process' and 'respect the privacy and impact upon the police members involved.'

Georgie thought the heavy-handed arson detective Bruner needed reminding of that. He'd been insensitive when he'd cited protocols to the local coppers. Enraged, Franklin had made trouble for himself. Again. And she was worried that, more than ever, for Sam and Irvy he'd have no boundaries.

She half-listened to Knight, speculating on how things had gone with Kendra. Literally on the wrong side of the police tape at the gate since Franklin had left and after Bruner had told her she had no place on the crime scene, she was cut off. Couldn't get updates from any of her cop friends. Resorted to brief texts to update Franklin on things she'd discovered of potential interest.

Waiting around here on the periphery wasn't an option. And she owed Hilda Getty after hanging up on her earlier. She pulled out her phone and dialled, mulling the woman's words, *I know something that I wish I didn't.*

———

Franklin tuned in and out of Howell's monologue as he swivelled from the house to the street and surrounds.

Several vehicles whizzed by their car. Nobody around on foot.

His attention pricked at '...the worst thing about fires is the destruction of evidence.' Howell held up a hand and added hastily. 'Apart from loss of life or injury, of course.'

Franklin shrugged. He understood what his partner meant.

But Howell kept going, painting a dire picture.

'By the time the scene's locked down, evidence has been damaged or destroyed by the masses of people and vehicles dealing with the fire. Something like this,' he meant the Korweingi incident, 'with rapid explosions and a raging fire and a tonne of water dumped on the site...it's going to be challenging to solve. Maybe the best we'll get is the cause of the fire.'

Franklin growled, 'You think that's good enough for Irvy and Sam?'

His partner went quiet and rubbed a hand over his balding scalp.

The radio crackled; nothing to do with them. Franklin drummed the steering wheel, anxious and aggravated.

Howell said, 'No, but it might be the best outcome we can expect,' as if there hadn't been an interval.

They both sighed.

'Who'd do this job?' Franklin muttered.

He rolled his eyes and caught his partner doing the same. Soon they'd be finishing each other's sentences.

'How much longer do we give her?'

They'd waited half an hour already. With so many things to do, they couldn't justify much more.

'Five minutes.'

Another three minutes crawled by, then a car slowed and indicated for fifty metres, before it turned into the adjacent property. The brake lights extinguished, but there was no movement from the car for a good ninety seconds. Then the driver's door creaked open. An old fella gripped the roof rail and hauled himself out. His movements were slow and ginger, like everything hurt, as he shut the door, tottered to the rear of the sedan, cranked open the boot and extracted two bulging shopping bags.

It was excruciating to watch. Without wording-up Howell, Franklin joined him.

'Let me help.'

He gathered the groceries with one hand and offered his free arm for support.

The fella clung to it. His face wrinkled in a smile. 'Give you a cuppa in exchange.'

Slightly tempting – they hadn't stopped for food or drink all day. Franklin said, 'Thanks, but can't,' gesturing to the unmarked car with Howell inside.

'We're colleagues of Irvy – on a job.' He didn't elaborate and the fella seemed unconcerned.

With small, slow steps they made their way to the front door. As he fumbled to guide his key into the lock, the old fella sniffed at the sky.

'Great day.' He cackled. 'For ducks!'

Intent on everything but the weather, Franklin hadn't noticed it start raining again. Water pattered his hair, sickening because it was an added problem for the investigation.

Maybe Howell's prediction was dead on – they would never get to the bottom of it?

He ushered the old fella through the front door and, on the way to the kitchen, turned on lights to counter the dimness. The tick of a clock drew his attention. Nearly 3.00pm. Only a couple of hours left before dark. So much still to do.

'Any idea where Kendra is?'

'Yep.'

The fella plucked a slab of cheese from the first bag and transferred it to the fridge door. His fingers had the look of a hoary tree.

Task done, he turned to Franklin and answered properly. 'She was helping out on an excursion today. Should be back at the school around-about now.'

———

Six rings. Seven. Eight. Eventually, it switched to, 'This is Hilda. Please leave a message after the beep.'

Georgie remembered her instructions and disconnected. But instead of returning the next call on her list, she regarded her silent phone.

Hilda was paranoid enough about her husband to know to save Georgie's number under a false name – wasn't she?

If she hadn't saved it, and Bob Getty saw those ten digits pop up on her screen, would he recognise it? Georgie had arranged their appointment via her phone. And mindful of the distance to Gordon from Richmond, she'd also confirmed it with him.

She told herself to chill. In the past, everyone memorised phone numbers, but with the reliance on technology these days, how many could they recite now? A few key numbers, usually.

Surely not a journo's number after two phone calls?

She bit her lip. It depended on whether Getty was as wary as his wife. Particularly if that journo or her questions this morning had worried him.

CHAPTER NINETEEN

A STRING OF MIDDLE-PRIMARY-SCHOOL-AGED KIDS JUMPED from the bus's bottom step and raced across the yard. The sweet ring of laughter floated above the sounds of arriving cars and slamming doors. Franklin hated that the innocence and pure happiness of kids was so short-lived. All too soon, life tested or ripped it from them – as he was about to do.

Howell propped on the bonnet of the CIU wagon. Franklin considered warning him he'd get a wet arse, but didn't have the energy.

Finally, a woman's hand appeared on the rail. Kendra supported herself as she stepped off the bus, clumsy for her belly that'd shot out since he'd last seen her. Safely down, she held out her hands to help two children much smaller than the rest: a boy and a girl. Irvy's youngest, except for the one in the oven, which must be five or six months baked.

Kendra spoke to Levi and Isla, then, as if sensing scrutiny, turned in their direction. Her hand cupped her belly when she and Franklin met eyes across the car park.

———

Georgie was returning calls as another came through. After hanging up, she retrieved her voicemail, half expecting it to be Hilda Getty. Be just her luck if they played phone tag for the rest of the day.

'It's me.'

Livia. Georgie pictured her mum with a pang.

'I heard...on the radio...' Livia hesitated. *'I hope it's none of your friends. It's not Franklin, is it?'*

She broke off. Then, *'Of course it's not.'* Tone bright now, either faking it or remembering that Franklin was seconded to the detective unit at Bacchus Marsh.

'Well, I'm here. No rush, I know you're always busy.' She blew a kiss.

Livia wouldn't have intended it as a guilt trip, yet Georgie squirmed. She had meant to touch base, kept forgetting. Couldn't do it now though because everything was a bit raw.

———

Kendra stood watching. All Franklin's senses switched to hyper as he and Howell passed through the open gate. His feet were heavy in his boots and nose quivered with diesel fumes from the bus. Howell's stomach rumbled, and the weak winter sun made brimming potholes in the bitumen glisten.

The tiny spitting image of Kendra clung onto her mum's legs, burying her face, and the little mini-Irvy flapped his arm in an excited wave. The taste of fear filled his mouth: metallic copper of blood. He'd bitten the lining of his cheek.

'Frankie!' Levi galloped up to meet them with his hands stretched in the air.

Franklin swung him up. Wiry arms ringed his neck and legs coiled his waist. As they neared Kendra and Isla, the middle boy in the family joined his mum and sister, though the other two weren't in sight. Levi chattered about their exciting day out, but all Franklin could think was, *They are going to be heartbroken.*

In front of the huddled Irvine family, he blanked. He'd practiced an opening but never imagined delivering it with three of the kids there.

He shifted his gaze to Howell, then back to Kendra. He watched her press a hand to her mouth. Terror filled her eyes.

———

Georgie figured she needed to leave it for Hilda to phone her back when she could safely. And as soon as she pocketed her mobile, she forgot about the Gettys and Hansen.

She scouted out DS Bruner. Surrounded by several uniformed and suited males and females with the air of those used to being in charge, she figured he'd be occupied for a while, briefing and coordinating the multi-levelled investigation.

She looked around and singled out a man in khaki overalls. He'd been speaking with Sven and Vlatka, but now stood by himself. Welcoming a chance to be potentially useful, she strolled in his direction.

———

Even little Levi had gone quiet.

Franklin broke the awkward silence. 'I'll drive you all home.'

Kendra stared at him. After close to a minute's lag, she dug into her big handbag and pulled out a chunky set of keys. The rest of her kids gravitated to them with suddenly too-old expressions. They couldn't know, could they? If they didn't, they definitely sensed something bad was happening.

He shepherded the family to their people-mover. Nobody spoke then or during the drive, not even to ask why Franklin was there and all so serious, or where Dad was, or why Mum had spaced out. Eerie to have a carful of silent kids. But at least they weren't crying. And at each check of the rear-view mirror, Howell was trailing in the wagon. A reassurance that he wasn't in this completely alone.

Once they entered the house, his partner offered to occupy the kids in the family room. Franklin and Kendra watched them.

Softly, he said, 'Is there someone I can call?'

She sighed. He took it for no or not yet.

'Where can we talk?'

Kendra blinked and seemed to process the question. She led him outside, across the lawn and through the side door of the garage to Irvy's man cave. The small space was barricaded off from the main shed by a row of old wardrobes and open shelves with a collection of empty beer cans and bottles on top. The walls and doors were decorated with footy and supercars posters. A bunch of photos pinned haphazardly on a corkboard hung above a beaten-up old couch along the window wall.

She motioned him to the couch, but it didn't feel right to sit. He stood with his back to the robes, observing Kendra pace, handle things, discard them.

She unpinned a photo from the corkboard and showed him – her and Irvy on a beach, sucking up an enormous blue cocktail through straws. She cradled the picture to her chest and sank onto the couch.

He took it as a sign. She was as ready as she could be for the news.

Then she beat him to it. 'I need to see him.'

Franklin crouched down and drew her gaze.

CHAPTER TWENTY

Noting a bunch of police personnel gathered away from the small group of firies continuing to make the burnt structure safe, and State Emergency Service volunteers setting up lights, Georgie took a circuitous route to avoid them all. By the time she'd joined the neighbour, he'd sunk to his haunches, hanging his chin low into his chest. His heaving sobs pierced into her as much as his broken posture.

She laid a hand on his shoulder as she hunkered down by his side, giving silent comfort until his tears were spent.

Roughly wiping his face with the long sleeves of his overalls, he let out a ragged breath. Georgie offered her hand to help him up. When he was on his feet, he gave a squeeze of thanks.

Only then did she say, 'It's been a terrible day.'

'The worst.' His words held an English burr.

'You live nearby, don't you?' Georgie hazarded, unsurprised when he pointed to the opposite property. 'Let me walk you home and make you a cuppa. You look like you need it.'

Though still puffy and red-raw, his eyes softened. After his nod, they matched strides, closing in on a white weatherboard cottage with a red roof.

Sweeping a hand over his home and the farm across the road, the man said, 'Theirs looked like this before the fire. Built by the same family, back when.'

Georgie noted an economy to his actions as well as his speech, which didn't alter while he led her to an annexe at the back, held the door, and ushered her into a compact and tidy mudroom. They shucked off their dirty boots, and he racked them upside down, then hung her jacket.

'WC through there, bath next door,' he nudged with his nose, 'and kitchen this way.'

She went through and filled the kettle, while he pulled out canisters, mugs and spoons, and invited her to call him Dave.

As the water heated, Georgie introduced herself, keeping it simple with, 'I'm a friend of the police members.' Not here as a journo.

It reminded her of Sam, then the others. Her nerves jittered with fear and anger at today's senseless and perhaps malicious injury and loss, and the wide ripples it would cast.

As much as she itched to move forward, Dave clearly needed to refuel.

She asked, 'How do you take it?'

'Tea with a touch of milk.' He pulled a carton of long-life milk from the fridge, flushing as he added, 'And three sugars, cheers.'

The kettle grew louder in the silence that followed. She dropped a teabag and three scoops of sugar into one mug and two spoons of coffee into hers, then pondered on the older man while the water came to the boil. The almost military neatness to the kitchen and what she'd seen of the farmhouse surprised her. Uncluttered, no frills, things aligned, no mention of a partner, no photos of family on display. She got the sense Dave lived alone but coped well with baching, managing all the housekeeping on top of running the farm.

That this proud and very together man had broken down in front of her earlier twanged her heartstrings.

They sat at the kitchen table with their drinks and a packet of jam tarts. Dave took a blackberry tart, broke it in half over his plate, then crumbled the whole thing without eating.

'It's a tragedy,' Georgie said.

'That it is.' He gazed at her, then back to the mess on his plate. 'I keep expecting to see young Ethan in his favourite top.' He tugged the fabric over his chest. 'It has an eagle on it. Or Bel with Ollie on her hip.' His fingers stilled. 'He was a little miracle.'

'Who?' She sipped her coffee, letting him steer the conversation.

'Ol-ol, as Ethan calls – *called* his brother.'

She cupped her mug with both hands, silently urging him to continue.

He did but it was obscure. 'Waited so long before joy, then grief, but eventually along he came. Such a happy little baby he is – *was*.' His features clouded at his second change of tense.

How much would he allow her in? She had to dig deeper and only hope he didn't clam up. The silent buzzing of her phone in her hip pocket distracted her momentarily. It stopped, then quivered once, signalling a message.

'Notice anything unusual about the family lately?' She kept it broad. Franklin had warned her not to lead the witnesses, tainting their testimony. And in her own experience, the wider she cast her questions, the greater the catch sometimes was.

Dave took a lemon tart. After a single bite, it met the same fate as the blackberry one.

Georgie drained her coffee while he considered her question.

'Nothing concrete, if you understand?'

'Yes.'

'I think they were a touch strained.' He didn't go on.

'They?'

'Bel and Alec.'

'Any idea why?'

He twitched. Then asked, 'What will happen now?'

His topic change threw her.

'Funerals and whatnot, and their farm, the stock, the dogs?'

A sad and complex question. One of many that couldn't be answered yet.

CHAPTER TWENTY-ONE

HOWELL WENT TO THE DRIVER'S SIDE OF THEIR UNMARKED wagon. 'Keys.'

Franklin dug them out of his pocket, bunched them ready to throw to his partner, and stared in shock at his shaking fist. He wheeled his arm and tossed the keys across the bonnet. He slid into the passenger seat, buckled up and shoved his hands under his thighs, hiding the shakes.

'What now?' Howell cranked the engine.

'Too late to go to the kindergarten, I suppose?'

'Didn't someone say Bel was on maternity leave?'

'Yep.'

Franklin gazed out his side window at a tree. Its leafless branches spread high and wide, their darkness popping against the striking luminosity of the horizon. Could be a good omen – tomorrow promising better weather and the worst being behind them.

He murmured, 'Even so, she worked there for quite a few years.'

He thought back to when he and Bel had met. On a job at

the kindergarten, a broken window that turned out to be purely accidental.

'She's a lovely person, by all accounts gets along with everyone, young or old.' He clocked his use of the present tense and swore silently. 'It's likely she was close to a colleague – or more than one.'

The older detective nodded, seeming to follow his train of thought. 'And if there were issues at home, she would've confided in them.'

'Good possibility, anyway.'

He didn't have to elaborate. They both knew plenty of people bottled things up. Pride stopped them admitting to any problem or worry. And the graver the issue, the harder they tried to conceal it.

'It's 4.30 – expect they'd be gone by now,' Howell said. 'Let's rack that for first thing tomorrow.'

'Then, guess we'd better go back to the scene and catch up with progress there.'

Franklin watched the branches of the bare tree bob in a wind gust. His mind was full of things he needed to do, and he only dimly noticed the tick of the indicator and their car make a U-turn towards Korweinguboora.

When they called it a day, whatever time that was, he'd head to Melbourne. See Sam's family. See Sam, if the hospital would allow it. Same for Denise. A stranger but he'd connected with her. Out there doing her job, just like Irvy and Sam, and now life would never be the same.

———

Georgie gathered up their empty cups, Dave's plate with the demolished tarts and her own unused one. She couldn't eat, and even the coffee sat uneasily in her stomach. The sights and smells she'd witnessed earlier had resurfaced while they'd chatted, and she really needed to be by herself for a while.

'I can tell.' Dave's British accent intensified with words that rang with resignation, maybe regret too. 'You have to go.' He rose, taking the dishes from her. He looked about to say more but moved to the sink instead.

Torn—*Stay or go? Could I hold myself together for a bit longer? Try to find out more or give him a break?*—Georgie observed the droop to his posture and figured he was done in too. But she sensed that Dave would open up further about his neighbours when he was ready, and that it could be pivotal to them unravelling today's events.

Today? All this has been just one day?

'Mind if I dropped in tomorrow?'

His face lit. 'That'd be brilliant.'

They shared their first smile. It lightened her heart, but on the back of it came shame. If only she could pop in for a cuppa without having to interrogate the sad man. If only they could nullify everything about this day.

———

As they pulled up near Goodlife Farm, Howell peered overhead. 'Air wing.'

A police chopper hovered over the farm. They did that in cases like this. Scoped the scene from above, took photographs. A normal step, but the *wuppa wuppa* sound would forever hold bad connotations for Franklin after today.

He tried to ignore the noise as Howell parked the wagon and they walked to the outer cordon. A glimpse of a distinctive frog-nosed black convertible parked in the throng of vehicles along the lane told him that Georgie was still around.

Hallsy logged their entry and lifted the police tape for them to duck under. Franklin felt her eyes on his back as they walked off, remembering that Howell had tasked her with watching out for the sarge when they'd left a couple of hours ago. But he was too drained to turn around and ask how Lunny was holding up.

His brain wouldn't switch off. Kept snapping back to Kendra.

Sick to his stomach, he visualised it blow-by-blow. How he'd explained the scene was sealed and she wasn't allowed there, and that the process was protracted, but Irvy would be taken back to town for the coroner to do what had to be done before his body could be released. He'd gently untied the rag and shown her what Crichton had salvaged. Kendra's voice shook as she'd pressed her fingertips to the metal police ID badge and whispered, *It's his Freddy.* He'd explained they could do a formal identification without her seeing him – *Better to remember him the way he was.* But she'd slapped him and told him to leave.

'Let's catch up with our blokes.' Howell motioned to a couple of the Ds from Bacchus Marsh.

It struck Franklin that they weren't *our blokes* to him. He belonged with the Daylesford crew, and he needed to know what was being done for Sam and Irvy from the top.

He shrugged a non-answer to his partner and took off across the paddock, straight for the local police commander. Kendra sprang into his mind again, and his cheek stung at the memory of her slap. He replaced the vision with a proper scan of the area, pushing down a mixture of hurt and anger.

The place had become a fully-fledged crime scene with tents and portable floodlights set up, more police tape ringing the smouldering ruin. Despite that, there was no sense of urgency. They had two members down, plus a family of four, and yet there was no sign of action here apart from the chopper doing its thing overhead.

Personnel stood in groups, sipping from coffee beakers or talking on mobiles. A few flipped through notebooks and jotted stuff.

He strode on. Jumped at, 'How's she doing?' from right behind him.

Franklin swivelled to Harty. He slowed his heart rate and gave his mate an abridged version of his visit with Kendra. Then he asked, 'What's the deal here?'

'You know how it is.'

He did but shook his head. He knew the process but hated any delay.

'Our people can't go in until the CFA has cleared it. Too much structural damage and the asbestos needs to be collected and removed.'

Harty pointed to five or six people on the periphery of the cordon around the fire site wearing decon suits and masks. 'AES are doing what they can though.'

Rage bubbled up. 'We need to be doing more!'

His mate stared at him. 'Yeah.'

Mick Sprague jogged over to join them.

Franklin said, 'What do you know, Slam?'

'This is the most fucked-up day we've had in the job.'

'Yep.' Franklin rubbed a hand over his jaw. 'What else?'

'We haven't managed to contact next-of-kin for the Murrays yet.'

'Made progress with the nurse?'

'Her co-worker confirmed the welfare check but felt *uncomfortable* enlarging upon that. Patient confidentiality, staff privacy, blah-blah. She did give us details for Denise's parents and her boyfriend. They've been notified.'

Franklin weighed whether the boyfriend could be a player in what'd happened. Couldn't rule it out. They couldn't rule anything, or anyone, in or out until they at least knew if they were dealing with an accident or arson.

'Any word on Sam and Denise?'

Harty glanced at Slam. He swallowed and breathed out through his nose. 'Both still fighting for life.'

CHAPTER TWENTY-TWO

GEORGIE FOLLOWED RILEY'S LANE TO ITS END, discovering a creek was the far boundary of Goodlife Farm. So the Murrays only shared a side border with Sven and Vlatka. Their other neighbours comprised whoever abutted them in the rear, which could well be the dazed woman who'd collided with her, along with Dave, and another over the road.

The creek twisted and turned in both directions. The rippling water reminded her of the call she'd missed earlier, and she checked her mobile.

Hilda Getty.

She connected to voicemail.

'*Miss Harvey, it's Hilda Getty. Don't ring me, sorry. I'll try again later.*'

'Damn.'

She pocketed the phone, and drew in a lungful of air and her surroundings. Her muscles softened with the burble of the water. There should be enough light left in the day to explore at least partway along the creek, and her torch app would get her out of trouble. The temptation to turn off from things for a short while was too strong to resist.

A fairly flat bank of rich red soil and grass made the first section easy going. As she trekked, Georgie faced into the clean air for an invigorating tingle on her skin. Listened to the wind rustle through the gum trees overhead, pings and bubbles from the water, bird calls of various tones, the low of cows.

Further along, the undergrowth thickened, and she picked her way through clumps of brown reeds and tussock bleached golden-yellow, and avoided patches of slippery moss and trailing blackberry canes. She was glad for her leather boots bracing her ankles and the winter cold making it unlikely she'd meet a snake. She stopped to gauge how far she'd come and what might lay onward. She could bring up a map on her phone, but it might well only give a guesstimate. She'd plod on.

A few minutes passed, and Georgie was glad she'd persevered when she came to a clearing on her left. Stranded wire fencing still separated it from the creek front, until she reached a wide gate. She leaned on the top rail of the gate, hooking a foot through the wire mesh, and gazed across the paddock.

Its gentle undulation meant as far as her eye could see was rolling, tranquil green countryside and a horizon of indigo over long smears of red and gold, with no hint of the deadly crime scene. It gave her an inkling of the couple who had chosen this place to make a home and a living for their family.

As the light faded, she traced a natural pathway leading from the gate. She was pulled to a spot where the grass had been trampled down with use – a ring of crude timber stools and a couple of PVC pipes spiked into the soil and angled towards the water. This was the Murrays fishing spot.

A lump filled the back of Georgie's throat. She sank onto a

stool unmindful of the wet seat, racking her brain for something useful she could do this evening.

Still clueless five minutes later, she gave up and backtracked along the creek, up the lane and to her car.

The Spider was hemmed in between a broadcast truck and a ute. But she manoeuvred the small car out of the space, completed a three-point turn, and breathed a little freer leaving the farm.

———

Franklin spied Lunny take off. One of the sarge's hands was buried in his pocket and he was rounded forward, the back of his uniform jacket hump shaped. He trained a torch on the turf and walked slowly in the direction of a scattering of mismatched outbuildings and a fenced vegie garden. Hunched over more with an icy wind gust.

Chewing over the MICA ambo asking his old boss if he was feeling okay, then Howell's request of Hallsy, Franklin asked himself why he hadn't checked on Lunny. Had he really been that busy with the investigation that he couldn't spare a mate a few minutes?

Honestly?

He knew Lunny would be doing it tough and wasn't sure he had enough in reserve to deal with it.

———

Georgie drove to Daylesford without recall of any of the trip. Her mind was busy, but no clearer on how to advance her inquiries tonight. At least she could be there to support Franklin and Kat.

Or so she'd thought until she let herself into the dark house.

She wandered into the front room and got kindling burning in the double-sided fireplace that defined the dining and lounge areas since Franklin had knocked down the wall separating them. She made coffee that she tipped out in favour of a large glass of red wine and loaded up the fire.

After she'd killed thirty minutes, she realised she'd probably spend the night here alone.

She switched on the TV for company. Flicked around and landed on a live update from Korweinguboora, partly through.

District Inspector Knight fronted the media, in the middle of two senior officers also in full uniform, with a younger woman in a smart suit standing at an angle to the group.

'Whilst numerous specialist police resources have been concentrated on this case, this is a major investigation, as you can imagine, and our members will continue to work methodically through the scene for some time.'

He paused. Reporters shuffled, and a female half-facing the camera secured her jacket against the windchill.

'As much detail as I can provide, at this stage, is that an initial explosion inside the house behind me then triggered a fast-moving fire, which was succeeded by additional blasts. Two police members have consequently been injured, along with a number of civilians.'

Knight raised a hand to quiet a murmur. Georgie's pen suspended over her doodle of his head – when did she reach for her pad and pen?

'I can confirm that two of the injured were treated at the scene before being conveyed to hospital. I can also confirm earlier reports that a number of deceased persons were located at this property, and that their identities will be released in due course.'

A young female piped up. *'We heard a police member was killed, District Inspector. Is that true?'*

'*What can you tell us about the family that lives here?*' a grizzled journo added. '*Are they among the fatalities?*'

Again, Knight held up his hand. '*I please ask for your patience as we piece together what happened here today. It is very early days, and we will provide regular updates.*'

Georgie noted backs straighten and chins lift as the journalists sensed Knight was nearly finished.

'*One line of inquiry revolves around a number of forty-five-kilogram LPG gas cylinders found here at the property. As part of the investigation, we will consider if, and how, they contributed to the explosions.*'

That grabbed her attention. And the journos reacted with a forward press of microphones.

'*We have posted an image of the cylinders on our website and Facebook page in that it might help jog someone's memory.*'

Intriguing, and Georgie thought deliberately ambiguous. She pulled up the image on her phone while the DI continued.

'*I ask anyone with any information that may assist our investigation to contact Crime Stoppers.*' He wrapped up with, '*I'm happy to take any questions, or you can direct them to my colleagues Commander Kelly or Deputy Commissioner Lester.*'

'*District Inspector, do you believe this is an act of sabotage?*'

'*It is one line of inquiry.*'

The voices droned on, and Knight's patience was tested when he had to repeat several aspects. Georgie's mind fixed on the gas cylinders, and their basic yet distinctive pattern to the collar. And something she couldn't pinpoint in the blur of today's events niggled.

CHAPTER TWENTY-THREE

THE GLOOMY AFTERNOON HAD PITCHED INTO DARKNESS about an hour ago. Why did this hellstorm have to go down on one of the shortest days of the year? Another curse for the firies and techies trying to do their thing.

Still, Franklin was able to navigate his way via the umbrella of light from the portable spotties and the sliver of moon above with only the odd flash of his torch. He found Lunny at the chook pen. His fingers were threaded through the chicken wire, and the mesh sagged where his forehead rested into it.

The sarge showed no sign he'd noticed Franklin's approach. He could still rethink this.

No, he couldn't. He said, 'Hey.'

Lunny didn't lift his head. 'John.'

Probably knew I was here all along.

'Tough day, Tim.'

Lunny's answering sigh made the chooks stir and cluck anxiously.

Franklin went to stand by his friend. He peered into the

pen. Couldn't see much in the shadows. He groped for what to say, but Lunny spoke first.

'Remember that crash we went to a few years ago?'

They'd worked a few horrors together. But Franklin thought he knew which he meant.

'Remember we went to Jim Crow, and fished and yarned about it afterwards?'

'Yeah.'

'Remember we talked about having to deal with the job or get out?'

Franklin closed his eyes, wishing he could shut his ears against what Lunny was building to.

'Well, it's my time...to get out.'

Franklin pictured the ambo, Shannon, and her concern when Lunny pressed his shoulder, and his bad colour. He tensed.

Shit. His ticker?

'You sick, Tim?'

Another deep sigh from Lunny. 'No. Well, a few warnings. Be worse than that if I don't get out. Or I'll lose my marbles. Or my wife.'

He laughed. An unhappy sound.

'Why don't you take sick leave and think about it? You've got plenty accrued.'

Lunny extracted himself from the wire mesh and turned towards him. The moon cast enough light to see his face.

'Nearly jumped back in spring, and this's the last straw. Mate, I'm done. It's only a few years early for my grand plan, anyway. And Maeve and I can do that travelling we've always dreamed of, starting with that South Pacific cruise we talked about a few years ago. We can spend more time with the grandkids and fishing. It'll be good.'

He smiled, a real one, and the tightness in Franklin's chest eased.

Lunny's smile drooped. 'My only worry is the station – who'll take over, whether they'll be any good. And what it'll mean to the crew.'

What's left of our crew.

Franklin squeezed his arm. 'It'll work out.'

The empty pit in his gut belied his words.

DAY TWO

THURSDAY 14 JUNE

CHAPTER TWENTY-FOUR

As soon as Georgie opened her eyes, she was washed with sickening dread, along with surprise that she'd managed to sleep after hours lying staring at the dark ceiling, listening to the creaks of the house, ticks of the clock in the front room. Hours of tossing to get comfortable. Dozes that she'd emerged from crying out, or muttering, before she'd crashed for a stretch that had taken her through to dawn.

She gazed at the empty pillow beside her. It was slightly skewwhiff but didn't look slept on. She peered under the doona. About half the sheet was rumpled. Franklin's side, smooth.

Had he even come home?

She rolled onto her back, pressing her hands to her temples to ease the tension. She strained for signs that Franklin or Kat were home. Just heard the damn clock.

Her phone was silent on the bedside cabinet. A bunch of messages banked up, nothing urgent or from him. No reply to her text letting him know she was here, to say if there was anything she could do. Hard to believe it was 7.10am.

Out of bed, the floorboards shockingly cold under her bare feet, Georgie shuffled to the bathroom to use the loo and to splash her face with water. In the kitchen, she made a strong, black coffee. Grief rolled in her stomach, and she had no appetite for food. What she needed, but feared, was an update on Sam and Denise's condition.

News on TV, Police Media or Facebook would all have something, but it might be little more than a rehash of yesterday's information. Still, she'd check. If that failed, she'd get onto Franklin, Lunny or the hospital.

She took her mug through to the living room to start with the TV, and nearly spilt her coffee when she saw Franklin sitting on the couch.

'When did you get home?'

He shrugged.

She offered him coffee or breakfast, but he shook his head, mute.

'Want to talk about it?'

He didn't look at her. Seemed a million miles away, but said, 'No,' hollowly.

CHAPTER TWENTY-FIVE

From astride his Kawasaki Ninja, Franklin watched his old crew flock up the driveway to park outside the station. Whether rostered on or not, each arrived early in full uniform and went in separately. None of the jostling or bantering that usually accompanied a briefing of the full team. Not that Lunny had called many over the years he'd been in charge.

Franklin waited until they were all there, then he rode up to park behind Slam's car. He drew off his helmet and left it on the Ninja's seat. Before he hiked the front stairs, he took several breaths, his exhales puffy clouds in the biting chill, and asked himself if he was sure. There would be no going back.

A grim internal voice said, *There is no going back.* He covered the stairs two at once, slipped through the front door, and strode to the lunchroom.

He froze, taking in the sight. They were huddled in a circle, arms slung around each other's shoulders and heads bowed.

Towering above the rest, Harty noticed him first, meeting his gaze over the top of the bent crowns. He nodded a greeting and stepped backwards to make space in the huddle.

Franklin latched onto his mates, looking down at the table they ringed. It held a bunch of photos printed on A4 sheets of Sam and Irvy taken at social dos—candid, happy shots—and a bowl of red camellias that he recognised from the garden of the station house next door. Maeve's touch, undoubtedly. He swallowed, but the lump in his throat didn't budge.

They stood like that for about five minutes. In silence, except for the crackle of the police radio in the adjacent room.

Lunny cleared his throat.

'We are family. In many ways, what we do and how we rely on each other makes what we have stronger than most blood relationships. I can't tell you how proud I am of each of you... and of Grant and Sam. Grant fought the good fight for twelve years, the last three with us. He lost the fight yesterday, but we will remember him. Rest in peace, Irvy.'

They murmured an echo, then reflected for sixty or so seconds. Franklin went over the police ode that Lunny had paraphrased, *With Honour They Served*, in his mind.

'Sam fights on, so send her your thoughts and prayers.'

Harty's arm tightened around Franklin.

'We're arranging counselling, and I want you to take it. We are police, but we are humans, and at times like this, we all need some help. We'll talk more about it later...' Lunny's voice cracked with, 'But now, I want you to know that it has been my privilege to head this team.'

Franklin glanced up. The sarge straightened and he stared at the wall.

'Today is my last shift – I'm taking early retirement.'

The knot of arms broke. Everybody spoke.

Slam was the loudest. 'You can't. We have to stick together.'

The sarge did a repeated headshake. He didn't seem able to answer.

'What about us?' Disbelief and dismay underlined Kong's question.

Franklin held out for a lull, and then said, 'I don't want the boss to go either. But he's made his decision, so I'm putting up my hand for officer-in-charge. Acting, at least.'

All eyes fixed on him.

'No way!' Harty exploded. 'What about CI?'

He brushed it off. 'If you'll have me, this is where I need to be.'

————

Georgie kicked over the Spider. As the engine warmed up, her mobile buzzed to life. Hilda Getty's name filled the screen.

She answered with simply 'Hello' in case the husband was setting a trap.

'Miss Harvey? Hilda Getty.'

'Good to speak. Sorry about—'

Hilda cut her off. 'The thing is, I made a mistake yesterday. I shouldn't have bothered you. It was really nothing. Silly, stupid. I'm sorry for wasting your time.'

She disconnected.

Georgie glared at her phone. Incredible. And unbelievable. The woman didn't strike her as silly or stupid, but rather as scared. That worried her. Had Getty forced her to backpedal? And what was it all about?

She'd intended to start the day with a check on farmer Dave. Then to try the property at the rear of Goodlife Farm – hopefully find the woman who'd walked into her and ensure she was okay. From there, she'd see what her careful questions uncovered.

Both could wait a few hours. Hilda's change of heart resolved her to take up where she'd left off at Gordon yesterday

– with Allan Hansen's de facto widow, if *de facto-widow* was a thing, and his sons.

She couldn't imagine Hilda's cryptic calls were unrelated to the man's death. She'd need to manufacture a reason to return to the Getty place as well. Hilda might talk face to face while she wouldn't over the phone. Or she could be in trouble.

———

It was done. Franklin had set the ball rolling and now it was in DI Knight's court. Meanwhile, he was still a suit, and it felt wrong to let his two work-worlds cross over this morning. So he asked Marty Howell to collect him outside the Daylesford cop shop.

Standing on the landing and watching the street for the unmarked, he suddenly craved a smoke. Nearly a year without relapsing, and mostly he was only half-tempted if people lit up in front of him. But now he wanted it so badly his hands tingled.

Enough time to nick up the street for a pack?

He shoved his hands in his pockets, imagining the taste of nicotine in his mouth and the feel of it running through his bloodstream.

A bubble of anger came from nowhere. At himself for even thinking about a smoke. At everything.

He got so preoccupied in his dark headspace that he didn't notice the unmarked wagon until a car door slammed.

Howell started up the stairs, but Franklin diverted him. He and his partner had things to review and act on that he didn't want his mates inside to know about until they had to. They were too raw from yesterday and now knocked sideways over Lunny's departure.

Howell gave him an intense look. 'Did you sleep at all?'

Franklin dodged the question, silently admitting if he had a clearer head, he would've given Howell different instructions. 'I'll meet you at mine. We'll grab a cuppa, go over what we have so far, then head to the kinder and the school. And I need to change.'

He gestured to his bike leathers.

His partner agreed and climbed into the wagon as Franklin mounted his bike. They convoyed for the short distance to his cottage on Raglan Street.

They didn't converse again until they were seated at Franklin's small kitchen table, coffees steaming, notepads and mobiles out.

'Right.' Howell scrutinised him. When Franklin didn't take the bait, he said, 'Heard something on the grapevine today. Wanna tell me about it?'

'Got a smoke, Marty?'

'But you quit.'

'That was before yesterday.'

'Kat'll kill me.'

'She's not here.'

Franklin hadn't seen his daughter since yesterday, but they'd texted and briefly spoken a number of times. Maeve had talked her into going to school today, convincing her not to miss her VCE GAT, but he didn't like the chances that she'd finish the test.

They stared at each other. Howell placed his pack and lighter on the table. Franklin took them outside, unsurprised when he was shadowed by the older detective. The first hit nearly buckled his knees. The next drag set off a coughing fit. But that smoke was bloody good.

'What you heard is right – about me and Lunny's job.'

Howell objected, and Franklin lifted his hands.

'It's not personal. Just what I have to do.'

'But—'

Franklin glared.

Catching on, his partner shut up.

'What did I miss from the morning briefing?'

Howell trailed him back into the kitchen and took a chug of his coffee. He ran through the limited progress the Bacchus Marsh team had made so far, along with updates from the AES crew.

'Still a way to go on determining the cause and origin of the fire.'

Franklin said, 'But they suspect the gas cylinders?'

'Yeah. They had to consider a drug lab, but it's now ruled unlikely. They're examining three intact cylinders from the scene, believed to be the same as the ones that blew.'

Franklin raised his brows. 'Question is *why* they blew.'

'Exactly.'

They brooded over that, then Howell went on.

'Denise Zachary is still critical, but the hospital is reasonably optimistic. Piecing things together—the shrapnel, their injuries, etcetera—we believe Sam was closer to the structure when the initial explosion occurred. In direct line of fire, she caught the brunt of the outward blast that turned ordinary household items into fiery missiles...the shockwave.' Howell groaned. 'The nurse had on a woollen jacket, so that also saved her somewhat.'

Franklin downed his lukewarm coffee, then surveyed the bottom of his mug.

'Irvy? And the Murrays?'

'Autopsies will tell us more. The thing we're struggling with most is the way the family was found.' Howell stopped and pulled out a photograph. 'Be prepared, mate.'

Franklin thought he was. He'd seen charred bodies in

person and in photographs. Worse, he'd seen Sam and Irvy. But he had to avert his gaze from these images.

Those mere seconds were enough to imprint them in his brain and to understand what Howell had alluded to. 'They were all lined up.'

'Yeah. All four in a row. The baby in a bassinet he would've been too big for.'

'Shit.' Franklin thought about the two little boys. Anger made coffee- and cigarette-flavoured bile rise to his throat. 'So it's looking like a murder–suicide?'

Howell grimaced. 'Maybe.'

CHAPTER TWENTY-SIX

THE WIDE GRAVEL DRIVEWAY CUT THROUGH THICK BUSH and promised something special. But it opened to a broad clearing with the residence the first thing in sight. A vertical-planked, flat-roofed affair, calling it ranch style would be generous. It was bland and bleak looking. And as Georgie parked the Spider, what she could see of the rest of the property didn't sway her opinion.

A sage-green tin shed dwarfed the house. The driveway appeared to continue in a racetrack loop around the house block, which was all grass and no garden. A dam and two horses in rugs were the only attractive features in view. Even the trees on the adjacent paddocks were stunted.

It set her expectations about the welcome she'd receive from the Hansens low. This could be a massive timewaster. She ought to have prioritised the Korweinguboora end.

She'd barely shut the car door when a guy around her age, between thirty and thirty-five, burst from the partly open roller door on the shed. With hands planted on his hips, he scowled as she approached. His likeness to Allan Hansen, especially his hawk nose and thick, red-brown mullet hairdo, had her convinced that this was one of his sons.

Georgie introduced herself. 'I'm very sorry for your loss.'

He eyeballed her.

'Bob and Hilda Getty send their regards.'

Not exactly true, but perhaps they would. She wasn't expecting him to hawk up phlegm and spit it between them.

'Would Jeanette have a few moments?'

A minute passed, and she considered repeating her question – clearer and louder. Maybe he was hearing impaired.

'Not for you, she wouldn't.'

So not deaf. And definitely not journo friendly.

'My piece is centring on Allan – your father?'

He nodded, conceding that at least.

'On your father and the hardships of farming. From my talk with Bob, I have some awareness of the issues you farmers face and how that puts stress on families.'

His cheeks blotched beetroot.

She clicked that he thought she was alluding to farmer–suicide. Raced on before he blew up. 'Your father's accident gives me a lead into this theme. But with a *feature* story,' hopefully, that'd appeal to his ego, 'it is so important to give a voice to the people, the loved ones, those affected. In this case, you and your brother and Jeanette, who have personal experience of what has happened, the precursors and repercussions.'

She squirmed. It sounded like drivel to her, but just maybe she'd draw his trust with her wordy, meandering pitch, a complete mess of what she'd prepared on the thirty-minute drive from Daylesford.

He shifted from hands on his hips into a crossed-arms position. It seemed encouraging. Sort of.

Georgie took a step towards the shed. 'Maybe your brother, then?'

He stopped her with a raised hand. Then he lumbered to pull the roller door all the way shut. Coming back, he gave her elbow a rough knock in what was apparently meant as *follow me* and led her to the drab house.

Her heart banged in her chest. What had she gotten herself into? And was it her imagination, or did he not want her looking inside the shed?

———

In hindsight, they should've come at a different time. A touch before 9.00am meant they had to walk past a huddle of parents, mostly mums, to enter the kindergarten. It also meant kids, staff and lingering adults were jammed together in the cramped foyer hanging coats, hats and bags. They were chattering, sulking, squealing or silent. Franklin sensed the hyper edge had nothing to do with whether they were morning people or not. Rumours had preceded their arrival.

The reaction to their entrance was an exaggerated silence, then uproar. Two men in suits and no kid – they might as well have whipped out a megaphone and announced, *We are police and we're here to talk about your dead teacher and friend, except we can't officially confirm that yet.*

Franklin knew two of the staff well – the leader and the teacher of the four-year-olds, who were both long-termers. The male he'd never met, and the third female he thought he'd come across, but didn't know whether in his capacity as simply a local, a dad or a cop.

He clocked their reactions. They all realised who they were and their purpose. He waited for a tell that'd indicate which person to prioritise. He saw it.

The leader met them, but he said, 'Mind if I borrow Yuki for a few minutes?'

She beckoned to her colleague in charge of the four-year-olds. 'Of course. Use my office.'

Good chance Howell understood his methods, and that this needed to be a solo interview, because he hung back when Yuki stepped forward.

She gave her customary little bow to Franklin, but a loud sob spoiled the Japanese greeting.

His face rumpled with sympathy. 'Let's talk.' He gently led her to the office, blocked out the bedlam with the door, then offered water and found a box of tissues.

'It is them?' She sniffed.

'It needs to be officially confirmed, but we believe so, I'm sorry. We're having trouble locating family.'

'Bel's parents are both gone, and she's an only child.' Yuki wadded a tissue against her nose. 'I don't know of other family. She talks of a Lucy often. She might be family...or a friend.'

Franklin nodded.

'Alec's father is a widower. He had a serious accident and moved to Ballan when he couldn't keep the farm.'

He tried to fit it together. 'The Goodlife Farm was his?'

'Oh, no. He never owned Goodlife.'

She saw he was still confused and explained. 'Bel and Alec worked very hard to save up and be approved for a mortgage. They moved in before they fell pregnant with Ethan.' She appeared to drift into the past. Returned to the present with a jolt. 'At the time of the accident, Ethan was going to school, and Bel was back at the kinder...they were well settled in at their farm. So when Alec's father couldn't keep his place going, he sold it and went into a unit.'

Yuki leaned forward. 'Bel suggested he live with them. But

he said no, she had enough on her hands without a crippled father-in-law.'

The usual pressures of a young working mother? A couple on the land?

He asked, but she was crying hysterically now, for her friend and her family. He stuffed more tissues Yuki's way.

While he wished he could back off for her sake, there was one thing he had to check. 'Anything out of character for Bel or the family lately?'

Her sobs lessened while she contemplated the question and mopped up with tissues.

'We were meeting at our favourite café on Tuesday.'

'You and Bel?'

'Yes, us two and Ollie. But she didn't come.' She dabbed her nose. 'And she didn't reply to my messages.'

'And that's strange?'

'Yes, absolutely.'

———

Apparently, Jeanette *Must've just ducked out.* Georgie didn't buy the two brothers' mock surprise. The gravel crunching under the tyres of the Spider and engine noise had alerted them to her entrance. It made sense that they'd notice any coming or going, and know full well if their stepmother was in or out.

She speculated whether they had brought her inside to ply passive intimidation or something more blatant. Well, she could bluff too.

'Never mind. I can come back and talk to Jeanette later. But now's fine for you two?' She pulled out a chair and sat at the kitchen table.

The guys exchanged an unsettled glance.

The hawk-nosed brother spoke for both. 'Look, we're not much for talking.' He affixed an apologetic face.

Georgie mirrored him. The insincerity in the kitchen was growing stifling.

'I understand this is a difficult time. But this could be a way to honour your dad. To share good memories of the farm here and perhaps others in contrast. The stuff people from cities just don't get about living and working on the land.'

The second guy scoffed, but again he left it to his brother to respond.

'You want us to talk about banks screwing us, suppliers screwing us, customers screwing us? Well, lady, we get by. We're,' Hawk Nose swung his eyes up to the left and seemed happy when he found the word, '*resourceful*. We don't ask for handouts. We do it our way.'

He stopped, catching onto daggers from his brother. They both turned to front Georgie. The set of their bodies toughened.

She swallowed, loud in her ears, but with luck, they hadn't noticed. She hid her intrigue in what the guy had *nearly* said and his brother's warning to shut up.

Gazing at the blank page of her notepad with her pen poised, Georgie used an upbeat tone. 'What a shame I missed Jeanette. What's her number – so I can arrange an appointment?'

They gave it to her. Why would they do that, really? They could've offered to pass on a message. But to give her the phone number when they didn't know if Jeanette would welcome the contact...odd.

Her suspicions about the Hansens multiplied.

CHAPTER TWENTY-SEVEN

ONCE THEY WERE CLEAR OF THE KINDERGARTEN AND ANY flapping ears, Franklin asked, 'Did you get anything?'

His partner clicked his tongue. 'Not really.' He summarised and sighed. 'You?'

Franklin filled him in.

'Interesting.'

They let that hang, both thinking.

Franklin pictured the woman he'd known for several years. Though he wasn't intimately acquainted with Bel, it didn't sit with him either, that she'd let her friend down without an explanation. He marked it in his mind to speak to Yuki again when she'd processed some of her grief. So far, she was the best-placed person to have inside knowledge of the Murrays' marriage and life.

'Right.' He straightened. 'We have two leads to follow. Why the breast care nurse called a welfare check for Wednesday morning. And why Bel missed her coffee date on Tuesday.'

He strode off in the direction of the primary school, Howell hastening to catch up. 'We might make that a hattrick at the school.'

———

Georgie dawdled getting into the Spider and drawing on her seatbelt. She pretended to use her mobile with her long, chestnut-brown hair veiling her face so she could watch the brothers, and for Jeanette.

The woman was a no-show. But the brothers went from standing with arms crossed and squared up to her, to the second brother taking a call, then panic mode – both throwing anxious looks beyond her parked Alfa and gesticulating.

She turned over the ignition, dragging out the process of easing the car into gear. She drove forward at walking pace, figuring it would be fun to see if it worried them if she took the driveway loop rather than do a U-turn.

By angling the rear-view mirror, she saw Hawk Nose yanked in by his jacket, so the brothers' foreheads virtually met. They spoke heatedly. Hawk Nose circled his arm, breaking his brother's grip. He made an angry swipe towards Georgie's car and then the way she'd come in.

She kept one eye on the car mirrors as she inched along the gravel, noting a medium-sized truck with high-slatted sides pull up the driveway and park beside the brothers. A thickset man jumped down from the cabin. She couldn't see his face, but noted their spirited discussion before she lost sight.

She hooked around the oval of the driveway considering why the Hansens were pissed she'd seen the truck. Then she passed a pen that backed onto an annexe to the rear of the large shed, crammed with sheep. They'd need their coats in winter, so they weren't there for shearing. They must be going on that truck.

Moving stock was normal on a farm, so why the subterfuge? Maybe she'd spent too much time around Franklin because her immediate guess was stock theft.

She needed proof. Without coming to a complete stop, she grabbed her mobile and shot a couple of photos, uncertain whether she'd captured tags or branding that would help ID the sheep.

She drove on, her pulse thrumming in her ears. If the three men confronted her, she didn't like her chances. She circled the farmhouse, her foot faltering on the accelerator when she passed a twin set of gas cylinders matching the image uploaded by the police last night. Yellow-and-red lightning-shaped pattern around the collar.

Georgie patted the passenger seat, feeling for the mobile she'd tossed aside moments ago. Her fingers clasped it, just as Hawk Nose emerged around the corner of the house, his posture aggressive.

Shit.

In a flash, she dumped the phone, smiled and drove off.

It took all her control not to plant it, stone chips be buggered. She appeared cool. She hoped.

———

The principal invited them to wait in his office while he relieved Ethan's teacher. He strode across the small space, touched the doorknob and let his hand drop.

His back still turned he muttered, 'I'm not sure how to handle this.'

He slowly pivoted. 'We get critical incident training, but you pray you'll never need to activate it, and when you do, you question everything.'

Obviously, he wanted something from them. Howell said, 'That's understandable.'

'We're supposed to get on with things as near to normal as possible. But then we're supposed to offer grief counselling to any student or staff member that needs it. Aren't they contradictory?'

Franklin saw his point.

'So, we're supposed to run the school day and classes as scheduled. But we're missing a good chunk of students today because their parents have kept them home.' He rubbed the bridge of his nose in a jerky motion. 'Like we've had an outbreak of something contagious.' He stopped rubbing and made an *of course* gesture. 'It really is, isn't it?'

He clearly expected them to fill the gap.

'Grief, shock? Yeah, it's spreadable,' Franklin agreed.

Howell gave him a sharp look. Apparently, not the right thing to say.

The principal went on verbalising his doubts. 'Perhaps I should close the school for the rest of today and tomorrow?'

Franklin kept his thought, *Who knows?* to himself this time.

'I meet all prospective families before they join us. And I make it my business to get to know them throughout their child's journey through our school. The Murrays were a conscientious couple, always wanted what was best for Ethan and Ollie, when his turn came. Incredible—'

Franklin lost patience. He couldn't solve the bloke's problems, and they had to get on with their interviews. He cut in. 'Nobody's been formally identified, so please don't name them at this stage.'

More contradictions. We're here to see Ethan's teacher, but can't confirm this involves him and his family.

'If you could get Ethan's teacher for us?'

The principal shot him a stunned glance, but finally left them alone in his office.

'Bring back memories?' Howell chuckled.

Franklin smiled back, but his past primary school days were the furthest thing from his mind. He was processing the little they'd learned at the kinder and his questions for Ethan's teacher. From there, he planned to focus on the welfare check.

The teacher came in three minutes later. She wore a long, letterbox-red woollen cardigan with oversized buttons and deep outer pockets. It looked cosy, but she draped it across her body as if chilled to the bone.

Franklin took the lead. Like the principal, he knew this teacher from way back. And as he'd done for both Yuki and the head, he opened with a disclaimer about official confirmation on the IDs still pending.

'I'm sorry, but we need to ask some questions.'

She undid, then rewrapped her cardigan even tighter.

They covered off a few basics, warm-ups that she could answer easily and without a sense of guilt. Guilt was a pain in the arse when it came to their inquiries. People felt it even when they needn't. For breaking confidences. For not doing more to stop the situation or protect the victim. For having no clue anything was wrong. And often the deepest kind came from *wanting* to help but being unable to.

He suspected the last of this teacher from her constant fidgeting with her cardigan as they talked. But Franklin pressed on, desperate to come away with even a single new fact.

While she answered his question, he chewed over the next he'd pose.

A phone rang in the outer room. Its annoying demand for attention tempted him to snatch it up and tell the caller to ring back. That whatever trivial thing was on their mind could in no way measure up to what they were dealing with.

At last, it shut up.

He cleared his throat. 'Can you think of anything unusual in the past week or so?'

Too broad, her gaze was puzzled.

'Anything Ethan said or did?'

Howell contributed, 'Or something he didn't do?'

She squirmed, dropping her eyes, then conceded, 'He missed school on Tuesday.'

Franklin's breathing shallowed while he willed her to go on. She didn't, so he urged, 'And his parents didn't let you know?'

'No.'

'Were you worried? Was that irregular? Did you call them to chat about it?'

Too anxious, Franklin. Too many questions at once.

'I'm sorry *now* that I didn't think much of it. I didn't want to bother Bel, and well, Ethan is,' she faltered, 'inconsistent.'

Her cardigan got rearranged again. 'With his challenges...'

'His challenges?'

'He's on the autism spectrum. He was diagnosed around the time Ollie came along.' She fluttered her hands. 'A lovely, lovely boy. But he has sleeping difficulty, attention deficit, and is incredibly literal, and well, you know how kids are, and even us adults? We are inexact, we generalise, embellish, and Ethan finds all that a problem. He's also oversensitive.'

She stopped, seemingly finished. But Franklin didn't believe they had the full picture.

'Oversensitive how?'

'To sound and touch. To change.' She waved, implying his sensitivity was hard to define, or all-encompassing.

Howell sat forward. 'And you put down young Ethan's absence on Tuesday to a kind of behavioural flare-up?'

She gave a bob of the head.

145

'Any inkling of a trigger for that?'

Good question. Franklin hung on the teacher's response.

She sighed. 'I'm sorry.'

There's the guilt.

'I just don't know.'

CHAPTER TWENTY-EIGHT

GEORGIE KEPT EXAMINING HER PHOTOS, ENLARGING THEM, scrolling over each portion. But she'd stuffed up. Without super-enhancing photo technology—and even that would only work if there was something to find—there were no discernible identifying marks on the flock.

She considered tailing the truck for an opportunity to take more pics and, if possible, to its destination. But while her classic convertible wasn't expensive by modern car standards, it was rare, and in the relatively quiet countryside around Gordon, conspicuous.

Instead, she settled on parking along the main drag with a handful of vehicles, hoping the truck would pass. Even better if the truckie stopped at the general store or café.

After forty-five minutes catching up emails, phone calls, drafting a short article for *Champagne Musings* and unsuccessfully trying Jeanette Roselle in between watching the road, she gave up. He'd no doubt hit the Western Freeway long ago. Or taken an alternative route out of town.

Before she drove to the Gettys, Georgie pulled up a fresh

sheet on her notepad and racked her brain, jotting several points.

First, what she could recall of the truck.

Isuzu. Single cab, white. Dirty-yellow metal-panelled sides with the same colour on the rails. Hard to see in the back section. Open top?

She dredged up four characters of the number plate.

WYU4??

Not enough. What were the last two digits? *No idea.* She gave up and moved on.

Gas cylinders at the Hansens – match to the Murrays?

She was almost positive.

Cause of primary explosion at the Murrays? How? Accident or deliberate? Common brand? Wouldn't police have said?

Connected or coincidence?

She screwed up her nose. No evidence, but instinct leaned to the former.

Need proof gas cylinders match. Find out what can about them.

Stock truck and sheep. Dodgy dealings? Stolen?

What other reasons could the Hansens have for their shiftiness?

Tax evasion?

They could just be unlikeable men but not up to anything unlawful.

What did Hilda want to tell me? Linked to all this? The gas, the sheep, Goodlife Farm?

Georgie plotted a timeline. Hilda was anxious to talk yesterday. The police revealed interest in the gas cylinders in the evening. The woman backed off this morning.

'Interesting.'

She stared out the windscreen at the gloomy, grey day. Her nerves took a low buzz.

———

Franklin pulled the unmarked wagon into the car park. Dread settled on him, which made no sense. He'd been to Ballarat Base plenty, on callouts and personal visits to friends, and not all doom and gloom stuff either. He supposed it was just too soon to be back at a hospital.

He parked, and they strolled to the main entrance, the blend of modern and period architecture trying its best to make the place inviting. They followed the signs to the cancer centre, and with every step, Franklin fought the urge to leave.

They were nearly at the breast care department when he spotted a public toilet and rushed for it, letting Howell think he was busting.

Inside a cubicle, he leaned against the door and breathed to steady his heartbeat. The odour of disinfectant overlaying urine added with his unease. His phone buzzed.

Georgie.

He rejected her call, just as he'd ignored those from Maeve and Lunny earlier. He tried to shut out the cubicle, the hospital. But it didn't help. His memory went to sitting beside Sam last night, after convincing a ward nurse to let him in. There for a couple of hours, maybe more, on strict instructions not to touch Sam or any equipment, and if he spoke to her, to keep it upbeat.

He'd watched her chest rise and fall as machines kept her unconscious and alive, brooding over what the nurse had told him. Sam had survived one surgery, with numerous to come. *If* she survived that long. Her life was counted in the miracles of minutes and hours. The nurse had explained why he needed to be careful with what he said in Sam's presence – it wasn't uncommon for medically-induced coma patients to have glimpses of cognisance.

Franklin had dwelled on that for a long while. He'd rather think Sam was peaceful, oblivious. He'd cried, silently, his head bowed, in case she could hear or see. Eventually, he wiped his face and talked to her. His throat scratchy, he went through every good time he could think of since she'd first walked up to the front counter at Daylesford, green and keen as probies come. He told her he was proud of her. She was a bloody good cop.

Her eyelids had twitched, and he regretted what he'd said. Why talk about work and how good she was at it? Even if she survived this critical time, her prospects of returning to the job weren't great.

———

Georgie left a brief voicemail for Franklin, plus an update by text. Her concern for him turned into thinking about what he'd make of her theory. And then she hurriedly reached for the ignition key. It was nearly 11.00am and she'd only ticked off a single major to-do item.

With déjà vu, she drove onto the Getty farm as she'd done twenty-six hours ago, when everything had been fine with Sam and Irvy, and at Korweinguboora.

Amid stepping out of the car, she pondered, *Is that true?* Or was the situation already dire at the Murray farm by then?

CHAPTER TWENTY-NINE

Denise Zachary's colleague made a show of checking her watch, highlighting that they were ten minutes late, five of those thanks to Franklin's meltdown in the toilet. Must be nice to work in a world where everything went to plan and to the clock.

He winced. That was unfair. Denise was paying the price for a day that had gone to hell. And it was on them to find out why.

The nurse fiddled with her watchband, wearing a glazed expression. Grappling with what had happened, he realised. Her fidgeting with the watch was unconscious.

Howell leaned forward in his chair, dangling his hands between his spread knees. Franklin sensed his partner would kick off the questions. Suited him.

'We're obviously interested in Denise's relationship with the Murrays.' Howell let his statement hang.

The nurse waited awkwardly.

Franklin put in, 'We gather Bel was a patient?'

Her brow wrinkled.

'Breast care patient,' he elaborated.

'Are you aware that breast cancer affects males too?'

Did she mean Alec was sick?

She talked on. 'They may represent only one per cent of our cases, but they shouldn't be forgotten.' Then she suddenly lost it. 'I'm sorry. I just can't believe it... *Denise. Den!*'

The word choked. Her grimace was pained. Then she added, 'And Bel.'

———

A shabby bitsa dog bolted up, and lunged back and forth, yapping at Georgie's feet as she left the Spider. She cringed at the racket and wasn't surprised when Bob Getty appeared from the midsized of three sheds. He pulled the door to, calling the dog to heel with, 'Henry.'

He joined her. 'Nice to see you again, Georgie.'

Agreeable enough manner and words, but she detected a rigidity to his posture that hadn't been there yesterday.

She shook his hand, spieling off much of what she'd pitched to the Hansens but more succinctly, and ending with a plea to honour Allan Hansen with this new, extended angle to her feature.

It crossed her mind that he might've received a warning that she'd been nosing around at the Hansens and to be prepared for her coming here. On the flipside, Bob had sanctioned her visit yesterday and welcomed a story about his friend. And besides an allegedly long and close friendship between the deceased man and Bob Getty, and Hilda's strange behaviour, Georgie still didn't know if or how Bob fitted in.

He scratched the side of his mouth, thinking. With a deep nod he said, 'He was a good man,' and started for the house. 'We'll talk over a cuppa.'

The smoke puffing from the chimney promised a cosy reprieve from the bitter winter's day, and a hot, strong caffeine hit tempted Georgie to go with it. But she wasn't here to just see the inside of another farmhouse.

She stayed where she was, forcing him to stop. Gazing around, she admired the property. More money here than at the Hansens? Or more pride?

'I'd love to talk while we walk, Bob.' She glided her hand to take in the paddocks, the dam, the sheds. 'So I can soak up the atmosphere for my story.'

Wide-eyed, she smiled. Ms Innocent. He did a series of fast blinks but shrugged, his zip-up parka rustling as his shoulders hiked. She angled subtly towards the sheds, but Bob steered her to a paddock with cows clustered together.

As they continued to traipse the farm, he answered her questions easily. His apparent comfort showing her the cattle, then his sheep, removed suspicion that they were stolen. His eagerness to keep her from the sheds sealed it in her mind that she needed to gain access to them to find out what he was hiding.

'Can you tell us when the welfare check was booked in?' Franklin added, 'And why?'

The nurse rifled through a filing cabinet and came back empty-handed. She typed a string of keys on her keyboard and paused, reading the computer screen.

She flinched. 'Looks like Den's behind in her notes.'

A regular occurrence was the sense he got. Confirmed by, 'She's always pressed because she gives people more time than she's got. Usually catches her paperwork up in a big hit every few weeks.'

Howell asked, 'Besides Wednesday morning's visit, did she have a recent appointment with Bel Murray at the farm? Or here?'

Exactly what Franklin wanted to know.

'You police have her paper diary.'

So they did. They should've gone through that thoroughly.

'But I can access her online calendar.' Again, she turned to her computer.

'The most recent was here, this Tuesday, at 11.00am. Bel missed it.' Her lips did a thin squiggle.

'What can you tell us about Bel's illness?'

The nurse glanced from Howell to her screen. 'I'll need to refer to legal first.'

'It could be beneficial to our investigation. The sooner you can help–'

'Look, I'd like to. But my hands are tied.'

Howell and the nurse kept talking, but Franklin's mind took leap over leap.

Mental state. Suicide risk. Police to help Denise gain entry and deal with whatever she found. Clear fears for the worst.

He supposed Denise had tried Bel several times, and surely Alec too. Apparently, neither had answered.

Or, on the other hand, Denise might've connected with one or both, but she'd been met with aggression, and she couldn't shelve her worries. So she'd enlisted police to buffer hostility and guarantee access to Bel.

Both theories seemed far-fetched yet made sense too. Ethan's absence from school without explanation, and Bel's missed breast care appointment in Ballarat and coffee date with her girlfriend in Daylesford. All on Tuesday.

An idea that began with Yuki became an increasing possibility. Could the Murrays have predeceased the explosion and fire on Wednesday morning? Franklin's skin prickled.

CHAPTER THIRTY

WHEN BOB CIRCLED BACK TO THE FARMHOUSE AND repeated his offer of a cuppa, Georgie's feet were numb and her hands frozen stiff, even though they'd been stuffed deep inside her leather jacket – the replacement to her old favourite ruined last spring.

'Definitely, thanks.'

It gave her the chance to thaw, recharge, and most crucially, with luck, to connect with Hilda. She didn't want to leave the Gettys without discovering the something Hilda knew that she wished she didn't.

They walked straight into the kitchen, finding Hilda at a computer on the table, her back to an old wood stove. She mumbled hello, giving Georgie a furtive glance, silently begging.

She caught the message and acted as if they were strangers. Which they were, excluding the phone exchanges.

Bob made drinks in the hush of people with little in common thrown together for a bit too long. Georgie sat near Hilda at the table and gazed around the room. She took in a couple of framed photos on the window ledge, a large Cobb & Co railway clock on the wall, and a vase on the table crammed with mauve-pink azalea blooms that she'd seen growing in the garden. Neat and homely, the room matched in with Hilda, whereas the broader property smacked of all Bob's.

'Here you go.'

Bob distributed the mugs, smiling widely, apparently buoyed by the assumption the interview was nearly over and he'd soon be done with Georgie. Hilda kept at the computer. It was looking like he wouldn't leave them alone. Until the landline rang.

Please be Bob that goes and picks up.

It gave a few more rings.

Please don't be Hilda.

Bob pushed back his chair, and Georgie's nerves buzzed as he left the room. She hesitated; it could be a spam call. But he droned on. In case he was quick, she stroked the azalea petals to imply they were talking about the flowers, angled only slightly towards Hilda.

She said softly, 'Tell me what's on your mind.'

The woman did a headshake.

'Look, I'm pretty sure I know.'

Hilda jerked, though she continued to front her screen.

'It'd be better if we spoke before...' Georgie didn't finish, letting Hilda fill in the gap with whatever she feared most. The cops, or her husband's cronies.

Bob's voice rose. 'Yep, yep, we'll see you on the weekend.'

He was wrapping up.

'You chose me, remember?'

Hilda made no response.

Not for the first time, Georgie wondered why she'd picked a journo to confide in. Maybe the mess the Gettys were in extended so wide that she didn't know who to trust, and she hoped Georgie would take it up, act on it as an anonymous tipoff, disguising it so nobody would ever suspect her source was Hilda.

Who knew? But Bob was saying goodbye.

'Ring me, Hilda.'

Her head moved, impossible to tell if it meant yes or no. Then Bob returned.

'Thanks for your hospitality and your time.' Georgie motioned. 'Mind if I take a few pics as I'm leaving?'

Annoyance shadowed the man's face. He smoothed it down, hooking his jacket from the chairback.

He was coming with her. Of course.

———

Franklin drove automatically, surprised when he passed the turnoff for Wallace and again going by the one for Gordon. He'd spaced out, blanking the radio and their surroundings, except for a basic level of traffic awareness.

He clicked the indicator for the Daylesford exit and realised his partner was talking.

He took the turn and listened.

'What do you reckon we'll learn when the hospital gives us access to Bel Murray's records?'

Franklin said, 'I think the nurse would've let it slip if Bel was in the clear.'

'Because in their line of work that is probably, sadly, unusual. So, she had cancer.'

'Yep.'

'And the situation warranted a welfare check,' Howell mused. 'Your guess on that?'

Suspecting he was being humoured, Franklin said, 'Denise Zachary believed Bel was a suicide risk.'

'It's looking that way, isn't it, mate?'

'Or, either Bel or Alec was in hostile denial.'

'And they all ended up dead.'

They drove in silence for a few hundred metres, then Howell went on. 'When I updated Darma from arson earlier, he said Bruner has already formed a theory.'

Franklin bristled. 'Of-bloody-course.'

'He might be a dickhead, mate, but he knows his stuff when it comes to arson and explosives. Anyway, Bruner wants us to do the legwork before he shares, and there are more i's to dot before he will announce it, but his prediction from the position and state of the bodies is that the Murrays were dead prior to the first explosion.'

He'd foreseen it, but Franklin's gut wrenched. He'd wished like anything to be wrong.

CHAPTER THIRTY-ONE

Georgie glanced at her phone. 1.30pm and still no reply to the voice or text messages she'd sent nearly two hours earlier. Had Franklin even received them? He could be in a black spot for coverage. Her mood darkened. Maybe he didn't rate her information.

She tapped her mobile on the steering wheel. Granted, what she'd discovered was tenuous. Even more so, her jumps connecting it with the Murrays. But her instincts and imagination had reaped rewards before, and Franklin normally listened.

She stared at sprawling paddocks of billiard-table green. The gently curving gravel driveway splitting them was lined with naked silver birches. Their smooth white trunks with dark knobbles formed a striking contrast to the browns and olives of the towering, multi-limbed gumtrees nearby.

Yesterday, she'd barely noticed how beautiful this part of the country was. The sickening events that'd occurred over this farm's boundary had obscured the elements that rendered Korweinguboora unique, gave it a *hidden secret* feel. Clean air, rich soil, ample rainwater and vivid greenness with a backdrop of bush. On any normal day, traffic would be local only. Peacefulness would be a hush like the snow she imagined layering the ground and dusting the trees.

The spell broke. They were no wiser as to accident, misadventure, or malice. Until that was clear, the number of people at risk was potentially huge. Perhaps even the neighbour living here, which if she'd guessed correctly would be the woman who'd knocked into her in a daze at the fire scene.

Georgie sighed, reviewing the last message she'd sent Franklin about an hour ago. She peered at the attachment. With Bob Getty in tow, this was the best shot she'd managed, with her focal point partly cut off. Yet the markings on the tank were unmistakable.

So why wasn't Franklin interested?

———

Howell stood next to him, neither talking as they watched the arson chemist and forensic crew pick through the ruins. *Ruins* was the only word to describe the Murrays' former home. It weighed on Franklin that weatherboard houses—his own included—went up like piles of matchsticks. Just add fire. And in this instance, multiple blasts swiftly expanding the blaze.

His phone vibrated with another call. They were coming in an endless stream today. He saw *Georgie* on the screen.

'You're not going to get that?' Howell asked.

Franklin pocketed his mobile and shrugged. Why try to explain what he didn't get himself?

———

Georgie chewed her lip. She was torn. Continue up the driveway and see if the neighbour was home? Or persist with Franklin? Or revisit Gordon and see what else she could dig up?

Might as well carry on here, and then drop in on farmer Dave. At least, she'd satisfy herself of the wellbeing of both neighbours. At best, she'd find a piece to the puzzle that led to the Murrays' final days.

Her gaze narrowed with a burn of anger and shame. Five lives lost yesterday and two teetering on the brink, with countless others irrevocably altered. Her efforts had to be levelled at more than piecing together a puzzle.

Truth for the victims. A form of justice for Irvy, Sam and Denise...and for the Murrays if they turned out to be innocents too. Answers for the families and friends who loved them all.

Closure, not so much. Experience had taught her that the concept had little place in the real world. You didn't move on from something like this. You tried to live with it.

She left the Spider at the bottom of the drive and slipped through the wide gate. Couldn't help checking her phone halfway along.

Franklin's silence frustrated her. Not only was she clueless as to what he thought of her groundwork, it also left her clueless as to what the official investigation had uncovered.

With a ripple up her spine, she acknowledged that anyone she'd met so far might be an accomplice or a perpetrator. But of what crimes?

CHAPTER THIRTY-TWO

FRANKLIN AND HOWELL STALKED INTO THE BACCHUS Marsh CIU rooms bang on time for the 4.00pm briefing headed by their boss, Detective Senior Sergeant Si Waldo. A sudden silence hit the gathering of detectives and uniforms. A whisper started towards the back of the room, followed by a hissed, 'Shush.' The sympathy on the face of one of the Ds made Franklin centre on the female detective by the bloke's side. Her hungry curiosity was easier to deal with...until he guessed she was about Sam's age and her undiluted interest reminded him of Sam's first day at Daylesford.

'John.' Waldo stopped, pinning his bottom lip with his top one. Then he muttered awkward commiseration.

Franklin gave a sharp nod, wishing a hole would swallow him through the floor. He stood cross-armed with his back to the majority of the room. His ears burned, and the craving for a smoke came on like a king-hit.

Thankfully the boss turned to the whiteboard, taking the crew's attention as he summed up the investigation so far and asked for updates.

'We're building a picture of the Murrays,' Howell added in turn. He outlined the key information they'd extracted from their various interviews today, concentrating largely on the kindergarten, school and hospital.

'So,' the keen female D said, 'it's pointing towards a domestic?'

The bloke beside her gave her a dig with his elbow, throwing a glare.

'Too early to call, team,' Waldo cut in.

Franklin's gaze moved from his boss to the photos stuck to the whiteboard, zeroing in on Sam and Irvy, smart in their blue uniforms. Their permanently captured smiles cut him deep. His arms unfolded. He sensed Howell stir.

'Mate–'

He dodged Howell's hand. A voice in his mind warned, *Shut the fuck up, Franklin.* But he couldn't.

'How do you think it'd go down with Kendra and her kids— Irvy's family—if we label this a *domestic*? Or Sam's mum and dad? The nurse's boyfriend?'

'John,' Waldo interrupted. 'We get it.'

Franklin looked over his colleagues until their expressions, ranging from embarrassment to pity, blurred together. 'Yep.'

He'd burnt his bridges this morning putting up his hand for officer-in-charge at Daylesford anyway. He walked out.

———

Georgie had drawn blanks all afternoon, including attempts to speak with Jeanette Roselle and Hilda Getty. And she'd run dry on ideas. She dialled a number that went straight to voicemail. She tried another that was answered on the third ring.

'Marty, I've been trying to get hold of Franklin. You wouldn't–'

Howell answered quietly, *'Hang on,'* and rustles suggested he'd covered the handset. After a minute, *'Sorry about that. Briefing was ending.'*

'Any developments?'

'Some, but still a way to go.'

'What do you think of what I found at Gordon?'

'What's that?'

She frowned. 'Franklin didn't fill you in?'

'Not sure he's been on top of his calls and emails today, Georgie.'

Just a beat off from casual.

'Is he there?'

'Hang on.' He repeated muffling his handset, coming back with, *'No.'*

Clearly bullshit.

'Sorry, Georgie.'

That bit she believed.

————

Franklin's phone went off and he fought the temptation to throw it out the window. He glared at it until it stopped. Howell peered his way, raised his brows and returned his focus to the road.

'What?' Franklin said.

The older detective did a long inhale-exhale. 'I was thinking how different things will be for you as OIC at Daylesford.' He clicked the indicator and pulled the wagon right. 'As the one in charge, you'll be stuck behind the desk a lot, slogging through paperwork.' He groaned. 'A tonne of reports. More overseeing, less active investigating.'

Howell gave him a glance adding, 'More phone calls and emails. Mate, you'll be the one your crew will expect everything of, from covering their shift to fixing their stuff-ups. The brass will want everything in triplicate and *no overtime*. The public will shake their fingers and demand the earth because *we're paying for that fancy new station* being built in Vincent Street. The local pollies will manipulate crime statistics whichever way suits their party, and if the press get wind of a rise in crime rates, you'll be drawn and quartered.'

Franklin hid a shudder of panic with a palm lift.

'So, I was thinking you'd better get used to dealing with your emails and texts.' His partner thumbed towards the mobile in Franklin's hand as it went off again. 'And answering your phone.'

Franklin shook his head, though Howell was dead right. He clicked to answer.

'*Can you talk?*'

It was Harty and he sounded weird. Thick – maybe with a cold. Fuck, he hoped he wasn't crying.

'Yep.'

'*What have you heard?*'

Franklin gave the latest in three sentences.

'*This is all on me.*' The *me* cracked.

Franklin hitched his arse higher in the passenger's bucket seat. 'Huh?'

'*If I hadn't switched shifts with Irvy to be with Melissa when—*'

'We all do trades here and there. Irvy agreed at the time, and if he wasn't fit for it on the day, he should've said.'

'*But—*'

'But *what*? You'd rather be the one dead?'

———

Needing a timeout, Georgie parked at the Korweinguboora reserve. Leaning on the Spider, she took in the four white goal and behind posts at each end of the oval, and the orange planked-and-bricked clubhouse ringed by scrub. Hers was the only car, and she spent a moment imagining the place on game day, or with a celebration on in the hall. Crammed with people and vehicles, aromas from the barbecues mingling with eucalyptus, laughter and chatter floating through the air.

She trudged across the potholed driveway, drawn to a cluster of primary-coloured playground equipment. At the foot of the spiral slide, a picture formed of Bel and Alec standing where she stood. It was shaped upon images police had released publicly with the family's names twenty minutes earlier.

In her mind, Ethan rounded the slide's curve. His brown eyes a little worried until he spotted his father, who had the same hair but shoulder-length, a stubbly beard with flecks of premature grey, and smiling eyes highlighted by small, round glasses. His mother's thick, wavy blonde hair framed her face, pretty with little or no makeup because of her wide grin, and she was cheering, with little Oliver on her hip. The baby's hands reached for windblown tendrils of his mum's hair tickling his cheeks.

The imagery was as real as if they were there. Oddly, Georgie's spirits boosted. She hoped they'd had times like that.

She moved on to the clubhouse, shadows reminding her that sundown was closing in. It was only a week to the shortest day, but an icy gust that made her shiver and burrow deeper into her leather jacket reminded her that the bulk—and worst—of winter was still to come.

Three plastic chairs sat in a nook at the front of the structure overlooking the empty oval. She chose the squat blue one and sank onto it. She'd love to light up. A smoke would warm her from the inside. Admittedly, she'd never stop at one, but she checked her pockets.

Instead of finding a stray ciggie and lighter, she pulled out a bundle of papers scrunched down from pushing her hands into her pockets for warmth. She registered they were the BRICC brochures she'd lifted from the breast care nurse's car yesterday morning, then forgotten.

Georgie stuffed them back into her pocket and bent forward, the chair creaking beneath her. She propped her chin in her hands, elbows on her knees, and watched daylight dissipate. Instead of enjoying the way the pre-sunset heightened then muted the colours of the foliage, she mulled over the smiling young mother actually suffering from cancer, and her husband and little kids going through everything she and her mum and sister had experienced with her dad.

Could it have pushed Bel or Alec over the edge?

She hated to think it possible.

CHAPTER THIRTY-THREE

GEORGIE'S MIND WAS AN EAGLE PICKING AT ROADKILL IN between cars flashing past. Her thoughts circled and swooped, but didn't quite lock on to any meat. Each time she came close, she was ricocheted back to the police station at Daylesford this afternoon.

She'd let herself in, and found Maeve in the kitchen arranging fresh flowers in the vase that was part of a memorial to Irvy and Sam. Without a word, they'd fallen into a hug. Harty and Slam had come in then. Harty had taken one look at their teary faces and buckled onto the nearest chair, sobbing like a bewildered kid. Slam had kept himself together by opening and shutting the fridge door continually, once freezing to ask if he should get Lunny to join them, then his pace revving up when Maeve said it was best to leave him be for now.

Very lucky thing no urgent calls came through on the police radio for that thirty minutes.

The thought of time gave Georgie a welcome diversion. She flicked on the TV at 5.49pm ready for the primetime

168

newsbreak, then returned to her computer to check the internet.

Nothing new from Police Media. Multiple hits from all the national print, radio and TV players. And plenty of regional coverage, especially the local areas of Daylesford and Ballarat.

POLICE INVESTIGATE FATAL GAS EXPLOSION AT FARM IN KORWEINGUBOORA

Several people have been killed following a gas explosion at a farm in Korweinguboora in central Victoria.

Neighbours reported a series of loud blasts and out of control house fire at approximately 10.00am yesterday morning.

Country Fire Authority trucks attended the scene within fifteen minutes, but the house was fully engulfed, and it took several hours for the fire to be controlled.

District Inspector Knight last night advised that two police members and a number of civilians were impacted by this incident, with several fatalities.

Two people were transferred by air ambulance to the Alfred Hospital, and they remain in critical condition today.

The fire destroyed the house, but nearby buildings were unscathed.

Anyone with information is urged to contact Crime Stoppers, and reports can be confidential.

Georgie recognised the article's inhibition. Stark, scant, all fact, no conjecture, written before the names were released. Appropriate yet inadequate.

She clicked on a story headlined 'Small Town Rocked By Fatal Blasts' by the *Ballarat Courier*. It began in much the same vein. But five paragraphs in it took a different tack.

... A neighbour, who did not wish to be named, told this journalist, 'It was a black day for Korweingi.'

He said, 'Smoke like you've never seen, and never want to see, filled the sky – like a nuclear mushroom cloud, it was.

'The smell was something I'll never forget either and the fire took the house so hard and fast that the firies couldn't save it.'

The man described the homeowners as a well-liked couple with two young boys aged eight and one but was unable to comment on whether they were home at the time.

'All I can tell you is, everyone around here loves them – they're a good lot and have never been in any trouble,' he added.

'How could this happen out here?'

Music heralding the newsbreak broke Georgie's concentration. After the anchor did her stock introduction, graphics filled the screen behind her with a familiar fire scene.

She said gravely, *'We go live now to Ballarat where District Inspector Knight has an update on the horror house explosion at a rural property in Korweinguboora yesterday morning.'*

─────────

In their stationary car, Howell stretched. His stomach ballooned and pressed into the steering wheel. 'I'm knackered.'

Franklin figured he should be too, but he was determined not to open that door. 'What's next?' They weren't far from Korweingi. 'Reinterview the neighbours?'

'Leave it to the morning.'

He silently agreed. While handiest in proximity, the neighbours weren't their highest priority. They'd given statements, and chances they had anything to add were slim. Return visits would be more worthwhile when they had fresh points to quiz them on.

Franklin went through a mental list. They hadn't spoken to any of Alec's friends yet. Needed to expand out Bel's world too. With their home destroyed, their computers, diaries, and the like had been wiped out, but something they'd said face to face or written in a text or email could be enlightening.

With so many to interview, a pressure headache built. He raced through his thinking.

Their crew had located a family member on Bel's side – an aunt living in Mornington. She'd been notified, but it was imperative that they talk to her personally. He glanced at the time on his mobile, calculated that if they left now, they wouldn't arrive until after 8.00pm, so that was another task for tomorrow. Maybe first up.

His insides jolted, remembering two things he'd intended to action directly after the briefing. He'd forgotten.

'Alec's dad in Ballan.' Like the aunt, he'd been informed, but they needed to follow up. His hands curled with frustration. 'And their cars.' He visualised the couple's vehicles in the carport at the farm.

Howell tilted his head, questioning with his saggy eyes.

'We need to see Alec's dad, then search Alec and Bel's cars.'

'Our lot have been over their cars.'

'No mobiles?'

'*Nothing* useful,' Howell stressed.

So, no suicide note.

'Okay, so let's get over to Ballan.'

Howell didn't start the ignition.

Franklin said, 'Let's go.'

Howell cracked a yawn. 'When the AES and coroner give us more, we'll know what we're dealing with and which way to run. Until then, we're blind mice. Scattering everywhere but ineffective.'

Franklin snorted.

'We've done everything we can for today.'

'Crap.'

His partner angled his way, drawing his gaze. 'I want to get to the bottom of all this too. For Irvy and Sam, mostly.'

Franklin knew he meant it, but found himself shaking his head.

'You're running on empty, mate – you just can't see it. You haven't slept in what – thirty-six hours? Nothing to eat either.' Howell's posture tightened. 'If this turns out to be anything other than a tragic accident, then the investigation will crank to the highest level, and we're both going to need every ounce of energy we can muster.'

―――――

DI Knight's presser basically reiterated the victims' names and the protracted nature of such an inquiry. When it ended, Georgie sat staring at the TV screen but didn't take in the rest of the news.

Lonely was a foreign concept to her these days. Her life was fuller than it'd ever been. But the emptiness of Franklin's cottage and his silence left her hollow. She found her phone, tempted to try him. Marty Howell had hung up in a hurry, but she'd squeezed in a plea for Franklin to contact her. And to get him to read her messages as she might've uncovered something useful.

She twirled her mobile in her hand as she used to do with cigarette packets in her smoking days. Should she take the hint and drive back to Richmond? Butt out of it all?

Yeah, like I'm good at butting out.

Still, maybe going to her place would be for the best. But not until she'd made a call.

'Katz? How are you?'

'*Fine.*'

Flat tone said otherwise.

'Are you coming home?' In the gap after her question, Georgie added, 'Should I make us dinner?'

'*No, I'm staying at Lisa's tonight.*'

None of the usual zing at a sleepover at her best friend's house. But at least she'd be safe, warm, fed what she could stomach. Someone was there for Kat. But what about her dad? Was he letting anyone in? Because it certainly wasn't Georgie.

'Have you spoken with your dad?'

'*This morning. Before school.*'

Kat didn't elaborate, and Georgie interpreted it as he'd

distanced from her too. She wondered if Kat was pushing away also.

She heard the teen take a quaking breath.

'Do you know how Sam is?'

'Apparently there's no change, Katz.' Georgie gripped her phone. 'That's a good thing. She's fighting.'

After a few more sniffling breaths, Kat whispered, *'Thanks, Georgie.'*

'You know I'm here for you? Anytime, anyway I can.'

'Yeah.' Her voice pitched. *'Have they said what happened? Why?'*

These were questions she should be able to ask her dad, especially as one of the investigators. While it saddened Georgie that he'd shut her out, she was twice as upset about him not properly supporting his daughter.

She leaned forward, wanting to shield Kat. 'There are plenty of things being said—in the media, out on the street—but in a case like this, the process takes time.' She didn't explain the ins and outs. It'd be too much grisly information. She hoped the teen wouldn't ask. 'We need to keep an open mind and wait for the coroner and specialists to work it out. All right?'

She had to press but got a weak agreement.

'Georgie?'

'Yeah.'

'Will you be there in the morning? I don't want to... I can't go to school. I didn't even make it through today.'

Georgie spoke through a lump in her throat. 'I'll be here when you get home, Katz.'

Nothing to stop her driving back to her own place, returning in the morning. Three-odd hours of driving was a waste though. And Franklin might turn up – as unlikely as it seemed. She'd stay. Even if she was clueless how to get through the night.

CHAPTER THIRTY-FOUR

'I GET YOU COFFEE.' MRS TESORINO FLAPPED A HAND IN what Franklin guessed was the direction of the kitchen. But she sat limply on the couch by her husband as if the suggestion had left her exhausted.

The thought of a drink curdled in his gut. Along with regret that he'd imposed himself on this family, thinking he had something to offer them in their grief. An improvement upon his phone message yesterday, presumably while they were at the hospital.

'No, thanks. But I could make you all one?'

Franklin went to get up, but dropped to his seat when Sam's parents gazed at him blankly and her sister shook her head. Nobody else reacted.

Mr Tesorino gathered the energy to say that Sam's older sister and husband were with her in the ICU.

His wife added, 'We take turns. They only let two of us with Samanta at once and for little,' she pronounced it *leettle*, 'bits of time. They tell us she needs quiet time to heal. We go back in the morning.' She patted her husband's knee.

Silence stretched. Not even a gurgle from the babies. Then a clicking began. Franklin followed the noise to an armchair in the corner. To the fingers of Sam's grandmother as they worked along a string of rosary beads. Then up to the old woman's moon face. Grooves suggested she laughed and smiled a great deal, but not now, as she desperately recited a prayer.

'We just don't understand.' It was the sister who said this. The small boy leaning against her leg had to be her son, their likeness was so strong. A thumb dangled from his mouth and his eyes were wide circles.

'We'll know more in the coming days.' Franklin clenched his jaw. *We'd better.*

'But why hurt Sam?' she insisted.

Her son made a whimper, muffled by his thumb. 'Aunty Sam?'

She shushed him, cradling him to her chest. Over her son's narrow shoulder, she silently begged Franklin for answers.

———

Georgie had forgotten to eat or put logs on the fire. She sat on the couch with an empty stomach and her arms hugging herself. Lethargy hauled at her joints, but she refused to give in to it, so she went to close the curtains. About a foot from the glass, she struck a barrier of coldness. A slap on her cheeks that snapped her alert as she pulled the curtains to.

Winters in Melbourne got cold, but winters here penetrated her bones. It was like she suffered from a visual illusion of the area. Wombat Hill's quaintness and small diameter made it easy to forget its altitude was similar to Mount Macedon and Mount Dandenong, and that even Daylesford's main street was about 500 metres above sea level. High enough for regular frost and occasional snow. The undulating countryside surrounding the town sucked in frigid air that lingered, often slowly dispelled over the day, then crawled back during the early-to-mid afternoon. Maybe one day she'd get used to winters here.

With the glass covered, the chill decreased. But Georgie got the fire going and made strong, black coffee, for warmth outside and in and to keep busy. Without debriefing with Franklin, she felt wrongfooted. Confused about what to put her efforts into.

————

After leaving the Tesorinos, Franklin didn't feel ready for what he had to do next. He rode around the CBD aimlessly and ended up at St Kilda. Fairly pointless thing to do at 9.00pm, unless it was mid-summer when it'd be around dusk. As it was, he parked at the beach and walked along the sand for a while in the murky darkness of night.

Grains crunched under his boots and the top of his leather jacket creaked as it whipped in the wind. He zipped it fully and chalked up another reason why he preferred freshwater. Quiet, unrushed, space to think. Not like this.

The waves crashing and receding on the beach assaulted all his senses. Salt on his tongue, brine filling his nostrils, a fine spray stiffening his exposed skin and wind lashing at his short hair. Worst of the lot was the constant noise.

Whenever he'd had a shit day in the job, or Kat tested him, if he didn't gravitate to the pub, it'd be to his favourite fishing spot. He'd throw a line in, but catching a fish would be a bonus. He'd let the fresh air and sounds of the countryside settle over him and soften the edges.

This place did the opposite. Busyness and noise. Fingernails scratching down a blackboard. He pivoted on his heel to leave.

Out of the headwind, he could lift his chin and look around as he retraced his steps on the beach. Admired the soft glow of the moon and lights reflecting off the pier onto the water, and the city skyline beyond.

Sand shifted under his boots, unceasing like the pummelling of the water. He attuned to both, and his black mood abated fractionally.

Nothing was better. Nothing was solved. But nothing was static either. As sure as the tide would come in and go out here at St Kilda, they'd advance the case tomorrow.

He needed to remember the headwind and shun distractions. All that mattered was Irvy and Sam. Getting to the bottom of what had gone down at Korweingi. And if some bastards out there had stage-managed or caused it, making them pay.

———

Everybody has their strengths, Georgie reminded herself. And it unlocked her brain. If this were an investigative story, what would she be doing? At times of the day when it was deemed rude to call or visit people, or at junctions when she had no clue who she should be interviewing and how to move the story forward – what did she invariably dive into?

Research.

She dragged her computer onto her lap and ran queries on the players she'd spoken to at Gordon. With a jolt, she realised Jeanette Roselle and Hilda Getty hadn't been in contact. She was more surprised about Hilda, yet still convinced the woman would cooperate, even if she were economical with the truth. She made a note to try both again.

Nothing particularly interesting popped up about the

Hansens or Gettys. Allan's death was apparently their five seconds in the limelight.

She did a tangent and googled the Murrays. For a family who had a relatively low profile until a few days ago, and who was only named among the fatalities two hours ago, there were a large number of hits.

Georgie started with one near the top published by *Best Kept Secrets*, a regional magazine.

COMMUNITIES MOURN BLAST THAT KILLS FIVE, LEAVES TWO INJURED

Korweinguboora is a town in the Shire of Moorabool in central Victoria, nearly halfway between Daylesford and Ballan and thirty minutes from Ballarat with a population of 600 or so people and around 200 properties, many with acreage. It is a small, close-knit community predominantly comprised of hard-working farmers. Cattle and woodcutting are the major industries. But, boasting clean air and pure water and rich soil, Korweinguboora is also renowned for roadside stalls with seasonal produce at many a farm gate, and truffles in the recreation reserve.

According to locals, 'Korweingi' is a little slice of paradise. Neighbours are friends. People borrow each other's things. They return them. They look out for each other. This community has just lost four of its own

in the greatest tragedy to ever strike their little town.

At around 10.00am on Wednesday morning, an explosion occurred at Goodlife Farm, which spiralled into an inferno that gutted the home of Alec (32) and Belinda (34) Murray, and their two sons Ethan (8) and Oliver (1). Several further blasts occurred during the blaze that took countless CFA volunteers hours to control and then make safe for police detectives and arson chemists to begin their investigation.

The bodies of all four Murrays were discovered in the charred remains.

Grant (44) Irvine, fondly known as 'Irvy', a senior constable at the nearby Daylesford police station, also died at the scene. Irvy leaves behind his widow, Kendra, and five young children aged between 3 and 8. Irvy and Kendra's sixth child is due on Father's Day. He or she will never know their dad.

Things like this don't happen in Daylesford either. It is a larger town that swells with tourists at weekends and over holidays and thrives on hospitality and health care. But where Korweingi is a little slice of paradise, residents of Daylesford claim their town is a larger piece of that same pie.

Two other people's lives were also irrevocably changed by this event. Samanta Tesorino (25), 'Sam' to everybody but her parents, Irvy's junior colleague, a constable

at Daylesford, and 'a shining star'
according to her supervisor Sergeant Tim
Lunny. And Denise Zachary (34), a woman
who has devoted her life to the care of
breast cancer sufferers, 'Den' works with
BRICC in Ballarat and is known for her
'huge heart'.
Sam and Denise are fighting for their
survival with critical injuries.
The third community mourning their own is
the one in blue. The police men and women
who strive to keep us safe. Irvy has served
his final shift and so might have Sam.
Nobody signs up to be hated, abused,
wounded or killed in the line of duty. They
join the police to make a difference. To all
of us.
This isn't a movie plot. It didn't occur in a
faraway place. It really did happen on
Goodlife Farm yesterday morning. It leaves
everybody from Korweinguboora to
Daylesford to Ballarat and to the Thin Blue
Line and far beyond mourning the loss of
five good souls. It is a tragedy for our whole
community. With shock and sadness,
everybody is asking 'why?'
The writer wonders if there can be a
satisfactory answer.

The journo erred towards sensationalism, yet Georgie couldn't fault the article. It drew the victims as the people directly involved and all those on the periphery. It was emotive. And depressing.

Flicking through the other new stories, Georgie judged them as syndicated versions with same-same content, nothing to add.

She then concentrated on the historic pieces. There weren't many. Bel and Alec both had mentions in local news.

Stories about the preschool, juggling motherhood and career, and learning through investigation and play painted an incomplete but warm image of Bel.

Alec remained more shadowy, beyond his passions for cattle and the land.

———

Sam's chest rose and fell. The rhythm didn't alter when he said, 'It's me, Sam... Franklin. I'm going to sit with you for a while.'

He said little else, worried it'd be the wrong thing, while the nurse who regularly came into the cubicle spoke chirpily to both her patient and him. As Marianne checked Sam's vitals, machines, and adjusted her position, bed and medication, he took in greater detail than the night before. Of Sam's sections of bare, undamaged skin. The dressings that covered her burnt face. The gauze pads where skin was taken from her thighs and grafted to her hands. The stocking sock that went to her knee on the unbroken leg.

He was grateful to Marianne for taking pity on him again tonight. Not blood family, he could be thrown out next time he tried. It surprised him that she let him stay at length, and assumed it was because he barely spoke or moved so as not to disrupt Sam's healing.

Whenever they were alone, he kept monitoring the equipment breathing for Sam, because as the nurse had let him in, she'd admitted what concerned them most was her airways. Saying, *It could be days until the swelling comes down in them. Until then* – Marianne had shrugged. Not exactly a confidence-inducing conversation. But Franklin had appreciated her honesty. And the kindness in her eyes.

He jerked out of a doze when an alert went off. His frantic gaze scanned the screens. Nothing flashing that wasn't before. Sam was as she'd been, as far as he could tell.

Staff surged from all directions, converging on the cubicle to the left of Sam's. After some time, the crisis passed, and they went back to what they'd been doing.

Apparently, the person had pulled through. Lived to fight another day. And when his watch reached 11.59pm, he realised Sam had too.

DAY THREE

FRIDAY 15 JUNE

CHAPTER THIRTY-FIVE

For the whole time that Franklin sat beside Sam's bed, he was on tenterhooks in case she arrested. The night slipped by while he stayed with her, amazed that the nurses didn't boot him out.

He dragged himself away from the Alfred and mounted the Ninja for the return ride to Daylesford at predawn, well and truly beating peak hour. With thin traffic, his run was uneventful. Didn't stop the crushing band of tension around his brain.

The sensation doubled when he arrived home.

Georgie's Spider sat in the driveway, the windscreen, boot and bonnet sheeted in thin ice glinting in the morning light. It must've been there all night.

———

Georgie jolted awake, unsure what had woken her. Then she recognised the sound of Franklin's bike throttling down to a stop. She raked her fingers through her hair to tame the mess and rubbed away sleep. A wide yawn made her ears pop. Rolling out of bed, she felt worse for the hour or so that she'd dozed.

She met him in the hallway. Went to reach out but stopped, reading the tautness in his body. His gaze wasn't cold so much as guarded. It left her at a loss. What to say or do?

In the end, she settled on, 'Are you okay?'

He answered with a jerky action. Confusing.

'Coffee?'

She supposed the sideways twitch of his mouth was meant to be a yes and an attempted smile of thanks, and a sinking feeling connected her heart and stomach. Franklin had built a moat around himself – and she got that. What he'd dealt with over the past few days on top of a career in policing would affect anyone. How to help him through it—*if* he let her in—that's what scared her.

And how would she live with what she'd seen at Goodlife Farm? Easy to imagine reverting to excessive alcohol, nightmares. Her time in counselling and the overexercised phrases of *introspection* and *closure* was two years ago, and she did her best to forget it. She shuddered at the thought of going there again.

Franklin's face furrowed. Maybe he'd seen her reaction. But in the next beat, he'd gone through to the kitchen, leaving her alone in the hallway.

———

The kettle came to the boil just as the back door swung open. Franklin knew it was Kat before he saw her. She had a habit of thrusting the door, making the venetian blind rattle violently, no matter what her mood. But why was she coming in at this hour? He massaged his temple, remembering her last text saying she was sleeping over at Lisa's.

'Dad! You're home!'

She looked so happy to see him. He gave her a hug.

'Gotta get ready for work.' He retreated, uncomfortable in the cross-gaze of Georgie and Kat.

'What about–' Georgie's question was drowned by Kat's, 'Have you slept? You look terrible.'

His mobile went off, saving him.

'John, Eddie Knight.'

Given names for his DI this morning? Unable to read his tone, Franklin kept his response neutral. 'Morning, sir.'

'Pop into Camp Street first thing, will you?'

Franklin's brows went up. A summons to the Daylesford station. What did that mean? His request was approved?

'Yes, sir. I'm expected at Bacchus for the morning's briefing–'

Knight cut in. *'I'll only need a few minutes.'*

He wasn't saying Franklin wouldn't be going on to CI afterwards. It left him conflicted.

'I'll be there in under ten minutes.'

Enough for a dunk in the shower, shave and fresh clothes. Ditch the coffee.

Knight rang off, and Franklin felt Georgie's stare. He met her deep-brown eyes.

'DI Knight.' He wished she'd leave it at that.

'And?'

Knew she wouldn't.

She waited.

'Meeting, that's all.'

Her gaze prodded. Unspoken, but another, *And?*

Taking a breath that puffed his chest, he figured it had to be said. 'I'm taking Lunny's job. Applied, anyway.'

'Dad?' Kat shouted. 'What the?'

More calmly, Georgie asked, 'What about CI?' But she looked as stunned as Kat.

He glanced away, focused on light zigzagging from the window and up the wall. 'It's the right thing.'

'Really?' Georgie's disbelief grated.

'How could you do it without talking to us?' Kat's voice shook.

Franklin started for the hallway, intent on his shower. He didn't need this.

'Dad?'

He froze. 'Look, it's my job. My decision.'

'Yeah, but we always talk about big things together, don't–'

'It's *done*.'

Like Georgie's stare had conveyed before, he could feel her hurt. But he still left.

CHAPTER THIRTY-SIX

Franklin rode off before 7.30am. Georgie and Kat sat at the kitchen table with their partly drunk coffees and untouched bowls of cereal. In moments where Georgie was thrown into stepping across the line from friend of the teen to a stand-in for her absent parent, her lack of experience was prone to trigger a fight-or-flight response. Out of her depth and first to admit it, also in no position of authority as merely the girlfriend of the teen's dad. And fairly or unfairly, she was pissed with Franklin for his treatment of Kat and for leaving her to deal with the aftermath of his announcement.

'Kat...' She trailed off.

The teen shook her head with a sad smile that aged her appearance to mid-twenties.

Harty leaned on the front counter, writing up a report and grappling with his hair as if it'd help him concentrate. He muttered a flat greeting, then tilted towards Lunny's office. Apparently aware Franklin was here to meet Knight.

Franklin knocked.

A pause. Then, 'Come.'

He went in.

Knight flashed him a smile. 'Sit.' He continued his phone conversation.

The office was all wrong. Stripped of Lunny's fishing gear, photos and World's Greatest Grandpa mug. Knight in the sarge's chair. Not having to sweep anything off the visitor's seat.

'Sorry for the delay.' Knight leaned over the desk, hand outstretched.

They shook.

'I won't keep you, John.' A brisk pull of his mouth. 'Terrible thing.' Another grimace. 'In the circumstances, I have taken Tim's resignation. But it's here,' he patted his chest over an inner pocket, 'for two weeks. Just as I have noted your request, John, I think it's imperative to let the dust settle before Tim makes such an important decision. I caution you, as I have Tim, not to act rashly. I've put him on medical. Can I offer you the same?'

'I don't need time off.' Franklin added, 'Sir.'

'You understand my position?'

No, but he nodded.

'Good, good. Well, that's all for now, John.'

Dismissed, he left the station after a short chat with Harty. He chewed over Knight's non-decision for the forty-minute ride to Bacchus Marsh.

His crap mood plummeted further when he entered the CI briefing room to find AES detectives Bruner and Darmawan standing up the front with the boss.

Kat called, 'What are you researching?'

Abandoning the rinsed cups on the sink drainer, Georgie joined her at the dining table where she'd spread out her work. 'A spike in farm thefts in the Moorabool and Hepburn districts, mainly.'

Her inquiries throughout the night had taken so many turns and tangents that it had taxed her sleep-deprived and stressed brain. She wasn't clear about what she'd discovered or its usefulness. Maybe talking it through would help.

'Has your dad mentioned cases of stock theft since he's been with CIU?'

The teen shrugged. 'Yeah, but not in depth.'

She sank onto a chair and dragged Georgie's notebook across the table. Her eyes followed the circles, doodles and scribbles over the page. She shook her head and pushed it back.

'Glad it means something to you.'

With a wry smile, Georgie flicked over a few pages. She summarised. 'Stock theft is on the rise in Victoria. Depending on what source you reference, its cost is half a mil to one-point-five million dollars per annum, and the reported theft of sheep has increased by around 129 per cent in the past year.'

She glanced at Kat. 'Sheep are apparently lucrative because of their value in both wool and meat. They are also harder to track than cattle.'

The teen wrinkled her nose. 'Who knew?'

Who knew that Kat could be distracted from worries about her dad and Sam? It spurred Georgie on.

'The cops have set up a dedicated squad,' checking her notes, she cited, 'the police livestock and farm crime specialist group. The local cops still do a lot of the legwork though. But most farmers don't bother making a phone call.'

'So those stats could be way wrong?'

'Yeah.'

'Why don't they go to police?'

'They don't have much faith in them. Apparently because they figure the cops are under-resourced and will prioritise other investigations over rural crime. There's also an element of dealing with problems internally rather than going to police. And consequences like ballooning insurance premiums can outweigh the benefits of police reports and insurance claims.'

'Kicking them when they're down.'

'Yeah,' Georgie repeated. 'And on the flipside, the cops blame failures in the national livestock identification system, falsified vendor statements, and slack or dodgy stock agents for driving up stock theft.'

Kat screwed up her face. 'Doesn't sound like an article for the magazine. Think it might be better for the *Weekly Times*?'

'Maybe.' Georgie hedged. Some things she couldn't share. 'It started with a feature story coming from a man's death—drowned in a dam—in Gordon last Friday. Did you see it on the news?'

At Kat's yes, she went on. 'But it's growing and going in a different direction.'

She'd landed on the messiest page in her pad. This one had an excess of thought bubbles, underlines and question marks because of her knowledge gap – her struggle to understand. The pace of her thinking and notetaking had ratcheted with glimpses of comprehension, and a growing sense it might not be stock thefts that connected with Korweinguboora but significantly worse crimes.

CHAPTER THIRTY-SEVEN

As various crew members recounted the leads they'd focused on yesterday and what they would pursue today, Howell edged up beside Franklin. When a smartarse at the back of the room commented and another detective bit back, Howell hissed under his breath, 'You managing?'

'Sure.' Too curt, so he said, 'Ta.'

'Did you talk to the boss?'

'Yep.' Franklin had tried to apologise to Si Waldo for walking out yesterday. Maybe not hard enough.

'Listen up.' Waldo regained control of the briefing. 'Ram and Darma have an update from AES. Ram?'

'Thanks, Si.' Ram Bruner stood front-and-centre of the room. Legs spread, chest expanded, sunnies on top of his bald dome.

He said, 'Here's what you need to know.'

Franklin groaned softly. Howell nudged him.

Bruner recapped for the detectives coming in late on the investigation. Concise and without dumbing it down. He rose a little in Franklin's estimation.

'Our stance is that the explosion and fire were quite possibly not deliberate. Not as such.'

The arson D let the outbreak of murmurs around the room subside.

'And the Murray family predeceased both.'

He'd had time to get used to the idea since yesterday, but Franklin's airways clamped.

The eager female detective's hand shot up. Bruner nodded. She asked, 'Do we know the cause of death, sir?'

'The coroner's waiting on toxicology and so forth, but the state of the bodies,' Bruner paused for Darma to fix a series of photos to the case board, 'tells us that they died prior. An accurate time of death is difficult to exactify in these circumstances, but we'll narrow it down.'

He was so confident that Franklin believed him.

Howell inserted, 'We have established movements for Bel and the children on Monday. Friends and neighbours are pretty vague about when they last saw Alec, saying each day on a farm is more or less the same. We're still building a picture of the past week, and we might uncover other instances of unreturned messages, missed calls and commitments – but we do have several for Tuesday and Wednesday.'

Darma agreed. 'This tallies with the coroner's preliminary findings suggesting TOD between twenty-four and thirty-six hours prior to the explosion.'

Franklin watched the young female wrestle with the impulse to repeat her question about cause.

'With regards to COD,' Bruner smirked at her showing he was aware of her impatience, 'we have four deceased bodies on mattresses and in a baby basket on the lounge room floor. Lined up in a row in front of a gas heater. Assumption for now is that they died of carbon monoxide poisoning.'

Shit.

Bruner's next words were drowned out. He waited for silence.

'Our chemists, forensics and the rest of our crew are slogging on with other aspects. And we're puzzling out what this information means for the investigation.'

Bruner gazed over the room. Nobody spoke or fidgeted.

'While it can't be discounted that all this could come down to a faulty gas appliance, albeit unusual because we have CO poisoning and a gas explosion, we can't rule out a murder–suicide pact.' He added tightly, 'That also goes for sabotage.'

Darma stuck more images to the case board. Close-ups of the dead family's top halves. Nightmare stuff.

Franklin's nostrils flared. What right did Alec or Bel have to take the lives of their partner and kids? To expose other people to a dangerous situation? To give no consideration to those who had to deal with the bodies, live victims, structural fire and gut-wrenching aftermath? He knew these were pressure-cooker situations that built until they burst, and, by that stage, who knew what mental competency the person had. Not much, if they figured death was the only way out. But it was still unforgivable.

Bruner waved a hand across the crime scene photos, lingering on an image of Irvy's body.

'That said, we believe there is more to this situation. That it connects with other inquiries spanning Victoria.'

'Fatalities?' someone asked.

Bruner let the question hang for a minute.

'Yes.'

CHAPTER THIRTY-EIGHT

KAT DISAPPEARED INTO HER BEDROOM. GEORGIE COULD hear her murmuring and assumed she was on her mobile. Lisa would be at school. Maybe she was talking to Josh.

Her stomach lurched. She hadn't given Josh much thought in the past few days. The young, local boxing coach wasn't just Kat's boyfriend, but also their friend, Sam inclusive. They all worked out at the boxing studio regularly. They'd all been involved in the Mount Dandenong disappearance, which brought them closer together afterwards. He'd be reeling like the rest of them. She should've reached out to him. He'd need it, but probably internalise his feelings instead. Had he shut out Kat? Is that why she hadn't mentioned him either? One man abandoning the teen at this critical time was terrible enough. Both the men in her life, unbearable.

But if they were talking now, that was a good thing. She'd find the chance to ask without coming across as nosy.

Georgie tossed up what to do. She was keen to run further online research and contact the CFA expert that was her go-to person on fires. With thirty-plus years' experience at the hose and in command, he was currently on the senior team at the CFA HQ in Burwood East.

The radio broke into her thoughts.

'It's 9.00am, and this is the news with Sally Newton.'

The newsreader opened with a stabbing in Melbourne, then a multi-car pile-up on the Hume, and a gaffe by the Lord Mayor. She finished with a brief reference to detectives *'...still working to piece together what caused the fatal explosion at Korweinguboora.'* Two days later and the tragedy had been virtually overtaken.

Not for the cops though, especially Irvy and Sam's colleagues. Not for friends and family of the victims. And not for her.

Georgie snatched up her mobile and dialled Hilda Getty, annoyed that she'd banked on the woman's conscience and been wrong. It went to voicemail, and she disconnected.

Next, she rang Jeanette Roselle, hazy about what she wanted from the woman, apart from an opening to return to Hansen's farm.

'Hello?'

Georgie introduced herself.

'What do you want?'

She spieled off the explanation she'd given the Hansen boys.

'Yeah, all right.'

She reared back in her chair. 'I'll be there around 10.00am.'

Jeanette's easy agreement made her suspicious. It could be a trap. Maybe the family was angling to find out what she knew or had guessed.

To be on the safe side, she saved the photos she'd snapped off at their farm and at the Getty place to her computer, then deleted the images from her phone, along with the emails and texts she'd sent Franklin.

She considered ringing him to make sure he'd seen them and to let him know where she was going. In half a second, she dismissed the idea. He'd frozen her and Kat out earlier. She doubted he'd even answer her call, let alone give a damn.

———

'Where do you want to start?' Howell asked as they left the office.

Franklin rubbed his chin, scraping bristles. He'd forgotten to shave.

'How about the neighbours?' his partner suggested. 'We need to pin down Alec and Bel's last movements.'

'Nah. Kendra's.'

'Mate.' Howell caught his arm. 'She made it pretty clear the other day that she—'

Franklin shook off his hand. 'She'd just lost her husband. Now she's had time for it to sink in. I'm a poor substitute, but she's going to need help.'

'From her family.'

'And that's not us?'

Howell responded with a deep exhale. He stayed silent as he led the way to the unmarked station wagon, and Franklin decided that was unspoken agreement.

It wasn't until Bacchus was behind them by ten minutes that his partner spoke. 'CO poisoning, huh? I mean, we knew there was something with the gas cylinders, but I didn't see that coming. Did you?'

Franklin shrugged. He couldn't see anything clearly on this case, but wasn't about to admit it. Not even to Marty Howell.

'Reckon this was all just a horrific accident?' After a burst on the police radio, Howell added, 'Still can't shake the picture of them lined up in a row in the living room. You too?'

He turned to Franklin, then went back to concentrating on the road ahead. His chest moved in a soundless sigh.

Franklin shut off the shocking visual of the dead family, and went to sifting through what they knew and how it fit together. His left hand balled as his anger rose. It would be no easier for anyone if it came down to the Murrays being too tight to maintain their heater. For the cost of what—a hundred or so bucks?—everything could've been avoided.

Tell that to Sam or Kendra.

Surely, Alec's dad would've given them the money. Or Bel's aunt.

Franklin pictured Alec. Nice bloke, friendly. What had Yuki said about Alec's dad? Had an accident and sold the farm, moved into town in Ballan. Bel had invited him to live with them, but he'd knocked it back. Too proud, maybe also too independent, to accept. If Alec was a chip off the old block, he was probably too proud to let his dad know about their money problems. Too proud to ask him or the aunt for even a small, short-term loan.

He snorted.

Howell made a comment that Franklin ignored. Then he spoke again and waited, as if he'd asked a question. Eventually, he gave up.

Should've already been to see the dad in Ballan. Franklin heated inside. So many things he should've already done. Still, Kendra had to take priority this morning.

In about fifteen minutes, Georgie would reach the Hansen farm. It hadn't been an easy drive so far, though a deluge of hailstones the size of marbles as she'd neared Leonards Hill had been the least of her concerns. The pounding of ice on the Spider had come and gone in under five minutes and left no damage that she could see, whereas there had been no turning off the flow of different thoughts and the mental slideshow of a series of faces.

The closer she drew to Gordon, the more her stress headache grew. Along with her recognition of what she *didn't* know. What the preliminary autopsies revealed. How the gas cylinders connected with the Murray incident. If the high occurrence of local stock thefts also tied in.

Without these facts, how could she know what she hoped to discover from the Hansens?

She shouldn't have pushed things with Jeanette Roselle yet.

On the other hand, maybe she should've tried harder with Kat. She'd knocked lightly and entered the teen's bedroom on her, *Come in*. It was the first time she'd ventured into Kat's private space with the usual teenager disarray of scattered folders, books, wrappers and who knew what under piles of clothes, and Kat dwarfed among it. Paler than she'd been at breakfast, but she'd smiled and assured Georgie, *I'm fine*. As was Josh. And that Georgie needed to go to work. Fine generally meant anything but. Georgie took the hint to leave it when Kat turned her attention to her phone.

Yep, she should've pushed with Kat and held back with Jeanette. Should've, could've, didn't.

Georgie flipped on the indicator. Under ten minutes from Gordon now. She gave a light shake to clear swelling black spots in her vision, and in the process was distracted by the horizon. It appeared to have stretched and sunken. Shades from pale silver to dark slate grey formed curved vertical streaks adjoining giant white cauliflower heads.

Part headache—part nature show, then.

She turned on the headlights as she admitted what she'd done this morning probably mattered less than tipping her hand by nosing around the Hansen and Getty places yesterday.

CHAPTER THIRTY-NINE

Franklin said, 'Stay there,' exiting the unmarked.

Howell gave him an unreadable look, then pulled out his notepad and phone. Maybe not happy about being excluded, but not going to push it.

As he neared the house, Franklin could've sworn Irvy called out, *Hold on, mate – got a crappy nappy to change, haven't I, Mr Monster?* His mind's eye saw Irvy give a dramatic growl before he scooped little Levi under an arm and carried him horizontally. The toddler was giggling his head off and his dad doing a running commentary of toilet humour.

In truth, his boots slapping the damp pathway was all he could hear today. No music or TV. No kids laughing or bickering. No Irvy and Kendra yelling or making up. No toys on the front lawn or other giveaways of the lovingly feisty family either, except for Kendra's people-mover.

With a jolt, he realised that Irvy's car wasn't here. Probably still parked at the station, it couldn't stay there indefinitely. He could make himself useful collecting it, but sitting unused in the yard here it'd just be a constant reminder of Irvy, wouldn't it? Maybe he could sell it for Kendra. No partner and soon to have her sixth baby, she'd need the cash and one less rego and insurance to pay each year.

He heaved out a breath and knocked on the front door. That was another thing he could do. Set up a fundraiser for the family, if the police association hadn't already – no, *even if* the PA had. Kendra would hate the idea of charity, but she'd accept it for their kids.

He stood waiting, the wind so cold it burned the skin on his ears.

Moron.

Why'd he come to the front? They always used the back slider that opened into the tiled family room, where dirty shoes didn't matter. Franklin had never been in the front rooms, but he had a recollection of Kendra mentioning, *A formal lounge is wasted on people like us.* She'd laughed about carpet and a tribe of kids not being a good mix.

At the scramble of a door lock from the inside, his stomach sank. That day, she'd added, *Not unless we ever have a visit from the cops*, and belly laughed. Not funny now.

The door opened slowly, as if it were immensely heavy, the effort too great. Franklin was drawn straight to the little girl gazing up at him. The dark circles and puffy bags under her eyes made him shake. The pre-schooler couldn't understand the finality of her dad's death, or the way he went, but she'd clearly absorbed the atmosphere of grief filling her world.

She pressed in against her mum, moulding herself around the belly holding her new brother or sister. Her fingers twisted a clutch of Kendra's dress. She stared at him, unblinking.

———

Georgie pulled on the Spider's handbrake and killed the motor. She listened to it tick while she checked her messages. Nothing from Franklin. Two voice messages: Sheridan Judd and Livia. Her editor and mum could both wait until after her interview with Jeanette Roselle.

Any other day and it would've been easier to reply immediately to a text from her best friend Bron than to remember to do it later.

Georgie reread it.

'Hey, GG! You two, dinner, ours, tomorrow night. Or we can come to DF if you're there. Let me and Jo help you through all this. We might be full of crap, but it's well-meant crap. Bron xx'

Clueless what to say to Bron, she put her mobile on silent. Franklin wasn't rostered on tomorrow, but she suspected she and Kat would be lucky to hear from him. They wouldn't see him. Or if he did turn up, it'd be a repeat of this morning. He might be there, but wouldn't really be present.

Her heart twisted. Leaving Daylesford would be disloyal to all her local friends. Kat needed support, especially if Josh was being flaky, and Georgie wanted to be there if Franklin realised that he did too.

She left the car and trudged towards the woman watching from the open doorway, her boots kicking up small stones as she walked.

She couldn't go to Bron and Jo's solo, and she couldn't let them come up here. Bron would see straight through Georgie's defences to her darkest fears.

———

Kendra let out a long sigh. Franklin looked from Isla to her mum. Her face was paper-white. Her lips trembled but nothing came out.

'Can I...' He couldn't finish the question. *Can I come in?* was too banal. *Can I fix it?* was impossible.

She sighed again, and as if they were joined, she and Isla stepped back to let him in. The hinges on the door complained as they rotated. The three of them hovered in the hallway. Franklin's mind was still blank. Or rather, his mind was stupidly busy, but he couldn't formulate a sentence.

They stood in awkward silence with a shrine of photos on the wall behind Kendra and her little girl. Portraits from Kendra and Irvy's wedding day; younger, thinner and in the groom's case, with more hair. Selfies of an exhausted Kendra and proud Irvy with each of their goo-covered, face-screwed-up, naked babies. School and kinder photos of the older kids. Family shots at Christmas with bonbons and paper hats. At Easter with hot cross buns and eggs in colourful foil.

'Maybe I shouldn't have...'

Kendra shook her head. Her mouth pulled, an attempted smile before she caught her bottom lip with her teeth, pressing so it made a white outline. Tension cut tracks across her brow. But it was the suffering in her eyes, so like her little girl's, that he couldn't look at.

In the distance, one of the kids cried, 'Mum?' Obviously frightened that Kendra would be taken from them next.

———

'Jeanette? Nice to meet you in person. My sympathies on the passing of your husband.'

Georgie outstretched her hand.

The woman shook it, then dropped it. She did a *come in* jerk. They went into the kitchen, sat at the table and stared at each other.

'How are you coping?' It was the best Georgie could think of as an icebreaker.

Jeanette made another little jerk. Maybe it was a nervous tick?

She didn't answer for nearly a minute. Then said, 'All right.'

Georgie swallowed. If she was going to pull an actual story out of this, she'd need to get the woman talking, using more than one or two words or non-verbal gestures. Ditto if she was going to gain anything useful towards her vague theory that the Hansen and Murray matters connected.

'Did Allan's sons fill you in?'

Jeanette did one of her judders.

Georgie took it as yes. She pictured Hawk Nose saying, *You want us to talk about banks screwing us, suppliers screwing us, customers screwing us?* She hadn't succeeded with the sons, but she needed Jeanette onside.

'Pressure on farmers is not a new thing.' She spoke quickly. 'I guess what the average person in suburbia, even in some regional towns, doesn't get is the *range* of issues. Not purely environmental: flood, drought, fire, infestation, and their financial impact. But also, taxes, tariffs, imports.'

She thought again of Hawk Nose.

'The average reader doesn't know how you need to be resourceful to get through the hardships of farming. For my feature, I want to draw a picture of you and Allan and your experiences on the land here, in Gordon. The stresses you tackled together and the upsides. I want to pull it all together with what happened to your husband and its effects on the farm, and on you, Allan's sons...'

Jeanette gave her a flat look.

Georgie waited, interested to see if the woman would fill the silence. What she'd say.

With a subtler tick, Jeanette said, 'Okay.'

Not off to a flying start. But Georgie was in.

CHAPTER FORTY

THE KIDS WERE LINED UP ON THE COUCH WHEN FRANKLIN and Kendra walked into the family room. Isla disentangled from her mum and squeezed in beside Levi. Oddly, they'd arranged themselves in size order, which didn't quite correlate to their ages. Levi, then Isla. Next came Logan, who was small for seven, and then Cody, who was actually younger than him by nearly two years. The oldest boy, Rhys, took up the opposite end to his toddler brother.

Franklin was pretty sure he'd gotten their ages and position in the family correct.

Kendra gave another hefty sigh as she clambered onto a stool at the island bar, then gazed at him absently.

'Oh, should've offered you a cuppa.' She went to rise.

Franklin held up a hand. He boiled the jug and glanced over to the kids. The way they'd aligned themselves made him flash back to the photos Darma and Bruner had affixed to the case board. The Murray family in a row by the gas heater. It was right up there with the worst things he'd sighted as a cop. He was grateful he hadn't seen the family up close, in person.

Unlike Sam. And Irvy.

He caught himself with his hand in mid-air holding a scooped spoon of coffee, and took a breath to clear the memory. With the mugs ready, he moved over to the kids.

'What can I get you lot?'

He forced a smile that didn't help the situation. They shook their heads. Wondering if he should go in harder, or take a different tack, he looked at Kendra. She gave a small headshake. He took it for, *Thanks for trying.*

Back to the drinks, glad to busy himself. He put Kendra's in front of her. From the array of platters, trays and containers across the bench, he took the lid off the fruit cake: something with health value, as Kat would say. Then rejected it and sliced up a chocolate sponge with jam and cream filling: something they might eat. He put a plate of it on the coffee table for the kids and one beside Kendra.

They drank their coffee. Nobody tried the cake.

His brain was sluggish. Noticing things, then processing them after a delay. It went back now to the flowers filling the room, all the sweets on the bench, and the casseroles in the fridge when he got out the milk.

'I thought you'd have family helping, friends.'

'They have been...they are. Everyone from the station has come.' Kendra's eyes widened. 'How's poor Sam?'

Franklin wet his lips. 'Unchanged.'

'Oh.' Her chest filled and deflated several times.

She backtracked. 'So many people looking out for us. I appreciate it, but just needed a break.'

His stomach fell. 'Sorry. I'll–'

'No, stay.'

They talked for a bit. Memories of Irvy. Inconsequentials like the car sitting at the cop shop that Franklin would deal with.

A tap came on the glass sliding door, and they glanced over. Howell stood outside, shuffling awkwardly on the spot. His nose was red with cold.

Franklin rose. 'I guess I should go. Get to work. But I'll stop by later. And just say—call me—if there's anything you need.'

He hugged her goodbye, awkward around her belly, then turned to leave. He startled when she grabbed his arm.

Her focus was clear, determined for the first time today.

'There is.'

He waited.

'Something I need. Irvy's eulogy.'

Cold wormed through him.

'I want you to give it.' She pleaded. 'Please, Frankie.'

CHAPTER FORTY-ONE

JEANETTE GRADUALLY OPENED UP DURING THE INTERVIEW. Her passions were farming and her late husband. On those topics, especially whenever she reminisced about the early days with Allan, her features lightened, and the nervous tick stopped. She even offered coffee. At one stage, she sobbed and laughed at the same time. Her age rewound by a decade in front of Georgie.

When the subject came around to Allan's sons and even the Gettys, Jeanette's posture closed in and her answers reverted to minimal words, often monosyllables.

Allan's death and the time around it was naturally difficult for her to talk about. Georgie readied herself for the woman breaking down. But instead, Jeanette's shoulders came back, squared, and her brow bunched while her pupils contracted to pinpoints.

Intriguing tells, but what caught Georgie unaware was that twenty minutes had already slipped by, and in that time the article had shifted from a lure in the hope it would lead to something to a tangible thing. Regardless of whatever else came out of Gordon, she had a feature story worth writing and suiting *Champagne Musings*.

'At that time...' Jeanette paused mid-sentence and tilted to the window, listening.

Belatedly, Georgie heard a vehicle—from the engine noise, a truck—approach.

Across from her, Jeanette stiffened. Georgie tried to read her, mind racing with possibilities. Her visit wasn't supposed to coincide with the truck, and Jeanette didn't want her to see what was on it? Or who was in it? Though the Hansen boys had ostensibly sanctioned the interview, they hadn't intended to let it happen, and Jeanette knew it? She'd said too much, or the wrong thing?

Georgie could go on, but she'd still only be guessing. She tuned into a heavy *thunk* as a door slammed, followed by two male voices she recognised: Allan's sons.

Jeanette's posture curved inwards as her breathing became noticeable. Light, catching inhales and heavy swallows. Battling tears. Trying not to fall apart.

Amazed it hadn't been sooner, Georgie empathised. 'Would you like to stop?'

They'd covered a lot; she almost had enough. One key question begged, though she'd leave it for now if asked.

Jeanette said, 'Go on.'

Outside, Allan's sons yelled to each other. Inside, their stepmother shrunk into herself.

'What do you see in your future – will you stay on the farm?'

'I–' Jeanette stopped. Her mouth twisted and her, 'Allan would want that, but–' strangled.

She covered her face and left the room.

Howell kicked over the engine and half-turned in his seat. 'Where to?'

If Franklin were honest, he'd say the public toilets at the Sailors Falls picnic area because he wanted to throw up. Vomiting the coffee he'd just drunk wouldn't help the nausea though.

He dropped his window and let the damp air cool his skin.

Fucking eulogy. Me?

He focused on Howell's question, running through a mental list. Revisit neighbours at Korweingi and Yuki at the kindergarten. See Alec's dad. Next thing, he was thinking about the eulogy again.

You've done it before, Franklin.

Didn't make it any easier.

Writing one's tough enough. But standing up in front, next to the coffin and...

Howell cleared his throat.

The brass had suggested the Police Academy Chapel in Glen Waverley, but Kendra told him, *Doesn't suit my man, does it?* She was tossing up between the chapel at the local funeral parlour or one of the churches. But she was certain on a few things. Irvy would want the iconic, black Daylesford chevy hearse. He'd want Franklin, Harty, Slam and Lunny to be his pallbearers.

'Franklin?'

Help her choose a coffin too? Fuck.

'Franklin?'

'What?'

Howell looked worried.

'Sorry, mate.' Franklin shook off thoughts of Irvy's funeral. 'Let's see if Alec's dad is home.'

———

Georgie gathered the used mugs from the table and took them to the kitchen sink. Rinsing them under the tap gave her a good excuse to look out the window. Not much to see. The same truck with high-slatted sides she'd viewed yesterday. Nobody visible.

She left the mugs on the drainer and wandered over to the fridge. It was covered in bills, takeaway menus, flyers for local events and snapshots.

One photo overlapping a business card for Mount Egerton Canvas Repair caught her attention. She unpinned it for a better look.

'That was a good day,' Jeanette said from behind.

'Sorry.' Georgie started to put it back, but the woman reached to trace her finger over Allan's image.

In the background, women in chambray shirts under sleeveless vests and wide-brimmed hats held leads attached to cows with shiny coats wearing numbers. Jeanette was among them. Hilda was there too, near another woman, and their heads were tilted towards each other. Hilda's mouth was ajar, and the woman smiled at whatever she'd said.

'Where was it taken?'

'Ballarat Show last year.'

'Did you win?'

'No.' Jeanette's smile was shaky. 'Went to someone's niece, I reckon.'

'That's Hilda and Bob, and Allan's boys.'

'Yeah, and Nance.' She pointed out the woman next to Hilda, her lips curving up more. 'And Cam.'

This fifth man in their group was thickset, similar build to the truck driver – could it be him?

Jeanette's smile vanished and she took the photo, reattached it to the fridge.

'You got enough?'

Her gaze had turned icy.

CHAPTER FORTY-TWO

F RANKLIN KNOCKED ON THE ARCHITRAVE AT THE FRONT door. Beside him, Howell shuffled his feet, trying to clean off mud or keeping warm. After a minute, he rapped again, this time on the security door itself. Then he took a couple of steps and leaned out a long arm to tap his knuckles on a large window.

Instinct told him the bloke wasn't home and a knot tightened around his sternum. Twenty-five minutes gone just getting here. If Alec's dad wasn't around, that dead time would be doubled before they made it to their next destination.

He rubbed at the burning knot in his chest and glanced at Howell, wondering if they should've called ahead. His partner did a small head wag. Might've been commiserating over the wasted trip. Or tuning into his thoughts and agreeing.

After more than two decades in the force, Franklin knew it was usually best to avoid giving grieving family notice of a visit. They'd either mutter in a lost, flat voice, *It's not a good time*, like anything would be after this, or explode, *You cops shouldn't be wasting time talking to us – you should be out there doing your job.* Meaning: find the culprits or answers. Forgetting the answers were often close to home.

Another sixty seconds went by, and Howell commented, 'Doesn't look good, mate.'

Franklin went up to the window and peered in at a small living room as neat, tidy and soulless as the brick veneer exterior of the unit. And empty.

Howell left the porch and scouted around, didn't get far with the units all attached with single garages connecting them to neighbours either side. He then approached the unit on the right.

Franklin noted Howell's ring of the bell and knock on the door went unanswered. Meanwhile, he tried the neighbour on the opposite side.

His knuckles were still touching when the main door opened. He gazed down through the security mesh at a petite woman. Silver-haired and thin, but a healthy glow to her cheeks.

'You're looking for Stephen?' With a snick of the lock, she ushered him through. 'Come in. Your partner too.'

Franklin brought out his ID. She laughed it off. A nice tinkly sound.

'You're police. I didn't come down in the last shower, you know.' She smiled, her web of wrinkles highlighting the truth in that.

———

Georgie drove into the Gordon township and bought a strong coffee. She sat inside the Spider, the windows fogging up, as she pondered over her interview with Jeanette. She had decent material for a story, which would help pay the bills. To be honest, it was more than a financial lifeline. And to be brutal, her editor had been justified in saying, *You haven't done much to impress me lately.*

She had been treading water in her work. But not just lately. For a few months. Maybe it'd stagnated after the flurry resulting from the Mount Dandenong missing persons case. Everything seemed too ordinary. Too pedestrian. And she'd disconnected. Oh, she went through the motions of pitching ideas, finding angles and wrangling with her editor for interest, but the appeal waned for her long before she'd filed each story.

The potential for this article seized her attention though. For the first time in a while, her pride in being an investigative journalist had reared its head. Chiefly because her research provided the perfect cover to contribute to the Korweinguboora investigation in about the only tangible way she could. What else could she do that others weren't already onto, or better equipped to handle?

But there was no denying it also appealed to her that writing on the subject offered a means to do justice to the many farmers who'd slid into debt and desperation during the Millennium Drought. Too many people assumed the rains over the past few years were enough. But even record-high rainfall in many areas was as effective as a band-aid on a fractured limb after countless years of devastation. And the drought hadn't yet broken for a substantial amount of eastern Australia, something far too many people were ignorant of. Prior to Georgie's assignment in the wildfire-ravaged town of Bullock eighteen months ago, she'd been among them.

Her opening needed to grab readers' attention and reverse the reflex reaction of, *It doesn't affect me.* When fresh food grew expensive or scarce, they'd soon be crying, but that would be long overdue. She had to make the farmer's plight relatable. The crises, the lack of genuine options, the lengths they'd go to in order to stay on the land.

Georgie sat her coffee on the dashboard and located her notepad and pen. Her ideas soon covered most of the page, her handwriting barely legible in her haste. She'd asterisked the query 'What can people do to help?' and jotted various offshoots. Support rural areas doing it tough. Buy fresh produce at farm gates, farmer's markets, and at cafés and restaurants with a paddock-to-plate philosophy that promoted their local community. Take farm stays or breaks at B&Bs. Spend money in these towns with preference to small businesses over large chain stores.

Georgie took another sip of coffee and grimaced at the cold mouthful. Her thoughts circled back to the lengths desperate farmers would go to. About how easily lines could blur. One small indiscretion could easily lead to transgressions of greater enormity. From cooking the books to stock theft...to manslaughter? Murder?

She bit her lip. Until now, she'd skirted around what had happened to Allan Hansen beyond doubting it'd been an accident, and trying to find a link between that and what had occurred at the Murray farm. But could the Gettys and Hansens be culpable for all these deaths?

She glanced at the notes on her pad and thumped back to reality. Yes, she had the bones of a good story and a bunch of half-baked theories. But it was a far cry from Walkley Award stuff. Where to from here?

The names Nance and Cam stood out on her page, and in her mind, so did Jeanette's sudden frostiness and end to the interview. The woman regretted mentioning them. Why? And how could Georgie trace them?

They politely refused lunch, but the neighbour insisted they get comfortable in her little front room while she made coffees.

She brought a pot in on a large wooden tray so loaded it dwarfed her, and Franklin tried to take it from her. But she chuckled. Saying, 'Away with you. I'm quite capable,' she set it down on the coffee table with not so much as a shake in her liver-spotted hands.

She plied them with drinks, cakes and muffins. Franklin nibbled at a muffin out of courtesy. His stomach tossed as he watched Howell wolf down a pile of the goodies.

Their host didn't eat or drink, just perched on her armchair, watching them but also the driveway. Looking out for Stephen Murray? Or habitually watching over her domain?

He put his money on the former and mentally paid the bet when she suddenly said, 'He's a broken man.'

Franklin abandoned the muffin.

'It's unnatural to bury your children.'

Sorrow filled her features. He followed her gaze to one of the photographs on the sideboard of a man in dusty camo gear, laden with flak vest, backpack and carrying a turbine rifle across his chest. Most of his face was covered, but his eyes mirrored the woman's.

'My son.' She focused on her lap. 'Mathew was a sergeant in the special operations command. In his second tour, he was shot in a skirmish with the Taliban and died in the military hospital two days later. He was thirty-three.'

Howell went to her side and laid a hand on her shoulder. She reached up, placed hers over his and gave it a squeeze.

'He was a change-of-life surprise.' She smiled. 'Oh boy, was he a surprise, but a good one. Our two oldest were already out of the nest, with the third just turned eighteen, when he arrived. My husband and I didn't play favourites, but Mathew was always our baby.'

Her gaze turned wistful. 'His dad and I were ever so proud when he joined up, and scared sick too. It was a blessing that his dad went before our Mathew.'

She swallowed. 'Six years ago, and I miss his hugs every day.' She blinked away tears, and looking at the framed photo added, 'He was such a great hugger.'

Franklin finally found some words. 'I'm sorry for your loss.'

'Thank you.' Her eyes turned in the direction of her neighbour's porch. 'But mine is nothing on Stephen's. His son, daughter-in-law and two beautiful grandsons.' She sighed, the sound catching. 'I have my other sons and their families. He has no family left.'

Howell retook his seat. 'Do you know when he will be back?'

'No. I'm sorry.'

'Has he spoken about his family much?'

'Oh, a little here, a little there, until over time I felt that I knew them quite well. And they visited on occasion and always stopped for a hello if I was in the garden.' She gestured at the shrubbery visible through her front window. 'Lovely people.'

She went to add more, then stopped. Gathering her thoughts or deciding if she should share them. Franklin sensed that it wouldn't pay to push her.

The three of them sat quietly until she went on.

'Since the...' she hesitated, then settled on, 'fire, Stephen has disappeared into himself.' She demonstrated a collapsed and rounded spine. 'But he's said one thing over and over.'

Franklin said, 'What?'

'He should've moved in with them when they asked – this wouldn't have happened then.'

'Why does he think that?'

She fluttered a hand. A small, twitchy movement. 'I'm not sure. He mumbled on about being selfish by trying to be independent, and what's the benefit in leaving your kids money when you're gone? When they need it while you're living?'

'They were in financial trouble?'

'It would seem so, wouldn't it?'

CHAPTER FORTY-THREE

PULLED IN THREE DIRECTIONS, GEORGIE REALLY WANTED to find out more about the Murrays. A revisit to their neighbours, perhaps an expansion of the net there too, might reveal a relationship with the Getty–Hansen lot. Friendship or business.

Then there was the agricultural angle to work to uncover who Nance and Cam were and how they fit into the picture.

But she also itched to advance her research into the upsurge of stock theft in the district and potential links with the Gordon families, plus progress how the gas cylinders connected these people to Korweinguboora.

Somehow these were all sum parts of the whole. She couldn't afford to prioritise wrongly. The Hansens were suss on her. The Gettys too. They might already be in cover-up mode.

Franklin tucked his business card between Stephen Murray's security door and its frame, and joined Howell on the nature strip by their unmarked.

'Got a smoke, mate?'

His partner pulled out a pack and lighter, but placed them on the bonnet of the station wagon.

'You shouldn't.'

'Neither should you.'

They both lit up.

Franklin inhaled, relishing the nicotine's ride through his body to his brain. Seconds later, after a slightly giddy sensation, came a wash of calm. He blew out the smoke and took another drag.

But this time, instead of soothing him, his heart rate sped up. And so did his mind. It flew from running over the neighbour's words to how Alec's dad was dealing with his grief. It could only be compounded by the coronial process. The delays in the relay of information and release of the bodies was torturing Kendra, and must be doing the same to Stephen Murray.

Franklin should ring the hospital and check on Sam. He should phone her parents again too. Their limbo was different to Stephen's and Kendra's. Their daughter was clinging to life, while who knew what her life would be like, the full extent of her injuries if she made it. *When she makes it*, he corrected.

Howell broke into his brooding. 'Where to now, mate?'

Franklin finished his smoke and ground it out harder than needed, frustrated. They needed to interview Stephen Murray about his son and daughter-in-law's monetary issues and Bel's health situation. Cancer was a bastard in so many ways. It was also an expensive business. If the family was already financially strained and Bel faced a long, costly health battle, during which period they'd continue to lose her income, if not permanently, could that have pushed them over the edge?

Murder–suicide though. He just didn't see it. But then he hadn't known the couple that well. Couldn't really know how they'd react. Likewise, he had no way of knowing if he and Howell weren't far from the full picture – or way off base.

'Yuki,' he said, not even realising he'd decided on their back-up plan to Stephen Murray. 'By all accounts, she was Bel's closest friend. She must be able to give us something more.'

———

Sheridan Judd's name filled the mobile screen. Georgie sighed and picked up the call.

'*What've you got?*'

The way her editor asked, told Georgie she didn't expect much.

'Well, actually...' She précised her story angle.

'*Good. You mentioned that a spike in rural crime ties in with this?*'

'Yes, but...' Georgie wished she could backpedal. What if it didn't fit? At least she'd held back on the gas cylinders.

'*I like it. The rest of it could be a bit namby-pamby–*'

'No, there's plenty of guts to the main thread.'

Her editor rabbited on. '*Our readers love your crime stuff. Ramp it up. Give them what they want.*'

Georgie held her tongue.

'*I want stats, loads of them, by the end of today. It's going to have to be good to knock Geoff's story off the cover.*'

'What's his story?'

'*The fourth coronial inquest into Azaria Chamberlain's disappearance concluded this week. What went wrong that her mother was convicted in 1982, then released in '86, and both parents' exonerated in '88, but it's only now official that a dingo did kill that poor baby back in 1980? Us, the media. That's what went wrong.'*

'It's a good story,' Georgie conceded.

'Make yours better and I'll bump his to second feature.'

———

Howell wanted to drive, and Franklin gave up the keys reluctantly. As passenger, he had more opportunity to think, not necessarily a good thing. He needed to shove all the extra stuff to the corners of his mind and focus on this case.

He mused aloud. 'So far, we know the Murrays were already dead before the explosions, the family had financial issues, and Bel probably had cancer.'

'Yeah, mate. And her health would've exacerbated their money tensions.'

'Did you manage to get Denise's diary?'

Howell threw a thumb over his shoulder. 'Darma's been over it, but reckons it can't hurt for us to take a look.'

Franklin stretched over the console and grabbed the diary from the back seat. From the sound of things, it'd be of little use. He flicked through the pages as Howell aimed for the kinder. Denise's jottings were appointments and reminders, which didn't tell him much.

'Was there a file for Bel in Denise's car?'

His partner shook his head.

'Must be at her house then.'

'Unless her co-worker only pretended not to find it.'

'Waiting for bloody legal to clear access for us.'

'Yeah.' Howell glanced at him. 'They might get back to us on that today.'

'Friday afternoon? It's likely to be Monday now.' Franklin slapped his leg. 'We know Denise catches up her admin in hits. Say you're slipping behind, where do you do that?'

'When you don't have time at work, or feel guilty about the excessive hours you're spending there? At home.'

'Do we have her address?'

'In my notebook. She lives in Bakery Hill, Ballarat, with her boyfriend.'

Franklin rubbed his temple. Why couldn't he think straight and deal with this case methodically? Everything seemed urgent – until the next thing came up. The number of dangling threads worried him, especially when he couldn't remember what they all were. Was this a constructive lead or not?

He thought so. 'New plan. Let's head there.'

Howell countered, 'Even if you're on the right track, her boyfriend's probably at the hospital.'

'Chance it. We need Bel's medical file. And we haven't interviewed him yet – might kill two birds with one stone.'

———

Judd wanted rural crime at the crux of the feature, so that was Georgie's priority. Stock theft or gas cylinders first though?

Gas set her thinking about the fiery blasts at Goodlife Farm, then pang with guilt. She should've called the hospital to see how Sam was doing hours ago.

She dialled, bounced through a number of departments and on-hold waits to learn Sam's condition was unchanged. Still critical.

Georgie disconnected and drifted into a memory from the previous summer. It was a melting hot day, and Kat, Sam and Georgie were enjoying an afternoon off together while Franklin worked his shift. Kat had suggested a dip in the old Hepburn pool. But when they'd rocked up, Georgie had looked at the water in the bush pool dubiously, and then at Sam who mirrored her doubt. Kat had said between giggles, *Seriously, you two are so city slicker, I can't even,* and eye-rolled. Dare accepted, they'd jumped into the murky water and slathered each other from head to toe in thick mud dug from the bottom of the pool.

Georgie smiled. Then, clear which path of inquiry mattered most, she sobered. But she needed all her notes and gear at hand. She fired up the Spider and nosed her car towards Franklin's place.

————

Howell moaned. 'Back seat. Inner pocket of my jacket. My notepad.'

Franklin dug it out.

'What's Denise's address?'

He found it as Howell diverted off the Daylesford road and onto the Ballarat freeway at the last moment.

'I'm not going to regret this, am I, mate?'

Franklin put the address into the satnav instead of answering.

————

Georgie took the turn onto Raglan Street, then veered off onto Camp Street instead of continuing to Franklin's. Her anxiety for Lunny had elevated yesterday when Maeve said it was best for them to leave him alone. Added with Franklin's bombshell this morning, she couldn't shake her concern.

She second-guessed the idea walking along the pathway to the police station house, but music magnetised her to the shed.

Inside, Lunny was packing a box, surrounded by stuffed garbage bags and taped-up boxes.

'Georgie.' Lunny didn't cease sorting items from the shelves, simply fluttered fingers in hello.

'How are you?'

He dodged the question. Said instead, 'Decluttering.'

He'd barely glanced at her so far. She knew this was his equivalent of Slam with the fridge door.

'Can I help?'

'No, thanks. Best to keep busy, and there's plenty to do before we vacate this place.'

She leaned on the wall. 'So it's true?'

'Yep. I've resigned.' Their gaze met. 'Best decision I've made lately.'

His hands busied again, but his words held a ring of truth.

Georgie said, 'And Franklin's taking your position?'

Lunny stopped with a remote-control device and toy helicopter dangling from each hand. His mouth twisted in something unsaid.

After a long interval, he muttered, 'Well. It's there for the taking.'

CHAPTER FORTY-FOUR

'Don't say it,' Franklin warned.

Howell chuckled, but didn't rub in that he'd predicted the nurse's boyfriend wouldn't be home. Franklin debated dialling the bloke's mobile, but his partner had probably nailed that too – he'd be by Denise's bedside at the Alfred in Melbourne. Five beds up from Sam. Phone switched off as dictated.

He walked across the verandah deck to the large double-hung window at the front of the house. Coloured leadlight panelling obscured the top half, but the bottom pane gave him a clear view.

The difference between the very traditional Californian bungalow exterior and muted colour scheme, and its bold, ultra-modern interior surprised him, but made sense. Definite stamp of a young couple.

He took in greater detail. Being at the front of the house and with its angled-off wall for the chimney, this room probably began its life as the lounge. But it was now set up as an office space for two with a square, white-painted desk on easel legs in the centre, and primary-red bookshelves and colourful abstract prints lining the walls.

A pink vest with a familiar logo draped the back of the swivel chair furthest from Franklin. Assuming that was Denise's side of the desk, he moved to the other section of the window for a better look.

He let out a groan, and Howell crowded in.

Franklin pointed to a stack of folders the same colour as the vest. 'What's the bet, Bel's file is one of those?'

———

As Georgie slammed the Spider's door, she heard the landline ringing inside Franklin's house. By the time she'd let herself in, the phone had stopped. Even as she dismissed it as a spam call, it restarted.

'Hi, Georgie here.'

'*Georgie! Sarah Cantrell.*'

Lisa's mum. Georgie's mind immediately went from *What's wrong with Lisa?* to *What's wrong with Kat?*

'What can I…'

'*Oh, sorry! It's just that I wanted to chat with Kat's dad or you to see how she's coping.*'

Georgie's anxiety rose. 'Has she been acting oddly?'

'*Nothing like that. We just haven't seen her since what happened to poor Sam and the others.*' After a small pause, Sarah said, '*Well, that is odd in itself.*'

'You haven't seen her? Has she been keeping to Lisa's room?'

'*No. She hasn't been here.*' Sarah sounded as confused as Georgie.

Kat had told her she was staying at Lisa's overnight. She hadn't been home. So where did she spend the night, and why did she lie about it? Whatever was going on, Georgie wouldn't drop Kat in trouble without talking to her.

'Oh, that's right. My mistake.'

She went on to assure the woman that Kat was fine, echoing the very phrase she hadn't believed that morning. While she talked on the cordless phone, she knocked on the teen's door, gave it thirty seconds, then went in.

All the teenager clutter as she'd seen it that morning. But no Kat.

———

'Not our day, is it, Marty?' Franklin hoped he could pull off the bluff. 'Before we head over to see Yuki, I'm gonna give Kat a bell. Wait in the car for me?'

Howell gave a good-natured, 'No probs.'

When his partner had climbed into the wagon, Franklin winced at his lie, then went to work.

He ran his hand over the top of the front door arc, copping a splinter but otherwise coming up empty-handed. He tried under the doormat and in the meter box. Found plenty of dust, a few dry leaves and some cobwebs, but not what he was after.

He contemplated the red-brick balustrade running between the pillars on the verandah. Across the top sat terracotta pots with flowering chrysanthemums in a range of colours, many much fancier than the type he'd traditionally bought his mum for Mother's Day as a young bloke.

Good a spot as any. He picked up each in turn and checked the muddy ring left on the brick ledge.

The key was under the last pot.

———

Georgie left a message for Kat on her mobile, not confident she'd struck the right note – caring but not clingy or controlling, not attempting to be mum to the seventeen-year-old.

Next, she cranked up her laptop for the latest on Korweinguboora. Didn't tell her anything new. A repetition of *A police officer and a nurse continue their fight for life at the Alfred Hospital,* and nothing official from the coroner's office.

She ran a search on gas cylinder explosions and came up with more hits than she'd expected, including one from a leading Australian LPG supplier aiming to debunk the myths.

Several tanks had gone off at the Murray farm. Georgie wanted to understand why and how, so she scanned the blog, jotting down the takeaways as she went.

She had to smile at the writer's firm finger-point at the media with claims that most accounts of propane-LPG gas blasts triggering tragic house fires were cases of sensationalism and false reporting in a ratings grab. They stated that in many of these situations, and contrary to the news stories, the tanks were actually found upright and intact.

Repeatedly underlining the fact that propane tank explosions were very rare, the writer said gas leak blasts often didn't even involve a cylinder. But if they did, it was liable to be a welding gas or other non-propane gas receptacle. And there always had to be an ignition source.

Georgie doodled on her pad as she made sense of the information in this blog.

The writer relied on the pressure relief valve, or PRV, in disproving propane-LPG tank blasts. They talked about experiments carried out in burning structures where tanks survived the fires without blowing up. That, while fire or another heat source would inflate the pressure of the gas in the tank, before the contents reached boiling, the PRV would release some gas to relieve the build-up. Thus preventing rupture of the tank.

But it also quoted an occasion in which a combination of extreme heat and temperature upsurge during a raging fire in a gas-bottle filling plant saw a handful of tanks out of the thousands stored there explode.

That kind of debunked their debunk theory with a, *Yeah, but it was only a few that blew up* excuse.

But several points were irrefutable. Gas leak explosion was usually caused by gas escaped from a faulty appliance or pipework and collected in an enclosed space. The problem was therefore probably inside the structure rather than outside, where any cylinders were generally stored. And it was just as likely to stem from bottled gas as natural gas.

Georgie overlayed those particulars with the farm incident. Irvy had entered the home in front of Sam, blasts ensued, and fire soon fully engulfed the structure. Several forty-five-kilogram LPG gas cylinders had exploded, whether or not the chain of events started with them. And police were very keen for information regarding the type of cylinders found at the farm.

Indisputably, there was a gas leak, in or out of the house. Gas had accumulated within the Murray home, and something triggered a blast inside the structure. The propane-LPG gas tanks outside were not as safe as the writer of blog wanted people to believe. They had exploded.

Were the leak and the fault with the gas tanks one and the same, or two different issues? A faulty stove or heater in the house and faulty PRVs on the tanks was possible, if not probable.

More importantly, were these faults accidental or deliberate?

Franklin slid onto the passenger seat and pulled the door to, blocking the icy air. 'Cold enough to snow out there.'

Howell nodded. 'Ballarat gets its share.' He eyed Franklin's left hand. 'Tell me you didn't?'

Flashing the file so he could see the name 'Murray, Belinda' in thick black lettering, along with a patient number and department logo, Franklin said, 'We can read it now. Then I'll take it back, and nobody needs to know.'

'Mate, you're treading a fine line.' But Howell added wearily, 'Open it.'

Stuck on the idea that the gas cylinders themselves were of interest to police, and their PRVs appeared to have failed, Georgie googled 'faulty pressure relief valves'. Easier than tackling other integral parts of the tanks.

Skimming through the hits, such devices could and did fail, on water heaters at least.

She tightened the query to information specific to propane gas tanks.

Propane 101 made it blatantly obvious that, like any working part, PRVs required proper maintenance and repair by licensed professionals. Valves could pop off. Debris clogged up in the mechanisms could cause valves to stay open and excessive loss of propane. Even filling tanks in hot conditions could be fraught with danger. Attempts at DIY repairs were likely to result in malfunction of the valve, failure to vent to the outside, and the tank rupturing.

Georgie thought about the police interest. She replayed in her mind the tanks at both the Gordon farms that matched the media release, the dodgy behaviour of the Gettys and Hansens, and the Hansens' determination to keep afloat.

Even if that meant diversifying into illegal and potentially dangerous dealings?

———

'What a waste.'

Howell had said the same thing when they'd met on an accidental death. Not even two years ago. Seemed like a lifetime.

Only their breathing filled the car for a few minutes. Lost in his thoughts, Franklin startled when Howell spoke again.

'Never even heard of this DCIS. You?'

Franklin shook his head.

'Remember what it's like when you have a newborn?'

From his side-vision, Franklin saw Howell vigorously move his head, answering his own question.

'What was it like for your missus for weeks after the birth? Mine said her body didn't feel like hers anymore, and sex was never going to happen again, or not for at least twelve months... Imagine finding out that minor pulled chest muscle is actually cancer. Non-invasive breast cancer, but it still means baby's ten weeks old and the missus is having a lumpectomy and radiation therapy.'

Franklin absorbed Howell's words, still taking in what they'd read in Bel's file.

Howell continued. 'Five years clear of cancer, they try for another baby and lose her at nineteen weeks. Then, miracle – Ollie comes along.'

Recalling what Ethan's teacher had said, Franklin put in, 'Which was around when Ethan was diagnosed with autism.

They certainly went through a lot in a decade. You'd never have known it.'

He'd never guessed they were anything other than a warm and happy unit. But everyone had public and private personas – what they showed the world, and the side they kept with their secrets. He ground his jaw. Bad stuff always happened to the nicest people, while those that deserved it skated through.

'On that, we haven't followed through on Ethan's recent flare-up,' Howell said tiredly. 'We need to consider what his special needs really meant for the family.'

'Another stress,' Franklin said.

Howell flicked the file between them on the console. 'Add it with the latest, Bel diagnosed with a secondary. She was facing more surgery, radiation, chemo.'

Franklin pictured the kinder teacher. 'Surely, you'd fight it – try and beat the cancer?'

The older detective slapped a heavy hand on the steering wheel. 'We're all different.'

'So they decided to take out their family?'

'It's looking like it.'

'But that way? And hurting others? I just don't get it.'

CHAPTER FORTY-FIVE

GEORGIE TOOK UP HER PHONE, THEN REPLACED IT ON THE table. Even without dialling, she knew Franklin wouldn't pick up, or return her call. Frustrated that they couldn't collaborate on this, she pondered how to find out what the police knew that would help her inquiries.

She retook her mobile and rang Matt Gunnerson.

'Gee! It's been a long time.'

'Sorry, Matty. It flies by, doesn't it?'

They spent a minute with chat and a promise to catch up properly soon, before Georgie said, 'I confess. I'm wondering what you've heard about the Korweinguboora incident. What your police sources are saying that's not out there yet.'

He was a gun crime reporter, as well connected to the cops as he was to the crooks in and around Melbourne and beyond. He had to know more.

Her question hung, and Georgie listened to background noise at his end. Judging by the confusion of voices and growls of traffic, he was in a throng outside court.

No surprise then, that he answered, 'Later, Gee.'

He couldn't talk freely. She understood, but the delay chafed.

She organised her thoughts. If she couldn't tap into what the police or Matty knew, maybe she'd have better luck with her go-to guy in the CFA.

He answered after a single ring.

'*Phillip Keogh.*'

'Phil, Georgie Harvey.'

'*Ah, my favourite journalist.*'

She laughed. 'I'd almost believe that if I didn't know how many journos you know through your work.'

'*Media liaison is what I miss in my new role. And strangely, being behind the fire hose.*'

'You love it all.'

He chuckled. '*Maybe not all the meetings. Speaking of...*'

Noting his limited window, she launched with, 'I have an interest in that fatal explosion and fire in Korweinguboora.'

'*Right.*' He sounded guarded.

'Are you able to shed any light on it?'

'*I can only talk about what's in the public domain.*' He hesitated and added, '*What you already know.*'

As she'd anticipated. 'Sure.' Georgie moved on. 'Then, can I run a few general questions by you?'

'*Of course.*'

'Propane-LPG gas tanks. Are some more prone to rupture than others?'

'*Keeping to generalities, yes, and particularly so when they have been tampered with.*'

She sat straighter. 'Happening much?'

'*Increasingly. When times are tough, people get innovative.*'

'How so?'

'*Petrol station drive-offs and number plate switches are off topic but good examples, and we often hear about them. But* some subjects are kept hush. I suspect because the police feel they are inherently more dangerous if they promote trends.'

'Such as?'

'Petrol syphoning, for one.'

'Yeah, I see that.' She steered Phil with, 'And gas tanks?'

He sighed. 'We've seen stupid things. The confusion for some people is that propane is the same as LPG, but not all LPG is propane.'

A bit cloudy on that, Georgie said, 'Uh-huh.'

'Take barbecues being used inside homes, for starters, and using car LPG in them, which is a mix of butane and propane. Some instances you can put down to bad judgment. Others, not so.'

Whether hurried by his next meeting, or heated by the theme, Phil spoke faster, and Georgie's pen skidded over the page as she raced to keep up.

'They'll try anything to save a buck. Especially if the gas has fallen off the back of a truck.'

'That's actually happening too?'

'There's a black-market trade for most things, Georgie.'

'True. What else?' she prompted.

'Lots to keep the dollar down.'

'Specifically, recently?'

'We've seen toxic mixtures of gas, the wrong types of hoses and connections, faulty valves, and unsafe tanks recycled illegally. We're working closely with the police on this because this isn't just people monkeying about. We're talking lethal stakes, and one or more rings prepared to cash in, regardless.'

The Hansens and Getty among them?

———

'You just missed her.'

Franklin's hands balled by his sides. His day of frustrations kept delivering. He'd forgotten that kinder kids knocked off at 12.00pm or 2.00pm depending on which age group. Never considered Yuki might've left for the day.

Howell viewed him strangely. Queried, 'Do you know if she was heading straight home?'

The leader said, 'I think so. She's having a hard day. With Bel,' her words trembled, 'you know. And the kids. She loved those kids.'

Not Alec though? Should they read anything into her not mentioning him?

'I told her I'd finish up here...not much to be done with half our kids absent today.' She hugged her arms to her body. 'They all know the family, between the kids and parents, and everyone is devastated, struggling to come to terms with it.'

She circled towards the table in the foyer where parents signed in. Boxed flowers and hand-drawn cards covered every centimetre. The tributes overflowed to underneath the table and along the walls.

Franklin jolted when the leader touched his hand. 'How is it all going?'

Staring at her fingers still pressing his skin, he wondered, *It all, the investigation?* Or an umbrella over everything, including the full fallout?

She went back to hugging herself. 'Do you know what happened yet? Have you made an arrest?'

Franklin fumbled for an answer. If only someone else was culpable and they could arrest them and mete out justice. Instead, it was looking more and more like Alec or Bel or both had engineered it.

Howell saved him. 'It's early days in a complex investigation. Could well be a terrible accident yet.'

She nodded. Her mouth moved in something unspoken.

Her lips pressed together as she forced a swallow. But she couldn't stop tears beading into heavy droplets, streaking lines down her cheeks.

Franklin swallowed too.

'We all miss her. Even though she was on extended maternity leave, she was always part of our team. She'd come to meetings where she could to stay involved, helped with open days and our little parties. She was dying to come back. Would've in a flash when Ethan settled down.'

She obviously knew nothing of Bel's latest illness. Was Yuki in the dark too? Franklin processed the rest of what she'd just said.

Sharper than intended, he asked, 'Did she resent not being able to work.'

Her dirty look with the shrill, 'Never,' made him believe it.

'She wished every day that Ethan didn't have to fight his battles. He was a delightful little boy, a special little soul, he just had a unique personality and needs. No, she never blamed him or resented him being on the spectrum. Herself now, that's as may be.'

———

Phil's meeting cut their conversation short. Georgie's pulse thumped in her temples as her fingers flew over her keyboard, drafting an email to the fire expert. She had gained an understanding of how the Murrays' tanks blew, despite being generally safe. But she didn't have enough information to join the dots.

She constructed a hypothetical situation bearing a resemblance to what had occurred at Korweinguboora, followed by a string of questions.

How did gas behave – did it float, sink or fill a space? Did all gases have that strong off-egg odour added, and if so, could people still be unaware of a leak? Could a fault with the gas cylinders cause such a gas build-up, or was her scenario more likely to involve an additional issue? And what might be a trigger?

Email done and sent, Georgie slumped with her elbows on the table, holding her head. Thinking over what she still didn't get about gas and explosions, what Matty might know about the case, and if Kat was okay. Waiting had never been her strong suit.

CHAPTER FORTY-SIX

As they pulled into Yuki's street, Franklin's mobile rang. He saw *Kendra* on the screen.

Shit.

Howell shot him a glance. He murmured, 'Shouldn't you start answering your phone?'

Didn't matter that he was right, Franklin still considered letting it go to message bank. But he owed a bunch of calls that he really didn't want to return because they'd be too heavy to deal with, especially to Harty, Slam, Georgie and Kat, plus several he figured he had to but wasn't in the headspace for at the minute. Best not add another.

'Kendra?' He caught himself before he added, *Everything okay?* Course it wasn't.

'*Yeah. I...*' Her voice fractured.

Franklin heard shrieks in the background at her end. He pressed the phone to his ear to listen. Kids hollering or crying, he couldn't tell exactly. Kendra began sobbing then.

'You need me to come over?'

She spoke, but so nasally and agonised that he couldn't decipher her words.

His gut churned with guilt and if onlys. If only he hadn't been chasing his dream to trade his uniform for plain clothes. They would have been a body up in the station, so Irvy could've taken a sick day and one of them would've gone on the welfare check with Sam instead. A clearer head and sinuses couldn't have prevented the whole catastrophe, but it would've saved Irvy's life, and meant Sam and Denise were physically unscathed.

Franklin knew he was a hypocrite. He'd told Harty that Irvy had agreed to trade shifts with him and should've said if he wasn't fit for work. But none of them would have done that, not already a body down in a station that always ran under complement. He'd told Harty off for blaming himself, but he was doing the same. It was like taking the blame would somehow make it different, or better.

Fuck, if only...

He came out of the fog when Howell shook his shoulder.

'What's up?'

Franklin looked around. They'd parked. He still held his phone, and when he put it to his ear, he could still hear kids' wails and Kendra's sobs.

―――――

Midway through making a coffee, Georgie recalled she still hadn't reviewed the brochures from the nurse's car. She went to her jacket and dug into the pockets, pulling out the crumpled bundle.

They covered everything from dog therapy, yoga, massage, relaxation, pampering, facials, art therapy, and cuppa and chat sessions, to information on wigs, risk of lymphoedema, and financial advice to help understand and cope with the monetary burden of cancer.

Fuck cancer.

Support services had improved since her dad's illness, but it wouldn't have made any difference in the end. He still would've died a horrible death and left Georgie, her sister and their mum broken.

But at least he'd had insurance to cover his treatment, his funeral, and to help them afterwards. Back then, she'd never imagined anything worse than losing Dad. Now, it struck her that families could rack up tremendous debt for medicines and on costs, often exacerbated by the patient's lost income if they were too sick to go in or lacked workplace flexibility around their medical appointments and bad days. Not every cancer patient died, but many slogged along, going backwards if not sinking, perhaps forever.

'I hate this.' Georgie's voice jarred in the empty house and rose with, 'I hate not being able to talk to you, Franklin.'

They could've helped each other deal with the harrowing thing that'd been inflicted upon their friends and the community. And if he hadn't cut her out, she'd have a better picture of the Murrays and what had happened at the farm instead of struggling to piece it together alone, and she could've helped the inquiry.

It came from nowhere. One, and then more tearing sobs that racked her body. Streams of tears. She couldn't get Sam out of her mind. Or Irvy.

Poor Irvy.

Georgie returned to the kitchen but rejected the unfinished coffee. The fridge beckoned. Yes, it was wrong in the middle of the afternoon and by herself. Inside her head, a familiar female from the past spoke, sprinkling in a tinge of worry with her non-judgemental, professional words. Saying, *Sit down. There's the water and tissues. How have you been sleeping? Have you cut back on the drinking?*

How was she sleeping? Mostly not, any sleep ending with visions of Goodlife Farm. Was she in control of her drinking?

'Until now.'

She yanked open the door and grasped a bottle from the top shelf. Twisted the lid and tossed it on the bench, while tilting back her neck and slugging down the beer.

———

Howell drew up the driveway behind Georgie's Spider, and Franklin's stomach sank. He couldn't deal with her shit. Anyone's shit. Kendra's was enough.

He stepped out of the wagon. 'I'll ring you when I'm done there, and we'll hook up.'

His partner signed *okay* with a thumb and index finger ring.

'You sure about seeing Yuki in the meantime?'

'I'll manage,' Howell said dryly. 'I've run the odd interview or two, you know.'

'Yep.'

Franklin had to let it go. He couldn't be in more than one place at once, and Howell didn't need him to hold his hand. He lifted two fingers in goodbye, shutting the door.

———

The approach of a car engine pulled Georgie to the window as Franklin exited from the passenger side. He leaned into the cabin. His low, deep tones reached her, though she couldn't hear what was said. She watched his back as he walked past the house to the rear of the property.

Deep down, she knew it. What he was going to do. She just didn't want to believe it.

The distinctive rev and engine growl came a few minutes later. And then Franklin rode down the driveway, donned in leathers and helmet. He scanned left and right before he pulled out. Not once looking back.

CHAPTER FORTY-SEVEN

Franklin went around the back. How often had he done this before? Pulled up at Irvy's, ridden virtually to the back door and clomped into the family room after a cursory knock. Like normal, yet dead wrong.

In contrast to that morning, the five kids were scattered over the room. Isla sat at a tiny table on a tiny chair sucking a tuft of her hair while she drew with a crayon clutched in her fist. Her two oldest brothers were squabbling. The other two sat separately, uncharacteristically pale and mute.

When he walked in shucking off his jacket, Kendra was rubbing her stomach and pacing. For a tick, Franklin worried that her baby was coming. She startled when she saw him, apparently oblivious to the motorbike's arrival, or his knock and entry.

She scurried to the island bar and picked up a packet that she bowled overhead at him.

'Take them. I'm not using any more of them.'

The package in his hand held a prescription drug. A sedative, he presumed.

'I don't want to be numb!' Kendra shouted. 'I need to know what's happening, deal with stuff, not be in an endless haze. I don't want him to be gone, but I need to *feel*. It's better to feel.'

She moaned, long and pained. Isla dropped her crayon and scuttled to her mum. She clutched the back of Kendra's legs and buried her head into them.

Franklin pocketed the pills, then he went to Kendra and opened his arms. She clung to him, their hug awkward around her belly. He jolted at a kick or elbow poke, the baby stretching or protesting inside its protective bubble.

'Did you feel that?' She leaned back. Eyes wide, she took his hand and pressed it to the fabric over her bump.

The baby thumped under his palm.

'It's going to be another boy.' She groaned, but her face softened. Almost a smile.

'For sure?'

'No, we never wanted to know for any of them until they came. But I think it's a boy.'

She still had her hand over his on her belly. Her fingers curled tightly with his.

She went on tiptoes, so she neared his height and repeated, 'I need to feel.'

He had to strain to make out her whisper.

'But it hurts, Frankie. It hurts so much.'

A lump blocked his throat, and he forced a swallow.

'I know.'

'No, you don't.'

Kendra freed his hand and clasped the front of his shirt.

She pulled him closer and hissed, 'We had the stupidest fight that morning. My last words to Irvy were *You're an arsehole*. He wasn't, ever. Annoying sometimes. Like all of us. I'm no angel, that's for certain.'

She leaned her head on his shoulder, muffling her voice.

'He was a good one, Frankie. My last words should've been *I love you, you great big sausage. You're my world.* But now I have to live with the fact that I was horrible to him just before he died.'

Franklin held her. 'Don't torture yourself. He knew you loved him, and you were his world too.'

'I know.' Her body trembled with silent tears.

After a bit, she murmured, 'I just wish I'd never wasted any of our words being mean.' She sniffed. 'We were supposed to have fifty...sixty more years.'

CHAPTER FORTY-EIGHT

GEORGIE WAS COLLATING STATS FOR HER EDITOR, ADDING to her research. Easier said than done with crime data frequently analysed annually or even decennially, and especially after sinking three—*or was it four?*—stubbies in two hours. On the plus side, the floaty feeling was a welcome respite. A few years back, she'd hit the booze too hard to enjoy the tipsy place she was in right now. Since then, she'd learned to be careful, to pace herself, and to tread the line between casual drinking and problem drinking.

Her counsellor, silent for nearly a year before this afternoon, sparked up for a second time inside her head.

Telling yourself that something is so, doesn't make it so, Georgie. Be sure you control the urges, not the other way around.

'I'm fine.' She lifted her hands. 'See, no shakes or anything.'

Just don't let it become a prop again, Georgie. Okay?

'Okay.'

'Talking to yourself means you're batshit crazy.'

Georgie whipped around to Kat. She hadn't heard her come in.

'No, it guarantees an intelligent conversation.' She held the teen's gaze. *Please let her have come in on okay.* 'You all right, Katz?'

'Yeah.' Headshake. 'Nah. I don't know. I don't want to talk about it though.'

With the *You can't play mum* predicament in mind, Georgie said, 'All right then, can you help me with this?'

Kat joined her at the table. 'What?' She slumped onto a chair.

'We need stacks of stats, stat.'

'You really are crazy.'

'Even if they're a little cloudy, I've got to give Sheridan enough juice tonight for her to bump my story to front page of the next issue.'

Kat rubbed her hands. 'Now you're talking.'

———

Much later than he'd expected, Franklin called Howell to let him know he was finished at Kendra's and ready to meet him to pick up their day.

'I'm at the office. PM briefing.'

Pissed, Franklin said, 'What happened to hooking up after Yuki and Kendra?'

'One of us needed to be here. Don't worry, I covered for you.' Howell fell over himself adding, *'Not that anyone would take issue with you doing what you needed to with Kendra. Or you taking time off, even.'*

Franklin got the impression that's what Howell wanted. Not a chance.

'What—'

'Look, I'd better get back in.'

'At least tell me what you learned from Yuki.'

His partner sighed. '*She's a mess, mate, but she wants to help. Bel didn't say too much, but with everything else, they really felt the cost of stuff for Ethan – special equipment, travel and lessons. It would've gotten very expensive as he grew up. Alec was dead against it—he hated labelling Ethan with autism or as on the spectrum apparently as much as he hated asking for charity—but Bel had started the process of applying for funding entitlements.*'

'And?'

'*Not much, but Yuki promised to write down what else she remembers, and check recent emails and messages from Bel for anything useful. I've gotta get back to the briefing.*'

———

They'd been at it for nearly an hour when Kat asked, 'Is that enough?'

Georgie weighed up the summary they'd prepared together. 'It'll do for Sheridan's purposes. I'll need to do more as I develop the story.'

'And you think it will be a front-pager?'

Her mind flit to all the loose strands from Gordon to Korweinguboora. There was potential for what she'd started to split into several stories if even some of her theories connected. And that even factored in those too close to her mates that she'd deem off-limits.

'Yes.'

'Cool.'

Kat was upbeat while they were occupied, but now bottomed out. Georgie took in the dark rings around her eyes and paleness of her skin. She considered the night she'd supposedly spent with Lisa and their wasted breakfast this morning. Had the teen slept or eaten at all in the past twenty-four hours or so?

'Sam's hanging in there.'

Kat perked up slightly. 'She is?'

Georgie nodded. 'Katz. Just know that this has sent a lot of people reeling. Admitting it doesn't make us weak... Don't bottle it up, will you?'

The teen let out a long breath.

'Want something to eat?'

Kat prodded her lower tummy gingerly. 'Nah.'

They sat quietly for a minute.

'Georgie? I think Dad might kill me.'

'Because you weren't with Lisa last night?' Georgie hazarded.

Kat gave her a stunned look.

'He doesn't need to know. Were you with Josh?'

'Yeah.'

'I get it. Just be open with me – I want to help.'

Georgie sensed that Kat had more on her mind but left it there, hoping she'd let her in.

She did. 'I'm late. I think I might be pregnant.'

CHAPTER FORTY-NINE

FRANKLIN TURNED OFF AT BUNGOWER ROAD, FOLLOWED IT awhile, crossed the highway, and then wiggled through a series of winding side streets to the address. A light shone from the front porch and another activated on sensor as he pulled the bike up the driveway.

He was expected.

After tossing around the pros and cons of phoning ahead, it'd been obvious that he couldn't risk just rocking up. Nearly two-and-a-half hours of riding, thanks to hitting a snarl through Burnley and a second on Peninsula Link, to result in yet another failed house call today would've done his head in. Though it hadn't been a day of complete failure. He'd gotten to Bel's file. They'd learned a little more about the Murrays.

He turned off the bike and leaned onto one leather-booted foot. The Ninja seemed wrong for this purpose, but his sedan would have to sit in the enclosure at Bacchus Marsh until he collected it. He drew off his helmet, and his cheeks smarted with the frosty sea mist.

He approached the front entrance of the bagged brick

house, ducking under several low branches of the bushy natives filling the front yard. He was expected, but wasn't wanted. The woman had hesitated before agreeing to the meeting, queried the lateness of the hour and necessity at all, but in the end had to because she couldn't cope with doing it over the phone.

The door gaped open, and a woman stood in the threshold. 'Detective Franklin?'

He nodded.

'Lucy Blakenish.'

'I'm sorry we had to meet under these circumstances, Lucy.'

They shook hands. Hers were bony. And very cold.

She whipped back her hand and wrapped her arms around her small frame. 'You'd better come in. I thought you'd be here sooner and have kept a lookout for you. It's freezing.'

A reprimand. Franklin didn't react as he peeled out of his jacket and boots. He trailed her through to a small room with a gas fire blazing.

A glance over the room told him this was a space occupied by one person. A lone comfy chair drawn up to the heater. Beside it, a side table with a mug on a coaster and an open book face down. Aside from the odd misfit, there was a uniformity to the artwork and types of books on the shelves you don't get with the mishmash of personalities of a couple or family. Lucy Blakenish had no kids, and if there'd been a partner must've decluttered when her circumstances changed. He recognised her garden in several of the photos she had on the mantel. She'd also featured colourful beach boxes, seascapes, rugged cliffs... and the Murray family.

Sadness weighed on him as he took a seat on the couch, too low and narrow for his long legs. Lucy Blakenish was another person bereft of family she loved and left totally alone after this tragedy. He couldn't help a stronger emotion: anger. At Bel and

Alec. If they did set out to hurt their family, did they never consider all the other people they'd shatter?

———

Kat had delivered her bombshell, flushed bright red, and then sprinted from the room before Georgie could say a word. The back door slammed, the blind banged loudly behind it. A moment later, running footsteps went past the window.

Georgie was too slow to pull back the curtains to catch the teen. She gazed into the darkness outside, listening to the wind rustling in the shrubs, their branches scratching on the glass and the weatherboards cladding the cottage. Pregnant or not, Kat shouldn't be out there by herself. Troubled and distracted, she could easily get hurt. Step in front of a car, or go hurtling over something unseen. But on the brink of adulthood, she wouldn't appreciate Georgie stalking her in the Spider or harassing her by phone. She'd decide if she preferred the company of Lisa or Josh. Or she'd come back when she'd gotten over her embarrassment and cleared her head.

Her mobile rang, and Georgie rushed to pick up, wanting it to be Kat.

'Gee. Sorry I couldn't get back to you earlier.'

Matty.

'I don't have long even now, so I'll have to make it quick.'

'No problem.'

'My police source told me two things I can't print yet, but are good as fact.'

Georgie tensed.

'The first is, the Murray family was dead well before Wednesday – all four of them. Police are aiming to narrow down the timeframe. But at this stage, it's a twelve-hour window between 10.00pm Monday night to 10.00am Tuesday morning.'

'They died at least a whole day earlier.' What was the implication of that?

'*Secondly, they died of CO poisoning.*'

'Shit.'

The warning signs had been there, but now it'd been confirmed. Georgie's mind dragged up the tragic death of two little boys, must've been around two years ago. Carbon monoxide had been their killer, and all the fault of an unserviced and faulty heater.

Was an awful, preventable accident the cause of everything after all?

Still so many questions.

'*My source is keeping his cards close on this, Gee. Understandable with two cops among the victims, though there is a plus side of this for the force.*'

Georgie couldn't see it. 'What?'

'*They tend to cop flack for welfare checks that don't go well. Without waiting for the facts of a case, plenty of people lay blame squarely on police for any flare-ups, particularly so when someone is hurt. Can be justly too. But I think this exonerates Irvy and Sam, don't you?*'

'Surely nobody's said—'

'Yes, they have,' Matty cut in. '*Dig around online and you'll see.*' He quickly added, '*Actually, don't.*'

———

Lucy Blakenish caught him staring at her photos. She moved to the mantel and retrieved one. Handing it to Franklin, she said, 'Magical moment.'

In the picture, Bel's hair was matted, her face lit up with exhausted joy as she gazed at the baby she cradled, slick with after-birth. By her side, a dewy-eyed and tired Alec held up a small boy observing his new brother in wonderment.

'Me and Alec shared being Bel's birth partner when both boys came, and they'd always wanted Ethan to meet Ollie as soon as he arrived. Bel'd had a rough labour, but the doctor allowed it.'

The woman sagged onto her chair by the fire and withdrew into herself for several minutes. Franklin tried to find a more comfortable position on the couch.

'I'm sorry you had to come so far to see me.' She clasped her hands together on her lap. 'And that I was brusque with you on the phone. I still can't believe they're gone.'

She shook her head repeatedly.

'Bel's father died when she was a little girl, did you know that?'

He said softly, 'No.'

'Her mother was heartbroken, completely lost. It made perfect sense for them to move in with me.' She waved a hand. 'The three of us in this small place, imagine. But it was marvellous, truly, even when Bel came of age. You wouldn't have thought three women could get along so fine.'

She floundered as if she'd forgotten where she was going with the story.

'I'd always thought it would be me.'

Confused, Franklin sat quietly.

'I said no to the only man I'd ever loved because I was so sure. And that meant I couldn't have children either, could I?'

He tried to make sense of Lucy's ramblings.

'Our mother died of breast cancer when I was sixteen and Cheryl ten. I became convinced that I'd get it...but it turned out to be my baby sister.'

Her gaze lowered to a spot near Franklin's socked feet.

'She died the year before Bel meet Alec,' she whispered. 'I

gave Bel away at her wedding, and I've always hoped that Cheryl was able to see how beautiful and happy her daughter was that day.'

Lucy choked. She needed space to recover, and they sat awhile, the hiss and hum of the gas heater the only noise. When she blew her nose, Franklin reckoned it was a sign to continue.

'I understand this is very difficult. Thank you for opening up.'

She nodded.

He considered which way to move. Lucy Blakenish and Stephen Murray were Bel and Alec's only living relatives, to his knowledge anyway. Interviews with friends and colleagues so far showed the couple in a positive light, but also flagged that they kept things private, whether driven by pride and embarrassment, or merely a natural reserve. Lucy had helped raise Bel with her sister. She'd stepped into the role of mum when Cheryl had died. He guessed she probably knew Bel better than anybody.

He contemplated her words *how beautiful and happy her daughter was that day* and wondered if Bel wasn't so happy down the line. How was the family dynamic, and how did Alec and Bel get along, specifically under the stress of the various problems they were dealt? What did Lucy know of Ethan's latest flare-up?

On the other hand, it'd be easy to segue to Bel's cancer.

In the end, watching Lucy labour to stay composed, he imagined she could rapidly disintegrate once they moved back the catastrophic loss of her only family. Best to start with the bigger picture.

———

Georgie replayed her conversation with Matty. She couldn't do what he urged: ignore the criticism aimed at Sam and Irvy. She went online.

HEAVY-HANDED POLICE 'WELFARE CHECK' TURNS DEADLY

Police are under fire yet again for heavy-handed tactics, this time for their part in a routine welfare check in small-town Korweinguboora on Wednesday morning that resulted in five fatalities.

Two Daylesford police officers attended an address in this rural town at the request of a medical professional, but the outcome of five deceased persons and two critically injured revives questions about over-policing, racial profiling, and mistreatment of mentally impaired citizens by our police officers.

Police in the northern district are currently under fire for their conduct of another routine welfare check on a man suffering from schizophrenia that was caught on video by neighbours.

Meanwhile, officers in Melbourne's inner west recently defended their over-response to what they perceived as threatening behaviour by a youth, which saw four police vehicles flock to the scene and ten officers tackle the youth to the ground.

Police regularly verify the safety and

wellbeing of individuals, often at the instigation of concerned family members, neighbours or medical personnel.

Georgie shivered off the cold and dirty slick of the article, while thankful Irvy and Sam hadn't been named. The Murrays predeceased the welfare check, so the visit and police involvement had no bearing on their deaths. The nurse, Irvy and Sam were all hurt doing precisely what such a call entailed.

Misreporting like this pissed her off.

With effort, she pushed it aside and went over the questions she'd put to Phillip Keogh. Her mind filled with the gas cylinders in the police statements and what she'd seen in Gordon. Still so many gaps, but the links were certainly growing.

She straightened suddenly, remembering the video she'd taken at the press conference at the Murray farm on the morning of the fire. She hadn't watched it back yet.

How could she have overlooked it?

She'd be angry with herself if a clue had been sitting on her phone for all this time.

———

Lucy spoke before him. 'I don't think a woman could have a better husband than Alec.'

Had she read his mind?

'They got along well?'

'Those two were made for each other.' Her smile softened her haggard grief.

265

'It's not fair – that some people seem to get far more than their share of bad luck, I mean. One thing after another...but they got on with it. They pulled together. What would break other marriages made theirs stronger.'

He wanted specifics. Waited.

'They got through all those miscarriages.' Lucy stopped, shaking her head.

How many pregnancies had they lost? Poor things.

'And the loss of their little girl...stillborn...she so nearly made it... Then finally, along came Ollie. But then Ethan was diagnosed, and Bel had her health troubles. Still, they pulled together.'

He nodded, hoping for more.

'The farm did reasonably well, but their overheads were too high, and income halved when Bel couldn't work. Alec picked up odd jobs where he could, to make ends meet. But it was robbing Peter to pay Paul: not enough cash, energy or daylight left for what needed doing at their farm, on their house. They wanted to give every bit of help they could to Ethan, and they wouldn't take a gift from me. I'm not rich or anything, but I could've spared some. But Bel wouldn't take it.'

A familiar story to what Stephen had told his neighbour. Franklin gave another nod.

'To top it all off, their roof had sprung more holes and Bel found out that she had a new round of health worries.'

'Health worries?' Franklin fished to see if she knew exactly what they were.

She bobbed her head. 'Cancer, invasive this time. Small amounts in both breasts and in the right lymph nodes.'

All the pain that'd lined her face talking about her mother and sister returned.

The drone of the gas heater filled the room for a few

minutes, while Lucy took unsteady breaths. At last, she met his gaze.

'We're fighters, us Blakenish women. Bel was going to beat her cancer. Or live as long as she could for her boys.'

———

Georgie pulled up the video on her phone and watched the entire recording of the presser. Then she replayed the slow 360-degree span of the crowd she'd taken before DI Knight had started.

While recording, she'd landed on the guy with the big belly after he'd bumped her, and then skimmed a little too quickly over the people directly behind her.

For the first few run-throughs, nothing jumped out.

But she played the footage again, and *there*.

She hit pause and squinted.

The neck-breather.

Playing on, he was in the frame, then not. But definitely the one in Jeanette's photo from the Ballarat Show that she'd called Cam. And almost positively the truck driver.

Georgie skipped to the end of the conference and the forty-five seconds of video as the crowd disbursed. Excited, she peered at the screen. Cam the neck-breather, talking to the pregnant-belly man, had turned and given her a clear view of the Power FM logo on his jacket.

DAY FOUR

SATURDAY 16 JUNE

CHAPTER FIFTY

FRANKLIN LEANED ON THE WALL NEAR THE PHONE AND shut his eyes, blocking the harsh white fluoro lighting. Not far off falling asleep standing up.

The day had been never-ending. The break he'd taken after leaving Lucy Blakenish felt like a distant memory. He'd sat on the little deck of a striped beach box on Mornington beach. Watched waves curl and break in the dim moonlight, salt misting his skin and hair, cold goose-bumping his skin. Propped against the door until he couldn't feel his arse, and wishing the rest of him would numb too.

What he'd learned from Lucy put things right in his mind about Alec and Bel. His instincts of them as a couple and separately, along with Bel's determination to fight for her life, not give in, had been affirmed by her last conversation with Lucy. She'd said that as soon as the hospital was ready to start her treatment, so was she. With the full support of Alec.

Not murder–suicide.

The missed appointment with the nurse—crucial to organise the first step—had made Denise concerned about Bel's wellbeing. She'd been right to be worried, but not for the reason she'd imagined.

But it wasn't enough. He had to find proof for the arson Ds and coroner. And answers for those left behind.

Cracking a huge yawn, he glimpsed his watch, surprised that midnight had come and gone. It was a new day. Better or worse than yesterday, time would tell.

Mustering his energy, he used the wall phone to let the nurse know which bed and patient name, and the bloke admitted him. His rank helped.

The walk through ICU added fatigue to his bone-weary body. How many of these patients would survive their crisis? What percentage would go back to life as they knew it? He knew negativity had no place here, but couldn't shake the black cloud that'd settled over him.

Movement within a nearby cubicle caught Franklin's attention, and he drew close to the curtain that gaped open. The patient moved her head, and for a moment, he thought it'd been a reaction to him. But her eyes did a roll as she exhaled. She seemed to be in discomfort.

'Back again, Franklin.' His favourite nurse had snuck alongside.

'Marianne.' He smiled with the greeting and nudged his nose towards the bed. 'How's Denise doing?'

'We're pretty happy. We've been able to wind back her sedation, and she's awake and responding. Her breathing is reasonably good. Her burns weren't as extensive as your friend's.'

'Because she was further back.'

'Yes, that saved her, and her woollen jacket.' The nurse gazed across to Denise. 'About fifteen percent of her skin tissue is burnt, mainly to her face and hands. Some of that is full thickness and some is only partial.'

Denise's head drooped. Asleep or just resting, Franklin couldn't tell.

'We grafted skin from her thighs onto her hands, like we did with Sam. But Denise's face wasn't as bad as it probably looked to you. It didn't need skin grafts. Under that dressing,' she patted her own face, 'is synthetic nylon sheeting with collagen in it which helps it adhere to the skin. Just temporary. Hopefully, her skin will be healed, and this will be all off, in ten or so days.'

'Wow.' Franklin shook his head. He considered the figure slumped over onto Denise's bed. 'How's her partner doing?'

'He's been her rock.' Marianne smiled widely. 'Speaking of rocks, he showed me the one he has in his pocket. As soon as Denise gets her clearance out of here to the burns unit, he's going to propose.' She pressed her palms and fingers together, clearly pleased.

A little of Franklin's gloom lifted. Denise's prospects were better than he'd expected. Had to wonder how long until she'd be able to wear her engagement ring. But still, she'd been lucky.

'And Sam?'

Marianne squeezed his shoulder. 'She's hanging in there. A fighter, that girl.' She propelled him up the corridor. 'Go see her.'

Momentum, and Marianne breathing down his neck, took Franklin to the foot of Sam's bed. He skimmed over her cubicle. The machines keeping her alive, monitoring her vitals. The teddy bear wearing an Italia scarf next to her head on the pillow, new since he'd last visited. Then the body lying in the bed.

Giving him a little prod, Marianne said in her chirpy tone, 'Sam, Franklin's here to see you.' She chuckled. 'It's very late. Special compensation for a special young lady.'

He took the seat at her bedside.

'Hi, Sam.'

Her machines beeped. Sam lay inert.

He reached for the unscathed part of her left arm, careful not to knock out the plastic tube.

She swallowed around the tube in her mouth. The first time she'd done that, that first night he'd sat with her, he hadn't realised that it was a normal, mechanical action even in unconscious patients.

He gently rubbed her arm. 'How you doing there?'

Sam swallowed, and her eyelids trembled. They opened a slit.

'Mate!' He leapt up and leaned over her. Watching her. Scared by the bleary look in her eyes.

Behind him, Marianne said, 'Sam? Well, hello there.'

'Oh, mate. Sam.'

Her eyes rolled back. Did she even know they were there?

Franklin bloody hoped so. 'Sam, it's good to see you.'

She blinked slowly. It had to be a good sign that she was awake, didn't it?

Her eyes widened. The lids fluttered. Slit. Then closed. She was gone.

CHAPTER FIFTY-ONE

GEORGIE ROUSED, HER CHEEK WAS SQUASHED INTO something firm, yet lumpy. Her hands were bunched under her chest. When she moved, her fingers shot with pins and needles and her back twinged. Everything stiff and sore from the unnatural position of being collapsed forward over her notepad and pens on the tabletop. Good thing she'd pushed aside her computer – unless she'd knocked it in her nosedive?

Groaning, she uncurled and eased out the kinks. The room was freezing. She must've been out of it for over an hour because the fire had died to a scattering of embers.

The mantel clock told her it was 7.03am. Apart from its ticks, the silence around her warned she was still alone. She checked anyway. No Franklin. No Kat. No messages from either.

'What the hell am I doing here if nobody wants me around?'

Her words reverberated through the empty cottage. She immediately wanted to suck them back. This wasn't about her. She could work as well from here as home, but it was a no brainer that if Franklin or Kat did return which of those was preferable. Just as it was a no brainer what her priority would be if they reached out. What she was doing on the article first and foremost was her way of helping to dig out answers about the Murray farm anyway. Earning her editor's approval and the front-page feature, connecting readers to the story, and her own satisfaction were only potential bonuses.

She restarted the fire, aware of the thump of a headache and a furry taste in her mouth. Drink had been her only bedfellow last night. She regretted it. But she perked up slightly, remembering that she had made a little headway in the small hours of the morning.

Georgie let the flames licking the kindling soothe her. She jolted at the click of the lock on the back door. Swinging in that direction, she wondered which one would walk through. The bang as the door shut and clatter of the blind revealed it was Kat even before she emerged, hesitated, then darted across the room.

Instinctively, Georgie's arms opened for a hug. She stroked the teen's long, softly curled hair, the same colour as her dad's. It was knotted and damp with dew. Her jacket was smeared with mud and moist too. How long had she been wandering around out there? Not the whole night?

'Thanks.' Kat untangled herself.

They stood warming their hands to the fire.

'Did you–'

The sound of the Ninja gearing down and its growl as it zipped up the driveway stopped Georgie mid-sentence and startled Kat. The teen began pacing and twisting her hands.

The back door opened and closed. Like rabbits caught in headlights, they froze and listened to Franklin's movements in the kitchen.

His steps approached, and Kat shot Georgie a panicked look.

She mouthed, *Don't say anything. Please.*

————

Georgie and Kat were both in the front room watching him as he came in. Franklin's chest swelled. His two girls had never looked so good, though they both looked wrecked. Dark-ringed eyes. Slept-on hair. Crumpled clothes. Mirrors of him, no doubt.

'Dad!' Kat hurled herself at him.

After a moment, Georgie joined their huddle. He clung onto them. Life was a bitch. Things changed in a heartbeat. He could lose them both any day. Or he could go on shift and not make it home, like Irvy.

He knew it. He loved them. But trembles took off inside him, and he extracted himself and moved to face the fire.

Apart from Kat's greeting, none of them had spoken. Tension crackled in the room. He knew it was probably all him, but instead of dealing with it, he took some wood from the basket and laid it on the fire. Poked around rearranging the logs and stirring up the flames.

Awkward didn't cover the way he felt when he turned to them.

C'mon, Franklin. Think. What's a positive to talk about?

'I sat with Sam last night.'

'How is she?' Georgie asked.

'She woke up around 12.30.'

Kat cried out, 'That's great!'

His mind went back to Sam's cubicle.

'I said hello and she opened her eyes.'

Georgie said, 'She responded to you?'

'I don't know. I think so, hope so. The nurse seemed happy. They'd taken her sedation down, and she'd been slow to come out of it. I think they were worried it was taking too long.'

He saw her excitement shrivel.

'It all happened in less than a minute. Her eyes opened, then she dropped back to sleep.'

'But that's good?' Kat pressed. 'She's getting better.'

Picturing Sam in her bed—with the teddy bear propped on her pillow, surrounded by the ICU gear, swathed in dressings, a leg in the air—was so intense that Franklin tipped back his head and took a deep breath.

Then he gazed at Kat and Georgie and swallowed heavily.

'I stayed until 5.30, but she didn't wake again. They're not completely happy. She's not squeezing their hands or reacting to stimulus as they'd like. They won't know for sure if there's any brain damage from the head trauma,' he cradled the back of his head where Sam's wound was, 'or the extent of it until she's fully conscious.'

Kat's face puckered. 'But she talked to you out there, didn't she?'

'Yeah. But she stopped breathing at least once after that. And she hit her head again after the initial injury.'

His daughter went white and whispered, 'Brain damage?'

Franklin jammed his hands into his pockets to hide their shakes. He had no idea how to make this better.

Georgie went to Kat and draped an arm around her shoulders. 'Katz, it's only a possibility. She woke up this morning. She responded to your dad. You know Sam. She's tiny, but she's tough.'

That earned a weak smile and a nod from Kat. Meanwhile, he went on watching his girls impotently.

***

'You guys want something to eat?'

Franklin said no, and Kat paled at the suggestion. They still needed to have *that* talk. At any rate, Georgie had to tackle it.

She took in the washed-out complexions of father and daughter. 'Have either of you slept in the past day?'

They grimaced, never looking so alike.

'Let's all try and grab some now?'

They stared back with matching hazel irises, the green and gold glints duller than usual.

Franklin cut his gaze to Kat. He must've recognised her need, if not his own, because he agreed.

Georgie saw the teen to her room, then followed Franklin to the one they shared, suddenly insecure. But he peeled back the doona for her to slide in. They were both still clothed.

They lay on their backs for a while, not talking. Her socked foot grazed his.

Georgie rolled to her side so she could see him. 'Do you want to talk, Jack?'

He tilted his head at her nickname, then gave her a sad look. 'Not now.' But he lifted his arm so she could snuggle into his chest and mould her legs and hips to his.

She had so much she wanted to say. To get him to open up, to help him, first. But also to share what she'd learned that might aid the investigation. If he'd reciprocate, they could be a team on this.

There'd be time after they rested. She probably wouldn't be able to fall asleep thinking about Franklin and Kat and Irvy and Sam, and having passed out for a few hours earlier this morning. But at least they were together, and he could get a bit of sleep.

CHAPTER FIFTY-TWO

GEORGIE STIRRED AND STRETCHED OUT A FOOT TO RUB against Franklin's. Reached further without striking any part of him, then cracked open her eyes. His side was empty. Amazingly, she'd slept, albeit not for long. And he'd left the bed.

It wasn't supposed to go that way.

She pulled her fingers through her hair as she padded from the bedroom to the kitchen. His jacket, boots, gloves and helmet were gone.

'Dad left half an hour ago.'

Georgie masked her dejection as Kat came from the hallway and joined her.

'He woke me up to say goodbye.'

At least he'd done that for his daughter. But if the teen had slept, it'd only been briefly.

Kat poked at the page fixed by magnets to the fridge. 'He's not rostered on today.'

'I don't think we're going to see much of him either way

until this case is closed.' Georgie pulled out a chair. 'Sit down.'
They both sat. 'Do you want to talk?'

'About this?' Kat clasped her fingers over her abdomen.

'How late?'

'A bit over a week.'

'Is that odd for you?' Georgie admitted, 'I'm all over the
place.'

Kat shook her head. 'I'm like clockwork.'

'Really? I've always had spotting, weird cycles. Chances
are, I'm late too.'

'No way.'

'You and Josh use contraception, right?'

Kat blushed. 'Yeah. Condoms.'

'And nothing…'

'Not that I noticed.'

Kat had divulged her secret, almost in spite of Georgie's
fumbling. But shit, imagine if she was pregnant.

Georgie had to think this through and tread carefully. She
didn't want to feed the teen's alarm.

'Seriously, I'm sure you're just late. Stress can do it, and you've
been under heaps with your SACs and swotting for your GAT
and exams. But I can go right now and get a pregnancy test kit?'

After a moment, Kat said, 'Not yet. Maybe it is just stress.'

Georgie stilled, struck by a fresh worry. 'You haven't missed
any assessments…with all this?' She waved, meaning both
Korweinguboora and the possible pregnancy.

'No. My SACs are up to date. I did my GAT—don't know
how it went though—and my exams are next week.' She
squirmed. 'I've skipped a few classes.'

'We'll talk to the school on Monday.' Georgie nudged her.
'Your period'll come soon, but we'll take the next step together
if it doesn't, okay?'

'Yeah. Thanks.'

'If you're feeling off, it's likely to be stress and PMS. It's quite common.'

'I hope so. I don't think Josh's ready to be a dad.'

'You haven't talked to him?'

Kat shook her head. 'I don't want to be pregnant. I'm not ready either. How would a baby look on my application to join the police?'

Still determined to follow your dad's footsteps then. Even after Sam and Irvy.

'More importantly, how would I juggle a baby and the academy?' Kat added.

———

Franklin trudged across the paddock next to the bloke. *Always something that needed doing yesterday on a farm*, he'd said with a shrug, adding they'd need to talk while he worked. Franklin sensed a half-truth in that. He dodged a cow patty, glad for his bike boots as he splashed in a puddle and the jacket insulating against the icy morning air.

'So, Alec and Bel?' he prompted.

'I dunno what I can tell you, really?'

They came to a fenced plot. The bloke went to open the gate and caved through his mid-section with a gasp, as if he'd been punched. 'Still can't believe they're all gone.'

Franklin had expected emotion. This was Alec's best mate. But the bloke's pain hit him strongly.

Sad, bewildered eyes drilled his. 'Know what happened yet?'

'We're piecing it together.'

'Yeah, yeah. Police talk.'

The bloke's hurt switched to anger. Easier for Franklin to deal with.

'Make sure you get the bastards.'

He nodded but made no promises.

Survivors needed to pin blame somewhere. Along the line, they usually blamed themselves with *If only I'd done this or that*. Bel and Alec and their shitty circumstances and an avoidable accident wouldn't cut it. Franklin wanted someone else to be held accountable more than ever.

The farmer's face worked through lifted, then crinkled brows, and downturned lips that quivered until he twisted his mouth. Finally, his jaw slackened.

Hollow-eyed, he got back to Franklin's question. 'They were doing it hard, money I mean. But aren't most of us?' He fanned a hand over his land. 'Still, we've got the best job in the world. Who'd wanna be stuck in an office?'

'True. That's not the bit I like about my job.'

'You like your job?' The bloke gave him a surprised glance, then ushered Franklin into the plot through the small gate. It banged and clicked shut behind them.

Franklin sighed, puffing a cloud. 'Not this part of it either.' He meant the deaths and the terrible injuries he was trying to get to the bottom of.

The bloke looked grim, understanding. He busied himself with his plants.

'We got together a fair bit. Me missus and our girls, and Bel and their little fellas got along like a house on fire.' He cursed and kicked the ground, his boots digging a semi-circle mound. 'Stupid expression.'

He gave Franklin a sheepish look and returned to checking the vegies.

'Alec and me, we've been friends since we were little

tackers ourselves.' He froze with his hand in mid-air, then let it drop. 'We *were* friends,' he corrected.

He gathered a large plastic crate and a garden fork, and loosened the soil before pulling out carrots and potatoes, loading up the crate.

'So, money was tight for them. And the roof had sprung leaks?'

'Yep.' The farmer moved on to hack cauliflowers off at the base.

Franklin commented, 'Lotta veg – for the stall out the front?'

'Yep. We do okay with it. Better than trying to sell into shops or wasting our weekends at farmers markets. You gotta diversify to survive in farming, 'specially nowadays.' He chuckled. 'Always something that needed doing yesterday though.'

Franklin smiled, then sobered as his mind went to the way the Murray family had died. Not public knowledge yet, so he had to be careful with his words. 'Were they cutting corners?'

The bloke brushed his cheek with the back of his hand. He straightened and ambled over to the beans, and started picking.

'Look, we get offers, you know? From fellas at the pub, things they reckon they have in surplus so they can sell cheap.' He added, 'I guess we've all got ourselves a bargain that way every now and then. Alec might've got some cheap stuff lately, but...'

Rising from his crouch, his wrinkled expression told Franklin the theory fit, but he didn't know specifics.

'How do we live without them?' He jabbed the air. 'I mean, *now* it's like they've just gone away for a day or two. Any tick and Alec will be on the blower suggesting we grab a beer. Or the girls will cook up a plan for all of us. But it's gonna hit properly soon, isn't it? They aren't coming knocking on our door ever again.'

———

Kat had disappeared into her bedroom, apparently to study. Georgie wandered back to the dining room, nursing her third coffee for the morning, and retrieved her notepad. A stir of excitement when she landed on the name Cameron McAlister. Announcer, local news presenter and all-rounder at Power FM, judging by what she'd found online.

She played devil's advocate to test her theories.

Cam, media guy from Ballarat, regular news reporter, covered the first press conference at Goodlife Farm.

By occupation, required to attend such a notable local event, particularly as it involved a Ballarat victim – though he couldn't have known about Denise yet. So, not remarkable for him to be there.

Except for his connection to the Hansens. His photo with wife Nancy (aka Nance) on Jeanette's fridge. Added with Georgie's growing suspicions about the Gordon lot, Allan's death, and links with Korweinguboora.

And *remarkable* didn't cut it to describe that.

She already had an address for C and N McAlister. Too easy. A blog on the Power FM site mentioned, *Our very own Cam McAlister from Miners Rest*. A White Pages search on the computer did the rest. But she couldn't drive straight out there and confront him or Nance. She had to strategise.

Georgie let her fingers do a little more walking online. She ascertained that Miners Rest was a town on the outskirts of Ballarat, and that in addition to any crops or livestock the McAlisters ran, they advertised farm fencing and slashing services, not necessarily great money-spinners with plenty of farmers doing their own. Between their farm, Cam's radio gig, and maybe the odd bit of slashing or fencing, they were spreading themselves around. Their own farm not enough to sustain them.

Hawk Nose had explained how tough it was on the land and that farmers had to be resourceful. The McAlisters must get tired juggling all those jobs though. Mighty tempting to branch out into something with a bigger pay day for less effort.

CHAPTER FIFTY-THREE

AFTER LEAVING ALEC'S BEST MATE, FRANKLIN DECIDED working through the rest of Bel and Alec's friends would be his priority this morning. Difficult calls. And he honestly didn't expect much to come out of them, but he had to exhaust every avenue.

The next address ran off Farm Road. As he throttled down for the approach, he backflipped and threw a U-turn instead. He wove through the short distance to Riley's Lane and stopped at the gate to Goodlife Farm. He couldn't bring himself to look at what was out front and kept his gaze averted.

Returning to the place where Irvy and the four Murrays had died knocked him worse than it had with Howell two days ago. He rode up the driveway and left the bike. The air still held a toxic pong. Ash blew across his path with a gust of icy wind. Torn blue-and-white crime scene tape snaked around scorched trees near the carcass of the house.

The fire, tonnes of water from the firies' hoses, rain since. Black sluice, melted plastic, burnt timber, warped metal, piles of rubble. Not much to show for a family's existence.

Franklin picked his way around the perimeter, intent on inspecting the gas cylinders. All gone, including the ruptured ones. Taken into evidence. Disappointing, even though he'd expected it.

He stopped at the front of the house, grappling with vivid memories. He skirted the spot where Irvy was found under charred wood and tin, a brick of dread in his gut, and moved into the structure.

Forensics had done their thing, sifted through the remains, removed anything of interest. No need to worry about disturbing evidence. But so close to where the Murrays had been buried under the upturned couch, he found himself tiptoeing through and saying, 'Sorry.'

Lives were lost on this spot. Their spirits might've stayed. He hoped they didn't mind his intrusion.

'Trying to put it together for you.' His voice sounded foreign. Lumpy, like his throat. 'I'm going to find the truth and put things right.'

As best I can.

Franklin spent a quarter of an hour in that room, picturing it before the fire. Remnants of the walls, wiring, pipes and flue told him approximately where the TV had sat and the position of the heater. He knew where the Murrays had laid and judged the couch must've been just beyond that. Perhaps pushed back from its usual position to make way for them on the floor.

He considered why the family was sleeping here. But that came with visions of the infant and baby that made him nearly lose the fight with queasiness that'd started when he had pulled up at the gate.

Enough. He crept through the rest of the wreckage. A partly melted dummy suggested he was in Ollie's bedroom. From a small number of books and toy cars and the surviving coils of a single bed base, he guessed the next one was Ethan's.

In a slightly larger room, he found a silver frame and blew soot off the glass over a photo of Bel and Alec's wedding.

Any clues the house had held as to what drove the family into the living room between Monday night and Tuesday morning had been destroyed by the explosions, fire and elements.

———

Georgie took the turnoff at Back Settlement Road and retraced her route of Wednesday to the Murray place. She caught sight of a blue-over-white bike ahead, its rider in black leathers. Even from the back, the way the rider synergised with the bike and the shape of his matt-black helmet made her thrust her hand on the Spider's horn.

She gave a long honk. But whether he heard it or not, Franklin sped off. She didn't give chase.

Sven and Vlatka were top of her list, but Georgie neared their farm and slowed the car to a crawl, then parked outside the gate for Goodlife instead. What she saw triggered a push-pull sensation within her. The same as what had compelled her take in Sam's injuries at this farm. Distressed fascination.

Out of the car, her gait unsteady, Georgie moved to the post-and-wire fence mesmerised by what hung from it. Bunches of flowers, some with cellophane and coloured paper, others wrapped in aluminium foil or tied off with string. Store-bought and hand-made cards. Posters and drawings. Many were protected from the rain and frost by clear plastic bags, A4 display pockets or cling film. The colours ran and cardboard wilted on those that weren't.

Her gaze returned to a large collage of names that surrounded a naïve drawing of a dad, mum, child and baby. Neat script near the bottom corner said, 'From your classmates at Daylesford Primary'. And as before, she locked on the three words in the centre scrawled in a rainbow of coloured markers. She whispered them. 'Rest in peace.'

She inched along, reading many of the cards. Written in almost illegible, unformed child's handwriting or neat, adult's script they pinged at her heart.

A kid had written, 'We love you. See you in heaven.' Heaven had been spelt *heeven*, scored out and rewritten.

Another wrote, 'I am sorry you are dead.'

Georgie stroked a little brown teddy holding a love heart stitched with 'Gone too soon'. She petted a rustic baby lamb with closed eyes and the initials B, A, E and O each sewn on the bottom of a hoof. Hand-knitted in less than three days.

Cards with stick-drawings of angels, crosses, and crying faces.

More flowers.

A poster covered in palm prints in primary-coloured paint from the kindergarten.

The offerings went all the way up to where the fence disappeared under water spilled over from the flooded front paddock.

Georgie couldn't stem her tears. She could only bear to read one more card and chose the large, multicoloured crayon rainbow arching over a simple house with wonky creatures she thought were cows, but what might have been a pair of ducks, or dogs. Inside, in green lettering, 'Dear Ethan. Sorry I said mean things to you. You can play with us. Your friend James.'

———

Franklin pulled off his helmet and heaved a sigh. Shouldn't have ridden off on Georgie. But he couldn't let her see him this flustered.

Was he ready to meet another of Alec's mates? He groaned. As he'd ever be.

He thought over his earlier visit. The only thing he'd gained was confirmation that the Murrays might've cut corners to save bucks. In hindsight, the bloke probably got more out of him stopping by than he did. An opportunity to talk about his mate and vent some of his pain without having to act strong and hold it together for the sake of his family.

If Franklin's morning amounted to listening to friends grieving the Murrays, he'd have to hack it, on the off chance that one of them did share the thing that could help him crack this inquiry.

———

Georgie cocooned herself in the Spider for several minutes. Swiped away her tears and breathed through the overwhelming sadness.

When she'd recovered, she sought out Sven or Vlatka, finding Vlatka under the bonnet of a ute.

'...and you'll be as good as new,' Vlatka murmured. She stood back, clutching a spanner. Smiling, satisfied.

Noticing Georgie, she said, 'Everything does better if you talk to it.'

She winked and tucked the spanner in the top pocket of her flannelette jacket. Green check today.

They shook hands.

'You want a drink, Georgie?' When she declined, Vlatka asked, 'The nurse and your friend the policewoman – how are they?'

'The nurse is conscious and improving. Sam opened her eyes briefly. They're both still in ICU.'

Vlatka's wishful look collapsed, but then she gripped

Georgie on the shoulder. 'They have survived the first days.' Her stare was as strong as her squeeze. 'They'll make it. You will see.'

Georgie hoped she was right.

'Wait a minute while I test this, eh?'

'Okay.'

Vlatka scrambled into the ute's cabin, fired up the engine and did a few revs. 'Perfect.' She exited and led Georgie over to a bench made of halved rough-sawn logs, bark unpeeled on the underside.

'We've had reporters here every day. Questions, questions, always with the questions.'

Georgie cringed. She was a reporter here with questions, though she wasn't here as a reporter.

'We have questions too. What have the police found out?'

She gave the version in the public domain.

'Good neighbours are hard to find,' Vlatka commented. 'We're lucky here. All ours are good. Bel and Alec and their boys...' She petered out.

They sat quietly.

'What will happen to their farm?'

They gazed over the paddocks separating the properties.

'I don't know.'

'Who would rebuild, knowing what took place?'

Georgie didn't answer. Couldn't.

'We'll keep looking after things until...' Vlatka held up her palms, which Georgie interpreted as, *Whatever comes.*

They both turned towards a male voice. Sven approached, talking to two red kelpies trotting alongside.

Georgie watched him fondle the ears of an all-red dog, then run his hand along the spine of the one with a white patch above its nose.

'Are they–'

'Yes, Bel's dogs,' Vlatka said. 'They couldn't stay over there alone.'

Good to know the dogs and livestock were being cared for.

'I turn my back, and you slack off, Vlatka.'

The dogs raced up ahead of Sven, who was chuckling. The smaller one bumped up against Georgie. She patted the kelpie's back, eyeing the weeping wound on her muzzle.

'Is her burn healing?'

'Yes, she will be fine.'

'Good.'

The three of them bounced around different topics for a short time, and the dogs grew bored and disappeared. When Sven touched on the gas explosions, Georgie jumped at the opening.

'Did you see the gas tanks the Murrays were using?'

They both nodded.

Vlatka said, 'We get ours from Beddoe in Daylesford.'

'Elgas,' Sven added. 'Didn't see any brand on theirs.'

'But they had like yellow-and-red lightning bolts around the top – cartoon-style?' Georgie checked.

'Yes.'

So had those at the Hansen and Getty farms.

She pushed. 'Have you seen them anywhere else?'

The couple exchanged an unspoken, *I haven't. Have you?*

'I would ask Klara and Lars.'

Sven agreed. 'Yes, Lars.'

She placed Klara. The other neighbour. She'd been alone when Georgie had dropped by previously. 'Lars?'

'Klara's son.'

CHAPTER FIFTY-FOUR

FRANKLIN WAVED, AS THE HUSBAND CURLED AN ARM around his wife and crushed her into his chest. They stood supporting each other while their two kids ran down the driveway after him, calling out, 'Bye!'

The kids were boys Ethan's age and a touch younger. Sheltered from his chat with their parents this morning, he suspected they had no idea what had happened to their family friends.

He still felt like a parenting novice with seventeen-odd years under his belt, so who was he to question the right or wrong way to handle this with kids of that age? But parents couldn't buffer what was said in the classroom or in the playground, so he hoped they'd break the news to their sons sooner than later.

His thoughts strayed to Kat. He knew he was letting her down. And Georgie. He just had so little to give them right now.

When this is over... Will it ever be over?

———

Her brain sluggish from poor sleep, little food, and too much coffee, Georgie took a moment to think. Sven had planted the seed that Klara and Lars must be her priority. After that, she'd visit Dave and the neighbour over the road from Goodlife Farm that she hadn't managed to connect with on Thursday.

At a glance to the sky and an unscientific decision that it wouldn't rain for a while, she left her Spider in Riley's Lane and took off on foot for some air and thinking time. Though Klara lived directly behind the Murrays, it seemed poor form to walk through the dead family's property. So she'd loop around. These weren't suburban blocks, but odd-shaped roads separating lots with acreage, making it at least a ten-minute walk.

Georgie circled an orange puddle that ran over most of the road, passed Sven on his tractor, and the driveway of his neighbours further along. Soon, the rhythm of her boots squelching on the gravel began to settle her. It also reminded her to tread cautiously with Klara and Lars. The way Sven had mentioned the son set off her antennae. He held reserves about the guy, whether based on instinct or fact. The guy might be a bit dodgy, or a lot. She'd have to skirt around to the tanks, not drawing attention to her interest. She couldn't refer to the Gettys, Hansens or McAlisters, or show photos, but she could inquire after strangers or atypical activity they'd noticed at the Murray farm.

Her phone buzzed in her pocket, on silent while she interviewed the neighbours.

Noting *Phil Keogh* on the screen, she answered fast.

'*Georgie! I thought it would be easier to talk to the questions in your email than write back.*' He hastened, '*Does now suit?*'

Not even halfway to Klara's place. 'Perfect, thanks.'

'If I miss anything you wanted to know, or you need me to go further, just say.'

'Sure.'

'First. You're on the right track about gas sinking, as you put it. It's heavier than air so it flows downwards and pools in low spaces in a room unless it has ventilation and air movement. Okay so far?'

'Yes.'

'Second. The off-egg smelly odorant to gas you commented on is mandatory. It's a lifesaver. Gas is odourless and colourless, so the additive is about the only way people can detect a leak.'

A raven announced itself with a rasping *kraa-kraa-kraaa-kraaaal*. It landed on the side of the road and watched her pass.

Georgie refocused. 'It stinks, so could someone still be clueless of a leak?'

'Good question. If it's a small enough leak, the smell might be negligible while the gas is still building up in an enclosed space. If they didn't notice the smell or a slight hiss or whistle from the gas line or appliance, perhaps because they were deeply asleep or ill, they might have no awareness of a problem.'

'Until it's too late?'

'Yes.' He redirected. 'But it's the by-product of gas that's the silent killer. When gas doesn't completely burn up—due to a faulty appliance, say—it emits carbon monoxide. The more of that in the air, the less oxygen available to breathe.'

They went quiet for a moment. Georgie's churning stomach made a heave. She held it down.

'There's still a chance they'd experience symptoms that'd warn them in time.'

She stopped walking. The raven hopped up and pinned her with its white eyes.

'Which are?'

'*Headache, dizziness, nausea, stinging eyes or throat, fatigue, breathing difficulties—*'

'Things that creep up on you. That you might mistake for coming down with a virus. That you might take paracetamol for, or think you can sleep off?'

'*Exactly.*' Phil's tone grew more sombre. '*And if inhaled in sufficient volume, carbon monoxide causes suffocation. Basically, drowning in gas.*'

'Drowning...'

'*Yes.*' He mumbled under his breath. '*Ah-hah, nearly missed your next question. It really is too broad, though. Too many variables as to cause. I'd suspect a heater. But it could be a stove, hot water service, any pipe connecting any of those appliances. It could be due to faulty repairs, wear and tear.*' After a beat he went on. '*Or deliberate. A toxic mixture of gas, as we touched on yesterday, is a possibility. And yes, there could also be issues with the cylinders outside and their fittings and fixtures.*'

The Murrays had died of CO poisoning before their house went up. The link between their suffocation and the explosion and fire confused Georgie.

She asked him to explain how both could happen.

'*Say a fault in the gas line or heater produced deadly CO emissions while the heater was in operation – perhaps linking back to the black-market trade in gas cylinders, bad fittings and mixes. After the damage was done there—*'

'After the victims had died of CO poisoning?' Georgie checked.

'*Yes. After that, a timer switched off the appliance, but gas continued to leak. With all the doors and windows shut, it had nowhere to go.*'

A long pause. Then, '*Speaking hypothetically.*'

She got the sense that Phil wasn't. But this was strictly off the record.

'And then?'

Gas is in demand as a combustion source, right? A small amount of gas can emit a large amount of heat. It's safe and effective, generally. But in the case of a leak, it is highly combustible. It spreads quickly and burns easily. If it goes up... think roman torch.'

'What are we talking for potential triggers?'

'Turning on a light would do it. Unplugging an appliance or using the phone might.'

Georgie's stomach heaved again. Her mind processed what Phil had told her.

'What would an influx of air do in that situation?'

'Fuel, heat by a mechanical impact, and oxygen...there's your fire triangle. The whole room would expand, windows would blow out, fire burn in.'

She put herself in Irvy's shoes. Heavy with a cold, misses the distinctive odour. Walks into the house bringing in a rush of air. Assuming the Murrays slept in the living room on Monday night, they probably had the lights off, curtains drawn. Reaches for the light switch and *boom.*

'Hang on.'

She held her mobile at a distance. Twisted into a crouch and vomited.

———

As Franklin hooked a leg over his bike, his phone rang. He didn't recognise the mobile number and let it go. The caller hung up and retried, same result. Immediately after that, his phone beeped with a new message.

Tempted to ignore it, yet ashamed at dealing with too many things that way, he considered all the dangling threads in this case and that it might be someone getting back to him with key information. He listened to the message.

'*Mr Franklin?*' It was a woman. Accented voice. Agitated. '*It is Samanta's mamma here.*'

There was a gap, and Franklin begged under his breath, 'No. Not Sam.'

The recording continued. '*Samanta, she's not doing so good. I thought you should know. They told us you've been sitting with her every night... You're a good man.*'

Another pause. Then her speed and stress escalated. '*The nurse... I must go.*'

Franklin lowered the handset. A scramble of internal talk started. He looked up at the lumpy grey clouds hanging low in the sky and fought to hold himself together. He jumped at a tug on his leather pants.

'Are you all right, mister?'

His gaze snapped down to the two little boys he'd just waved goodbye to. Their faces were pictures of fear.

'Yep.' He swallowed and tried to smile. 'Got a tummy ache.'

The smallest boy clutched his belly and moaned. The brothers dissolved into giggles.

If only all the worries pressing in on him could be so easily fixed.

———

Georgie panted, still hunkered down. She coughed. Had to finish this call. 'Sorry, Phil.'

'*Alright there?*'

'Overload. But thank you. I'll let you go.'

She tucked her phone in her pocket, staring at the pool of bile near her boots. Acid scorched from her stomach up her oesophagus, to her throat. Her eyes burned with tears from the effort of retching. Tears she didn't want because she had to stay strong.

'Shit.'

The raven gave a longer gurgling croak. Half a metre between them. Gawking, its hackles extended.

'It's fucking Russian roulette.'

Whatever money-making scheme the Gettys, Hansens, McAlisters and cronies had cooked up, if they were responsible for what went wrong with the Murrays gas tanks, they were killers. That went for whether it had caused either or both of the CO leak and the gas build-up inside the house, and even if Allan Hansen's death was accidental.

How many of those tanks are out there?

Which ones are dodgy?

How many could leak or blow any minute?

Worse. How many people were at imminent risk of ending up like the Murrays, Irvy, Sam, Denise?

'Fuck you, Franklin. I need to talk to you about this.'

Georgie retrieved her mobile and rang him, still too weak-legged to rise.

Voicemail.

'Ring me, please. It's urgent.'

She began an SMS to him, intending to give details. But a forest-green, long-wheelbase four-wheel drive pulled up.

'Georgie!'

Farmer Dave leaned out the window, his face creased with concern.

She made do with a match to her voice message, but typed, 'Really urgent!' and sent it to Franklin.

'You don't look at all well.' With emphasis on *at all*, he sounded very English.

She flushed, embarrassed.

He rummaged around in the cabin. 'They're clean – to

wipe your chin and your jacket.' He wielded two tissues, then climbed from the truck.

Dave tucked a hand under her elbow. 'Up she goes.' He hoisted her to her feet easily. She tried to brush off his help, but he insisted. 'Let's get you back to my place for a cup of tea and freshen up.'

He led her to the passenger side and virtually pushed her up and inside. 'Sorry, it's a true workhorse, not one of those fancier Land Rovers.'

It was basic, tough in design, high off the ground, and suited him exactly, reminding Georgie of often-eccentric farmers getting around their estates on British TV shows.

The need to see Klara and Lars was greater than ever. But she couldn't rock up stinking of sick with bits splashed on her. Georgie's butt banged in the seat as the Land Rover bumped through muddy ditches. She resigned to the enforced reversal of her plans.

CHAPTER FIFTY-FIVE

Franklin's phone vibrated with a missed call while he left a message for Mrs Tesorino. He then contacted the hospital, asking for ICU. He was put through, and it rang six times before a female answered. His mobile received an SMS alert as he asked for the latest on Sam. The nurse told him practically nothing—'*Critical, no visitors except her parents'*—harassed, needed elsewhere. She added, '*Sorry,*' and hung up.

Not even rank would get him in to see Sam this morning. He couldn't fix her as he had the little boys. That made it vital for him to make headway today. He pulled on his helmet and steeled himself.

Set to crank over the bike, he remembered the new message. He pulled off his lid and checked it. Georgie. Urgent. He'd be furious if she wanted to talk about feelings, but he returned the call.

She answered on the first ring.

'You said it was urgent?'

He heard her inhale sharply.

I'm an arsehole.

302

She said, *'It is. But I'm with someone. I'll call you back as soon as.'*

'All right.'

'Jack…'

'Yep. Ring me back.'

They disconnected.

He refitted his helmet and stared through the visor as he revved the bike to life. Three more friends for Alec and four for Bel on his list. Would they yield anything? Could he make better progress elsewhere? Following up with the neighbours or family or Yuki? Speaking to the fire captain, Rohan Crichton? Expanding his inquiries with a door-to-door through Korweingi?

All these things had been ticked off, but not by him. Something must've been missed.

———

After she'd cleaned up in the bathroom and used her finger to scrub her teeth with toothpaste from the shaving cabinet, Georgie found Dave in the kitchen. He offered tea. She ended up brewing him one and pouring a glass of water for herself, while he dug around in the cupboards.

'Brilliant.' Triumphantly, he angled a package for her to see. Four tarts with half white, half chocolate iced tops. 'Neenish tarts will settle that squeamish belly of yours.'

The thought of a sickly-sweet mouthful of mock cream, raspberry, chocolate and icing brought an alarming jolt in her stomach, but she smiled and placed the tarts on a plate for Dave.

They drank, he ate, they talked. Soon, he was on the subject of the Murrays, but her mind wandered to her mobile when it pulsed mutely in her pocket.

Was it Franklin? No, she was supposed to ring him back. Hilda Getty? Kat? A break in the case? News on Sam?

Dave let out a sigh ringing with pain. 'I miss them more than I can believe.'

She twinged with guilt and gave him her full attention.

'How could such a thing happen to such a nice young family?'

He dipped his chin towards the collar of his khaki overalls. His body shuddered with silent tears. Georgie patted his hand. He captured hers and held it in a crushing grip.

'Are your police friends close to making things clear to us?'

'The coroner will prepare a report. The police will let us know when they can.'

Dave would find no comfort in the gruesome details, and she couldn't tell him.

She added, 'I think their interest is largely in the gas cylinders at Goodlife.'

At his blank look, she pulled up the image that the police had publicised.

'Ah, yes. I remember seeing that.'

Georgie perked up, then registered the ambiguity. 'On the news?'

'No, no. Outside Alec's.'

She tamped down a bolt of excitement. 'Oh?'

'Chuffed, he was. He'd found a supplier with terrific prices and bought a few extra in case the price rose. He offered to get me some, but I didn't need any then. Can't afford to tie up dosh before it needs spending.'

'You didn't see the supplier or...' She left the question unfinished.

'No. He'd been and gone.'

She sighed inwardly.

Eyes wide, he said, 'The police dropped by to ask questions

– what I knew about Alec's tanks was one of them. I couldn't think then. It only came back when you brought it up now.'

'Dave, if that's all you know, it wouldn't have made a difference.'

His face contorted. She could relate.

———

Franklin tried another of Alec's mates. His knock went unanswered, and as he turned back to his bike ruing the wasted call, a bloke yelled, 'G'day, Franklin! Long time.'

He looked across to the side fence and clocked the bloke hanging over it. He'd coached two of his four boys so far in the Under 15s.

'Not that long. I've only taken this season off.'

The bloke grinned.

Franklin crossed the yard, and they chewed the fat briefly.

Abruptly, his mate said, 'You'll find him,' he pointed over Franklin's shoulder, 'down at the club. His middle daughter is right into her netball, and he goes along to watch her wherever she's playing. Stays for the footy when it's at home, and there's plenty happening down there today.' He snapped his fingers. 'You know him. Great bloke.' He held his hand a foot above his and Franklin's heads. 'Tall. Ginger.' He stroked his chin. 'Beard.'

'Not Frogman?'

'Yeah.'

Franklin considered with one stop at the combined netball and football club, he could chat to Alec's friend and loads of locals.

Smile shrivelling, his mate said, 'You here about, you know... Korweingi?'

Franklin nodded. 'Know anything that might help?'

'Nah. They were friends of theirs,' he nudged towards next door, 'and they were around a bit, but I didn't really know them, you know? Just to say g'day to. They're not taking it well.' He repeated the nudge move. 'They were tight, you know, good mates. The league's wearing black armbands this weekend to mark respect. Doesn't bring them back, but, does it?'

CHAPTER FIFTY-SIX

GEORGIE RETRIEVED HER PHONE MESSAGE AS SHE SET OFF from Dave's home to the neighbour she was yet to meet.

'*Georgie-girl! Guess who?*' Bron went on. '*I take it you and Franklin aren't coming to ours tonight?*'

Georgie slapped her forehead. She'd forgotten to reply to the invitation.

Her best friend's tone swapped from light reproach to concern. '*Seriously, I get it. But call me when you can. I can be your sounding board, I'm good at that.*'

She rang off, and Georgie mentally promised to buzz Bron later. She immediately dialled Franklin, got his recording.

'Sorry, me again. Speak soon as.'

She could see them phone tagging all day.

She hung up as she reached the neighbour's front door. After ringing the bell, knocking and giving them a few minutes to answer, Georgie called out. But nobody responded. Not home. Probably a timewaster anyway – they were out whenever she stopped by.

She hurried to the Spider, running through her priorities.

Klara and Lars first, and then she'd tackle the Cam and Nance angle. Hopefully, Franklin would be in touch in the meanwhile. Two heads and working twice as fast would be a huge relief.

————

Franklin's mobile rang while he chatted with a bunch of parents hanging around the netball court. He sneaked a glance, anxious not to miss an update on Sam from Mrs Tesorino.

Georgie.

Wincing, he slipped the phone back in his pocket. A familiar figure caught his eye.

'I need to rush off.' He apologised, pressing his business card in each hand in case they recalled something of note.

'Rohan! Hold up.'

The Daylesford fire captain halted and gazed around, tracking the voice. He waved to Franklin and waited while he jogged over.

They shook hands.

Rohan fixed him with a shrewd look. 'Still looking for answers?'

'Yep. We're making progress but not quickly enough.'

'Fatals are always shocking.' Rohan's lips compressed. 'But when it's kids, nothing we do is enough, is it? Can't bring them back. Can't give them back their future.'

'True.'

A whistle blew on the netball court. Cheers erupted. Both seemed to mock Franklin's efforts. Nearly noon, and he had bugger all to show for the morning.

Rohan watched him intently.

Legwork was the greatest game of lotto. Odds weren't great.

Could get lucky early, after a long time, or never. Still had to try.

'Any scuttlebutt your end?' Franklin rolled a hand, acknowledging the broad scope of his question.

'Doubt I know much more than you do, mate. But if it's any help, we've had other incidents involving gas tanks recently.'

Franklin stilled.

'Nobody hurt, not seriously. But they blew. Just like the Murrays'.'

'Know why?'

The firie replied, 'Recycled tanks that shouldn't be in circulation with worn or wrong fittings.'

Franklin sensed more. 'And?'

'A concoction of gas that should never be used inside a structure.'

———

Georgie struck it lucky and unlucky. Klara and Lars were both at home. They were having coffee in the narrow sunroom annexed to the back of a cottage of around the same era as Dave's. Together. In jeans, jumpers and socks, not dressed to go outside.

Her hope to quiz them separately dashed, she accepted a coffee as an icebreaker.

Klara motioned her to the spare armchair. It was awkward. The chair angled to the window for the view, and from her side vision Georgie saw Lars staring at her. She had to perch sideways to connect with the mother and son. The guy looked away. He slugged back his coffee and balanced the empty mug on the arm of his chair.

Georgie cradled her hot drink and began with neutral subjects, taking the opportunity to assess the two. Both had square-shaped heads topped with wheat-coloured hair, and wide-set eyes that they used expressively. Klara engaged with the conversation, talking easily. Occasionally, the trace of a European accent popped through. Lars glowered at his socked toes mostly. When he spoke, it was short, direct, in a strong ocker accent.

He surprised her by bringing up the Murrays. 'So, he did them all in, or what?'

Georgie's back stiffened. 'I heard it was an accident.'

He scoffed.

'You know otherwise?'

Lars folded his arms with his thumbs pointed up.

The cocky prick didn't realise he'd helped her cut to the chase.

She said, 'I heard there was a problem with the gas cylinders...and maybe an appliance inside.' The police had put the gas tanks into the public arena, which made it topical. She had to be careful not to reveal too much though.

Silent buzzing in her pocket distracted her. A sudden string of calls and message alerts on her phone. She mentally eye-rolled, thinking one would be Franklin. The rest?

Lars lifted his brows slightly.

'Who do you use for your gas?'

Klara swayed her mug towards the kitchen they'd walked through earlier. 'We've got a combustion wood stove for heating and cooking, solar and mains power for the rest, and a backup diesel genny when all else fails. Never needed gas here.'

Lars went back to staring.

Georgie adjusted her thoughts. 'Did you notice anything out of the ordinary at the Murray place recently?'

He sniggered. 'Can't see much of their place through that.' He jerked his head.

She followed his movement and registered the dense

cluster of gumtrees along the horizon that went as far as she could see. This wasn't going well.

Klara shrunk into her chair and pinned her attention on her son. Yielding to him.

'Yeah, true,' Georgie admitted, and his look said, *Dumb bitch*. She dipped her chin as if embarrassed. Long strands of her hair hid her scrutiny.

'Have you seen any people hawking gas, or odd activity, or newcomers around lately?'

His jaw knuckled, then Lars went deadpan. Except that his gaze narrowed. 'Nup.'

CHAPTER FIFTY-SEVEN

FRANKLIN CHEWED OVER WHAT HE'D LEARNED FROM THE netball parents, Rohan Crichton, and a couple of friends of the Murrays.

He added in Bruner's comments at the briefing at Bacchus. *More to this situation... Connects with other inquiries.*

The arson bloke had revealed these included fatalities. But he hadn't elaborated beyond alluding to their cases ranging over the state, not just this district, explaining Rohan's limited knowledge. Franklin reflected on why it didn't ring any bells with him either. Decided that it'd been kept out of the media spotlight – otherwise they'd have been all over it, re-hashing it after the Murray event.

Arson were holding their cards to their chests, even with the crew assisting them. Clearly, they were on the trail of something big. How close were they? If they shared, time could be spent on sound lines of inquiry, instead of chasing shadows.

He racked his brain for what else Bruner had said. It seemed long ago, not yesterday morning.

The family had died of CO poisoning well prior to

Wednesday and had been sleeping in the living room. The specialists had reservations about the blasts and fire being deliberate – but they were treating it as a possibility that the family's deaths were.

Everything Franklin had learned so far pointed the opposite way. The Murrays had had their troubles, but they were fighters that pulled together in adversity. He needed to know if their tanks had the bad mix of gas that Rohan had seen before and/or if they were illegally salvaged.

If so, as far as he was concerned, whoever had supplied them were murderers fivefold at Korweingi alone. His stomach dived, remembering Sam. Her deterioration.

He tried Mrs Tesorino. Reaching message bank, cursed.

'You look like shit, John.'

Franklin whirled around to the very familiar voice, ready to quip, *You look like shit too, boss.*

His mouth opened and shut. Lunny had never looked better. Bright and sparky in his navy tracksuit and white runners, whistle hanging around his neck. Pink glow to his cheeks and white hair fluffed up in the breeze.

His old friend smacked Franklin's back and gave him a double-handed shake.

'Here to see the boys play?' Lunny rubbed his hands. 'They're doing good under my watch.'

Franklin nearly replied, *Don't get too comfortable. I'm taking back the reins next season.* But everything had changed. Lunny wasn't his boss. Knight was keeping him in limbo. Next season, he might be back in uniform as officer-in-charge at Daylesford, or filling in until they found a body the brass deemed more suitable. His mind strayed towards what he'd given up with CIU, but he cut off the thought. Regardless, would he be able to recommit to coaching the boys?

He settled for answering the question. 'No, I'm working.'

Lunny retreated by a step, a tell-tale that he didn't want to know. 'Maeve's been asking about you. She's worried that you're making a mistake taking my position.'

'Tell her I'm fine.'

'Are you?' Lunny hiked his white brows.

'Yep.'

'I'm done with the force. If I stayed, it'd be the death of me in the end.'

Lunny studied his face. His sage expression made Franklin uneasy. It was like he'd seen through his veneer of holding it together. His lack of sleep or food. The darkness that'd taken grip.

'Take care, John. I'd hate for you to go down that path. The job's not everything.'

———

Back in the Spider, Georgie cranked the engine and heating, then listened to her messages.

Josh, returning her call from yesterday morning with, *'I'm cool. Speak to you later.'* His tone said he wasn't, but to back off for now, please.

Second came Sheridan Judd, excited by the stats that Georgie and Kat had put together. Then warning, *'Your story had better live up to your hype to get that front page.'*

Livia came third, doing her mum thing, always there for her but never crowding.

Lastly, Franklin.

Damn, we did miss each other again.

Hard to hear him for background noise, she pressed the phone to her ear. She made out: *'I'm doing interviews. Try you after...'* and the melancholy slip of his voice with, *'Sorry.'*

She understood that this case was personal, but hated what

it was doing to him. She took off, not sure where to go or what to do, yet in a rush.

———

Franklin watched Lunny's back until he disappeared among a cluster of parents. A movement caught his attention, and he saw a redheaded teenager in a red, white and blue netball dress waving, then drop her hand, dejected. She joined a huddle with her teammates. Noting the black armbands each girl wore, his throat stung.

Not many redheads here this morning. On the off-chance, he charted the direction she'd been focused on, running his gaze up the embankment between the netball court and footy oval to a big bloke grasping the galvanised rail with both hands.

He climbed the grassed mound.

'Why?' Frogman kicked a fence pole. 'Can't be... It's not right.'

A moment too late, Franklin realised he was sobbing between the words. The bloke twisted, must've heard him approach. Recognition flashed in his swollen and red eyes before Frogman lifted a forearm to scrub his jacket sleeve over his wet cheeks. He sniffed up snot.

'What do you want, Franklin?'

He laid a hand on the bloke's shoulder. 'Answers. For you. For everyone.'

Alec's mate gave a sharp nod.

———

Georgie noticed the time and flicked on the radio. With luck, she'd be back in range for reception.

'It's twelve o'clock, and this is the news with Sally Newton.'

315

Just made it.

'First, the latest on the fatal gas blasts at Korweinguboora on Wednesday.'

She raised the volume.

'At a press conference this morning, senior police revealed that the young mother, father, child and baby all died of carbon monoxide poisoning prior to the incident that claimed the life of a Daylesford policeman and critically injured two others.'

'Shit.' She should have tuned into Power FM. If he was reading the news today, Cam McAlister's delivery of the bulletin might've been telling.

The newsreader transitioned to the next story while Georgie drove on. She was closing in on the Western Freeway and the point where she'd have to decide which way to travel.

'If I were the Gettys, Hansens and McAlisters, what would I take from that update?'

It depended greatly on how culpable they were.

Unsafe tanks hooked up on the outside of the Murray house had contributed to the destruction of the property and increased the danger to the emergency crews on site.

But if that was all, the gang might breathe easy.

On the flipside, everything rested on them if the faulty tanks or bad gas mix that they'd supplied actually caused a malfunction inside the house that had killed the family by suffocation, and subsequently, a build-up of gas that had led to the explosion that blew Irvy away. Or a variation of that.

Then, they'd be running scared.

'Hilda Getty.' Georgie breathed the name. 'She's the weak link.'

CHAPTER FIFTY-EIGHT

HALF THE DAY HAD SPED BY. STILL BUGGER ALL TO SHOW for it. Franklin weighed hanging around longer at the footy ground, visiting more of Alec and Bel's friends, or Stephen Murray in Ballan.

The peal of his phone interrupted.

'Mr Franklin?'

He recognised the speaker. 'Mrs Tesorino. How's Sam?'

'She's not so good.'

His dread grew in her pause.

'But doctors are making her steadier.'

He breathed out. 'Thank goodness.'

'Sì, yes.'

A thick drop wet his nose. Franklin swiped at it, and glancing up was surprised by the heavy, granite-grey clouds gathered above. Thunder rumbled, swelling to a loud growl. The earth trembled under his boots.

'She has an infection, so her lungs aren't so good. But we keep believing. She's a strong girl, our Samanta, sì?'

'Has she woken up again? Said anything?'

'No.' Some of her optimism drained. 'Not since when you are with her.'

Franklin shook off his gloom. It crept back while they spoke for another minute, rain splatting the ground around him. It poured when Mrs Tesorino rang off.

He loped for cover under the commentary box as the rain turned to sleet. Ice slashed at the tin roof and scoreboard a few metres to the side, drowning out the ring of his phone. But he felt the vibration.

No idea who was calling, but he'd given out his number to over twenty people this morning, so he had to answer.

'Mr Franklin? It's Yuki, from the kindergarten.'

Glad he'd answered.

'Mr Howell said to contact one of you if I thought of something.'

'Go on.'

'Well, when the thunder and rain began just now, I remembered something Bel told me. I am not sure it is relevant.'

Her nervousness bothered him. She might hang up any moment.

'Anything could be a help.'

'Really?'

'Absolutely.'

'When we confirmed our coffee date on Monday, Bel said that Ethan was more stressed than usual.' Her voice quivered, particularly when she said Bel's name.

'Did she say why?'

'The ceiling in his bedroom had a leak, not extensive, but enough for Alec to shift his bed and put a bucket there temporarily. But... Ethan always had a difficult time coping with things when they weren't as they should be. Do you understand?'

'Yes.'

'The rain and thunder just now reminded me that Bel also

said the bad weather in the past week or so had made Ethan very agitated. He'd said the wind and rain was too loud, too angry. He'd insisted they all sleep in one room to keep safe.'

Hence, the mattresses and bassinet in the front room. Franklin enjoyed a glimmer of satisfaction as another part of the case slotted home. Short-lived.

He needed more, but Yuki was grieving her friends and struck him as a sensitive young woman. No way he could blatantly bring up the gas situation.

'Besides leaks in the roof, did Bel mention anything else around the place that needed maintenance?'

A bit broad, he rebuked himself.

She didn't answer, and he thought the call had dropped out. 'Yuki, are you still there?'

'Yes.'

She was crying, and he felt like an arsehole for pushing her, but had to know. 'Did she?'

'No, I don't think so.'

The thunderstorm quit almost as abruptly as it'd started. Georgie pulled the Spider onto the gravel verge of the Ballan road. Stupid to go off half-cocked. She parked, sloshed in a puddle as she stepped from the car. Bracing air winded her.

She drifted towards the fence and looked over green rolling paddocks and the trees and hills beyond, in what she thought was the direction of Korweinguboora. Lowing drew her gaze to a herd of cows and their calves. Ears pricked and watching her, openly curious. Many were black, a few black and white or black and tan. A solid red-coated cow trotted up. Several of its mates trailed.

'Hi there.'

The cow listened, fixing her with glossy chocolate eyes fringed by long red lashes.

'What should I do?'

But Georgie already knew her next move. She retrieved her phone and dialled. It rang and clicked to voicemail. She remembered her instructions and hung up without leaving a message.

She'd have to wait and hope that Hilda Getty found her conscience and an opportunity to call back.

Meanwhile?

The cow came up to the fence. Georgie checked for electric wire and tentatively reached over. The hair on its forehead wasn't as soft and silky as it appeared – not as coarse as some dog coats either. The cow nudged her hand gently as if saying, *More*. Others crowded in behind the red cow, and she retreated to the Spider, worried they'd break through the wire.

On the way, she decided that the cows were a sign that she was on the right track. Half an hour. If Hilda didn't ring by then, she'd proceed to Miners Rest.

CHAPTER FIFTY-NINE

AFTER THIRTY-SIX MINUTES, GEORGIE DECIDED THAT IT was pointless waiting any longer. On her way to Miners Rest, she tuned into Power FM. The on-air talent was a female with a voice perfect for popular radio – husky and matey, confident in her chit-chat about local happenings or when listeners rang in and introducing songs. No mention of Cam McAlister. That increased the risk she'd run into him at Miners Rest.

Would he recognise her? She'd blended into the crowd of journos at Korweinguboora, like many, recording on her mobile phone. Just another female, albeit one he'd been close enough to breathe on.

But what if the Hansens or Gettys had flagged her interest? She'd given them her *Champagne Musings* card. They could track her down on the website, or on LinkedIn or Twitter. Even the bulk of her freelance stories bore her headshot.

She pushed down her misgivings and concentrated on the road. Traffic on the freeway was light and mostly moved in the same direction, outbound. Her route was simple, stay on the highway as it skirted Ballarat to the north, then follow the

Maryborough and Clunes road until her turnoff. Still thirty or so kilometres of straightforward driving.

Ample time for thoughts to thud in her mind.

Fear couldn't deter her. But a blunder could be disastrous.

What if they'd already gone into cover-up mode because she'd tipped her hand too early? If they shut down and then sprung up somewhere, sometime down the track, potentially hurting more people, she'd hate herself.

She sympathised with farmers doing it tough. She intended to write the best story she could to feature their plight. While it was a shitty thing to do, it didn't take a giant leap to understand the temptation to steal stock or farm gear. But what drove this lot to these extremes?

The Spider's tyres drummed on the bitumen. The radio presenter chattered, then cut to a song.

Georgie considered the Hansen boys. Her impression of them – resentful bullies, the world owed them types. Why shouldn't they take a shot at easy money? Not their fault if there was collateral damage, was it? That's how they'd think.

Their father remained cloudy, but she suspected Allan had been the driving force of his family and his sons were apples from the same tree. And it was easy to imagine his wife Jeanette having no say among those three men.

Bob Getty struck her as a wily man. Driven by the game as much as profit. One word for Hilda – subservient. She went along with whatever Bob wanted and tried to overlook her qualms.

No doubt. Hilda was Georgie's best shot. But the woman hadn't gotten in touch. Nor had Franklin rung back, which for once wasn't necessarily a bad thing – it gave her the chance to scout the McAlister place at Miners Rest and pursue Hilda to develop a bigger picture.

———

Franklin's decision to leave the sports precinct was quashed by a fresh influx of kids and adults for the footy. He ignored the tribe from Buninyong. Coming from a small place south of Ballarat, they weren't likely to provide a strong lead. He homed in on familiar faces and those donned in the Doggies colours.

While he canvassed the locals, his fury that the arson crew was keeping them in the dark bubbled. Between chats, he drew out his phone, tempted to call Bruner or Darma and tear shreds off them. They were wasting time and resources working blind. He'd demand they reveal what they knew so he could focus his efforts effectively.

Dumb idea, Franklin.

Ram Bruner would take great joy in shutting him down. Darma might've shared the diary and a few other restricted aspects of the case with Howell and Franklin, but he'd draw the line at this. Very clearly, the arson Ds were slowly, carefully, getting their ducks in a row, but this needed sorting now. He'd be no better off for drawing attention to himself. In fact, it'd be the opposite. They'd suspend him.

No badge. No official capacity.

Wouldn't stop him, but it'd be a pain in the arse.

———

'She's not out of the woods just yet.'

Is he talking about me?

Sam's eyes were weighed down, but brightness seeped through the skin of her lids – she thought so anyway. If only she could break through this fuzzy sensation and force them open, she could be sure, and then she'd ask the man why he sounded worried.

One of her hands was lifted and turned, not as if in giving comfort. Like being inspected.

A female said, 'We'll take the staples out of her hands tomorrow.'

Staples? What the?

It didn't make sense.

And she didn't get these people talking in soft, serious voices. Or the clatters, beeps and steady in-and-out whooshing.

She went to nothingness. Then her insides dived with horror. Reliving flashes of the Murray farm. Irvy there, then gone. Her uniform on fire. Her hair. Denise screeching. Her frightful injuries.

A male said, 'She's still unresponsive? Nothing further since last night?'

No, no, I'm not!

Sam tried to speak. Nothing. She strained to move her head, hand, foot, anything to show she was with them. They went on talking around her, about her, but not to her.

The woman who'd taken her hand said, 'It's the body's way. Saving energy for healing.'

Her tone was calm. It held a conviction that Sam would make it.

'Aren't you finished your shift, Marianne?'

A small groan, then, 'Double.' She chuckled.

'I'm not happy.' Yet another male. 'She's not where I would like her to be by this stage.'

Sam didn't like this man. He was too negative. She wanted to scream or cry. Her eyes burned with unshed tears. They hurt so much. Like they were on fire.

CHAPTER SIXTY

HE ANSWERED HIS PHONE. 'JOHN FRANKLIN.'

Silence. Then, *'Detective Franklin?'*

'Yes?'

'Stephen Murray. Alec's father.' The words held a tremble.

'Thanks for calling.' Franklin added his condolences.

This gap stretched longer. Was he crying?

'Sorry for the delay. I couldn't...'

'It's fine...it's a difficult time for you,' Franklin reassured him.

The bloke's shrill moan made the hairs on the back of Franklin's neck stand. He blanked on what to say. Stood planted on the slushy grass copping odd glances, listening to shouts, grunts and trills of whistles. Then applause and the clamber of appreciative honks from car horns. A goal, apparently for the Doggies.

Stephen Murray's keening receded. Still heart-wrenching.

'What can I do to help, Mr Murray?'

'Stephen.'

Breathing came down the line.

'*The radio said they were poisoned. Dead before the fire. I don't understand.*'

Why hadn't the family been informed before the public? They shouldn't have learned it this way. *Shit.* He needed to speak to Lucy Blakenish in Mornington asap. The biggest problem here was that he didn't have the full picture himself.

He was groping for a response, when Stephen said, '*Can you please come and see me? I'm at home.*'

———

Nightmare stuff trying to recce Miners Rest. The McAlister farm sat outside of the township among large properties. Its neighbours ran a few cattle and sheep, a dotting of horses, but the majority of paddocks nearby were under crop or lying fallow. Few trees. Only a gentle swell to the land. Little to hide her conspicuous convertible.

After her initial rapid pass through the area and by the farm, Georgie's head swam, and her stomach groaned. She needed sustenance, though food held little appeal. And she also needed to space out her sweeps past the McAlister place to avoid being spotted.

Miners Rest was too small for anonymity, and too close for a sufficient interlude, so she drove into Ballarat and found a bakery. A plain grainy roll and a strong coffee filled her, and with it, the side trip extended to sixty minutes.

She chanced another drive-by. Travelled as slowly as she dared.

From her online searches, she knew the McAlisters had a neighbour to the left and were otherwise ringed by minor roads. She approached from the neighbour's side, taking in a dwelling and outbuildings set well back, accessible by a long gravel driveway. The land was carved into regular rectangular paddocks at different stages of rotation: growth, cultivation and crop stubble.

A border of gumtrees appeared to define the boundary – where the McAlister property started. All grazing land to the right of the scrappy hedge with several overflowing dams and limb-dropping gums, judging by the pile of broken branches heaped at their base. She made out cattle in a far paddock, and sheep and alpaca sharing the first front one. The farmhouse sat twenty or thirty metres from the road. As she reached the cross-intersection that formed the other side boundary, Georgie noted two large tin sheds and a sign for 'C & A McAlister, fencing & slashing'.

She went left, and slowed more as she contemplated the sheds. She crawled a little further along and swivelled for a final look. Clear view of the back of the house. Two gas cylinders hooked up under a window. She braked, grabbing her mobile. Zoomed its camera in and snapped several photos showing the pattern around the tank collars.

———

Behind the security door stood an older version of Alec Murray. He beckoned to Franklin with a hand missing all its digits. His gait listed as his left side moved in a stiff-legged hitch and roll. No wonder he'd had to give up his farm.

They went through to a small living room, the mirror image to the neighbour's unit. They took seats, and Stephen sandwiched both hands between his thighs as if hiding the deformity.

Lucy Blakenish had battled to restrain her anger when Franklin had phoned her before riding over to Ballan. Stephen's bewildered hurt was tougher to take. The air temperature dived by several degrees in the period that

Franklin was with him. Light faded to a miserable grey. It cut him up to leave the grieving father without all the answers. He gave him as many as he could. Promised the rest soon.

As he readied to leave, Stephen's face scrunched.

'Alec told me he'd got a great deal on the gas.'

Franklin knew better but still prickled with hope. 'Did he?'

'Yeah, I told him, if it sounds too good to be true...' Stephen pressed his lips together. 'Never imagined this though.'

Franklin gave him a few minutes. Then asked, 'Did he talk specifics?'

Stephen looked up, squinting. He breathed out through his nostrils, annoyed with himself. Then he brightened.

'If I remember rightly, he said something about the gas coming from out this way.' He waggled his head. 'Gordon, I think?'

Inching forward on the couch, Franklin said, 'Did Alec mention any names?'

He watched the older bloke dredge up a memory.

Their gaze met. Stephen said, 'Only thing I can think of is Rufous. But I might've mixed it up with a story about a dog?'

———

Georgie had hit a wall. She couldn't hang around Miners Rest any longer. And until she heard back from Hilda Getty and Franklin, confronting the McAlisters or going to Gordon would be a huge mistake.

Exhaustion pulled on every bone and muscle in her body, while she contended with regular waves of nausea. Though the thought came with a twinge of guilt, and even though it was only mid-afternoon, she craved crawling under the doona, snuggling up to Franklin's pillow and disappearing into oblivion for a little while.

As she drove back to Daylesford, cold air whistled through every crevice it could find, chilling her inside the Spider, despite the heater on full blast. The small car rocked with strong gusts that pitched the canopy of trees hanging over the road into a frenzy.

It matched her thinking. All the way, she probed what she knew and what she didn't, and tamped down her fears that she'd messed this all up.

Could she have concocted a fantasy?

She reviewed it and came back to the worst scenario. Her theories were bang-on, but she'd let the gang get away with it.

———

Gordon boasted an eight-hour cop shop. Chances were 3.30pm on a Saturday wouldn't fit into those hours. Meanwhile, the larger, 16-hour station here in Ballan, all of approximately a minute's ride from Stephen Murray's unit, was a better starter. Might still be a flop, but worth a try.

Thoughts rolled in Franklin's mind as he covered the short distance.

Rufous, maybe from Gordon, could be a dog – needle and haystack stuff. Was it even worth the question?

Do you have anything else to go on?

Nope.

He pulled up outside the station and drew off his helmet, eyeing the marked four-wheel drive parked outside. Maybe this'd be his lucky day.

The front office was empty and silent when he entered. Two minutes later, the door off to the side opened and a female in uniform came through backwards, pushing it with her arse. She turned to him, holding a mug in one hand and a folder in the other.

'Hello.' She smiled.

Franklin had never seen such a pointy chin and wide mouth on a woman. Both formed triangles, the effect highlighted by her dark hair strained back in a bun. Impossible not to smile back.

'Do I know you?' Now she laughed. Loud, genuine. 'Sorry, that sounded like a pathetic pick-up line.' She plonked down the mug and folder, and cocked her head at him. 'But you do look familiar.'

He introduced himself and brought out his police badge. 'I'm attached to Bacchus CIU.'

'Ah, seen you about then. You can put away your Freddy.' She flapped a hand, then offered it for a shake. 'Viv.'

She rubbed the widows peak of black hair high on her forehead. 'What brings you here?'

'We're working a number of jobs,' sufficiently vague, 'and a name came up, a bloke from Gordon. It may or may not turn out to be anything.'

'What've you got?'

'Rufous. Ring a bell? Anyone go by that name from Gordon who's come to your attention recently?'

'It's clearly a nickname.' Viv rubbed her hairline again. 'It's not much. Nothing else you can share?'

He blew out a breath. Tell her more, or not?

Viv watched the conflict on his face. 'Don't worry. I know how it goes. Not at this stage.'

She leaned on the front counter. He waited.

'Well.'

He perked up.

'An Allan Hansen drowned in Gordon back on the eighth.'

Franklin recalled it. Didn't see the connection.

'For all intents and purposes, an accidental closed-head injury. But any sudden death must be looked at, right?'

He nodded.

'Homicide came in, coroner took a look. Some of your CI mob, plus me and my offsider, we all helped with interviewing family, friends, neighbours. All hunky-dory.'

He wished she'd stop beating around the bush.

'One of them referred to the deceased as Rufous.'

Franklin puffed out his cheeks.

Viv studied his reaction. 'You didn't expect that?'

'Nope.'

'Like the coincidence much?'

'I'm not a fan of coincidence,' he admitted. 'How did he drown?'

'In his mate's dam.' She gave it thought. 'The mate was Robert Getty, Bob. We all thought an accident.'

They shared a long look.

'How'd that come about? Not exactly swimming weather.'

Viv laughed, a tougher edge to it this time. 'Apparently, the two men were fixing the tractor in Getty's shed, and Hansen went to get his toolbox from his ute because they needed a bigger shifter. It appeared that he'd tripped, falling forward to knock his head on a tree.' She palmed the spot. 'Then he went nose-first into the drink.'

'Getty didn't hear anything?'

'He had no clue, he said. When he'd realised Hansen had been gone too long, he went looking for him. Found him floating face-down.'

Her eyes probed his. 'Still not able to share more?'

CHAPTER SIXTY-ONE

GEORGIE PULLED UP THE DRIVEWAY. SMACKED BY THE prospect of rattling around alone in the empty house, her mood flat-lined. She ought to go to Kendra's. She'd phoned, but needed to rally around and offer love and help in person. It would be heartbreaking though.

'Tomorrow. I'll go tomorrow.'

She went to the back door ready to slip her key in, but found it unlocked. Her spirits rose – someone was home. And even better, when she came into the kitchen, Kat wrapped her in a bearhug.

'I'm such a derp.' Kat smiled widely. She dragged her jacket off the back of a chair and shrugged into it, then dove into a pocket.

'I don't need this.' She wiggled a paper bag. 'Won't for ages. Maybe you will before me.'

She handed over a light package as her happiness flickered. 'How's Sam?'

Georgie gave a palm-lift. 'I'm sorry. I don't know anything beyond what your dad told us this morning.'

That feels like days ago, not eight or nine hours.

Kat sagged.

'She woke up earlier today – that's a good thing, yes?'

'Yeah.' She perked up. 'Of course.' She went to the door, throwing behind her, 'I'm going to Lisa's.'

As soon as she'd gone, Georgie peeked into the bag. A three-pack early detection pregnancy test. Kat had a lucky save.

Keep it or toss it? Best keep it, in case of another scare. Everything crossed, that didn't happen though.

She went into Franklin's bedroom and stashed the box in one of the drawers he'd cleared for her, after wrapping it in his old shirt that she used as a PJ top. That done, she sat on the bed drawing off her boots, and resisted crawling under the covers.

There had to be something useful she could do.

She checked her phone. Even turned it off and back on. Nothing wrong with it. A new email popped up, trivial matter. No unread texts. No fresh voicemail.

That meant zero from Hilda Getty and Franklin. Still.

Georgie's sigh echoed in the empty house.

'C'mon, think.'

It was cold, and she could warm herself three ways by cutting a load of wood, bringing it inside and lighting a fire.

That killed nearly twenty minutes, but it hadn't brought a brainwave.

So by rote, she went to her computer and updated her notes. Then she googled the morning's presser.

Just three paragraphs long, it virtually duplicated the radio piece.

She broadened the search parameter to capture the most recent articles on Korweinguboora. Read the third headline and murmured, 'Oh, shit. No.'

POLICE REVEAL FAMILY OF FOUR DEAD BEFORE BLASTS IN POTENTIAL MURDER-SUICIDE

The police investigation into a fatal explosion and house fire at Korweinguboora on Wednesday morning has taken a horror twist today with new information indicating that it may be another domestic violence statistic for Victoria.

At a press conference this morning, District Inspector Knight said, 'It is believed that the family died during the night of Monday 11 June.'

This puts their deaths at twenty-four to thirty-six hours prior to the first reports of blasts and a fire at the property.

The district inspector went on to say, 'The coroner's initial findings are that carbon monoxide poisoning was the cause of death for all four family members.'

Following today's press conference, distraught members of the local community arranged an emergency memorial for Alec and Belinda Murray and their sons Ethan and Oliver at the Korweinguboora Recreation Reserve.

Despite the short notice, the gathering brought together over one hundred residents, but it ended at 2.55pm due to a

**heated clash between several people in
attendance.**

Georgie was gobsmacked. In the interval after she'd left Klara
and Lars and before she'd driven by the rec reserve on her
return from Miners Rest—around three-and-a-half hours—the
local community had come together, scrapped and dispersed...
and this article had been written and published online.
  Keen to know what had caused the clash, she read on.

**On one side were those who deemed the
incident a dreadful accident, while their
opposers took the view one or both parents
executed a grisly murder—suicide or double
suicide.
A neighbour, Mr Lars Agaard, who lived
next to the family for approximately ten
years said, 'It's terrible to think about and
goes to show how easily someone can snap.'
Although he never witnessed any
altercations at the adjacent property, Mr
Agaard added, 'But everyone knew they
were having dramas.'**

Georgie paused again, picturing Lars with his arms folded,
cocky. But saying this on record? 'What a prick.' She continued
reading.

Another neighbour, Mr David Perry, disputes Mr Agaard's claims stating, 'Alec and Bel were a nice young couple, and they would never harm their baby and little boy.'

Past president of the now-disbanded Korweinguboora Football Club, Mr Clancy said, 'It saddens me that we're a community divided by opinions about what happened to this family, but we are all deeply traumatised.'

Mr Clancy demanded that police divulge the full details.

This incident also claimed the life of a senior officer at Daylesford Police and critically injured his colleague and a member of the public.

Police were unable to comment when contacted this afternoon but continue to urge the public to come forward with any relevant information.

As she finished the article, Georgie's hand covered her mouth. Processing what she'd read with her eyes shut, she saw Dave, distressed, sickened by the slurs against his friends made by people like Lars. Highly likely, crying. Mortified afterwards.

She guessed Vlatka and Sven would've been at the memorial too, though they weren't quoted in the article. She'd only seen their gentle, generous natures, but easily imagined them vigorously defending their neighbours. They might've even got physical.

And other friends and kin of the Murrays? They'd be shattered that people thought Alec or Bel had deliberately killed their family, by these accusations out there for the world to dissect, enjoy, debate.

Her mind skipped to Geoff's story on the Azaria Chamberlain case, comparing the situations. As far as the Murrays were concerned, even if the verdict of accident came in, and whether the rest of the truth ever came out, some people would always believe the worst of them. They'd forever say, *He got away with it*, or, *They were in it together*.

Because some people liked to think the worst of others.

Because of trash like this that went to air, or online, or in print.

Because some journos and editors lacked ethics.

She hated her job in that moment.

CHAPTER SIXTY-TWO

Franklin nursed a coffee in the café on the ground floor. He chewed over his chat with Viv, regretting the timing of the incoming phone call that had made his decision for him. She had given every impression that she was a good one and might've offered further valuable local insight. But when Mrs Tesorino had asked him to come, he'd left for the hospital immediately.

'Mr Franklin.'

The now very familiar voice of Sam's mum cut into his thoughts. She and her husband circled the table to sit opposite him. Both groaned as they flopped into their seats as if exhausted.

They looked shattered too. Had an ashen tinge to their skin not completely due to the harsh-white fluoro lighting that wouldn't be doing him any favours either.

'Mr and Mrs Tesorino.' Franklin shook hands with the couple.

She scoffed, 'Too much,' insisting they use given names.

He nodded. 'Can I get you a coffee or tea?'

'No thanks, John,' Paola said.

'How is she?'

Dino floated a downwards-facing hand side-to-side while lifting his brows. Completely ambiguous to Franklin.

'Samanta looks a bit better to us, doesn't she?'

Dino agreed with his wife. '*Sì*.'

'The doctors are a little,' as he'd noticed on Thursday it came out *leettle*, 'bit worried though.' Paola twisted her gold wedding band. 'Her lungs aren't so good and...' She hesitated, glancing at Dino.

He crossed himself. 'And her heart is weak.'

Franklin jolted, kneeing the bottom of the table. His coffee spilt. A passer-by, her face marked with the same tightrope-walker signs as the Tesorinos, rushed over to mop it up with paper napkins.

'Thanks.'

They shared a sympathetic look before she wandered off.

Paola tried a brave smile. 'Samanta'll be okay.' Her accent had thickened, and it sounded like *hokay*. 'But Dino say to me, "Tell John Franklin to come sit with her."'

Franklin's pulse raced.

Is she that bad?

She must've sensed his stress. She grasped his hand. Hers was tiny, like her daughter's, and only half-covered his. 'Samanta'll come good. But she looks up to you, you know this? She wants to be as good as you in the police.'

He choked out, 'She's already better than me.'

She swayed her head. 'It would mean a lot, you coming to see her.'

Dino added, 'It will make her better.'

Whether they spoke with confidence, bravery or longing, Franklin locked onto what they'd said. He couldn't get the right words out, trusting his eyes told them he, too, hoped his visits would help Sam.

Paola nodded. 'We go home now to see my mamma and the rest of our *famiglia* for a little while. The nurses know to let you in to see Samanta.'

The three of them rose and walked to the exit together. As they parted, Paola brushed aside his handshake and raised her arms. He leaned down to hug the small woman. When they pulled apart, Dino did the same, thumping Franklin's back several times.

CHAPTER SIXTY-THREE

THE FLAMES MESMERISED GEORGIE, LIQUEFYING HER
muscles as she watched them lick the logs and listened to the
hungry rumble, crackle and pops from the fireplace. The rock
riff of her phone broke her trance.

She turned in the direction of the music, noting that the fire
and the illuminated mobile were the only sources of light in the
room. Coming to her feet and padding over to the dining table,
her gaze flicked to the window. Pitch-black outside. Must be
closer to 6.00pm than 5.00. She'd lost over an hour, reeling
from the latest article, troubled by the angst mushrooming from
the Korweinguboora tragedy.

Georgie's sluggishness vanished when she spotted Hilda
Getty's name on the mobile screen. She slapped around on the
tabletop, couldn't find what she needed. She switched on the
lamp.

There!

She snatched the digital recorder and aligned it by her
mobile, activating it with nervous hands.

Your last chance with Hilda...and she's the weak link. Get it right, Harvey.

She answered the phone with just, 'Hello?' holding back in case it wasn't Hilda. Clicking speakerphone on, she leaned over, steadying herself on the table with a hand either side of the devices.

'Miss Harvey? Georgie?'

The voice came through clearly for the recording.

'Yes, Hilda. Thanks for–'

'You need to stop calling me. I can't help you.'

'No, Hilda. I know you're scared. I understand.'

'No, you don't!' the woman shrilled. *'Bob, he's not someone you cross. I made a mistake saying anything.'*

'But I don't think you did. You want the truth to come out, don't you?'

'Listen to me! If I told you, even part of it, I'd end up like Allan.'

Georgie pressed her palms down harder. 'Dead, you mean?'

'Yes!'

'Bob would kill you too and make it look like an accident?'

'Yes. He's clever. You need to leave this alone, or you'll be next.' Hilda's panic flared. *'Look, don't call me again.'* She added flatly, *'It's too late anyway.'*

She hung up.

Georgie tried Franklin. Reached his voicemail.

She replayed Hilda's cryptic message over and over, dissecting every word and nuance in the woman's tone.

It's too late.

Did Hilda mean *it's too late* for her – she feared for her own life?

Or *it's too late*, Bob Getty was already coming after Georgie?

Even, *it's too late*, the gang had covered their tracks?

Or all of the above?

CHAPTER SIXTY-FOUR

SAM HURT EVERYWHERE, LIKE BURNING GRAVEL RASH inside and outside her skin, yet the pain was buffered.

Maybe this is shock?

So calm, despite the hazy pain. Her mind wandered. Was this how it felt to be dying?

She thought she heard Franklin, but reckoned it was a dream or hallucination. She went with it.

'Oh, mate.'

He had a nice deep voice. He never struggled to project it, not like her. She let the sound lull her.

Maybe I'm not dreaming, but I'm already dead? How would I know? Does somebody tell you? How do you know not to carry on with everyday life anymore?

Sam drifted to thinking of Nonna. She was fascinated by death and hung on stories about people being brought back to life, wanting to know what happened between physically dying and coming back. Sam guessed the reason Nonna found it interesting was that it was the second-best thing to knowing what it was like to go to Heaven.

Nonna would like to know that Sam could see an aura of brightness...even though she thought she had her eyes closed. And that Franklin was telling her he'd had a break today, digging up information on a Rufous, or was it an Allan?

None of this makes sense.

But it wouldn't if she were dead, would it?

DAY FIVE

SUNDAY 17 JUNE

CHAPTER SIXTY-FIVE

At 10.00PM, GEORGIE HAD LEFT A MESSAGE FOR Franklin. Pissed off. *Where are you? Can't you at least phone? I've got crucial information.*

She'd tried him again at midnight. Hung up on his voicemail. Nerves thrumming. Thinking, *Has something happened to you, Jack?* Dwelling on his behaviour in the past days, she made a leap to, *Have you done something to yourself?*

Her next attempt came at 1.30am and bombed, annoying and worrying her in equal measure.

Bone tired, she willed her mind to switch off. Denied just a short while of nothingness when her imagination filled with visions. Of the horror at the Murray farm. Sam's burns. Franklin's reaction. The bodies in the burnt ruins.

By 2.30am, Georgie was battling anger, fear and a desperate need for action. She considered calling Marty Howell or Tim Lunny – hell, anyone who might know where Franklin was, or have had contact with him. She went back to Howell and the sarge. Maybe she shouldn't wait for Franklin but use one or both as a sounding board?

He'd hate it though. She procrastinated, putting off a decision until dawn. Not altogether optimistic he'd beat the deadline.

Attempting sleep once more, her internal slideshow jerked around with scenes at Gordon. Faces: the Gettys, the Hansens. The photo on Jeanette's fridge. Gas tanks. The stock truck. Bob Getty telling her, *Nobody could've seen it coming. An accident.*

That morphed into Hilda's visible fear during Georgie's visit, and the fright in her tone yesterday. The ambiguous meaning of the woman's words echoed in Georgie's mind until she raced to the toilet and vomited.

She'd never puked so much in her life.

'There's no way? No, course not. But...'

She pulled up the calendar on her phone, counted the days, the weeks. Repeated it, with the same result. She collected an object from the bedroom, then went into the ensuite. Stared at the little wand with a thousand thoughts crowding in for ages before she peed on it...and for much longer afterwards.

'Now?'

It brought back memories of the baby that would've been a toddler if it had lived. Her and AJ's child. She'd been so mixed up back then. Not ready by any means, or in the right place. Honestly not sure she'd ever cut it as a mum.

'And now? With Jack's baby?'

How did she feel?

Georgie retched and swivelled to the toilet. The bile was a noxious black colour. Her insides burned like they were coated in paint stripper. She went on until she gagged with nothing coming up and her head threatened to burst. Then collapsed on the floor, panting.

Nine weeks. Too soon to be safe.

But Baby Two was already one week luckier than Baby One. She cupped her breasts. Swollen and tender, like last time. No morning sickness with her first. Apparently, that didn't mean anything, it had nothing to do with the miscarriage, but being so sick made this one tangible, more real. Then her rational side reminded her that Korweinguboora could be a good part responsible for her nausea.

After she'd recovered, Georgie stashed the test, cleaned up, washed her face, brushed her teeth. She gazed at her reflection in the mirror over the basin. Wasn't able to read herself.

She heard a sound and her stomach flipped. She watched her expression stiffen as anger fizzed. Strode into the kitchen as he came in.

———

Georgie glared at him across the room. Franklin was tempted to walk out, but stabs of guilt in his chest told him to man up and cop whatever she had to say.

Neither moved. The expanse of the kitchen seemed to swell to twice its size.

'What the fuck, Franklin?'

He winced, not exactly clear about what he'd done but hazarding, 'I should've called you.'

'You're kidding. I've been trying to talk to you since yesterday. No, *actually*, I've been trying to talk to you for days.'

'Not just you – I haven't been on top of calls, messages, since Wednesday.' His mind spun back to their telephone tag yesterday, then the hospital. 'I went to see Sam again. Her parents asked me to come.'

She flinched, thrown by that.

The fridge kicked to life, filling the sudden silence.

Georgie said tentatively, 'Is she improving?'

'I don't know.' His honesty startled him, and he regretted not filtering when she pressed a hand to her mouth. 'I'm sure she can hear and that she's close to coming out of it, but she didn't move or anything.'

He held back what Sam's parents had said, rejecting the doctors' concerns. She'd show them they'd underestimated her heart.

Again, the fridge hum dominated.

Georgie shook her head sadly. Then she turned steely.

'Come in here,' she beckoned.

He followed her to the dining room and saw the table covered in papers.

She waved towards the clutter. 'What we can do for Sam is right here.'

He gave her a puzzled look.

'Sit down, let me talk.' She pulled out two chairs. 'I have to start at Wednesday morning...'

CHAPTER SIXTY-SIX

GEORGIE CLICKED STOP ON THE DIGITAL RECORDER AND heaved out a deep breath in the silence after Hilda's last words. Without many digressions, she'd told all.

Franklin had looked shell-shocked since the moment she'd mentioned Allan Hansen and her suspicions about his sudden death. But he'd flashed with distinctive emotions as he strove to keep quiet through her narration.

Shame with, 'If I'd picked up my fucking phone...'

Alarm when he echoed her worry, 'Might already be too late.'

Naked fear when he said, 'You put a target on your back!'

She dimly heard his comments on Hilda's admission that her husband had murdered Allan, while the clock ticked, marking time passing, stoking her anxiety. Her mind turned to her glaring omission. She prickled with guilt, but now definitely wasn't appropriate.

Franklin plucked up a photo of the gas cylinders she'd snapped at the McAlister farm and aligned it with one from the Gettys. They weren't good quality, but it was enough to confirm the design and type matched. He dragged a pic of the suspect sheep next to the others.

'You've put all this together on your own?'

Georgie bristled at his surprise, then shoved her resentment aside when she saw the admiration in his look.

'If we'd worked together...' He rubbed a hand over his face. 'Wasted days. My bloody fault.'

He met her gaze with bloodshot eyes. 'I was getting there though.'

Now it was her turn to shut up and listen, as he detailed what he'd uncovered, plugging some of her gaps.

Who'd have thought they could circle so closely and yet be so far apart?

She reached for him, but he shied away. 'What do we do now?'

Franklin rose, stretching. His spine clicked.

'I need to get the crew together at Bacchus, and the arson Ds too, bring everyone up to speed and–'

She bit. '*You* need to?'

He frowned at her. 'Yeah–'

'Uh-uh. I'm in this too.'

'You're not a cop.'

'Stating the obvious, Franklin. But I won't be cut out. I can fill in the things you don't have first-hand knowledge of.'

'Nope.'

'I'm coming.' She stood. 'It's smart anyway. While I'm driving, you can make your calls. And you'll be able to bring back your Commodore afterwards.'

Her mind strayed to, *After what exactly?*

Franklin's face locked down.

She played her best card. 'Either we go in together, or I'll tail you in the Spider, which will make you look like a real dick in front of the crew. Your choice.'

CHAPTER SIXTY-SEVEN

FRANKLIN PACED THE WIDTH OF THE ROOM, CHAFING AT the wasted time.

'You do realise it's Sunday, Franklin?' a smartarse asked. He had the heavy, bleary-eyed look of a big night and not enough sleep.

'It can't wait.'

Someone sniggered across the room. He didn't know what about specifically but flushed anyway.

At least half the crew thought he was a moron. Take a ticket as to why. Seeing him crack it and walk out the other day. Pulling an urgent briefing this morning. Having his girlfriend tag along.

He scanned the room as a local D dawdled through the door. She yawned widely and groaned. A round of fake applause followed, probably from the same smartarse.

He stifled his own yawn, and did a series of blinks in an effort to clear the sandy, gritty sensation in his eyes.

'Hello, Franklin.'

He recognised the voice. 'Viv.'

She was smiling.

He took in her uniform. 'You on shift at Ballan?'

'No. It's my day off...and I wouldn't want to be anywhere but here.'

'Good to have you.'

She wiggled her fingers and crossed the room to join a cluster of blokes.

Franklin ticked off a mental checklist. Viv, two Bacchus uniforms, and all but one of their detectives were here. He flicked to his watch. Nearly 7.00am. How long would it take for Bruner and Darma to arrive from Melbourne? He couldn't start without the arson Ds, but the extra delay rankled. It could mean the difference between nailing the Getty mob and letting them slip through their fingers.

Marty Howell came into the room carrying a carton with three coffee beakers. He went over to Georgie and gave her one. They talked for a while, shooting glances in his direction. Then Howell joined him, proffering the spare coffee.

'Thanks.' Franklin took a gulp. It took a little edge off but intensified his cravings for a smoke.

'You've got this, mate.' Howell gave him a grim nod.

His partner's support settled a few more nerves.

Franklin had updated Howell on the road from Daylesford. Howell had rattled off a few astute questions, then offered to contact Darma or Bruner, while Franklin called their boss. He'd started with a grovel for his stuff-up at the briefing on Thursday, but Si Waldo had told him, *Park that, it's old news. Just get on with it.* Full credit to him, once he was in the picture, Waldo seemed as impatient as Franklin to get the crew into the office. And from what Howell had said, he'd had a similar response from Darma, though Bruner's attitude was as yet unknown.

He glanced at the wall clock and swore under his breath.

7.15am. Every minute they wasted here was an extra minute to the side of the Getty mob.

He blamed himself. At least two days had been shot by him piss-arsing around, not talking to Georgie. Then anger displaced his guilt. If the arson crew had shared everything instead of holding back, Georgie wouldn't have had to push things with the Gettys, putting her on their radar. And they'd have closed the Murray case, along with Hansen's murder, and, very likely, a string of stock thefts.

Nothing would surprise him less than finding the missing sheep from Greendale and pigs from Colbrook were at the hands of Getty's lot.

———

Georgie hung on the periphery and drained her coffee. She eavesdropped on conversations. Many were complaints about a ruined sleep-in or rest day. Others compared theories on why they'd been ordered in.

She skimmed over Franklin's colleagues, to Marty Howell who was organising papers on a desk at the front, and then to Franklin himself. She read his body language as he balled his empty paper cup and lobbed it into the bin. Getting more keyed up by the minute. Doing a lot of time checking and muttering to himself.

She couldn't go to him. The team would razz them both, and Franklin might lose it completely. She willed him to get a grip.

Hang in there, Jack. This thing is nearly over.

———

The last locals straggled in together, but Franklin's attention left the room. To the voices of Ram Bruner and Pandu Darmawan.

He didn't think, just strode into the hallway where they were talking. He went straight up to Bruner and grabbed a fistful of his shirt front and tie, twisting them.

'You're a cockhead.'

'Whoa-there.' Bruner's eyes flashed, but he laughed. A mocking note.

Franklin fought the urge to knock the bald bloke's lights out.

'Let him go.' Darma thrust an arm between him and Bruner's barrel chest. The tall, lanky bloke wedged them apart and dragged Franklin a metre from the pack.

Still grappling with Franklin, Darma stared intently through his glasses. 'Whatever you think he's done, you're wrong.'

Franklin rotated his wrist towards Darma's thumb and pulled to retract his hand. Darma clamped on harder and hauled him in until his mouth and Franklin's ear were an inch apart.

'I have every respect for you as a copper, and every sympathy for what you're going through. It must be hell.'

Franklin quit fighting him.

'But you need to back down. Ram can come across as a bruiser, but he's good at what he does.'

'We lost time not working together.'

'What are you talking about?' Darma sounded genuine.

'You blokes left us in the dark. If you'd shared what you had on the other cases, we'd have known who to target instead of running around with our heads up our arses.'

'We didn't—'

Franklin cut in. 'All we needed was names.'

Darma released him and splayed his hands. 'We weren't sitting on names. We've been hoping for a break like this. Meanwhile, we've put what we could in place to be ready for it.'

The air went out of Franklin. He looked at Darma, earnest behind his lenses. Then he turned to Bruner. The big bloke had smoothed his shirt and tie, and he stood yacking with his team and scratching at his beard with an eye on Franklin.

———

Drawn by Franklin's voice, Georgie entered the hallway as a gangly guy wearing glasses pried Franklin off another with a trimmed beard and polished bald crown. Both dressed in suits. She recognised them from the Murray farm as detectives from the arson and explosives squad. She dredged their names from her memory.

Howell arrived at her elbow. They watched Darma talk down Franklin, and Georgie let out a relieved sigh. Howell gave a low whistle.

'He's a loose cannon here. What's he been like at home.'

Georgie snorted softly. 'Overall? Not there. Literally.'

They shared a look, then faced back to Franklin as he approached Bruner, offering his hand. The two men shook, and the arson detective led them into the briefing room. Things were kicking off.

Turning to trail the group, Howell said, 'He'll be fine once this is all over.'

She lifted her chin in agreement. 'Yeah, of course.'

CHAPTER SIXTY-EIGHT

With all the background covered, Si Waldo directed them to, 'Take five.' He moved in front of the large projector screen casting a shadow over Georgie's photos. Added, 'Use this opportunity to clear your schedules for the rest of today.'

While the CIU boss conferred with Bruner and Darma, bodies stretched and shifted en masse. Most members made calls or plugged messages on their phones. Many rushed off as if desperate for the toilet or a strong coffee. Noise erupted all around.

Franklin stood back, observing. Several workmates nodded his way or came over to thump him on the back. He thanked them, but uneasily. Happier when they crowded around Georgie, shook her hand and showed her the respect she deserved.

As the minutes went beyond five, the volume hiked. Those around him buzzed with optimism, excitement. He tried to pin down what he felt. Dread. But mainly bloody-minded determination to bring down the mob responsible for the carnage at Korweingi.

Waldo clapped twice and awaited silence.

'This is a complex and potentially high-risk operation. It's going to take time to coordinate the warrants and resources we'll need to pull off three simultaneous raids.'

Whoops. Chat broke out, drifting to an end when the CI boss held up a palm.

Grim, he said, 'Time, of course, is something we're short on. We strongly believe that the suspects are readying themselves for cover-up or getaway. We cannot let that happen.'

Waldo ceded to Ram Bruner.

Bruner said, 'The safety of every member—every one of us out there today—is of paramount importance.'

Murmurs hummed around the room.

'Our objective is to apprehend these suspects,' he pointed to the screen, which now displayed seven headshots, 'without fatalities or injuries.'

Franklin glared at the images of the Gettys, the McAlisters, the two Hansen blokes and their stepmother. His attention returned to the arson D when he went on.

'There will be additional parties attached to this ring, so we need these suspects,' Bruner jabbed towards the photos again, 'in top shape for interrogation. Everything must be executed safely and by the book. Our goal is to bring down the entire ring once and for all, and to ensure we get the right result in court.'

He stopped. Then checked, 'Understood?'

Muttered agreeance around him. Franklin nodded. Nobody wanted it more than him.

'Darma?' Ram Bruner swivelled to his offsider, who took the lead.

'Our best outcome is what Ram just outlined – a swift, safe

and successful exercise. But we need to consider what we might encounter out there. Number one, firearms. Several registered weapons at each of our three target addresses, at least.'

He let that sink in.

'With the history of what happened at Korweinguboora last week, and other recent incidents, number two is accidents involving volatile gas cylinders.'

Heads bobbed near Franklin.

'Three,' Darma's tone sharpened, 'intentional triggers – setups to make those tanks blow.'

The female D next to Franklin muttered, 'Fuck.'

'And four.' Darma spread his hands wide.

Franklin took it to mean any number of mantraps.

CHAPTER SIXTY-NINE

GEORGIE INCHED CLOSER TO RAM BRUNER AND PANDU Darmawan, pretending to read an email on her phone while throwing glances at the arson detectives.

Bruner appeared agitated, fidgeting with the tail of his tie. 'How long for the warrants?'

Darma held up a finger, listening to a message on his mobile. He disconnected. 'Another hour?'

Georgie detected a small question mark on the timing.

'It's been four already – 12.30 now.' Bruner puffed his cheeks. 'And CIRT?'

She pricked up at the mention of the critical incident response team. Fast-response specialists in high-risk jobs and kitted out with a greater range of equipment than general duties police, though not as high up the ranks as the hardcore men and women in black belonging to the special operations group: the soggies.

'One CIRT van's on the way now with five on board. We can get started with them when the warrants are in, or wait for the soggies?'

'Can we?' Bruner scuffed the floor with his toe. 'Should we?'

They struck Georgie as rhetorical questions, but Darma answered. 'I think we have sufficient people-power. No mean feat taking into account the short notice and being a Sunday.'

He went through it; she guessed not for the first time.

'We'll have three crews of five led by Si Waldo, you and me. We've got three coming from our office,' Darma paused, 'and they should be here any minute. We'll share them, along with CIRT, Waldo's 2IC, Howell and Franklin.'

'Yep,' Bruner said. 'Hang on.'

He answered his phone, stepping aside.

Georgie's mind tacked from mild curiosity about the incoming call to surprise that Bruner would include Franklin in the raids after their confrontation this morning.

Over the next minute, she swung to quietly freaking out. She'd half-expected Franklin to be named, knowing it was a matter of *Try stop him.* She fancied that Darma and Waldo had driven the decision, recognising how invested he was and that they wouldn't be on the right trail without him. Or her, but she was a civilian and no way in hell would they let her go.

But in the context of CIRT and SOG, Franklin's front-line involvement worried her. This was dangerous stuff. Her eyes found him across the room, talking to Howell. He'd barely slept since Wednesday. Was he an asset or liability out there?

Bruner returned and Darma continued.

'We'll top up with whoever Waldo recommends of the CI team or uniforms. Backup crews of a further four each for cordon and containment. SOG and BRU on call if we need them, and that'll leave a couple back here.'

When Darma stopped, Georgie belatedly figured out that BRU was the bomb response unit.

Scary shit.

Bruner made a noise that crossed a growl and sigh.

She couldn't interpret it and risked a glance, catching him nod. She looked at Darma as his lips curled slightly – possibly relieved to have appeased his boss and happy that they were organised.

She hoped so. But it could be another hour or longer until the crews hit the ground. Such a long spell since her conversation with Hilda Getty. What if the gang had already cleared out?

Bruner voiced her concern. 'And meanwhile?'

Before Darma could answer, Si Waldo entered, followed by several of his crew. They carried pizza cartons, trays of coffees and bottles of water.

Waldo yelled, 'Lunch is up!'

When the answering clamber subsided, Darma said, 'We've got unmarked cars monitoring things.'

Georgie held her breath. Let it out after, 'Looks good so far.'

———

Franklin munched on a slice of chicken pizza, then swallowed it down with a mouthful of coffee. Across the room, he saw Georgie gag and bin her lunch.

His wasn't going down much better, but he kept eating because he had to. Darma had tapped him on the shoulder and told him he was on his crew hitting the Hansen property. The detective had warned him to fuel up because today's work could be completed in the next few hours, or stretch into the afternoon.

Franklin took a second pizza wedge as three suits joined Bruner and Darma. He placed them; they'd been with the arson Ds at the Murray place. He watched them chat and joke, and then turn serious. While he ate, he tossed over his chances of talking his way onto Bruner's team. Considering he'd gotten physical with the bloke this morning, not great. But he'd try. Getty was their man, and he wanted to be there when they brought him down.

He washed down the pizza and nabbed another piece. Now that he'd started, the empty pit of his stomach needed more.

His mind sprinted on. The rest of the personnel would show up shortly. They'd have a final briefing, splitting into the various raid and backup crews.

Then as soon as the warrants arrived, it was on.

He located Georgie again and tried to catch her attention. Now might be the only chance for them to grab a minute.

———

A female officer passed in front of Georgie, towering over her five-foot-seven. She wore a different uniform to the general duties police, and Georgie couldn't help staring at her, impressed by her heavily kitted out vest, belt and pouches around her thighs. Had to be part of CIRT. Likewise for the guy in the same gear who flanked her.

They talked as they crossed the floor. Georgie took in the deep timbre of their voices. That their heads slowly rotated around the room, surveying the personnel, the photos still on the projector screen, the detritus of the meal break. More than the silver at his temples and prominent creases around his eyes marked the guy as the unit boss for her. He had a presence, an authority to his posture and gait that the cops in the room reacted to with gapes, hellos or by parting to make way.

Three CIRT guys walked in the wake of the female and male. Georgie contemplated if that denoted the hierarchy of the group, just as the newcomers homed in on Bruner and Darma.

Conversations tailed off as everyone fastened on the huddle of plain-clothes detectives and uniformed specialists filling the front section of the room. Soon the hush of expectation strayed into a low buzz.

With a fleeting touch to the small of her back, Franklin came alongside. They shared a look. Georgie's mind crowded with the things she wanted to say, but in the proximity of so many cops, self-censored. Franklin seemed to do the same.

She mouthed, *Be safe*, and he nodded, as Waldo said, 'Listen up, team!'

CHAPTER SEVENTY

At 1.12pm, Darma announced, 'We're on.'

A cheer went up, and cops disgorged from the room. A uniformed officer walking past at the wrong moment had to squash up to the wall rather than fight the flow of bodies travelling to the car park.

Two minutes later, only three people remained in the briefing room – Georgie, a young female detective, and a stout general duties cop with an alarming pink tinge to his skin and soft wheeze. They perched in a row on tables opposite the projector screen and whiteboards.

'Get either of you a coffee?' the male offered.

'I'm good.'

'No, thanks.'

Georgie pressed her palms together, trying not to think. An impossibility.

Hearing the detective sigh, she asked, 'Hanging in there?'

'Yeah. I just *really* wanted to be involved. Hands-on, you know?'

'Me too,' Georgie admitted. 'Though I knew there was no chance.'

The male cop patted his large belly and chuckled. 'I think we know why I'm not out there.'

The female laughed with him. Then she said, 'And I *know* it's just seniority working against me. Last one in, least experience, and we need a D here for contingencies. All that, still.' She sighed deeper. 'However long it takes, it's going to feel five times as long for us, isn't it?'

'Yep.'

Georgie's eyes travelled over diagrams on the whiteboard that resembled game-day strategies for an AFL football match. She reminded herself, *They know what they're doing.*

She moved closer to the screen filled with the seven suspects' faces, resting her gaze on Bob Getty. When Franklin had convinced Bruner to add him to his team, he had stood in exactly this spot. His small smile hadn't softened the flinty stare fixed on Getty.

She reran her parting words to Franklin, *Call me when you've got him,* and his tight nod.

CHAPTER SEVENTY-ONE

To the timeline, Bruner and Darma's teams had taken positions in proximity to their target addresses. In the thirty minutes since, Franklin had periodically rasped a hand over his stubble, anxious to get going. But neither of the Gordon crews could move until Waldo's lot reached Miners Rest.

Eventually, yet right on schedule, Waldo called in. *'Whisky, in place.'*

Bruner acknowledged, then checked with the other two team leaders, 'Everyone set to go?'

Darma came through clearly on the radio. *'Delta, ready.'*

'Whisky, ready,' Waldo shot back.

Franklin's body crackled with tension.

'Backup crews set?'

The various cars gave their callsigns and an affirmative.

'We ready?'

Bruner lowered a direct look at each of his members on the benches.

He lingered on Franklin, who said a resolute, 'Yes.'

'Yes, Sarge,' the arson D on their crew replied.

The driver and the second CIRT officer sitting beside Franklin pulled down their goggles. The driver tweaked the chin grip on her helmet and said, 'We're good.'

Bruner spoke into the radio. 'Bravo, ready. On my count. Three, two, one!'

Their driver floored the CIRT van, covering the final span to the entrance of the Getty property, through the open gate and up the gravel driveway. Franklin glanced rearward once as a backup vehicle parked near the entrance. Buoyed by the knowledge that Viv and three other good cops were in the car.

They came to a stop midway between the farmhouse and a cluster of sheds. Franklin noted that the passenger side of their van angled away from the windows overlooking the drive and the front doors of the largest shed. It gained them protection and an unimpeded exit. He took in a curl of smoke from the chimney on the house. A giveaway that someone was in there... or a ruse?

They piled out through the sliding door on the passenger side. The female CIRT officer trotted towards the farmhouse, and Franklin and the arson D shadowed in single file. The CIRT's offsider and Bruner moved swiftly around the back.

Franklin's breath puffed white clouds into the cold air as he brooded over the flaws in their plan.

The unmarked cars keeping each place under observation were certain all parties were home. That made him suss. Were they expected? Were they going to be ambushed? Or would they surprise the suspects in the act of clearing every trace of their crimes?

He moved fast but landed his booted feet as lightly as he could, still thinking. They couldn't afford to divide their crew over every structure – too vulnerable, safety in numbers, the area too vast. They had to check each in turn. The snag being the suspects could be in different locations, or wait until they were on them and then split up.

Rain suddenly pelted down, knocking on the ballistic vest snug over his back. Bruner was optimistic that the bleak weather would benefit them. He'd said, *It'll keep them inside.*

Franklin jogged on, with a bare few metres left to travel, shooting a glance up at the sky. Bruner might be right. Still, that didn't mean in the house. Could be in the main shed. Or any of the others. He was very conscious of the pistol in his left hand. Glad for it.

A dog barked. Went silent. One or both Gettys were about then. But Franklin couldn't be certain where the sound had come from. House or shed? No idea what breed either. Could be a problem.

They covered the last stretch of open ground and came to crouch at the front wall of the house, near the entrance.

The CIRT officer whispered through her radio with an arm held high. Dropped it. Yelled, 'POLICE! COME OUT! SHOW ME YOUR HANDS!'

Franklin shouted, 'POLICE! COME OUT!'

They heard Bruner yell at the rear of the house.

The dog barked once. So quickly, still couldn't pinpoint where.

The CIRT did a countdown, then another hand signal. 'WE'RE COMING IN!'

Bruner's voice echoed her in the distance.

The CIRT tried the handle. She stepped aside for the arson D to ram it. Timber splintered, the lock gave, and the door flew open. It banged against the wall.

Weapons raised they moved in, now calling, 'POLICE! DON'T MOVE!'

They continued to yell the warning as they began a systematic sweep, and then, 'Clear!' when each room was eliminated. They converged in the hallway as Bruner exited the next room along. He pointed behind him. Franklin dodged around the shoulder obstructing his view to see into a bedroom. A blind billowed out from an open sash window.

Bruner said, 'They've gone that way.'

'Both?'

He admitted, 'Unknown.'

Franklin slipped up to the window, held back the blind and eyeballed the scene. He spotted a churned patch in the garden bed directly below. Could be where one or two people had landed. No discernible trail after that. He scanned a broader area, drawn to the nearest outbuilding. Just caught sight of the side door swinging shut.

———

Georgie paced the briefing room at Bacchus Marsh. She tried to ignore her heavy bladder, loath to duck out for even a minute. The twitch of paper as the male cop turned the pages of the local newspaper made her jittery.

Wall clock, watch; they both said the same thing. The crews had left the checkpoint at 2.10pm. Add five minutes to drive in. Then what? How long did it take to complete a search, make arrests? She pictured the three farms. It all depended on where the suspects were and what contest they put up.

A call came through on the radio. Georgie stilled, nailing onto the cop as he perked up, listening too. Then he shook his head, though she already knew it wasn't the news they wanted.

She flicked to the time, aware it was pointless. Couldn't help thinking, *How long before they report back?*

———

Bruner and the two CIRT officers were running the show here, but Franklin chafed for action. At least one, and maybe both, of their suspects were in the shed. They should have gone straight in. Why hold back?

Because it feels too easy.

He hated the thought. But the sitting duck idea had settled as a band around his chest since this morning, as much as he'd tried to shake it off – not that the Getty mob were the sitting ducks either.

We are.

Why would they sit here waiting for the cops?

He could see why Bruner and CIRT didn't want to jump.

———

The female detective glanced up from her computer. She gave Georgie a sympathetic smile.

'It could take a while.' She studied Georgie's face. 'This must be awful for you.'

Tempting to deny it or shrug it off. Easier to do nothing.

'That's why I don't date guys in the service. First thing I find out is what they do. They have to be in normal jobs.'

Wasn't that a tad hypocritical?

The detective misinterpreted Georgie's silence. 'It's a good post here, but we still deal with some terrible things.' Troubled, she said, 'I need to disconnect after knock-off, don't want to talk about it mostly, and I don't want to be worrying about my guy either, whether he'll make it home safely.'

Georgie winced.

'Oh, sorry. I wasn't thinking.'

'No harm.'

The male cop cleared his throat loudly and rattled the

newspaper, and the young detective went back to her computer with red dots on her cheeks.

The radio crackled.

Georgie's hands bunched together.

Let this be it.

She sensed the detective come beside her.

'*The McAlisters are in custody. Repeat, Cameron McAlister and Nancy McAlister are both in custody, and we'll have them back at Bacchus Marsh post-haste.*' A moment passed. Then Waldo added, '*All Whisky team safe.*'

The three of them cheered, clapped.

Georgie hurried to the list of their suspects on the whiteboard and gave Nance and Cam thick red ticks with a grand flourish. 'Two down!' Thrilled, yet her inner voice kept saying, *C'mon, c'mon. Call in.*

CHAPTER SEVENTY-TWO

After Waldo's update and some back thumping, they turned serious.

'We're ready then?' the female CIRT asked.

Nods all round.

She said, 'Move out.'

They exited the house faster than they'd gone in. The two CIRTs sprinted to the access door that Franklin had seen pulled shut. The rest moved to the cover of their van.

When the CIRTs were near the tin wall, crouched to provide smaller targets and ready to spring, Bruner called through the loudspeaker, *'This is the police! Come out!'*

The dog erupted into frenzied barking from within the shed. This time nobody stopped it.

Franklin shifted his pistol in his hand for a better grip. His eyes were skewered into the front access door. The two arson Ds were covering the main door and the perimeter of the shed between them. Moderate rain obscured their view, particularly annoying because Franklin had to continually wipe dots from his safety glasses. His mind did a strange sidestep, comparing the grey duco of the van to the horizon.

'Robert Getty! Hilda Getty! This is Ram Bruner from the police. For your own safety, I want you to come out the front with your hands raised.'

Franklin's gaze went to the CIRTs. The leader signed to her 2IC. He covered her with his longarmed rifle as she went to bang on the side wall.

A male yelled, 'Get off my property.'

The CIRTs repositioned. Franklin refocused on his door.

Bruner said through the speaker, 'Bob, we can't do that. We need you and Hilda to come out. Show your hands.'

'GET THE FUCK OFF MY LAND!'

At a stir from Bruner, Franklin saw the bloke knead the back of his neck.

He didn't like Getty's tone either. His arse started to cramp from being in the same pose. He changed it up, clocking the arson D taking a double hold on his pistol. Franklin wondered if he'd used it before – discharged it at a suspect. He had, and would do it again if necessary. He flexed his fingers around his own weapon.

Bruner's arm moved, bringing up the mic. He clicked it on, then off, pressed it to his forehead thinking, then held it to his mouth.

'Hilda, come out the front. You don't need to stay in there.'

Franklin stared forward, willing the woman to appear. They believed she was the lowest part of the mob's food chain and best off the scene as soon as possible.

'Hilda–'

A boom cut off Bruner. Holes peppered high in the front wall of the shed, above the main door.

'Shotgun!'

'GET DOWN!'

They ducked for cover.

Getty yelled, 'And you dickheads at my side door have five seconds to move to the van!'

The CIRTs scrambled back, guns outstretched.

Bruner's offsider said, 'He can see all of us.'

'Cameras.' Franklin scoped the walls, noting a couple of blemishes that could be hidden cameras. 'Shoot them out?'

'No.' Bruner did a cut motion with his hand.

'Five...'

The CIRTs signalled they were coming in.

'Four...'

'Bob, hold your fire!'

'Three...'

Franklin saw Bruner swipe away a bead of sweat. *'Bob, the two police officers are retreating. They are coming around the front—'*

'Two...'

'Hold your fire!'

The CIRTs jogged up, dived behind the van.

With another boom, spray erupted through the wall they'd just vacated.

CHAPTER SEVENTY-THREE

GEORGIE WAS SITTING WITH HER CHIN IN HER HANDS. THE other two hadn't moved for ages either. Paralysed by waiting.

It feels wrong.

She couldn't shake the sensation. Stupid when it'd been less than sixty minutes.

The radio came to life. Darma's voice and callsign. The three of them gathered in.

'Jeanette Roselle has been safely apprehended.'

The uniform grabbed the mic. 'And the two Hansens?'

'Negative.'

'Shit,' the female detective muttered what Georgie had thought.

'We have detained two males with Roselle, but they are not the Hansens. We believe these males were with her to provide a decoy.'

'The Hansens got away?'

Darma hesitated. *'For now.'*

'Do you have any leads?'

'Yes. Put out a KALOF for that truck Georgie saw here on Thursday.'

The detective whispered, 'That's a request for local units to keep a lookout for the truck.'

Georgie smiled her thanks, though she knew that.

'Did we progress that lead yet?' Darma asked. 'Do we have a full plate and ownership details?'

'Hold on.' The uniform scrambled through his notepad, while the detective scurried to her computer.

Georgie suggested, 'Can we cross-check the partial against the vehicles registered to the Hansens or their address?'

'Yes!' The detective looked relieved and typed furiously.

In under a minute, she said, 'WYU499. Owner is Allan Hansen, the Gordon address.' She rejoined them around the radio.

The uniform relayed the information to Darma. 'Do you know what direction the truck is travelling in?'

'Neighbours said west.'

'Say Ballarat, then. Hold on, Delta.'

He put out the KALOF.

Darma thanked him. 'Any updates on Bravo team?'

Her hopes dashed that Darma had learnt something off-air, Georgie did an eyeroll.

'Negative,' the uniform replied.

The detective squeezed Georgie's shoulder.

———

After the second gunshot, Franklin's body surged with energy and his senses went hyper. On the back of that, hearing Darma's report that he had Roselle in custody, but her stepsons were on the run, ramped up his responses even more.

Bruner flattened against the van as if he needed the

physical support. He said, 'This is not good,' with a shudder. Not what Franklin would've expected from the burly detective.

Rapid, shallow breathing came from Bruner's offsider who was fidgeting like crazy. A bad egg smell drifted from his way.

You farted, you bastard.

The bloke reddened, and Franklin pitied him.

The CIRTs were talking softly between themselves. Their tone stayed measured.

Just another day in the office.

He glared at the shed and wondered how Getty was doing. Was he feeling the pressure like the blokes from arson? Was he about to take another shot at them?

The female CIRT directed them into a huddle, while her colleague maintained constant scrutiny of the shed with a small rhythmic arc of his head.

'Ram, you've done a good job, but we need help here.' Cool and calm. Just stating fact.

Bruner nodded. Grateful, if his wide eyes and dilated pupils were any indication.

'We need our colleagues. Can you arrange to get them here asap?' She delegated it to the second arson bloke and waited for his yes.

'And we want an additional CIRT van on the road now for backup here or to help in apprehending the Hansens, plus SOG on alert. Got that?'

'Yes, ma'am.'

'My boss is the best negotiator in the unit, so we'll be in good hands.'

She let it fully sink in – they were involved in a siege with an armed offender.

'I'll take it from here until he arrives. If that's acceptable to you, Ram?'

Officially deferring to him, yet telling him.

'Of course.'

'Thanks. You made a good start.'

Really? Two pot shots so far.

Franklin knew that wasn't fair.

The CIRT adjusted her weight, ready to move. 'My priority is the status of Getty's wife and defusing the situation.'

CHAPTER SEVENTY-FOUR

GEORGIE HEARD THE WORDS SHE'D DREADED SINCE THE units had left the Bacchus Marsh station nearly two hours ago. And again as an echo in her mind. *Siege. Shots fired. Armed offender. Possible hostage.*

'Anyone hurt?' the uniform asked.

'The status of Hilda Getty is unknown. We have spoken to Bob Getty, but we haven't sighted him or her. No way of knowing the condition of either at this stage.'

'But the Bravo team?' Georgie butted in.

The uniform cop relayed her question over the radio.

'All good.'

She breathed out.

'We need you to redeploy the CIRT crew over here.' Bruner's guy went on. He and the uniform continued with logistics for a further two or three minutes, but Georgie's only awareness was that Franklin and his crew were okay.

For now.

When the room went quiet barring the detective and the

uniform cop working their phones, her thoughts turned to Hilda Getty. Her guts tumbled. Hilda had reached out, then run scared, and Georgie had informed on her.

Right thing to do. Only thing to do.

Hilda was complicit. She knew what her husband had done. What he was still up to. She'd ultimately decided not to speak out, but then let it slip.

Georgie's sympathy ebbed. Hilda was not an innocent in this. She'd had choices.

But then she pictured Hilda in the farmhouse kitchen and replayed their conversations mentally. From their phone calls and brief face-to-face contact, she recognised her as a woman who'd been worn down by degrees over the years. She knew she'd find it hard to forgive herself if Bob harmed Hilda in any way.

———

'Bob, Hilda. I am Jacquie Tobin, and with the police too, as you'll have noticed. I'm giving Ram Bruner a bit of a break.'

The CIRT paused, allowing Franklin a moment to adjust to thinking of her as Jacquie. A person. Just like all of them, Bob and Hilda Getty included. He understood that to be her aim. Seem interested, stay in charge, but not pushy.

'Listen, we just want to make sure you're both okay. All right? A good start would be hearing from you both.'

Jacquie created the illusion they were in no hurry here. Just chewing the fat. Working things out.

'Hilda? How are you doing there?'

Franklin tensed, thinking, *C'mon Hilda.*

The rain maintained a constant drumming on the van roof. Bruner's offsider snuck alongside Franklin, still breathing as if he'd been out for a run. The dog hadn't let up barking. Otherwise, quiet from the shed.

'All right then. Bob, how are you going?'

'Fuck off.'

'Listen, I can't do that. But I am here to help you both. You and Hilda.'

Jacquie let that sit. Franklin appreciated her sense of timing and calm, but he had to dig into his reserves, honing his body and mind. Who knew how this would go?

'Listen, Bob, Hilda, can you come out the front and talk to us? Just come out. Empty hands. All right?'

'Why nothing from Hilda?' Franklin muttered under his breath.

'Hilda, we've spoken a little with Bob. We'd really like to hear from you now. Just a few words. Let me know how you are.'

'That bloody dog,' Bruner's offsider mumbled, shaking his head. 'If it shut up for a minute, we might be able to hear her.'

'I doubt we've missed anything.' Franklin kept his voice low.

'Maybe she's not in there. Done a runner.'

Franklin almost hoped so. Preferable to dwelling on her in the shed with Bob and a shotgun, and her silence.

Then again, he didn't want any of these lowlifes getting away with what they'd done.

'We don't even know it's them in there. They could be decoys, like at the Hansen place.'

Franklin hissed, 'I don't think anyone would put their hand up to impersonate the Gettys in this, do you?'

'No. It's just...' The bloke trailed off.

Franklin got it. He wanted a miracle. A reroute to a different, better scenario than their reality.

'Hilda? Listen, let's talk.'

Jacquie clicked off the mic and stared at the shed.

The arson bloke got his wish and the dog shut up.

The hairs on Franklin's neck lifted in the same instant that a woman shrieked. Within the shed.

CHAPTER SEVENTY-FIVE

WALDO AND THREE OF THE DETECTIVES WHO WERE ON HIS raid crew marched the McAlisters down the corridor and parked them in separate interview rooms. The CIRT officer who'd gone out with him hadn't returned, and Georgie recalled they'd all been transferred to the Getty farm.

On a high from the arrests, they spewed back into the briefing room, talking animatedly and firing tasks at the female detective they'd left behind. She rushed about grinning, happy to be actively involved now.

As she stopped to collect papers from a desk, Georgie asked, 'What can I do?'

The detective threw up her hands before dashing from the room.

'My gut agrees with our initial assumption,' Waldo was saying. 'The way they gave themselves up, their cooperation with keys and the like, all corroborates that neither McAlister is a major player. They got roped in by their old mates Hansen and Getty, for extra hands and storage space.'

A female arson detective spoke. 'The crew haven't finished the search yet–'

Waldo cut her off. 'We already have enough to stir the pot – get them talking while we're waiting. Our lot will be out there a good few hours yet, going through the house and sheds thoroughly. I want to get cracking on this now – emphasise anything we can use to help the situation at the Gettys.'

That threw water over their enthusiasm. For a few moments, they all stood glumly.

'Do you think they'll lawyer up?'

Waldo shrugged.

Georgie stole forward. He cocked his head.

'Georgie?'

'For what it's worth, I think the women are close.' She arranged her thoughts. 'Jeanette Roselle has a photo with the whole lot of them on her fridge. My sense is that it's special, a keepsake. And when she pointed out Nance, there was real warmth to it, you know?'

Waldo and the arson detective both nodded. Waldo's 2IC looked engrossed, and the other guy blank.

'Anyway, Nance and Hilda are sharing a moment in that photo. There's something intimate about their posture and expressions.'

'Intimate?' The third detective wiggled his brows suggestively.

'Not like that,' Georgie said. 'I think, concentrate on Nance and her friendship with both women, but especially Hilda. That's going to be her Achilles heel.'

Waldo slapped his hands together. 'Good. Thanks, Georgie.' He told his team, 'Let's get cracking.'

———

An unmarked drew up adjacent to the grey van. Franklin watched the three CIRTs who'd been on Waldo and Darma's crews slip out and into the back of the van in a slick action. The other car left.

As the unit leader beckoned to Jacquie, Franklin sidled in too, determined to be across things. It meant that Bruner and his offsider had to remain outside.

'Where are we at?'

She gave her boss a rundown.

'Good. You've built a rapport with Getty, and we've already had one negotiator switch.' He gestured outside, in the direction of Ram Bruner. 'So you keep going. We know there's a woman in there with Getty now. We have to think it's his wife and that she's hurt, or frightened, or both.'

'Yes, Sarge.' Jacquie was nodding and Franklin caught himself mirroring her.

'Coax them into talking. What does Getty want or need – even if he doesn't know it? Until he's talking, we can't work with him. Same for Hilda.'

'What else can we do?' Franklin butted in.

'Jacquie will be out there with you for eyes too, but we need you lot to be vigilant,' the leader replied. 'Anything that hints we have a problem, I need to know. We can only imagine what's going on in there between the Gettys. High emotion. High risk of escalation.'

A burning tingle crawled up Franklin's spine. 'Understood.'

'I'll run an assessment. Look at how to contain the situation and keep it from turning more violent. It'll help to know what matters to them.'

Obvious, yet daunting. Franklin breathed loudly, impatient.

'Me and my team will throw everything at it.'

The leader used his nose to loop in his crew and the

equipment in the van. Franklin took in the audio and visual gear, tablets and further array of mobile office paraphernalia. Out of his league, he found it overwhelming and reassuring.

'Let's go.'

———

A fresh influx of energy came with the return of Darma's unit; Jeanette Roselle and two men around the age of her stepsons in tow.

'We only have one interview room available.' The young detective flushed.

Georgie seesawed between her and Darma as they tackled the problem.

He said, 'I'll take that, I want to start with Jeanette. Where can we put the men?'

'Meeting room? Lunchroom? Boss's office? Holding cell?'

Darma pushed his glasses up his nose and looked around, assessing. He had only brought back two detectives as he'd had two CIRTs on his crew, and Georgie deduced it wasn't enough personnel for three separate interviews, on top of Waldo's couple in progress and the room shortage.

'Park them in the meeting room,' he decided and signed to a member of his raid crew. 'You're on babysitting for now, I'm sorry.' He hooked his finger at his arson colleague. 'You're with me.'

CHAPTER SEVENTY-SIX

FRANKLIN SLIPPED OUT OF THE VAN AND UPDATED BRUNER and his offsider. Jacquie went back to her post with the microphone in hand.

'Bob, Hilda, this is Jacquie. I'd like you to talk to me. We heard Hilda give a bit of a noise back there. You can imagine we're a little concerned for her, Bob. Can you let us know how you are, Hilda?'

Dead air from the shed, except for the dog that'd started barking again when the unmarked delivered the extra CIRTs.

'Bob, then. Listen to me. Let me know how you're going. And how your wife Hilda is. Then we can talk about what's happened today.'

Franklin's frustration was like a rising whistle in his ears. This was useless. He considered what the unit boss had said – they were assessing the situation. But background checks and all talk on Jacquie's side and no action otherwise wasn't going to resolve things.

He snuck towards the van's rear and pulled out his phone.

———

Georgie fumbled to answer her mobile. 'Jack? You've broken the siege? Got Getty?'

'Nope. We're still here.'

Her mood flattened, turned anxious. Franklin sounded wobbly. She put it down to high stress. Normal in a case far from everyday, even for a seasoned copper like him, wasn't it?

He hadn't rung with good news. She asked, 'Why are you calling?'

'The CIRT need to know what makes the Gettys tick, particularly Bob. What we might be able to use to manipulate him, to bring down the heat. And fast.'

'And so–'

'They're running checks and doing their thing. However long that takes, it's already too long. None of us have met the Gettys. You have.'

'Briefly. So what can I do?'

'Is there anything you can remember from your visits or talks with Hilda that can help?'

'Shit. Bob did most of the talking – about farming, their property, history there. Allan's death, of course.' She thought hard. How much of what he'd told her had been lies anyway?

'C'mon, Georgie.'

'Sorry. I'm trying.'

She filtered her memories: what had been personal, valuable? Pushed herself with *Think. Quickly.*

'I didn't see much of the house.' She tapped her temple, summoning up a visual of the kitchen. 'I can picture two photos on the window ledge. They were wedding photos, in matching silver frames, with Bob and Hilda, a bride and groom, and one bridesmaid and her male partner. Same people in the second photo, everyone a little older, and roles interchanged. The women must be sisters – Bob and Hilda's daughters.'

'Hang on.' Muffled sounds. *'Did they mention any names for the family?'*

'No.'

'At least it's something.'

'Not much.' She hated that she hadn't done better. 'They have a dog, a little shabby bitsa thing.'

'We've heard it.' Dry tone.

'Its name is Henry.'

————

Franklin relayed the extra information to the CIRT boss.

'Good. It's a start. Thanks, mate.'

He'd been dismissed. He climbed from the van as the bloke told his crew, 'We need names and contacts for the daughters. I need to speak with them.'

Franklin's phone vibrated with a text message. From Georgie.

'Got someone asking what Nance and Jeanette can tell us about the family.' She'd put a crossed fingers emoji.

He eyed the shed. Getting late in the day, it was as if the dimmer switch on the light had been turned down. He didn't fancy the siege continuing well into night.

Said under his breath, 'C'mon, Georgie.'

Franklin rearranged his body. His hips and back had a dull ache. His toes were chilled inside his boots. From here, he could see the shed and Jacquie, still striving to get through to the Gettys.

'Bob, let's talk. It's growing cold out here. What's it like in there?' She waited a few beats. *'Bob, Hilda, are you cold? Do you need some blankets?'*

Jacquie lowered the mic, sighing softly as she timed her next try.

Bringing it back up, she said, *'How about something warm to drink or eat? I'll help you with that if you both let me know how you are. Talk to me, then we can work out how to help you with what you need.'*

A buzz alerted Franklin to a new SMS from Georgie. 'Jeanette won't help.'

He huffed.

On the back of it came, 'But Nance has given us names.' Georgie had listed them and included after the second name, 'Lives in Echuca.'

He darted into the van and fed the information through.

There was a spark in the boss's eyes when he said, 'Nice job, you and your girlfriend.'

Franklin nodded, returning to his place, as Getty said, 'I'm all right.' He whirled front-on to the shed amazed that Getty was talking. Strained though, probably a combination of stress and projecting his voice from the building.

'Why are you still here? I want you to leave. I want you to go. NOW!'

'I hear that you want us to go. You sound pretty upset there.'

'I bloody well am upset.'

'Yes, Bob. And what about Hilda? How are you feeling, Hilda?'

'I want you to go.'

'Bob, listen, I hear you. But can we speak to Hilda too?'

'No. NO!'

Jacquie kept calm. *'Bob, it's good that we're talking. Can you tell me more about how you're feeling?'*

'How I'm feeling? I want you to leave us alone, that's how I'm feeling. You have no right being here.'

Sweat broke on Franklin's lip and he wasn't the negotiator.

Jacquie—no, all of them—walked a tightrope. Any tick, a single slipup, and Getty would blow.

Shit, he hoped not literally.

Franklin backpedalled and replayed Getty saying, *I want you to leave us alone*. Us, plural, him and Hilda. He was acknowledging her for the first time today. Had to be a good omen, didn't it?

CHAPTER SEVENTY-SEVEN

GEORGIE FIDDLED WITH HER MOBILE, COMING DOWN WITH a bump. Her usefulness had been short-lived. Here she was, back in the briefing room with the uniform cop, while the young detective flit in and out, making phone calls or computer queries and running messages between the interview rooms. Back to being out of the loop and clueless, pretty much.

'Just us again.' The uniform chuckled.

The longer the afternoon grew, the greater her combat with mental fatigue. So how did this guy stay so cheery? Georgie wondered if he'd dodged an unpleasant task on the front counter or boring patrol by being assigned to the CI team today. Or maybe his mental endurance was greater, and that's why he carried a badge and she had a press card.

I'll have to contact Sheridan soon.

Her deadline of 7.00pm tonight loomed. In three hours, she had to deliver or let her editor know Geoff had earned his front page. She had nothing—no confidence she'd file before cut-off and no energy to care—everything invested in the Getty siege.

'Any sightings of the Hansens?'

'We'll get them.' The cop smiled. 'We're stretched tight with the backup crews all tied up searching at the Hansens and McAlisters. But Ballarat has put extra cars on specifically, and a second CIRT unit is out there looking and ready to assist.'

'Do you know what they've found at the farms so far?'

His smile bobbled his cheeks. 'Christmas! The McAlisters made a half-arsed attempt to get rid of the tanks they had. We're still fishing them all out of their dam.' He laughed. 'We've also got a growing paper trail. And I reckon Waldo and his friends will get that lot talking.' He waved in the vicinity of the interview rooms. He leaned forward. 'It looks like the Hansens cleared out in a hurry. Find them and the truck, and it'll be the icing on the Christmas cake!'

———

'Some blankets.' Getty was finally listing his needs. 'Hot soup. There's a big thermos in the cupboard over the fridge.'

'Okay, Bob, you want some blankets and some soup in the thermos. I can help with that. Before I get them sorted for you, how about Hilda just letting me know she's all right? Can we do that, Bob?'

Jacquie lowered the mic and conferred with her boss. Franklin came closer, heard the snippet, 'older daughter.' She whispered, 'How do you want me to play it?'

'Get Hilda talking in exchange for the soup and blankets first.'

She nodded.

'Hi there, again, Bob and Hilda. So I'm going to get those things for you, no tricks.' A second, then, *'We are not going to ambush you or anything. I want everyone to stay safe here, okay? But listen, Hilda, can you talk to me?'*

Franklin swivelled around to the shed. Light was fading fast, and it concerned him that setting up spotlights would be necessary yet posed a potential trigger for Getty. A reminder they weren't here just to check on welfare, and they had the big guns with them in the CIRT unit.

On the positives, Jacquie was getting through to Getty. She'd gained his trust, offered him something he needed in a trade for something simple that he could give.

Franklin thought the next person they'd hear from would be Hilda.

———

'*We have the Hansens!*' came through the police radio.

Georgie snapped a look at the uniform cop. He'd jumped up and almost danced on the spot.

Over the air, he said, 'Both of them?'

'*Yes. One has a minor injury. We'll have to get him cleared by the hospital before we can bring him in. The other is parcelled up and ready to be delivered back to Bacchus.*'

Georgie said, 'And the truck?' just as the uniform transmitted the question.

'*Full of goodies. We've got the bastards with a bunch of tanks, and stock and farm gear that'll prove to be stolen.*'

'Well done.' The uniform added, 'I'll let the boss know.'

———

'This is Hilda Getty.'

The woman's voice lacked the strength of her husband's, but Franklin made out each word. His heart thumped at the breakthrough.

Her cadence increased with, 'Bob has not hurt me.'

After that came a sound that puzzled Franklin. He glanced at Jacquie and Ram Bruner. They had braced and stared forward. The other arson D had his gun arm stretched out as he wheeled left to right.

They'd all sensed something wrong too.

'I am alright,' Hilda repeated, rushing on with, 'but Lachie is–'

'SHUT UP!'

Franklin echoed, 'Lachie?'

Bruner groaned. 'Is Lachie the dog?'

'No, Georgie said he's Henry.'

'Fuck. There's someone else in there with them.'

Jacquie's mouth twitched. She lifted and lowered the mic a few times. Franklin couldn't believe how calm she still appeared. As far as he was concerned, the shit had just gone off the radar here.

'Hilda, stay with me there. You said you're unhurt – I'm happy to hear that. But Lachie? Could I talk to Lachie?'

They were flying blind. Voices in the grey van grew animated before the boss came to the door and filled them in. 'They have two grandsons by the younger daughter. One is Lachlan – they call him Lachie.'

'The other grandson?' Franklin shot a look from the CIRT leader to the shed and back. 'Is he in there too?'

'We're working to find out.'

CHAPTER SEVENTY-EIGHT

THEY HAD TEN OR FIFTEEN MINUTES OF DAYLIGHT LEFT, and the rain was a persistent drizzle. Neither Bob or Hilda had answered Jacquie's questions about Lachie, or spoken since.

Franklin came to a boil. He ducked into the van. 'We have to do something.'

The boss ended a radio conversation, then answered him. 'Stay calm, that's the first thing.'

'I want to go in.'

'We're nowhere near ready to discuss things like that. Sit.' The boss waved him to the opposite bench. 'The rest of the family has been accounted for. Bob picked up Lachie this morning – to go firewood collecting, he'd said. Lachie's brother couldn't go. Tonsillitis.'

'Lucky for him.' Franklin bunched his hands under the table. 'Lachie doesn't deserve to be trapped up in this. We have to get him out.'

'I understand, Franklin. Give us time. We want to bring this thing to a close without anyone being hurt.' He held up a hand to curb Franklin's response. 'Primarily, our priority is the safety of Lachie, and secondly, his grandmother. Got it?'

He nodded. 'Let me take the soup and blankets over. I'll ask Getty to release Hilda and the kid in exchange for me.'

'It's too soon to ask for a hostage exchange. But I'll let you take the soup.'

———

Darma and Waldo had put their interviews on pause and converged on the briefing room.

Georgie's legs went to complete jelly as they came in. She fell to the nearest chair.

Waldo's top lip pulled over the bottom one.

'What's the strategy now that a child is involved?' Darma asked.

The uniform's joviality had shrivelled with the latest radio update. 'CIRT believes that Bob Getty is a man with no way out. From what the McAlisters have told you, it makes sense, doesn't it?' He turned to Waldo.

'True. Nance said it wasn't until they were too deeply in that she realised how well he'd manipulated each of them, probably most of all, Allan, his best mate. Getty had convinced them that their setups suited storage better than his, and they were better at the hands-on or logistics, but he'd contribute equally as organiser and by occasionally holding things for a day or two.'

Georgie frowned, trying to piece it all together. 'So what? He assumed he'd get away with it all? His mates might get caught, but they'd take the fall? Worst case, they'd talk, but you,' she spanned a hand over each of the cops, 'wouldn't have enough to charge him?'

At murmured yeses, she went on. 'So he never prepared for

this, and in desperation this morning, when it dawned on him that he might be in trouble, he decided to use his wife and grandson to get him out. How, exactly, even he doesn't seem to know.'

———

The CIRT leader's last words of warning rang in Franklin's ears as he laid down his weapon and presented his hands.

'*See there, Bob? John is unarmed.*' Jacquie breathed out and in beside Franklin. He shook inside, but took strength from her control and matched her breathing.

'*We've shown you what's in the package – it's the blankets and the soup you wanted. We wrapped it to keep it dry. John is going to bring your package to the front access door of the shed.*'

She marked Franklin's route with a finger, though everything she'd said was clear.

'*Bob, John is unarmed,*' she repeated, '*and he is not going to attempt to surprise you. He will lay down the package. All I want in return is that you open the door wide enough to show him that your wife Hilda and young grandson Lachie are both in good health.*'

Exhale. Inhale. Exhale.

'*Then John will back away from the door, and he will return over here. Do you understand, Bob?*'

'Just give me the bloody stuff.'

'*Bob, John is coming over now with what you need.*'

Jacquie nodded to Franklin, his cue to gather up the item and start the short but slow walk from the shelter of the van to the shed.

'*But he'll stop where he is,*' she emphasised the next bit, '*unless I have your agreement. Listen, Bob, I'm only asking you to show him that Hilda and Lachie are fine.*'

'Just show him, and that's it?'

'Yes, Bob. You have my word.'

'Tell him to hurry up.'

Jacquie said off-mike, 'Go. Good luck, Franklin.'

His boots sploshed on the wet gravel. He continued the breathing pattern, steady in and out, noting that in the time it had taken the crew to flesh out the plan and for the two arson Ds to make soup and find blankets, it'd gone dark. White light shone from the van, highlighting the black shadows.

He couldn't help pacing up his steps and breaths as the shed loomed in front. Two metres from the door, he called out, 'Bob, I'm about to place your package on the ground.'

From the shed came a scrambling noise and some whispering. The door lever turned as Hilda's voice lifted, still muffled. The door cracked a centimetre. A double *click-chung* made his stomach drop. The dog's barking went frantic. Then, *BOOM*. Deep, powerful, loud. A woman screamed and a child cried as a spread of pellets pierced the metal in front of him like grotesque firecrackers.

Franklin dived down.

What the fuck?

———

They'd formally suspended all interviews for now. An officer remained with each suspect, the rest crowded into the briefing room, even those who weren't attached to this case.

The horror within Georgie reflected on every face.

The tubby uniform cop leaned over the radio, ready to pounce.

Over the airwaves, '*Shot fired!*'

Around the room, 'Jesus.'

'Shit.'

'Was it Getty again, or us?'

————

'Hilda? Lachie?' Franklin stayed low. Naked without his pistol, out in the open, potentially mere metres from the shooter. But his fear for the woman and child overrode everything.

'Bob, Hilda, can you tell me what just happened?' Jacquie said through the speaker.

They'd had a breakthrough with Getty. What went wrong? Why did he do this? How bad was it?

Franklin called, 'Are you hurt?'

He snake-walked a little closer. He had to know if Hilda and Lachie were hurt and how badly.

'Stand down, Franklin. Take cover,' came over on his portable radio.

He ignored the CIRT boss and wriggled closer. A metre chasm between him and the shed now.

'Are you hurt? Bob... Hilda... Lachie? Please talk to me.'

The gap at the door grew bit by bit, and Franklin flattened himself with his cheek pressed into spiky aggregate, his head covered with his hands. He twisted so he could watch with one eye.

'Stop there!' Jacquie instructed.

The door stilled.

'Before you come out, listen to me. Put down the weapon. I repeat, drop the gun. Then I want you to walk out the front – slowly. Make sure there is nothing in your hands. And wait for further directions from me.'

Franklin's heart pounded. His breaths were pants. If Getty came out with the gun, what should he do? Tackle him to the ground? Focus on disarming him? Protect Hilda and the boy?

'Bob, Hilda, Lachie? Can you acknowledge my instructions

please?'

Nothing.

Franklin pushed the steel caps of his boots into the gravel, prepared to use it for traction to spring up and move in.

'Bob? Hilda?'

The door shifted, the space widening.

Fuck. This is it.

He could only see darkness inside initially. Then he spotted a faint glow in the distance. Into the scope of the white light from the van, the toes of two small gumboots shuffled up. He twisted his head further, his neck shooting with pain. A little boy hesitated in the doorway.

'Stop there! Please show me your hands. Come out slowly.'

A hand latched onto the boy's shoulder as a larger pair of farm boots came into sight. Both figures advanced sluggishly, giving Franklin a visual of an older woman. Had to be Hilda. Was a third set of boots about to emerge from the shadows— Bob Getty's—and were all three linked in a human chain?

'DROP THE WEAPON! DROP IT NOW!'

Hilda started sobbing. Lachie looked too traumatised to cry. They were halfway between him and the shed. Franklin weighed what to do if Getty materialised behind them.

'PUT DOWN THE GUN, HILDA!'

Only then did Franklin notice the shotgun dragging muzzle down behind her. The blood spattered over her clothes.

The woman kept hobbling forward.

'Are you hurt, Hilda?' Franklin did a backbend, bringing his torso off the ground for a better view. His arms were up, submissive.

She didn't react. Deafened by the blast or shock.

The woman and child made it three metres past him. Then Hilda's fingers let go of the gun, and she crumpled to the ground clutching Lachie.

DAY SIX

MONDAY 18 JUNE

CHAPTER SEVENTY-NINE

SHERIDAN JUDD WANTED HER STORY. NOT THE ORIGINAL one – no, her story about yesterday, the culmination of incidents of the past week. For once, a real-life drama that involved Georgie—*her* reporter—coincided with the magazine's publication schedule. It would still be hot news when *Champagne Musings* hit the streets on Thursday.

Her editor glossed the plea with an extra twenty-four hours to file, front page guaranteed, and a bonus.

Not even tempting. Not even to report with satisfaction that Lars Agaard and a growing list of scumbag accomplices were facing charges along with the gang's ringleaders.

Georgie would not sell out Franklin and the coppers on the raids. She wouldn't be the journo to put Hilda under the spotlight and expose how she chose her grandson over her husband because deep inside her heart she knew none of them would make it out alive otherwise. Hilda had foreseen it when he'd killed Allan, and it'd been cemented when he forced her and Lachie and the dog into the shed with his shotgun.

Running her gaze over her study, the feeling that not a lot

had changed, yet everything had, swamped Georgie. Her tortoiseshell cat sat next to the computer where the warm air escaped. The golden retriever lay under the desk with her head weighing down Georgie's feet. Her housemate, Maz, would've spoilt them rotten, but they always missed her. They were part of the reason she'd come home to Richmond after lunch via a stop in at Kendra's. She also needed to spend a day or two catching up with Livia, Bron and Jo, and to pack a fresh bag for her return to Daylesford. Franklin had suggested it.

She flicked over the bookcase that had replaced the jarrah planks on stacks of red bricks, and she ran her hand over the top of the salvaged blackwood desk, swivelling in the leather chair AJ had gifted her. She'd done this so often...procrastinated at her desk.

Georgie sighed and Molly stirred. The dog breathed out loudly through her nostrils, then flopped back over Georgie's feet. Phoebe rose, arched up, circled around, and then curled back where she'd been, purring softly. And Georgie went back to staring at the computer screen.

The timing was wrong for her original story, and it didn't rate the extended deadline, front page of this issue or bonus. But Judd had promised it'd go on the next front page, if good enough.

So, though it wasn't urgent, Georgie should be ploughing on. Still plenty of research to run and weave in. Then she'd need to brief their photographer and hit the road for a photo shoot, clearly not at the Getty or Hansen farms.

Instead, she pulled up an article published online earlier this afternoon by *Best Kept Secrets* with the byline Georgie Harvey.

A journo I know quite well.

She chuckled aloud, her conscience easy because this story

she could write, and she'd anonymously donate her fee to the police association.

COMMUNITIES BOLSTER IN THE AFTERMATH OF HEARTBREAK

With the effects of climate change, taxes, tariffs and competitor imports, rural communities across our vast nation from north to south and east to west are under constant pressure. Yet when faced with natural disasters of flood, fire, drought and infestation, or tragedies such as what happened in Korweinguboora last Wednesday and Gordon yesterday evening, they pull together, take stock and find a way forward.

'We will help each other,' says Dave Perry, a neighbour and friend of the Murray family who died in Korweinguboora. 'We'll get through this together.'

Similarly, taking control and responsibility for life-and-death situations in precarious and distressing environments is a job requisite of emergency service workers. The need for emergency-preparedness is a growing reality, as the services try to prepare and plan for adverse events, and when they do occur to quickly absorb, adapt and respond to them, and following that, promote community recovery.

'It's all part of the job,' admits Senior

Constable Mick Sprague, one of the members at Daylesford Police proud to have been a friend and workmate of 'Irvy' who was killed in the Korweinguboora explosion and fire. 'We're doing it tough right now, but we'll keep doing what we do to keep the community safe.' Emergency responders have a mandated duty of care, while the rest of us are largely bound by the ethics of community and humanity. But over the past week country Victoria has demonstrated the ability and readiness for individuals to provide emergency care, first-aid and shelter, or assist with evacuation and protection of life and assets. A marrow deep inside that doesn't prevent us falling but enables, even drives us to get back up and to lend a hand. 'We've got this,' said Shayna, a resident of Gordon who knew the two local men killed in separate, yet allegedly connected incidents less than ten days apart. 'We're resilient. Always have been and will be again.'

Resilience is a beautiful part of human nature, but we all struggle on occasion. It's the degrees that vary. A brave façade and fighting words can conceal a person crumbling internally.

That is why the R U OK? movement encourages us to reach out, connect, talk and support each other through life. It is far

**better when truly worried about someone to
go even further and ask, 'Are you having
thoughts of self-harm?' than to do nothing.
If the answer is no, they might open up
further. If the answer is yes, they need help
now. It might save their life.**

**One incident can trigger post-traumatic
stress disorder. Or it can be the cumulative
effect of repeated exposure that comes to
boiling point. It is not only first responders
in the emergency services that suffer acute
or chronic reactions to trauma. It can as
easily be the reporter on the scene, or the
family member, friend, neighbour or
passer-by who witnessed the event or
assisted in the aftermath.**

**The full story about Korweinguboora and
Gordon will flow in due course. Now is a
time to grieve. It is also a time to celebrate
our resilience and our sense of community.
But in that, we need to trust our guts and
ask R U OK? if concerned. Then listen to
the answer.**

Georgie's eyes filled as she finished rereading her article right
up to the crisis line numbers that she'd included at the end. It
wasn't perfect, but neither was life. She also wished it was as
easy as asking, *Are you okay?* when it came to the person most
important to her. She had done that in different ways and at

different instances already. But alone, she couldn't make him answer or better.

———

Marianne met Franklin as he came through the door and matched his stride up the corridor.

'How's she doing?'

'Fighting on.' The nurse smiled.

He read unease in her expression, but also reassurance. She believed Sam would make it over this hurdle, and the big one coming soon. When later this week, they switched off the machines doing everything for her and waited for her to breathe by herself and come out of the coma properly.

'She's young, fit, strong. In better shape than most of our patients.'

'She earns it. Works out five days a week, takes two rest days and mixes up her routines. Puts me to shame.' He chuckled. 'Makes me feel my age.'

'You're a young buck yet.' Marianne laughed softly.

Franklin looked to the left as they passed a cubicle, taking in the empty chair and then the bed. A stranger, a square-faced bloke with yellowish-white hair, stretched virtually from the pillow to the foot rail.

He halted, his heart doing a few extra beats. 'Denise?'

'She got her rock this morning.' Marianne wiggled her left ring finger. 'Three-point-five seconds after she got her clearance to the burns unit.' Her laugh tinkled.

'That's good news.'

'The type that we like,' she agreed.

Five beds up, they stopped, both gazing at Sam.

'Well, I'd better get back to it, while you visit.' Marianne swivelled on her soft-soled shoes, then stopped. 'Sam's good news is coming.'

Franklin nodded, grateful for her optimism. She left, but he didn't move into the cubicle immediately. Just watched the lights on the machines around Sam, and the regular rise and fall of her chest.

'Hi, Sam.'

He pulled the visitor's chair up to the bed. He noticed her teddy bear had toppled nose down and propped it up on the pillow next to her, then adjusted the scarf so Italia was readable.

In a familiar action, he held her arm.

'We got them, mate.'

He held his breath for a response. She swallowed. No discernible movement behind her eyelids.

'I hope you can hear me.' Franklin's throat thickened. 'Got so much to tell you.' A catch in those words. 'I don't know where to start.'

For a few minutes, he arranged his thoughts and watched Sam.

'I guess it should be with Bel and Alec, and their little boys.'

His voice deepened and his eyes welled, and he couldn't stop it. 'It's a shame you never got to meet them.' His lips quivered. 'You would've liked them. And it's good to know they never intended any of this – for them, or you, Irvy and Denise to be hurt. Just hard luck and bad choices on their part.'

If she could hear him, she wouldn't miss that he was crying openly now.

Fuck it. I'm human.

'I forgot. Before I go on, good news on Denise...'

He talked and talked, backtracked, hesitated, sniffed and wiped his eyes every now and then. Often, he stilled, certain she was with him, and searched her face, her hands for a sign. Nothing, but he still believed she was listening to every word.

Marianne came by with a box of tissues while he was talking. She squeezed his shoulder, then left.

Franklin told Sam the whole story. He choked on parts, chuckled at others. Said, 'Still can't believe how it ended in Gordon,' at least twice.

'Sam, mate, it's time to come back to us. You can take some more time off to get better, then come back to the job. If not operational, you'd be great at other stuff. Maybe training.'

Knowing the truth about what had happened, that Getty had paid his price and the rest of those responsible would too in due course, surely this would be her turning point. A weight lifted from his body.

DAY TEN

FRIDAY 22 JUNE

CHAPTER EIGHTY

FRANKLIN'S LIPS MOVED SILENTLY. HIS FACE CREASED AS
he struggled with the words he'd written and practiced over
and over. Georgie wanted to stroke away the worry that had
overtaken his laughter lines. But the gulf between them seemed
impossible.

He checked his watch, and Georgie glanced at hers.

Nearly time to go.

Across the room, Kat murmured to Josh. Georgie couldn't
hear what was said, but he rubbed her back, leaning in close,
answering. They looked old for seventeen and twenty. But they
had each other. More than Georgie could say for certain about
her and Franklin.

She turned to him as his chest puffed with a deep breath.
Her hand touched her abdomen, still flat, but she'd soon show.
She hadn't told him yet, was saving it for when things were
better for him, and for them. She wrapped both arms around
her waist, desperate to believe and determined to fight for it.
But watching Franklin battle his demons, it scared her that the

Korweinguboora incident might've claimed another casualty in him.

Franklin drew his jacket from the back of the couch and slipped it over his crisp white shirt and black tie. His best suit. Used for weddings and funerals. He had lost weight in the past nine days and fiddled with the pants, yanking them up before he cinched his leather belt by a couple of notches.

Again, she restrained herself from helping. Everything from the way he held himself to his shortness when he spoke, warned her off. Maybe after today, after he'd given Irvy's eulogy and they'd buried their friend, he'd begin to heal. Whether he reached out to her or a counsellor or elsewhere, it didn't matter, so long as he did it.

Franklin's gloom deepened, and Georgie fretted harder. How would he go when they rolled through the memorial slideshow? Or when they played *American Pie*? It was inevitable; it was Irvy's favourite song and he'd cranked it out at every occasion. The lyrics always poignant, but today they'd take on a new, personal meaning for them all.

He dipped into an inner pocket of his suit jacket and pulled out his phone. 'John Franklin.'

He listened for thirty seconds.

'No...'

His head shook. His skin blanched.

Georgie tensed. *What's happening?* She glimpsed Kat push Josh aside and focus on her dad, alert to something very wrong.

'No. She can't be...'

A hand gripped his head as if he'd been pierced by a shooting pain. The one holding his mobile fell to his side. His fingers splayed, and the phone clattered to the floorboards.

'Dad?' Kat cried out. 'Is it Sam?'

Franklin acted shell-shocked. Unaware of any of them or where he was.

His hand clenched into a fist by his thigh. 'No!' Anguish and fury rang through the word. He punched a hole in his plaster wall. 'Sam!'

'Oh, God, no.' Kat moaned.

Georgie wheeled around to see her cant backwards, slide down the wall to collapse on the floor, her legs stretched out in front. Josh stood beside her. He brought up his arms and tucked them around his neck.

Coldness ran through Georgie. She shivered, as she silently cried, *No, it can't be. I don't believe it.*

Around her, all sound muted. Colours bleached monochrome. She couldn't take one step. Not to Kat or Josh. Not to Franklin. She didn't know if she was crying. But her hands trembled as she cradled her midsection, protecting the new life inside her.

'Not Sam. She has her whole life ahead.'

Had she said it aloud, or thought it?

In her stunned, cold paralysis, her sluggish mind went to Franklin. She made a slow arc. He turned from the wall at the same time. His misery so tangible, she knew it was true.

Irvy's funeral day.

And now Sam's dead.

Georgie's gaze skated over Franklin, Kat and Josh. They would find a way forward, one way or another. They would remember how it used to be. Maybe someday they would share memories, smile and laugh again. But nothing would ever be the same.

She met Franklin's eyes knowing that, with Sam, today a little bit of each of them had died.

Dear reader,

We hope you enjoyed reading *Black Cloud*. Please take a moment to leave a review, even if it's a short one. Your opinion is important to us.

Discover more books by Sandi Wallace at

https://www.nextchapter.pub/authors/sandi-wallace

Want to know when one of our books is free or discounted? Join the newsletter at

http://eepurl.com/bqqB3H

Best regards,

Sandi Wallace and the Next Chapter Team

While you wait for Sandi Wallace's next novel,
you might also enjoy these collections of
her short crime stories:
On the Job and *Murder in the Midst*

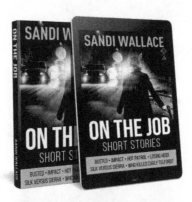

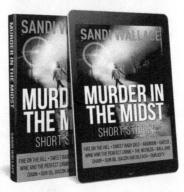

To read the first chapter of *On The Job* for free, please head to:

https://www.nextchapter.pub/books/on-the-job

ACKNOWLEDGMENTS

With this book, I wanted to pay tribute to the men and women who fight the good fight for the community and are injured or killed in the job, and to highlight some effects of post-traumatic stress disorder, which has a high incidence rate among all the emergency services, but can afflict anyone. If you are experiencing a personal crisis or considering suicide, please reach out to family, a friend or helpline.

While several factual cases helped inspire this book, all characters and events are a work of fiction. This was a technically complex story to write, so I am grateful to the various experts who assisted me. Any mistakes are my own.

Thanks to David Spencer, then attached to Victoria Police Media & Corporate Communications Department, Film and Television Office. Dave helped me with crimes relating to gas cylinders and the technicalities of gas explosions. Thanks also to Anthoula Moutis of Victoria Police, Film and Television Office and to Joanne Morrison for further policing information.

Keith Pakenham, who at the time of our discussions was Victoria's Country Fire Authority Digital Media Co-ordinator, has attended something like 6500 calls as a volunteer and an employee of the CFA since 1983. Keith was generous with his insights into the behaviours of gas and fire, and the procedure for the volunteer country firefighters in my fictional scenario.

I mention BRICC in this book, which is a cancer centre based in Ballarat providing critical services in the care, treatment and research for patients in the region, though all descriptions in this story are imagined.

My appreciation goes to fellow crime writers B. Michael Radburn, Chris Hammer and L.J.M. Owen. Thanks also to the whole team at Next Chapter, along with Isobel Blackthorn, Raylea O'Loughlin, Sharon Gurry, Judy Elliot and Marianne Vincent.

Very special thanks to you, my wonderful readers, for all your messages, emails and reviews letting me know how you have enjoyed my stories. I'd love you to join me on Facebook or Instagram or follow my website.

Lastly, I can't thank Glenn enough for encouraging and supporting my dream.

ABOUT THE AUTHOR

Sandi Wallace's crime-writing apprenticeship comprised devouring as many crime stories as possible, developing her interest in policing, and working stints as banker, paralegal, cabinetmaker, office manager, executive assistant, personal trainer and journalist. She has won a host of prizes for her short crime fiction including several Scarlet Stiletto Awards and her debut novel *Tell Me Why* won the Davitt Award Readers' Choice. Sandi is currently at work on a psychological thriller. She is still an avid reader of crime and loves life in the Dandenong Ranges outside of Melbourne with her husband.

Connect with Sandi at

Website www.sandiwallace.com
Amazon www.amazon.com/author/sandiwallace
Goodreads www.goodreads.com/author/show/
8431978.Sandi_Wallace
Facebook www.facebook.com/sandi.wallace.crimewriter
Instagram www.instagram.com/sandiwallacecrime
Pinterest www.pinterest.com.au/sandiwallace_crimewriter/

Black Cloud:
How Many Lives Can One Incident Shatter?
ISBN: 978-4-86745-151-9
Published by
Next Chapter
1-60-20 Minami-Otsuka
170-0005 Toshima-Ku, Tokyo
+818035793528

3rd April 2021